Remember Me

VOLUME ONE

Remember Me

REMEMBER ME

THE RETURN

PART I

CHRISTOPHER PIKE

Hodder
Children's
Books

A division of Hachette Children's Books

Text copyright © 1989 Christopher Pike

First published in the USA in 1989/1994/1995 as three separate paperbacks
by Pocket Books, a division of Simon & Schuster Ltd

Remember Me first published in Great Britain in 1990
by Hodder and Stoughton Ltd

Remember Me: The Return first published in Great Britain in 1995
by Hodder Children's Books

This edition published in 2010 by Hodder Children's Books

A Catalogue record for this book is available from the British Library

ISBN-13: 978 1 444 90126 9

Typeset in Berkeley by Avon DataSet Ltd, Bidford on Avon, Warwickshire

Printed in Great Britain by Clays Ltd, St Ives plc

The paper and board used in this paperback by Hodder Children's Books
are natural recyclable products made from wood grown in
sustainable forests. The manufacturing processes conform to the
environmental regulations of the country of origin.

Hodder Children's Books
a division of Hachette Children's Books
338 Euston Road, London NW1 3BH
An Hachette UK company
www.hachette.co.uk

For Pat

REMEMBER
ME

CHAPTER 1

Most people would probably call me a ghost. I am, after all, dead. But I don't think of myself that way. It wasn't so long ago that I was alive, you see. I was only eighteen. I had my whole life in front of me. Now I suppose you could say I have all of eternity before me. I'm not sure exactly what that means yet. I'm told everything's going to be fine. But I have to wonder what I would have done with my life, who I might have been. That's what saddens me most about dying – that I'll never know.

My name is Shari. They don't go in much for last names over here. I used to be Shari Cooper. I'd tell you what I look like, but since the living can see right through me now, it would be a waste of time. I'm the colour of wind. I can dance on moonbeams and sometimes cause a star to twinkle. But when I was alive, I looked all right. Maybe better than all right.

I suppose there's no harm in telling what I *used* to look like.

I had dark-blonde hair, which I wore to my shoulders in layered waves. I also had a fringe, which my mom said I wore too long because it was always getting in my eyes. My clear green eyes. My brother always said they were only brown, but they were green, definitely green. I can see them now. I can brush my fringe from my eyes and I feel my immaterial hair slide between my invisible fingers. I can even laugh at myself and remember the smile that won 'Best Smile' my junior year in high school. Teenage girls are always complaining about the way they look, but now that no one is looking at me, I see something else – I should never have complained.

It is a wonderful thing to be alive.

I hadn't planned on dying.

But that is the story I have to tell: how it happened, why it happened, why it shouldn't have happened, and why it was meant to be. I won't start at the beginning, however. That would take too long, even for someone like me who isn't getting any older. I'll start near the end, the night of the party. The night I died. I'll start with a dream.

It wasn't my dream. My brother Jimmy had it. I was the only one who called him Jimmy. I wonder if I would have called him Jim like everyone else if he would have said I had green eyes like everyone else. It doesn't matter. I loved Jimmy more than the sun. He was my big brother, nineteen going on twenty, almost two years older than me and ten times nicer. I used to fight with him all the time, but the funny thing is, he never fought with me. He was an angel, and I know what I'm talking about.

It was a warm, humid evening. I remember what day I was born, naturally, but I don't recall the date I died, not exactly. It was a Friday near the end of May. Summer was coming. Graduation and lying in the sand at the beach with my boyfriend were all I had on my mind. Let me make one point clear at the start – I was pretty superficial. Not that other people thought so. My friends and teachers all thought I was a sophisticated young lady. But I say it now, and I've discovered that once you're dead, the only opinion that matters is your own.

Anyway, Jimmy had this dream, and whenever Jimmy dreamed, he went for a walk. He was always sleepwalking, usually to the bathroom. He had diabetes. He had to take insulin shots, and he peed all the time. But he wasn't sickly looking or anything like that. In fact, I was the one who used to catch all the colds. Jimmy never got sick – ever. But, boy, did he have to watch what he ate. Once when I baked a batch of Christmas cookies, he gave in to temptation, and we spent Christmas Day at the hospital waiting for him to wake up. Sugar just killed him.

The evening I died, I was in my bedroom in front of my mirror, and Jimmy was in his room next door snoring peacefully on top of his bed. Suddenly the handle of my brush snapped off. I was forever breaking brushes. You'd think I had steel wool for hair rather than fine California surfer-girl silk. I used to take a lot of my frustrations out on my hair.

I was mildly stressed that evening as I was getting ready for Beth Palmone's birthday party. Beth was sort of a friend of mine, sort of an accidental associate, and the latest in a seemingly endless string of bitches who were trying to steal my boyfriend away. But she was the kind of girl I hated to hate because she was so nice. She was always smiling and complimenting me. I never really trusted people like that, but they could still make me feel guilty. Her nickname was Big Beth. My best friend, Joanne Foulton, had given it to her. Beth had big breasts.

The instant my brush broke, I cursed. My parents were extremely well off, but it was the only brush I had, and my layered waves of dark-blonde hair were lumpy knots of dirty wool from the shower I'd just taken. I didn't want to disturb Jimmy, but I figured I could get in and borrow his brush without waking him. It was still early – about eight o'clock – but I knew he was zonked out from working all day. To my parents' dismay, Jimmy had decided to get a real job rather than go to college after graduating from high school. Although he enjoyed fiddling with computers, he'd never been academically inclined. He loved to work outdoors. He had got a job with the telephone company taking telephone poles *out* of the ground. He once told me that taking down a nice old telephone pole was almost as distressing as chopping down an old tree. He was kind of sensitive that way, but he liked the work.

After I left my room, I heard someone come in the front door. I knew who it was without looking: Mrs Mary Parish and her daughter Amanda. My parents had gone out for the night, but earlier that evening they had thrown a cocktail party for a big-wig real estate developer from back east who was thinking of joining forces with my dad to exploit Southern California's few remaining square feet of beachfront property. Mrs Parish worked as a part-time housekeeper for my mom. She had called before I'd gone in for my shower to ask if everyone had left so she could get started cleaning up. She had also asked if Amanda could ride with me to Beth's party. I had answered yes to both these questions and told her I'd be upstairs getting dressed when they arrived and to just come in. Mrs Parish had a key to the house.

I called to them from the upstairs hall – which overlooks a large portion of the downstairs – before stealing into Jimmy's room.

'I'll be down in a minute! Just make yourself at home – and get to work!'

I heard Mrs Parish chuckle and caught a faint glimpse of her grey head as she entered the living room carrying a yellow bucket filled with cleaning supplies. I loved Mrs Parish. She always seemed so happy, in spite of the hard life she'd had. Her husband had suddenly left her years earlier broke and unskilled.

I didn't see Amanda at first, nor did I hear her. I guess I thought she'd changed her mind and decided not to go to the party. I'm not sure I would have entered Jimmy's room and then let him slip past me in a semi-conscious state if I'd known that his girlfriend was in the house.

Girlfriend and *boyfriend* – I use the words loosely.

Jimmy had been going out with Amanda Parish for three months when I died. I was the one who introduced them to each other, at my eighteenth birthday party. They hadn't met before, largely because Jimmy had gone to a different high school. Amanda was another one of those friends who wasn't a real friend – just someone I sort of knew because of her mother. But I liked Amanda a lot better than I liked Beth. She was some kind of beauty. My best friend, Jo, once remarked – in a poetic mood – that Amanda had eyes as grey as a frosty overcast day and a smile as warm as early spring. That fitted Amanda. She had a mystery about her, but it was always right there in front of you – in her grave but wonderful face. She also had this incredibly long dark hair. I think it was a fantasy of my brother's to bury his face in that hair and let everyone else in the world disappear except him and Amanda.

I have to admit that I was a bit jealous of her.

Amanda's presence at my birthday party had had me slightly off balance. Her birthday had been only the day before mine, and the whole evening I remember feeling as if I had to give her one of my presents or something. What I ended up giving her was my brother; I brought Jimmy over to meet her, and that was the last I saw of him that night. It was love at first sight. And that evening, and for the next few weeks, I thought Amanda loved him, too. They were inseparable. But then, for no obvious reason, Amanda started to put up a wall, and Jimmy started to get an ulcer. I've never been a big believer in moderation, but I honestly believe that the intensity of his feelings for her was unhealthy. He was obsessed.

But I'm digressing. After calling out to Mrs Parish, I crept into Jimmy's room. Except for the glow from his computer screen, which he was in the habit of leaving on, it was dark. Jimmy's got a weird physiology. When I started for his desk and his brush, he was lying dead to the world with a sheet twisted around his muscular torso. But only seconds later, as I picked up the brush, he was up and heading for the door. I knew he wasn't awake, or even half awake. Sleepwalkers walk differently – kind of like zombies in horror films, only maybe a little faster. All he had on were his underpants, and they were kind of hanging. I smiled to myself seeing him go. We were upstairs, and there was a balcony he could theoretically flip over, but I wasn't worried about him hurting himself. I had discovered from years of observation that God watches over sleepwalkers better than he does drunks. Or upset teenage girls . . .

I shouldn't have said that. I didn't mean it.

Then I thought of Amanda, possibly downstairs with her mom, and how awful Jimmy would feel if he suddenly woke up scratching himself in the hall in plain sight of her. Taking the brush, I ran after him.

It was good that I did. He was fumbling with the knob on the bathroom door when I caught him. At first I wasn't absolutely sure there was anyone in the bathroom, but the light was on and it hadn't been a few minutes earlier. Jimmy turned and stared at me with a pleasant but vaguely confused expression. He looked like a puppy who had just scoffed down a bowl of marijuana-laced dog food.

'Jimmy,' I whispered, afraid to raise my voice. I could hear Mrs Parish whistling downstairs and was becoming more convinced with each passing second that Amanda was indeed inside the bathroom. Jimmy smiled at me serenely.

'Blow,' he said.

'Shh,' I said, taking hold of his hand and leading him away from the door. He followed obediently, and after hitching up his boxer shorts an inch or two, I steered him in the direction of my parents' bedroom and said, 'Use that bathroom. This one's no good.'

I didn't wake him for a couple of reasons. First, he's real hard to wake up when he's sleepwalking, which is strange because otherwise he's a very light sleeper. But you practically have to slap him when he's out for a stroll. Second, I was afraid he might have a heart attack if he suddenly came to and realised how close he'd come to making a fool of himself in front of his princess.

After he disappeared inside my parents' room, I returned to the bathroom in the hall and knocked lightly on the door. 'Amanda, is that you?' I called softly.

There was a pause. 'Yeah. I'll be right out – I'm getting some kitchen cleaner.'

Since she wasn't going to the bathroom, I thought it would be OK to try the knob. Amanda looked up in surprise when I peeked in. She was by the sink, in front of the medicine cabinet and a small wall refrigerator, and she had one of Jimmy's syringes and a vial of insulin in her hand. Jimmy's insulin had to be kept cool, and he'd installed the tiny icebox himself so he wouldn't have to keep his medication in the kitchen fridge downstairs where everybody could see it. He wasn't proud of his illness. Amanda knew Jimmy was a diabetic, but she didn't know he needed daily shots of medication. Jimmy didn't want Amanda to know. Well, the cat was out of the bag now. The best I could do, I thought, was to make a joke of the matter.

'Amanda,' I said in a shocked tone. 'How could you do this to your mother and me?'

She glanced down at the stuff, blood in her cheeks. 'Mom told me to look for some Ajax, and I—'

'Ajax,' I said in disbelief. 'I wasn't born yesterday, child. Those are drugs you're holding. Drugs!' I put my hand to my mouth. '*Oh, God.*'

I was a hell of an actress. Amanda just didn't know

where I was coming from. She quickly put down the needle. 'I didn't mean to—' she began.

I laughed and stepped into the bathroom. 'I know you weren't snooping, Amanda. Don't worry. So you found the family stash. What the hell, we'll cut you in for a piece of the action if you keep your mouth shut. What do you say? Deal?'

Amanda peered at me with her wide grey eyes, and for a moment I thought of Jimmy's expression a moment earlier – the innocence in both. 'Shari?'

I took the syringe and vial of insulin from her hand and spoke seriously. 'You know how Jimmy's always watching his diet? Well, this is just another part of his condition he doesn't like to talk about, that's all.' I opened the medicine cabinet and fridge and put the stuff away. 'It's no big deal, is what I'm saying.'

Amanda stared at me a moment; I wasn't looking directly at her, but I could see her reflection in the medicine cabinet mirror. What is it about a mirror that makes the beautiful more beautiful and the pretty but not exceptional less exceptional? I don't understand it – a camera can do the same thing. Amanda looked so beautiful at that moment that I could imagine all the pain she would cause my poor brother if her wall got any higher. And I think I resented her for it a tiny bit. She brushed her dark hair back from her pink cheek.

'I won't say anything to him,' she said.

'It's no big deal,' I said.

'You're right.' She nodded to the cupboard under the sink. 'I suppose I should have been looking down there.'

We both bent over at the same instant and almost bumped heads. Then I remembered that Jimmy was still wandering around. Excusing myself, I left Amanda to find the Ajax and went searching for him. When I ran into him, coming out of my parents' bedroom, he was wide awake.

'Have I been sleepwalking?' he asked.

'No. Don't you remember? You went to sleep standing here.' I pushed him back into my parents' bedroom, and closed the door. 'Amanda's here.'

He immediately tensed. 'Downstairs?'

'No, down the hall, in the bathroom. You almost peed on her.'

Sometimes my sense of humour could be cruel. Jimmy sucked in a breath, and his blue eyes got real big. My brother's pretty cute, if I do say so myself. It runs in the family. He's the solid type, with a hint of refinement. One could imagine him herding cattle all day from the saddle, playing a little ball in the evening with the boys, taking his lady to an elegant French restaurant at night where he would select the proper wine to go with dinner. Except he would mispronounce the name of the wine. That was Jimmy. He was totally far-out, but he wasn't perfect.

'Did she see me?' he asked.

'No. I saved you. You were about to walk in on her when I steered you this way.'

'You're sure she didn't see me?'

'I'm sure.'

He relaxed. Jimmy always believed everything I told him, even though he knew what an excellent liar I was. I guess he figured if I ever did lie to him, it would be for his own good. He thought I was a lot smarter than he was, which I thought was stupid of him.

'What's she doing here?' he asked with a note of hope in his voice. I couldn't very well lie and tell him Amanda had come over to see him. When I had been in the bathroom with her, she hadn't even asked if he was home.

'Her mom brought her over. She's downstairs cleaning up the mess from the cocktail party. Amanda wants to ride to Beth's party with me.'

'Why's she going? Is she a friend of Beth's?'

'Not really. I don't know why she wants to go.' I had to wonder if Amanda had had time to buy a present, if she even had the money to buy one. She and her mom didn't exactly enjoy material prosperity.

'Is she still in the bathroom?' he asked.

'I don't know. You're not going to talk to her, are you?'

'Why not?'

'You're not dressed.'

He smiled. 'I'll put my jeans on first.' He started to open the door. 'I think she's gone back downstairs.'

'Wait. Jimmy?' I grabbed his arm. He stopped and looked at me. 'When was the last time you called her?'

'Monday.' He added, 'Four days ago.'

'That was the last time you talked to her. You called her yesterday. You called her the day before that, too. Maybe you should give it a rest.'

'Why? I just want to say hi, that's all. I'm not being fanatical or anything.'

'Of course you're not,' I lied. 'But sometimes it's better, you know, to play a little hard to get. It makes you more desirable.'

He waved his hand. 'I'm not into all those games.' He tried to step by. I stopped him again.

'I told her you were asleep,' I said.

'She asked about me?'

'Yeah, sure.' I wasn't even sure why I was so uptight about his not talking to her. I guess I couldn't stand to see

Jimmy placed in a potentially humiliating situation. But perhaps I was just jealous. 'We have to leave for the party in a couple of minutes,' I added.

He began to reconsider. 'Well, I guess I shouldn't bother her.' He shook his head. 'I wish her mom would tell her when I've called.'

'Jimmy—'

'No,' he said quickly. 'Amanda really doesn't get the messages. She told me so herself.'

I couldn't imagine that being true, but I kept my mouth shut. 'I'll drop sly hints to Amanda tonight that she should call you tomorrow.'

He nodded at the brush in my hand. 'Isn't that mine?'

'Yeah, mine broke.'

'You have a dozen brushes.'

'They're all broken.' I gestured to our mom's make-up table behind us. She never went out of the house without fixing herself up for an hour. Some might have called her a snob. I had called her that myself a few times, but never when my father was around. We didn't have a lot in common. 'And Mom wouldn't let me use one of hers.'

'What did Amanda ask about me?'

'If you were getting enough rest.' I patted him on the shoulder. 'Go to bed.'

I tucked Jimmy back in bed so that he could be

fresh when his alarm went off at three in the morning and finished getting ready. When I went back downstairs, I found Amanda and her mom in the kitchen discussing whether a half-eaten chocolate cake should be divided into pieces before squeezing it into the jammed refrigerator.

'Why don't we just throw it in the garbage?' I suggested.

Mrs Parish looked unhappy about the idea, which was interesting only because she usually looked so happy. Maybe I should clarify that. She wasn't one of those annoying people who go around with perpetual smiles on their faces. Her joy was quiet, an internal matter. But if I may be so bold, it often seemed that it shone a bit brighter whenever the two of us were alone together. I could talk to her for hours, about everything – even boys. And she'd just listen, without giving me advice, and she always made me feel better.

Jo, 'Little Jo', had given her a nickname, too – 'Mother Mary'. I called Mrs Parish that all the time. She was a devout Catholic. She went to mass several times a week and never retired for the night without saying her rosary. That was the one area where we didn't connect. I was never religious. Oh, I always liked Jesus, and I even went to church now and then. But I used to have more important things to think about than God. Like whether I should try to have sex with my boyfriend before I graduated from high school or whether I should wait until the Fourth of July and the fireworks. I wanted it to be a special moment. I wanted my whole life to be special. But I just hardly ever thought about God.

I'm repeating myself. I must be getting emotional. I'll try to watch that. Not everything I have to tell is very pleasant.

Back to that blasted cake. Mrs Parish felt it would be a waste to throw it out. 'Shari, don't you think that your mom might want some tomorrow?' she asked.

'If it's here, she'll eat it,' I said. 'And then she'll just complain about ruining her diet.' I ran my finger around the edge and tasted the icing. I had already tasted about half a pound of it earlier in the day. 'Oh, wow. Try this, Amanda. It's disgusting.'

Amanda looked doubtful. 'I'm not a big cake person.'

Mrs Parish suddenly changed her mind about saving it. 'Maybe we should throw it out.'

'You don't like cake?' I asked Amanda. 'That's impossible – everybody likes cake. You can't come to Beth's party with me unless you eat cake. Here, just try it. This little piece.'

I could be so pushy. Amanda had a little piece, along

with her mother, and I had a slightly larger little piece. Then I decided that maybe there was room for it in the refrigerator after all. I didn't care if my mother got fat or not.

Mrs Parish sent Amanda to check to see if our vacuum cleaner needed a new bag. For a moment the two of us were alone, which was nice. I sat at the table and told her about the party we were going to, while she stacked dishes in the dishwasher.

'It's for Big Beth,' I began. 'I've already told you how she's been flirting with Dan at school. It really pisses me off. I'll see the two of them together on the other side of the courtyard, and then when I walk over to them, she greets me like she's really glad to see me, like nothing's been going on between them.'

'How do you know something *is* going on?' Mrs Parish asked.

'Because Dan looks so uncomfortable. Yeah, I know, why get mad at her and not at him?' I chuckled. 'It's simple – he might leave me and run off with her!'

I was forever making jokes about things that really mattered to me. I doubted that even Mrs Parish understood that about me. I may not have been obsessed with Daniel the way Jimmy was with Amanda, but I couldn't stand the thought of losing him. Actually, I honestly believed he cared for me. But I continued to worry. I was never really cool, not inside, not about love.

'Is Dan taking you and Amanda to the party?' Mrs Parish asked, carefully bending over and filling the dishwasher with detergent. She had an arthritic spine. Often, if we were alone in the house, she would let me help her sweep the floor or scrub the bathrooms. But never if anyone else was present. I'd noticed she particularly disliked Amanda knowing she needed help.

'Yeah. We're picking Jo up, too. He should be here in a sec.' I paused. 'Mary, what do you think of Dan?'

She brightened. 'He's very dashing.'

I had to smile. *Dashing*. Great word. 'He is cute, yeah.' I took another forkful of cake, although I needed it about as much as I needed another two pounds on my hips. 'What I mean, though, is do you like him? As a person?'

She wiped her hands on her apron and scratched her grey head. Unlike her daughter's, her hair was not one of her finer features. It was terribly thin. Her scalp showed a little, particularly on the top, whenever she bent over, and she was only fifty. To be quite frank, she wasn't what anyone would have called a handsome lady. She did, however, have a gentle, lovely smile.

'He seems nice enough,' she said hesitantly.

'Go on?'

'How does he treat you?'

'Fine. But—'

'Yes?'

'You were going to say something first?'

'It was nothing.'

'Tell me.'

She hesitated again. 'He's always talking about things.'

'Things?' I asked, even though I knew what she meant. Daniel liked *things*: hot cars, social events, pretty people – the usual. Since the universe was composed primarily of things, I had never seen it as a fault. Yet Daniel could be hard to talk to because he seldom showed any deep feelings or concern for anything but 'things'.

Mrs Parish shrugged, squeezing a couple more glasses into the dishwasher. 'Does he ever discuss the two of you?'

'Yeah, sure,' I lied.

'You communicate well when you're alone together then. That's good. That was the only thing I was concerned about.' She closed the door on the washer and turned it on. The water churned. So did my stomach. I pushed away the cake. I'd heard a car pulling up outside. It must be Daniel, I thought. I excused myself and hurried to the front door.

I found him outside opening our garage. Graduation

was a couple of weeks off, but my parents had already bought me my present. I can't say what it was without giving the impression I was spoiled rotten.

It cost a fortune. It was fast. It was foreign.

It was a Ferrari.

Oh, my car. I loved it. I loved how red it was. I loved everything about it. Daniel loved it, too, apparently. He hardly noticed my shining presence when I came out to greet him. He fell in love with my car at first sight.

He had taken longer to fall in love with me.

I had officially met Daniel after a high school play in which he played the lead. I have an incredible memory for facts, but I cannot remember what the play was about. That says a lot. He blew me away, and he wasn't even that great. He had forgotten several lines, and he'd been totally miscast. None of that mattered, though. He just had to strut around up there under the lights, and I felt I just *had* to go backstage afterwards and commend him on his artistry. Of course, Jo had to drag me kicking and screaming to his dressing room. I was sort of shy, sometimes.

Since we went to the same school and were in the same grade, I naturally knew *of* him before we met after the play. I would like to record for posterity that the reverse was also true, that he had noted with approval my existence the four years we had spent together at Hazzard High. But the first thing he asked when Jo introduced us was if I was new to the area. What a liar. He didn't want me to think I was too cute.

But he asked me out, and that was the bottom line. He asked me out right there in front of his dressing room with Jo standing two feet away with her mouth uncharacteristically closed. Later, it seemed so amazing to me that I wondered if Jo hadn't set it all up beforehand. But she swore to the day I died that it wasn't so . . .

I must talk about his dashing body. It was smooth and hard. It had great lines, like a great race car. Except Daniel wasn't red. He was tan. He hugged the road when he moved. He had legs, he had hips. He had independent rear suspension. We used to make out all the time in his bedroom with the music on real loud. And then, one warm and lustful evening, two weeks before Beth's birthday, we took off our clothes and *almost* had sex.

I loved to think about sex. I could fantasise six hours a day and not get tired, even if I was repeating the same fantasy with only slight variations. I was a master of slight variations. But one can think too much. When we got naked together in bed, things did not go well. Daniel couldn't . . . Oh, this will sound crude if I say it, so I'll say instead that I shouldn't have overdone it comparing him to my Ferrari. Yet, in a sense, he was as *fast* as the car. I left the room a virgin.

He was *so* embarrassed. I didn't understand why. I was going to give him another fifty chances. I wasn't going to tell anyone. I didn't tell anyone, not really. Maybe Jo, sort of. But she couldn't have told anyone else and had enough details to sound like she knew what she was talking about. Unless she had added details of her own.

Daniel and I had other things in common, other *things* we liked to do together. We both enjoyed going to movies, to the beach, out to eat. That may not sound like a lot, but when you're in high school, it often seems like that's all there is.

Anyway, when I went outside to welcome Daniel, he was in ecstasy. He had turned on the light in the garage and was pacing around the car and kicking the tyres like guys are fond of doing when they see a hot set of wheels. I didn't mind. He had on white trousers and a rust-coloured leather coat that went perfectly with his head of thick brown hair.

'Did you have it on the freeway today, Shar?' he asked.

'Yeah, but I didn't push it. They told me to break it in slowly over the first thousand miles.'

'This baby could go up to one forty before it would begin to sweat.' He popped open the driver's door and

23

studied the speedometer. 'Do you know how many grand this set your dad back?'

'He wouldn't tell me. Do you know how many?'

Daniel shook his head. 'Let's just say he could have bought you a house in the neighbourhood for the same money.' He went to climb inside. 'Are you ready to go? Can I drive?'

'We can't take it. Amanda Parish is here, and she's riding with us. And we have to pick up Jo.'

Although Joanne had introduced the two of us, Daniel didn't like her. It would be hard to pinpoint specifically what she did that bothered him, other than that he was a boy and she had a tendency to make the male species as a whole feel inferior.

I had no idea what he thought of Amanda.

He showed a trace of annoyance. 'You didn't tell me.'

'I didn't know until a little while ago.' The Ferrari had no backseat. 'We can go for a drive in it tomorrow.'

He shut the door, sort of hard, and I jumped slightly. To be entirely truthful, I never felt entirely comfortable around Daniel. He strode towards me and gave me a hug. His embraces were always unexpected.

'Hi,' he said.

'Hi.'

He kissed me. He wasn't an expert at lovemaking, but

24

he had a warm mouth. He also had strong arms. As they went around me, I could feel myself relaxing and tensing at the same time. I didn't know if other girls felt the same way when their boyfriends embraced them. But when his kisses grew hard and deep, I didn't mind.

'Oh, sorry,' we heard behind us a minute or so later. Daniel let go, and I whirled. There was Amanda, as pretty and as unprepared as when I walked in on her in the upstairs bathroom. Her big eyes looking down, she turned to leave.

'No, it's OK,' I said, taking a step towards her, only mildly embarrassed. 'We should be leaving. Stay here. I'll go say goodbye to Jimmy and Mother Mary. Be back in a moment.'

Amanda stopped. 'What did you say?'

I suddenly realised I'd brought up Jimmy. 'If Jimmy's awake,' I said quickly, the remark sounding thin in my own ears. 'He was asleep a few minutes ago.'

Amanda stared at me a moment. Then she muttered, 'Say hello for me.'

'Sure.'

Jimmy was awake when I peeked in his door. He motioned me to come and sit on his bed. His computer screen was still on, and, as always, I found the faint white light hard on my eyes.

'Why don't you just turn it off?' I asked, gesturing to the monitor.

He smiled faintly, his muscular arms folded across his smooth chest, his eyes staring off into space. He was in a different mood now – more contemplative. 'I might wake in the night inspired.'

'The way you get around in your sleep, you wouldn't have to wake up.'

'I was dreaming about you before I bumped into you in the hall.'

'Oh? Tell me about it?'

He had just opened the window above his bed, and a cool breeze touched us both. Later, I thought it might have been the breath of the Grim Reaper. It was a warm night. Jimmy closed his eyes and spoke softly.

'We were in a strange place. It was like a world inside a flower. I know that sounds weird, but I don't know how else to describe it. Everything was glowing. We were in a wide-open space, like a field. And you were dressed exactly as you are now, in those slacks and that blouse. You had a balloon in your hand that you were trying to blow up. No, you *had* blown it up partway, and you wanted me to blow it up the rest of the way. You tried to give it to me. You had tied a string to it. But I didn't catch the string right or something, and it got away. We

26

watched it float way up in the sky. Then you began to cry.'

Far away, towards the front of the house, I heard Daniel start his car. He wasn't a good one to keep waiting. But suddenly, I didn't feel like going to Beth's party. I just wanted to sit and talk with my brother until he fell asleep. I pulled his sheet up over his chest. The breeze through the open window was getting chilly now.

'Why was I crying?' I asked.

'Because the balloon got away.'

'What colour was it?'

'I don't know. Brown, I think.'

'Everything's brown to you! What was so special about the balloon?'

He opened his eyes and smiled at me. For a moment I thought he was going to ask me about Amanda again. I felt grateful when he didn't. 'I don't know.' He paused. 'Will you be out late?'

'Not too late.'

'Good.'

'What's the matter?'

He thought a moment. 'Nothing. I'm just tired.' He squeezed my hand. 'Have fun.'

I leaned over and kissed him on the forehead. 'Sweet dreams, brother.'

He closed his eyes, and it seemed to me he was trying

to picture my balloon a little more clearly so maybe he could answer my question about it a little better. But all he said was, 'Take care, sister.'

People. When you say goodbye to them for the last time, you'd expect it to be special, never mind that there's never any way to know for sure you're never going to see them again. In that respect, I would have to say I am thankful, at least, that my brother and I got to talk one last time before I left for the party. But when I got downstairs, Daniel was blowing his horn, and Mrs Parish was vacuuming the dining room. I barely had a chance to poke my head in on her as I flew out the door.

'We're going,' I called.

Mrs Parish leaned over as if she was in pain and turned off the vacuum. 'Did you bring a sweater?' she asked, taking a breath.

'Nah! I've got my boyfriend to keep me warm!'

She laughed at my nerve. 'Take care, Shari.'

'I will,' I promised.

But I lied. And those little white lies, they catch up with you eventually. Or maybe they just get away from you, like a balloon in the wind.

CHAPTER 2

I let Amanda sit in the front seat with Daniel. His Audi didn't have much of a backseat, and since I'm a lot shorter than Amanda, I figured it was only fair. I'd always been kind of sensitive about my height. I won't tell you exactly how tall I was — suffice it to say that I was only an inch taller than Little Jo and that she hadn't got her nickname by accident. A lot of people thought Jo and I were sisters.

Amanda perked up once we got on the road. Or at least she began to do more than nod her head and smile faintly. Amanda was awfully shy. Maybe it was the sugar in the cake that got her talking a bit. For a girl who didn't like desserts, she had gone to enough trouble to sneak back into the kitchen and grab another piece of the chocolate monster. As Daniel raced towards Jo's house at warp eight, Amanda fought to balance the cake between a napkin and her mouth. She must have known how paranoid Daniel was about getting crumbs on his upholstery.

'Thanks for inviting me to the party,' Amanda said between bitefuls. 'I've been cooped up in the house all day painting.'

'I'm glad you're coming,' I replied. In reality, I had not invited Amanda. She had invited herself through her mother.

'You're an artist?' Daniel asked. 'What were you painting?'

Amanda hesitated. 'Our bathroom.'

'Really?' Daniel said. Amanda could have told him she'd been cleaning toilets; he was amazed. He had obviously never painted a wall in his life. His parents were almost as well off as my own, as were the parents of most of the kids we went to school with. Amanda was our token pauper. I sometimes kidded her about it.

'What colour?' I asked.

'White,' Amanda said.

'White's so boring,' I said. 'Why white?'

'It's all the same to me,' Amanda said.

'You must be colour-blind,' I said. 'You're as bad as Jimmy. He keeps telling me I have brown eyes.'

'What colour *are* your eyes?' Amanda asked.

'Look at them,' I said, slightly exasperated. 'Can't you tell?'

Amanda glanced over her shoulder. 'It's too dark. Are they green?'

'Good girl,' I said. 'We'll let you live.' Daniel took a corner at the same speed he was taking the straight. 'Hey, Dan, slow down. It's only a party we're going to.'

'I just don't want to be late,' he said. 'Jo had better be ready.'

'She'll be ready,' I said. 'Jo is always ready.'

Jo wasn't ready. I told Daniel and Amanda to wait while I ran in to get her. Jo's mother answered the door. I didn't mention this earlier, but Jo's mother and Amanda's mother were sisters, which meant, of course, that Jo and Amanda were cousins. The reason I didn't mention it before was because Jo and Amanda were so different I forgot they were related. Their mothers were even less compatible. The only thing they had in common was that they both were divorcées. Mrs Parish would have given me her right arm had I needed it, but Mrs Foulton wouldn't have twisted her left wrist to let me see her watch had I asked the time. The lady wasn't hostile towards me, just *busy*. That was her excuse for everything – she had *so* much to do. She was head nurse at a hospital with a million hospital beds, and Jo had grown up practically an orphan. That was Jo's excuse for being so weird.

But Mrs Foulton *was* hostile towards her sister. She loathed Mrs Parish. Jo said it was because her mother blamed Mrs Parish for the collapse of her marriage. Years ago Mrs Parish was supposed to have had an affair with Mr Foulton. When Jo told me the story, I didn't believe a word of it. But that was one of the things with people older than your parents – it was impossible to imagine they had ever had sex.

'Oh, Shar, Jo's in her room,' Mrs Foulton said when she saw who it was, quickly pushing open the screen door before turning back to the kitchen, a cup of coffee in her hand, a cigarette in her mouth. It always cracked me up to see someone in a starched white medical uniform with a cigarette in her mouth.

'Thanks,' I said, stepping into the house over a pile of newspapers and magazines. Mrs Foulton had *so* much to do, how could she possibly have time to clean up? Yet it was a beautiful house, a big house. Mrs Foulton didn't have to kill herself going to work every day. Her husband had left her with enough bucks to give her the leisure to follow all the afternoon soap operas. It was Jo's opinion that her mother was obsessed with helping people because she felt guilty about not really liking them.

'Off to work?' I asked.

'I *am* at work,' the lady replied, throwing her coffee

32

into the kitchen sink and stubbing her cigarette out on the top of an open beer can. 'This is my "lunch break".' She picked up her car keys. 'Tell Jo I don't want her bringing her Ouija board to Beth's party.'

'I don't think it's going to be that kind of party, Mrs Foulton.'

She stopped at the door, digging in her bag for her lipstick. When she wasn't in a hurry, she could be attractive. She had a great Roman nose, very authoritative. I couldn't imagine Mr Foulton having left her years ago for a roll in the hay with Mrs Parish. Then again, I couldn't remember when Mrs Foulton had not been in a hurry, nor had I ever seen Mrs Parish anything but patient. I often wondered what Mr Foulton must have been like. Jo wouldn't talk about him.

'How do I look?' she asked, touching up her lips.

'Like a nurse,' I said.

She flashed me a dangerous smile. 'You're worse than Jo. Who's that out in the car? Dan?'

'And Amanda, yeah.'

Mrs Foulton brightened, which was the equivalent of smog forming a rainbow. Amanda was the one person Mrs Foulton felt – besides those dying in hospital beds – was worthy of her time. She threw her lipstick back in her bag. 'I'm going to say hi to her. Bye.'

'Goodbye, Mrs Foulton, and you take special care of yourself, 'cause we love you so much.'

'Shove it, Shar.'

I found Jo in her room carefully combing her hair. She had only recently begun to worry about her appearance, the way most girls did at age nine. She had fallen in love. His name was Jeff Nichols, and he was Big Beth's boyfriend. I knew it was going to be a hell of a party.

Jo was fascinated with the occult. She was into the usual New Age fads such as astrology and crystals. Yet she leaned towards the darker edge of the esoteric circle. Nothing excited her more than a method to tap into a supernormal power. Her latest craze was a magnetic pendulum that she said could be used to *broadcast* or send substances into a person's body from any distance. When I was sick with a cold the week before Beth's party, she had called and told me she had broadcast vitamin C into my throat. It was ethereal vitamin C, of course, but she said it worked as well as the real thing. I can't say I felt a thing.

Did she believe in all that stuff? I don't know. When I was alive, I never gave it much thought, and now that I'm dead, I consider myself too close to the subject to voice an objective opinion. But Jo was no one's fool, that I can say.

'Dan's got the car running,' I said as I stepped into her room. Friends at school who knew of Jo's interest in the supernatural were often disappointed when they visited her house and discovered that her bedroom was perfectly normal. In fact, it was usually the cleanest place in the house. The only things in her room that suggested her hobby were a box of incense and an incense holder on top of her chest of drawers.

Her appearance was also fairly normal. Although we resembled each other, her hair was dark enough that I made fun of her every time she described herself as a blonde. We had the same petite builds, the same kind of mouths that laughed at the same kind of jokes. But whereas I did have *striking* green eyes, hers were at best hazel. She did have great taste in clothes, however. I was forever borrowing outfits from her. The yellow blouse and green trousers I wore to Beth's party actually belonged to Jo.

'Tell him I'm going to be a minute,' Jo said, finishing her hair and hurrying to the closet.

'It'll take me more than a minute to walk down to the car,' I said, sitting on her rock-hard bed. Jo also practised yoga and would never stand for a mattress that would let her spine sag. 'You look fine. Let's just go. I don't think Dan's in the best of moods.'

Jo glanced up from digging in her closet and grinned. 'Does Spam feel uncomfortable around you now that you two have engaged in bestial activities together?'

'I didn't say we had sex.' Jo always called Dan 'Spam'. I had long ago ceased trying to free her of the habit. It is interesting that I was one of the few people Jo never gave a nickname to, and I was her best friend.

'Yes, you did,' Jo said, finding what she was looking for, which appeared to be a lump of metal. 'You said he undressed you, you undressed him, and then the two of you let things take their natural course.'

'Stop,' I pleaded. 'We have to drive to the party in the same car in a few minutes, for Christ's sake.' I paused. 'What's that? Another magnet?'

'Yeah.'

'What happened to the last one?' I asked as I picked up a small pile of typed papers lying on her bed.

'I still have it. But this one's stronger. It's used for a different purpose.' She squeezed it into the pocket of her black trousers. Like any good witch, Jo loved to wear black. 'We can talk to the universe with this one. We'll play with it at the party.' She gestured to the papers in my hand. 'You know what that is?'

'What?'

'A short story by Peter Nichols – Jeff's brother.'

A couple of years back, when I was a sophomore and he was a senior, I had shared a biology class with Peter. He was great – he could crack me up like no one could. He would tell me these totally ridiculous stories about all the weird things that kept happening to him. For example, once he told me how he picked up an old man with a white beard hitchhiking, and how the old guy started telling Peter his whole past history, beginning with when Peter was in second grade right up until Peter helped the Hazzard High baseball team win the city championship. Peter had an amazing arm – his coaches said he had pro potential. He also had an incredible way with words. I could picture the old man and his story perfectly. Before the old man got out of Peter's car, he also told Peter what his future would be. I remember how Peter smiled and shook his head when I asked what the guy had said.

I must emphasise that Peter was not – at least to the best of my knowledge – interested in the occult. I don't know why he told me that story. Usually his stories were about crooked cops and crazy people he constantly ran into while simply walking down the block.

Peter died not long after that – some kind of car accident. I missed him terribly. He had been the best part of my day, and I always felt I'd known him all my life.

I instinctively dropped the papers when Jo said his name. 'Oh, God,' I whispered. 'Peter. How did you get this?'

'Jeff gave it to me,' Jo said, picking up the sheets and sorting them into a neat stack. 'He gave me a whole bunch of Peter's stories. He wanted to see if I could help get some of them published.'

'Peter wasn't a writer. He was always playing baseball. When did he have the time to write? He never showed me any of his stuff.'

'He never showed anybody. Jeff only found the stories a couple of months ago at the back of Peter's closet. You should read this one.'

I don't know why the news disturbed me so. I brushed off Jo's attempts to hand the story to me. 'Why are you reading them? Are you trying to get on Jeff's good side?'

Jo didn't flinch at my remark. It took a lot for her to show she was hurt. 'I'm doing this because I want to,' she said in a normal tone of voice. 'He was a pretty good writer, and he had great ideas. But he seldom finished anything. That's one of the things Jeff asked if I could do for him – put some endings on Peter's stuff.'

I continued to feel uneasy about the whole thing but couldn't pinpoint the reason why. Could it have been that the mention of his name had triggered a wave of painful memories? I asked myself.

Jo wrote for the school paper and was acknowledged to be Hazzard High's sole master of grammar. She tried to hand me his story again. 'You should read it,' she said.

I finally took it and glanced at the title: *Ann's Answer*. 'What is it?' I asked reluctantly.

'It's about a girl our age who buys a VCR and then discovers it can tape tomorrow's TV programmes today. She starts out taping the local news, spotting all the tragedies that are about to happen, and then she goes out to try to prevent them.'

'How does it end?'

'He never finished it.'

'But what was the last thing that happened to this girl?'

So my middle name was Ann, I told myself. He hadn't written the story about me. Yet the icy breeze that had blown through my brother's window earlier that night felt as if it had taken a detour into Jo's bedroom. And her windows were all closed. A cold sweat broke out on my forehead. *Omen* might be the word for what Jo said next, and for the balloon Jimmy watched float away. I suppose it was all a question of interpretation. A part of me must have seen the black axe rising slowly into the air above my head.

Maybe Peter had seen the same axe.

But of course he'd seen it. Far more clearly than I.

'She taped a programme of a news story that was about herself,' Jo said.

I swallowed. 'Had she died?'

'The tape was jammed in the machine. She didn't get to see the entire piece, only the beginning where her name was mentioned and her picture was shown. Then Peter stopped.'

'He stopped?'

'In midsentence. But read it. It's fun.'

I handed the papers back to Jo. 'I'll wait until you write the ending.'

CHAPTER 3

I had forgotten to tell Jo that Amanda was in the car. The fact didn't seem to faze Jo. She may have had little in common with her cousin, but there was no known hostility between them. Jo climbed into the backseat with me, however, a seating arrangement that may have been unwise. Dan had once complained to me whenever Jo and I got together, we drowned out the rest of the world. Remembering the remark, I endeavoured to be quiet. Jo immediately took it upon herself to make up for my silence.

'Spam,' Jo said to Dan as he pulled out of her driveway. 'What did you get Big Beth for her birthday?'

Dan frowned. I could tell he was frowning even though I was looking at the back of his head. He frowned whenever Jo spoke to him. 'Why don't you call people by their real names for once?' he asked.

'All right, Daniel,' she said. 'What did you get Elizabeth for her birthday?'

'Earrings,' he said, flooring the accelerator and racing up the street as if he were late to his own wedding.

'What?' I asked, amazed. 'I got her a present from both of us. You didn't have to get her something.'

'What did you get her?' Jo asked me.

'An old Beatles album,' I said.

'Beth has a CD player,' Daniel said.

'Elizabeth hates the Beatles,' Jo said.

'Oh,' I said. I had been aware of both facts, but there had been a sale on Beatles albums at the store.

'What did you get her, Bliss?' Jo asked Amanda. Jo had once explained the choice of nickname to me. Apparently, in India, the Sanskrit word for 'bliss' is *ananda*, which Jo obviously thought was close enough. Her reasoning might have had an element of sarcasm in it. Amanda seldom smiled.

'I didn't have a chance to stop at the store,' Amanda said softly. If I hadn't been so overwhelmed with disgust at Daniel's having gone to the trouble to buy Beth a separate gift, I probably would have told Amanda she could put her name beside mine on the album.

'Isn't anyone going to ask what I got her?' Jo asked, fiddling with the pink tissue paper on the package in her hands. A moment of silence followed. 'Specimen jars,' Jo said finally. 'My mom got them from the hospital for free.'

'You can't give Beth that,' Daniel said, irritated.

'Sure I can,' Jo said. 'She'll think they're crystal.'

'She's not that stupid,' Daniel said.

'She's pretty stupid,' I said.

'And we'll tell her they're crystal,' Jo said. 'Hey, slow down, Spam. The party won't start until I get there. What's the hurry?'

'I always drive this fast,' Daniel said.

'Is he always this fast?' Jo asked me.

'Always,' I said without thinking. The question, and answer, might have been innocent enough, to start with. Except Jo suddenly burst into hysterical laughter.

'*Always?*' she asked, gagging.

I gave her a hard poke in the side – too late. I didn't have to see Daniel's face. I could feel the vibes. They were *bad*. He knew that Jo knew he had not performed up to expectations when we had gone to bed.

'What's so funny?' Amanda asked.

'Nothing,' I said.

We drove the rest of the way in silence.

Big Beth met us at the door. Her parents' condominium was on the top floor of a four-storey building that overlooked the ocean. It had a view, of course, and it had been built with lots of money. My father had been involved in the construction. The soundproofing in the walls between the condos was excellent. Beth had her CD player up loud and pumping, and there wasn't one complaint. I handed Beth my gift as we went through the door. A fool could have told what it was. Beth glanced at it after saying hello and smiled.

'It's not a painting, is it?' she asked hopefully.

'It'll never wear out on you,' I said, remembering her CD player. My eyes flickered to Daniel. Whenever someone is madder at me than I at them, it is hard for me to stay mad. Guilt, I suppose. Daniel handed Beth his tiny box, and you would have thought he had given her an engagement ring. She planted a kiss on his cheek, gushing.

'You shouldn't have,' she said.

'No problem,' he said, by no means pushing her away.

'It's your birthday, for God's sake, he had to get you something,' Jo said, quickly scanning the room for Jeff Nichols. He was standing alone in the corner of the room, a beer in his hand. He didn't even glance over at us. Why a shy, intelligent fellow like Jeff Nichols was going with someone like Beth was beyond me. Jo's eyes lingered on him a moment before she turned back to Beth and handed her the specimen jars.

'Whatever you do, don't shake the box,' Jo said seriously.

Beth nodded and pressed her ear to the package. Don't ask me to explain it.

Yet I'm giving the wrong impression of the girl. Beth was not totally stupid, nor was she a complete knockout. She did as well as I did in school – As and Bs – and her SAT score was high. It's my belief that she had cultured her air-head qualities to pacify her subconscious anxieties about her looks. Guys often say there's nothing sexier than a girl with brains, but just watch them drool over *Playboy*'s Miss September, whose turn-ons are sincere guys and windy nights and whose turn-offs are rude people and dogs that bite. I mean, it's no wonder that a girl like Beth with breasts out to the moon would develop the idea, while growing up in a society as superficial as ours, that if she just smiled a lot and didn't demand regular cerebral stimulation, guys would be more likely to ask her out. That's my theory, at least, but then again, what the hell do I know?

Beth had more to her body than a chest. She had a bumpy nose, two ordinary brown eyes – devoid of even a hint of gorgeous green – and a head of brown hair which, although long and straight, didn't shine in any light.

All the guys at school thought she was sex incarnate, and she wasn't even that pretty. And as I said, I think she knew it. Studying her as she stood next to cool, soft Amanda, I thought Beth looked like nothing to worry about.

'I'm sorry,' Amanda said to Beth. 'I didn't have a chance to get you a present.'

'That's OK,' Beth exclaimed, hugging Amanda, whom she scarcely knew. 'I'm just glad you're here!'

'You're shaking the box,' Jo warned Beth, silently muttering *Christ* under her breath. For his part, Daniel kept silent.

And so the party began, and at first it was a fairly ordinary affair. I won't go into every blessed detail. Beth's parents were gone for the night. We ate a little. We danced a little. We ate some more. We gossiped; lots of people came and went, so there was plenty to gossip about. And all the time I kept my eyes on Daniel and Beth, and Jo kept her eyes on Jeff and Beth, and the world went right on turning. Nothing out of the ordinary happened.

There are, however, a few things I should mention before I get into Jo's idea of entertainment. Beth opened her presents close to eleven o'clock, and even though it was early, the party had begun to thin out. There couldn't have been more than a dozen people left when Beth sat in the middle of the floor in her pink summer dress and proceeded to break every one of her nails. She really did – each time she dug into a fresh package, she ripped another manicured nail. It was excruciating to watch.

'I should have bought you a bottle of calcium supplement instead,' Jo remarked, busting up the group. Beth laughed at the joke, but I could tell she hadn't appreciated it. Yet all was forgiven a moment later when she opened Jo's present. To be fair, the specimen jars at Mrs Foulton's hospital were a bit larger and more elaborate than the usual. But in no way did they look like expensive crystal. When Beth unwrapped them and held them up for the room to see – a hint of utter confusion in her eyes – Jo broke in with smooth sincerity.

'I know they're not the usual crystal,' she said. 'But I thought you would like something different for your collection.' Jo added humbly, 'They're from China.'

Beth beamed and hugged Jo. I almost died. The rest of the room nodded and tuned out. Only Jeff gave any sign that he knew Beth was being suckered, and it was a faint sign at that; he finished his beer and silently crumpled the can between his palms. Amanda sat quietly in the corner, casting me furtive glances, probably wondering if I was going to lose it, or maybe still embarrassed that she had nothing for Beth to open.

Daniel's earrings had diamonds in them. Diamonds! They sparkled as he helped Beth put them on her earlobes. Again, I almost died. I almost cried. I almost said something. But what could I say? Daniel hadn't said much to me all night. I knew he was still pissed at me for speaking to Jo about his excitable bedsheet manners. I was afraid that if I spoke then – or even later – I would ask why and he would say bye.

I began to think it was a stupid party.

Beth finally finished with her presents. ('Oh, Shari, the Beatles! My favourite!') Several more people left. Then Beth brought up the idea of swimming. The condominium complex had one huge heated pool and two steaming Jacuzzis. But how would we go swimming, I wondered, without bathing suits? That was no problem for those who had been told in advance to bring their suits, I soon learned. Daniel was one of those people. And strangely enough, Amanda was also one. Apparently, after asking her mom to ask me for a ride to the party, she must have called Beth directly to see if she really could come and had received the word on the suits. Daniel and Beth had theirs on under their clothes.

'We could go skinny-dipping,' Jo said as we watched everyone except Jeff parade out the front door. Jeff was standing alone on the balcony drinking another beer when Jo made her suggestion. He had been putting them away all night, one after another, but he did not seem drunk.

'No,' I said. 'I always feel naked without my clothes on.' I nodded towards the dark balcony, which lay – relative to our cosy spot on the living room couch – beyond an intervening kitchen. We could see Jeff's silhouette against the night sky, the shadow of his beer can resting on the supposedly strong and secure wooden rail. 'Besides, this is your chance. Go give him a bite.'

'I think he wants to be alone,' Jo said.

'He wouldn't have come to a party if he wanted to be alone.'

'He had to come to the party. It's his girlfriend's birthday.'

'His girlfriend's not here. She's gone swimming with my boyfriend.'

'You're not upset?'

'I'm not?' I asked.

'They were the gaudiest earrings.'

'Gaudy costs money. You should have given her used specimen jars.'

'Who says I didn't? Are you really upset?'

'I don't know. Are you really afraid to talk to Jeff?'

'I don't know,' Jo said and sighed. 'Yeah.'

'Do you want me to talk to him?'

'I don't care. Just don't tell him I love him.'

'Do you love him?' I asked, surprised. I hadn't realised he meant that much to her. Coming to the party was probably hard for her.

Jo began to make a flip remark, at which the two of us were masters. Then she paused and lowered her eyes. 'Yeah, maybe. I don't know. Do you love Spam?'

I stood. 'I always hated it when I was a little kid.'

Before going out on to the balcony, I made a quick stop in Beth's bathroom. But it wasn't because I'd been drinking beer. I was never into depressants like alcohol and health food. I liked good old blood-rushing caffeine: coffee, Cokes, Pepsis. I'd had all three that night.

The design of the condo was common for the beach area, although it would have been unusual a few miles inland. It had two master bedrooms, which meant, of course, that the condo's two bathrooms were located in the bedrooms. Beth's room had the better view, with a wide sliding glass door that led directly on to the west-end balcony that overlooked the ocean. But it was smaller than her parents' room and, being next to the kitchen, was also less private.

When I finished in the bathroom, I joined Jeff

outside on the balcony without having to backtrack to the living room.

He was lighting up a cigarette when I first stepped into the night. That is my last impression of Jeff Nichols – the side of his rugged face in the orange flare of a wooden match. He wasn't particularly handsome. He had none of the warmth and humour in his face that his older brother had had. His bone structure was not well defined, and he didn't have to narrow his eyes for you to feel he might be angry. Still, you had to look at him. He had magnetism, buried deep, perhaps, and probably rusty, but pulling hard. He was unlike most of my friends – he didn't give a damn what anyone thought of him.

We'd only talked a few times at school, although we shared a couple of classes. Sometimes it seemed to me that he purposely avoided me.

'I hope I'm not disturbing you?' I asked.

He glanced over, waved out his match, and took a drag on his cigarette. 'No.'

I went and stood with my hands resting on the smooth-sanded railing, six feet from Jeff. The view of the ocean at night was nothing – all flat, black, and depressing. It depressed me then, that's for sure. Or maybe it was the faint sounds of splashing and giggling I could hear coming from the far side of the complex.

Jeff seemed kind of down, too. I wondered if he was remembering Peter. He wasn't saying anything, and I felt I had to speak.

'It's a nice night,' I remarked. It was essentially warm, with layers of cool, damp air drifting up to the balcony – not unusual for that close to the sea.

'It's all right.'

'Am I bothering you?'

He shrugged. 'I'll probably be going home soon.'

'Before Beth gets back?'

'Maybe.'

'Jeff?'

'What?'

'Nothing. I just wanted to, you know . . . say something.' That was clever. What I wanted to say was that he shouldn't be with a girl who would put specimen jars in with her crystal collection and that I missed his brother, too. Jeff had idolised Peter, the way Peter could stand on the mound and make another team's hitters jittery just by the way he chewed his bubble gum. Peter had been funny but cool, without having to act it.

'I wish I'd brought my suit,' I said. When he didn't respond, I added, 'I wish Dan had told me we'd be swimming.'

'Maybe he forgot.'

I may have imagined it, but his reply seemed to contain a note of sarcasm. 'You two don't know each other very well, do you?' I asked.

'No.'

'That's too bad.'

He peered over at me. Neither the lights in the kitchen nor those in Beth's bedroom were on. I couldn't see his eyes; nevertheless, I shifted uneasily. 'For whom?' he asked.

'For the two of you. I mean— What do you mean?'

Jeff looked back towards the ocean, took another drag off his cigarette. 'Never mind, Shari.'

I moved a step closer to him. 'You don't like Dan, do you?'

'Why ask?'

'Come on, Jeff.'

'Dan, he's OK.' He shrugged again. 'If you like assholes.'

I did not appreciate the remark. Yet I think it disturbed me mainly because it reflected on me as Daniel's girlfriend.

'You're the asshole,' I said, deciding that any sympathy I might have felt for him had been misdirected.

'I suppose.'

'What's your problem?'

'I don't have any problems.'

'You've got an asshole for a girlfriend.'

It was not a particularly nice thing for a sweet little girl like me to say, I admit. I half expected him to throw down his cigarette and walk away. Yet his upper lip curled into a slow smile beneath the glow of his cigarette. 'She's not that bad. She's too good for him.'

'For who?'

He shook his head, and now he turned to leave. 'Nothing.'

I hate it when people start to tell me something that I will hate and stop right in the middle. That's my only excuse for saying what I did next. It *was* cruel.

'You know, Jeff, you're such a shallow jerk compared to your brother.'

He stopped suddenly, and I wished I could have reached out and retrieved my words. Like in the car with Dan on the way to the party, I only had to look at the back of his neck to feel the bad vibes. He turned slowly, though, casually raising his cigarette to his mouth and sticking it in the corner in such a way that I thought it would fall out any second. It was too dark for me to read his expression clearly, and I was glad.

'He used to tell me stuff about you,' Jeff said. 'He thought you were all right. But I always thought you didn't know what was going on. I just had to look at the way you strolled along with your head up your ass.' He pulled out his cigarette and dropped it, crushing it beneath his black boot. Then he cleared his throat. 'Yeah, and he died, Shari, and you haven't changed. Not in my book.'

He went inside but didn't leave. Jo met him in the kitchen, and I saw the two of them sit down on the living-room sofa together and talk. Maybe they talked about me. I never did know.

Neither did I know that I had less than two hours to live.

I turned back to the ocean. It was black. Then I looked straight down. A concrete sidewalk ran just below, alongside a plot of green grass lit by a hard white globe on top of a shrunken lamppost. It was a long way down.

CHAPTER 4

I could tell you how I died. How my skull cracked open and the blood gushed out. All the gory details. But gore is for the living. Fading mortals don't always close their eyes when becoming naked spirits, but they seldom watch. At least, I didn't.

Jo played a strange part before the fun started – and ended. But before even that, Bliss told me all about Big Beth and Spam. I think I understand now why Jo was always giving people nicknames. The living really have only one point of view – their own. Oh, there are wise men here and there on earth who can see things as others do, but they are rare. Most people can't see other people as quite as real as themselves. It is forgivable when you realise they have to see everyone from inside a body that can be in only one place at one time. When I was alive, some people at school seemed to me like little more than mannequins in a store window. They were simply there for my greater shopping enjoyment.

Jo must have had the same problem. For her, Daniel was easier to relate to as Spam because Spam was a *thing*, and she could always return a thing to the store if she didn't like it. And Big Beth was like a cartoon character; Jo could change the channel on the set and watch another cartoon if she was no longer amused. Or she could pull the plug, and they would all be gone. All of them.

I believe her nicknaming people gave Jo the feeling that she had control over her environment.

But I'm digressing. While Jo and Jeff sat in the living room, I went back into Beth's bedroom and lay down on her bed. I figured if she could swim with my boyfriend, I could wrinkle her sheets. I didn't go straight from the balcony to the bedroom. I discovered that the sliding glass door I had used a few minutes earlier automatically locked when I closed it. I had to re-enter the condo through the kitchen and return to the bedroom. Jeff and Jo didn't even look up as I went by. God knows what they were talking about.

I had a headache. I was tired. When I lay down, I had no intention of sleeping, but I must have. I didn't dream, however. My omens were over for the night. Except for one last big one. Before my headache blossomed into a skull-shattering mess, the gang rehearsed my funeral.

Amanda awakened me. She was sitting on the bed by my side when I opened my eyes. Her black hair looked so long and lovely to me right then, I remember thinking how awful it would be if she were to go prematurely grey. I knew from a picture album Mrs Parish had shown me that her mother had. Amanda must have blow-dried it after swimming.

'What time is it?' I muttered. My headache was worse than when I had lain down.

'After twelve.'

I sat up. 'Is the swimming over?' Amanda had changed back into her clothes. She stared at me for a moment with her grey eyes before answering.

'Most of the kids have left,' she said.

The condo did seem unusually quiet. 'Where's Dan? Is he back?'

'No.'

'Where is he?'

She looked down, and even in the gloom I could see the lines form on her forehead. 'I don't know how to tell you this, Shari.'

'What?'

'Dan and Beth are still out.'

'So?'

Amanda took a breath, her hair hanging over the side of her face. 'I was walking back when I remembered I'd left my watch by the diving board. I went back to get it. Dan and Beth must have got out of the pool. They weren't there. But I . . .'

'What?' I demanded as she paused. She glanced up.

'They were in the Jacuzzi.'

'So?'

'They were naked.'

'No. How could you tell?'

'I could tell.'

I swallowed, and my throat wasn't merely dry, it was parched and bleeding, like my soul. I have a confession to make. Daniel was a lot better than I've described him. He wasn't just a pretty face. He had style. He was funny. He had done a lot of nice things for me. He had taken me to the prom in a gold-plated Rolls after pinning the biggest corsage of the night on my long white dress. I liked him, I really did like him. And all those doubts I had about him and Beth – deep down inside I knew I was just being paranoid.

I hated Amanda right then for telling me I had been right all along.

'What were they doing?' I asked.

She shook her head. 'Nothing.'

'What?' I insisted.

'They were kissing.'

'And she had her top off?'

'Yes.'

'How could you be sure?'

'I could see, Shari. There was enough light.' Amanda shook her head again. 'I shouldn't have told you.' She started to get up. I grabbed her arm.

'What else were they doing? Was he fondling her?'

Amanda broke free of my hold and retreated to the end of the bed, where she stood and looked down on me. 'I'm sorry,' she said.

I laughed out loud for a second. 'What are you sorry about? She wasn't kissing Jimmy – if you would even care. You know he was home when you came over? You could have said hi. I know how much you love him. Anyway, I don't care. Dan can do what he wants. You can do what you want. I ain't going to stop you, sister. The whole world can go to hell for all I care.'

Amanda left. And I cried, alone and to myself.

The party should have ended when Dan and Beth returned. I should have openly accused them, ignored their pleas of denial and forgiveness, and then stormed off into the night with Jo chasing after me to make sure I was

OK. The problem was that when Dan and Beth finally did come through the door together, I was too heartsick to speak, and Jo was still busy entertaining Jeff on the couch. It struck me then that my best friend might actually find reason to celebrate the news of Dan and Beth's passionate public petting.

The party *would* have ended if Jo hadn't insisted we talk to the universe after everyone finished dressing. She pulled out her magnet.

'I read about this technique in a book on Taoism,' Jo said, holding up the magnet so that we could all see that it had a brass cap over one end. 'It was originally used thousands of years ago to diagnose health problems. It allows you to question the body directly about what's wrong with it.'

'Is it like a Ouija board?' Beth asked wearily. Even I could sympathise with her. Beth was afraid that Jo was going to get out her Ouija board, as she had done at so many parties before. This is not to say that Jo insisted others share her fascination with the occult or that she couldn't sometimes liven up a dead party by invoking a few dead people. It simply meant that Jo never knew when it was getting late.

'It's similar but different,' Jo said.

'Oh,' I said.

Jo cast me a look that said she knew I wanted to leave but that she also thought we should let the magnet decide when to call it a night. 'Why don't I demonstrate it rather than talk about it?' she said.

'What do you need?' Jeff asked, seemingly interested. He had put away his cigarettes and didn't look nearly so fierce in the light as he had in the dark. There were six of us in the room right then – Amanda, Dan, Beth, Jo, Jeff, and myself – all arranged in a rough circle in the cluttered living room. Sad six, one short of lucky seven.

Jo smiled at Jeff. 'A body.'

'I have one,' Beth volunteered, raising her hand, showing more enthusiasm now that her official boyfriend had made the whole matter respectable with his question. Daniel looked at her and smiled, the bastard.

'We know,' I said, sitting on the floor against a wall.

They ignored me. They wanted to talk to the universe. Only Amanda appeared uninterested. Or else afraid. She continued to hang back in her corner chair. She might have been afraid of what I was going to say. Or else what the universe might know. I suppose we all have our secrets.

But Dan and Beth weren't afraid of anything. They gathered around as Jo slid on to the floor. 'What's the heel like on those shoes you're wearing?' Jo asked Beth.

'They're all right,' Beth said, not having the foggiest

idea what Jo was asking. Jo leaned over and gave Beth's sneakers a brief inspection.

'They'll work,' Jo said. 'Lie down flat on your back.'

'What are you going to do?' Beth asked, now a tad nervous.

'I'm going to put this magnet on the floor at the back of your head,' Jo said, doing precisely that as she spoke. 'And then I'm going to take your ankles in my hands and ask your body questions. When your body wants to answer yes, one of your legs will get longer than the other.'

'Why don't you use her nose?' I asked, thinking of Pinocchio and telling lies and that sort of thing. No one seemed to care. They continued to ignore me.

'Are you serious?' Dan asked.

'You'll see,' Jo said. 'One leg will actually get longer than the other.'

'How does that happen?' Jeff asked.

'Her hip must rotate,' Jo said, cradling Beth's shoes in her palms. Beth had closed her eyes and appeared to be concentrating hard on something unknown to the rest of us.

'No, how does her body know to respond?' Jeff said.

'No one knows,' Jo said. 'Somehow the magnet triggers an answering reflex in the body.'

'Why did you cap one pole of the magnet?' Jeff asked.

'The book said to do it,' Jo said. 'It doesn't work otherwise.' She turned her attention to Beth. 'How do you feel?'

'Different,' Beth whispered.

'Should she feel different?' Daniel asked.

'No,' Jo said, looking down and pressing Beth's heels together. 'Your body must be in good alignment. Your legs are exactly the same length.'

'Thank you,' Beth said.

'She probably has her hips worked on regularly,' I said.

One person in the room didn't ignore me this time. Daniel caught my eye and stared. I stared back in such a manner that I made it clear I knew what had happened in the Jacuzzi. And somehow I knew he was thinking of the comment Jo had made in the car on the way to the party, about how fast he always was – thinking about what an untrustworthy bitch I was. There was something unhealthy in the way we looked at each other right then.

'Is today Beth's birthday?' Jo asked aloud, simultaneously raising Beth's heels off the floor. Jo then nodded for Jeff to check Beth's leg lengths.

'They haven't changed,' Jeff said.

'It's not working?' Beth asked, obviously worried that her body might not be connected to the universe. Jo was unconcerned.

'Think for a moment,' she said. 'It is after twelve. Today is the day after your birthday.'

'Ask an affirmative question,' Jeff said.

'Is Beth a girl?' Jo asked, again raising Beth's feet up. I was too far away to tell, but apparently there was a shift in the length of one of her legs. Jeff leaned forward from his place on the edge of the couch and nodded his head.

'There is a slight difference, yeah,' he said.

'It's not that slight,' Jo said, continuing to keep Beth's heels tightly pressed together. 'The right leg is now an inch longer than the left.'

'And this is her body's way of saying yes?' Jeff asked.

'Yes,' Jo said.

'You can only ask yes-or-no questions?' Jeff said.

'You'd be surprised how much information you *can* get,' Jo said. 'Now, I know what you're going to say, but go ahead and say it anyway.'

Jeff shrugged. 'Beth heard you ask the question. She knows she's a girl. Her body's response could have been subconscious.'

Jo smiled. 'What if I told you it doesn't matter if I say the question aloud or if I just *think* it?'

'You want me to think about being a girl?' Beth asked, frowning, her eyes still closed.

'The legs will still shift?' Jeff asked.

Jo let go of Beth's ankles, climbing to her knees and scooting towards Jeff. 'I'll whisper three questions in your ear that we already know the answers to,' she said. 'Then we'll see if her body responds correctly each time.'

They had a brief huddle, and then Jo got back to Beth's ankles. Since the rest of us didn't know the questions, the demonstration was not exactly overwhelming. When it was done, however, and Jeff had finished comparing Beth's leg lengths, he nodded his approval.

'You did them in the same order you told me?' he asked Jo.

'Yes,' Jo said.

'What did you ask?' Daniel asked.

'First I asked if Beth was pregnant,' Jo said. 'And the answer was no. Her heels didn't shift.'

'Thank God,' Beth said, smiling. It struck me then how cool Beth was playing it for someone who had only a few minutes earlier been sinning in a hot tub with a guy who didn't belong to her.

'Then I asked if Beth was alive,' Jo continued. 'And as I raised her feet off the floor, her right leg got an inch longer. Right, Jeff?'

'It did, yeah,' he said thoughtfully. I suspected that if he knew about Beth's unfaithfulness, he would have cared less. But he did seem to be totally absorbed in what Jo was doing. And she knew it. Her cheeks were flushed with pleasure.

'My third question was if it was Saturday morning,' Jo said. 'And once again, Beth's legs moved.' Jo glanced down at Beth. 'Are you uncomfortable? Can we keep using you to ask our questions?'

Beth squinted her eyes without opening them. 'Yeah, but turn off that lamp. The light's bothering me.'

Jo gestured to Daniel to turn the light off, although it was clear Jo still did not understand why Beth should feel any different. The rest of us pulled in a little closer, including Amanda, who finally came and sat on the floor beside me. The door to the balcony in the kitchen lay wide open. I could feel the night air on my bare feet; it seemed to hug the carpet like a cool sheet. I wanted to go home. My headache refused to go away.

'What should we ask?' Daniel asked.

'Anything,' Jo said, a glint in her eyes. She again took hold of Beth's sneakers. 'Anything at all.'

'Ask if there's going to be another war,' Daniel said.

Jo asked the question out loud, raising Beth's heels a foot or so off the floor and then checking for a shift in leg length. Now that I was close enough to see, I realised the shift was genuine. It was clear-cut.

'Yes,' Jo said.

'Oh, no,' Daniel said, distressed. The poor baby, I thought. The bombs would probably catch him in bed with his neighbour's wife. God, how I wanted to grab that magnet and glue it to the back of his head so that every time he lied his left leg would get shorter and he would trip and fall on his face.

'Of course there's going to be another war,' I said. 'There are small wars going on all the time. Ask if there is going to be another world war in the next twenty years.'

I noticed that Beth's heels returned to an even keel the moment Jo set Beth's feet back on the floor. At the back of my mind, I wondered if Jo was tugging on Beth's ankle whenever she wanted a yes answer.

Jo asked about another world war. Beth's leg shifted a tiny bit.

'What does that mean?' Jeff asked.

'That there might be,' Jo said, obviously taken off guard.

'Did it say in the book you read that a slight movement means maybe?' Jeff asked, obviously not trusting Jo a hundred per cent on this point.

'Yes,' Jo said quickly.

'Ask if I'm going to be rich,' Daniel said.

Jo asked. Beth's right leg didn't budge.

Jo laughed. 'You're going to be a poor can of Spam, Dan.'

Daniel frowned. 'Ask if I'm going to live to an old age.'

'Yes,' Jo said a moment later.

Daniel perked up. 'Am I going to be happy?'

'No,' Jo said. Beth's heels had not moved. Daniel sat back, discouraged.

'I don't know how a magnet can know my future,' he said.

'It's not the magnet,' Jo said. 'It's only the trigger. It's Beth's body that's answering our questions.'

'Her body might have some effect on your future,' I muttered.

That time my comment did not go unnoticed. The room became filled with tension. Yet no one said anything. What was there to say when we had God to talk to? Jo wasn't going to let my bad mood spoil the festivities. She nodded to Amanda.

'Anything you want to know, Bliss?' she asked.

Amanda got up slowly and crawled over beside Jo. 'Can I do it myself?' she asked.

Jo smiled. 'It takes a little practice. Why don't you just let me ask for you?'

Amanda gestured to Beth's feet. 'But you just ask the questions and lift her heels up. I can do that.'

'But why not let me ask?' Jo asked.

'She wants to ask something private,' Jeff said.

Amanda nodded. 'Please?'

'All right,' Jo said reluctantly, moving away. 'But be sure to have your question clearly in mind, or it won't work.'

The magnet did work for Amanda. Sometimes Beth's right leg would get longer when Amanda thought her question and raised Beth's feet, and sometimes Beth's legs would stay the same. It was eerie watching Amanda go through the routine silently. Amanda asked many questions. Or else she asked one question a number of times. I didn't know why I got that impression – that she was hung up on one point. When she was done, she stared off into empty space for a few seconds.

'Are you satisfied?' Jo asked.

'One question,' Amanda said. 'Is this thing always right?'

'I've found it to be,' Jo said carefully.

Amanda looked at her. 'But I just asked it if it was always right, and do you know what it said?'

'What?' Jo asked.

'Maybe,' Amanda said.

Jo motioned for Amanda to scoot aside and took hold of Beth's feet. 'Does the leg-length reflex in Beth's body always respond correctly to our questions?' Jo asked.

Beth's right leg got more than an inch longer.

'Yes,' Jo said.

'That's not the answer I got,' Amanda said. Because she was so often solemn, it was difficult to tell if the magnet had upset her. But she certainly didn't appear to be bursting with joy.

'You must have done it wrong,' Jo said.

Amanda thought a moment. 'Maybe.'

Jo let Jeff ask his questions next. He questioned her out loud, not worried about what we thought. He let Jo handle Beth's feet.

'Is everything in our lives predestined?' he asked.

Jo frowned down at Beth's shoes. 'Her heel budged slightly.'

'Is there a yes-or-no answer to my previous question?' Jeff asked.

'No,' Jo said.

Jeff was getting awfully heavy awfully fast. 'But are certain things in our lives destined?' he asked.

'Yes,' Jo said. 'It's very clear this time.'

'Is the force that we understand as God *directly* answering these questions?' Jeff asked.

'No,' Jo said, and she seemed disappointed.

'Is there a God?' Jeff asked.

'Yes,' Jo said.

'Is he as we imagine him?' Jeff asked.

'No,' Jo said.

71

'Is there life after death?' Jeff asked.

Jo paused.

'Of course there must be life after death if there's a God, Jeff.'

'Ask,' he insisted.

Jo asked. 'Yes,' she said. 'I told you.'

Then he asked the question that on the surface started me on my long fall to my death. He definitely must have had Peter on his mind. 'Is someone who was once alive but is now dead using this leg reflex to try to communicate with us?' he asked.

'Yes,' Jo said.

'Did we know this person when he was alive?' Jeff asked, sitting forward.

'Yes,' Jo said.

'Is this person anxious to talk to us?' Jeff asked.

'Yes,' Jo said, letting go of Beth's feet and looking at him. It was then I noticed that Beth had fallen asleep. She wasn't snoring or anything, but I could tell by the way she was breathing that she was out of it. Jeff had lowered his head and was thinking. Amanda was doing much the same, her expression lost behind a curtain of hair. Daniel shifted uneasily.

'This is creepy,' he said.

Actually, that was an acute observation. The atmosphere

in the room had definitely changed. It was no longer simply tense. It was distorted, as if the room we were in had somehow been overlapped with another room, a place almost the same but not quite. The room felt *heavy*.

'Beth's gone to sleep,' I said. 'Let's call it a night.'

'No,' Jo said suddenly, firmly. She shook Beth's feet. Beth opened her eyes.

'I'm floating,' she whispered.

'We have to find out who we're talking to,' Jo said. 'Right Jeff?'

Was Jo trying to win Jeff's favour by giving him a last chat with his brother? The idea struck me as so perverse I almost screamed. But screaming's not supposed to be cool. There are times, though, when it can save your reputation. Oh, yes, indeed.

Jeff touched Jo on the shoulder. I could practically see the thrill go through Jo's body. It has been said that nothing is as powerful an aphrodisiac as a brush with the supernatural. Well, maybe I'm the one who said it. But Jo was primed. She wasn't going to deny Jeff anything. Beth had closed her eyes again.

'Did you bring your Ouija board?' he asked.

'No,' Jo said.

'I need more than these yes-or-no answers,' Jeff said, his hand still on her shoulder. 'I want whole words.'

Spirits were fine, but this was real male flesh that had ahold of Jo. She nodded quickly. 'We can do it without a board.'

'How?' he asked.

She swallowed. 'One of us can channel this entity.'

'Not me,' Daniel said and giggled foolishly.

'How?' Jeff asked.

'I can put one of us in a hypnotic trance,' Jo said.

'Who?' Jeff asked.

'Shari,' Jo said.

'No way,' I said.

'Why Shari?' Jeff asked.

'It has to be someone I've known all my life.'

Now, Jo was Amanda's first cousin and had known Amanda all her life, but I didn't bring that up. I imagined Amanda would be too shy to invite an entity into her body. Also, I suddenly had a change of heart. I decided I wouldn't mind channelling. My reasoning was simple: it would put me in a perfect position to stop all the nonsense. Once Jo *thought* she had me hypnotised, I was going to say all us entities were exhausted and wanted to go home to sleep.

'All right,' I said. 'What do I do?'

Before we could proceed, we had to wake Beth up once more – no small feat. We got her eyes open, but before

74

she could climb into a vertical position, she passed out again. It was almost as if having the magnet resting at the back of her head had drained her. When she finally was sitting up, I noticed that her eyes looked glazed.

Jo made me lie on my back on the floor in the spot Beth had just vacated. Surprisingly, the spot was not warm. Jo told Daniel to bring a blanket from the bedroom, and he covered me to my chin. Then Jo turned off all the lights and lit a red Christmas candle, which she set on the glass coffee table, off to my right. It was pretty dark, but I could still see everyone clearly enough to identify them. Jo positioned herself just behind my head and had the others kneel around me. Amanda was on my right near the candle, Daniel and Jeff were to my left, and Beth was hanging out near my feet. I thought the whole set up typically New Age.

The candle flame caught my eye. I had always been fond of fires – those of the safe and sane variety – and I found the steadiness of the burning orange wick oddly comforting. I wished, though, without knowing why, that the candle had been any colour but red.

'We're going to start the same way as we did when we played that "dead girl" game at Tricia's party,' Jo said. 'Does everyone remember? We'll pretend that Shari is lying here about to be buried. We'll talk about her as if she's dead. Just as important, we'll try to *feel* as if she's dead. We should get sad. But unlike the other game, we won't start to talk about how light she's getting. We won't try to lift her into the air with our fingertips. When we have her in a deep trance, we'll start to ask her questions, just as we asked the magnet. Only Shari should be able to answer us out loud. All right?' Everyone nodded. 'Close your eyes, Shari, and just listen to my suggestions. *You* don't have to worry about anything. *We'll* take care of everything.'

I closed my eyes and thought back to the last time we had played the 'dead girl' game. I hadn't been one of the subjects, but the two girls we used, Tricia Summers and Leona Woods, did get amazingly light after we went through the whole burial ritual. In fact, it had taken only one finger each from Jo and me to lift Tricia all the way to the ceiling. She had seemed as light as a feather. Amazing, I had thought at the time, yet I was glad they weren't going to be floating me into the air. I was afraid of heights.

'Take a deep breath, Shari,' Jo said, her voice soft but firm. 'And let it out slowly. Feel the air leaving your lungs. Feel the life leaving your body. That's good, that's fine. Now, take another breath, and again let it out very slowly. And this time, feel your heart slowing down, becoming faint. Listen to me, Shari, and don't be afraid. You're going to be all right. It is only your body you're leaving behind, not your soul.'

It may have been because I was tired, but the suggestions had a profound effect on me. I started to relax immediately. The tension in my shoulders and neck began to dissolve, and I could feel the pulse of my headache diminishing. It was almost like Jo had said – my actual heartbeat was slowing down. The muscles of my back eased deeper into the carpet. I began to feel as Beth said she had, as if I were floating.

Jo continued her suggestions for a while – I'm not sure exactly how long – and then there seemed to be a long period of silence. I was still conscious of my body, of where I was, and yet at the same time, I felt removed from the situation. I didn't even feel like thinking. I just wanted to drift, like a balloon on the wind. But even though I was relaxed, I didn't feel content. The wind was pulling me along, but I wasn't sure if I liked the direction it was taking me. I was afraid, however, to try to move, to stop what was about to happen.

That was it right there. I *was* a tiny bit afraid. Despite what Jo had said about my being safe, I felt as if I were about to lose something precious to me, that I had, in fact, already lost it. The idea of Daniel kissing Beth in the

Jacuzzi flashed across my brain, and with it came a stab of pain. Then it was my brother's face that I saw swim by and fade away, drowning in the darkness inside. Daniel's voice came to me from far off.

'She was a good friend of mine. We had a lot of good times together, and I'm going to miss her.'

That was all I heard him say. Two lines about his poor dead girlfriend and not one word about how much he had loved her. My sorrow deepened and, with it, the darkness. It was suddenly so dark inside that it seemed as if I were about to be devoured, soul and all.

I was no longer floating. I was sinking, and fast. I don't believe I could have opened my eyes if I had tried. It was Jeff Nichol's turn to remember Shari Cooper.

'I really didn't know her that well, not as well as my brother did. I suppose if I had known her better, I would have liked her more. We never talked that much. It's too bad she's dead, though. It's a real shame.'

None of them sounded sad. It was almost as if they were remembering someone they had murdered. Amanda spoke next.

'I didn't know her very well, either. I knew her brother better. But she loved her brother – Jim. She was crazy about him.'

She sounded like a record that had already been

played. Beth went to speak next. She was a broken record. I remembered that was what I had got her for her birthday, a Beatles album from the discount bin. I could remember the party. I knew I was still at it; I hadn't disappeared into the ozone. I knew everything that was happening and that it was only a game. Yet a portion of me, a huge portion, continued to fall, deeper and deeper, down through the earth to where it hid its most terrible secrets. They could have already lowered me into my grave and covered me over with dirt.

Beth couldn't speak. Some kind of entity must have crawled inside her and bit her tongue while she lay on the cold floor. Jo spoke instead. *She* sounded sad.

'She was my best friend. She was more important to me than anything. I used to tell her everything, and now she's gone. I can't believe it.'

Jo had to pause to collect herself. Yet she, too, seemed far away. I felt that if I were to reach out to touch her, I would snatch only thin air.

'But she's still alive to me, because I won't forget her,' Jo continued, her voice gaining strength. 'None of those who have died is really gone. They're always near, speaking to us in whispers we don't ordinarily hear. But occasionally we can hear them, *if* they find someone to speak through.'

Jo paused again. She might have cleared her throat. Or I might have cleared my own. I couldn't tell what was happening. I had stopped falling finally, but I doubted if I would be coming up for air soon. Something strange was happening, stranger than all that had previously transpired. Maybe it was a delayed reaction to discovering I was now an *ex*-girlfriend. Perhaps it had something to do with Jo's suggestions.

Then again, it could have been one final omen.

When Jo spoke next, a weight of sorrow heavy enough to crush the world descended on me from nowhere and everywhere at once. I felt it on top of my chest, crunching my ribs, my heart.

'Who are you?' Jo asked.

My voice sounded. But it was not mine. It was not me.

'Most people would probably call me a ghost,' the voice said. 'I am, after all, dead. But I don't think of myself that way. It wasn't so long ago that I was alive, you see. I was only eighteen. I had my whole life in front of me . . .'

Someone gasped. Someone else cried out a name – *Peter*. More cries followed. Everyone was talking at once. The candle had been knocked over. There was a danger of fire.

I snapped out of my trance. At last my body was my own again. For a moment. I threw off my blanket and jumped up. At first, I couldn't see a thing. I wasn't even sure if I had my eyes open. The room was pitch black. Then Jeff turned on the lamp near the sofa, and the glare hit me like a hot flare. Jeff was mad at me. They all were.

'Why did you stop?' he demanded.

'You shouldn't have jumped up,' Jo said.

'You were faking that,' Daniel said.

I wasn't a fake, I wanted to shout at them. But I couldn't get out a word. I was too choked up. When I looked around at their faces, I couldn't find a trace of a thing I had assumed had been with me all the days of my life to one degree or another. There was no love. Daniel just wanted to be back in the tub with Beth. Jo just wanted to be alone with Jeff. I hung my head low, smelling smoke. Amanda was on the floor at my knees, turning the toppled candle upright. The red wax on the carpet was blood red and still hot. But my body was cold; I was shivering. I felt so overcome with loneliness right then that I thought I would be consumed and die of it.

'What is it?' Amanda asked, her clear, cold grey eyes holding mine.

'Nothing,' I whispered. 'It's nothing.'

I ran from the room then, through the kitchen and out on to the balcony and into the night. I remember standing by the rail, feeling the smooth wood beneath my shaking fingers. I remember seeing the flat black ocean and thinking how nice it would be if I could only exercise my magical powers and fly over to it and disappear beneath its surface for ages to come. I remember time passing.

Then things went bad.

I felt a sensation. It was not one of being pushed; it was, rather, a feeling of rising up. Then of spinning, of being disoriented. I saw the edge of the condominium roof, the stars. There were only a few of the latter, and they weren't very bright. Not compared to the lamppost standing beside the cement walkway, which suddenly began to rush towards me at incredible speed. It was only in the last instant that I realised I had gone over the edge of the balcony. That I was falling headfirst towards the ground.

I didn't feel the blow of the impact. But I do remember rolling over and looking up. Now there were millions of stars in the sky. Orange ones and green ones and blue ones. There were also red ones. Big fat red ones, whose number rapidly grew as I watched, blotting out all the others in the heavens, until soon they were all that remained, part of a colossal wave of smothering hot wax.

I blacked out. I died.

CHAPTER 5

When I came to, I was home in bed, lying on top of the sheets in the dark. At first I didn't question what I was doing there. Many times throughout my life I would wake up in bed and not know what the hell was going on. I was a deep sleeper; in fact, it was normal for me to take several minutes after sleeping to figure out what planet I was on.

On the other hand, I did feel *strange*. I was mildly surprised when I sat up that I wasn't dizzy. For some reason I expected to be dizzy. Yet when I paused to ask myself why, I had no answer. I remembered being at the party, but I didn't remember the end of the party. Certainly, I had no recollection of falling to my death.

I climbed to my feet and walked to the open door and peeked out. As I have already mentioned, my bedroom was off a hall that overlooked a large portion of the downstairs. Because most of the downstairs lights were off, it was natural that I wasn't able to see well. Except I couldn't see for what appeared to be the wrong reasons. It was less dark than it should have been; the walls and furniture were not glowing or anything, but they weren't exactly not glowing, either. They were brighter than they should have been with nothing shining on them.

Then there was the *stuff* in the air. It was the stuff, I decided, that was blurring my vision. It was everywhere, translucent, vaguely gaseous, and flowing, very slightly, around the entire room, up the curtains and over the bookcase. In fact, the vapours actually seemed to be flowing *through* the walls. I blinked my eyes, but it did not go away. And yet I had to wonder if I was really seeing it at all. It was very fine, almost invisible.

I walked down the hall to Jimmy's room and stuck my head through his partially opened door. He was asleep, lying on his back, his sheets thrown off, his right arm resting behind his head. If I hadn't known that he had to get up early, I would have tried to wake him up. The feeling of dislocation refused to leave me, and I wanted to talk to him about it. But I left him alone. His computer was still on, of course.

I went downstairs. My parents were in the kitchen; I heard them talking before I actually saw them, and even before I went inside and joined them at the table, I thought they sounded different. My mother had one of those high-society voices that could be the embodiment of charm when she was in a good mood and nothing short of bitchy when she wasn't. My dad had a deep, authoritative voice that never changed no matter what his state of mind. It certainly never sounded muffled, as it did now. Their words seemed to be coming to me through a layer of invisible insulation. Yet I mustn't overemphasise the effect. I could understand what they were saying. They were talking about money.

'Hi, Mom. Hi, Dad,' I said as I stepped into the kitchen and grabbed ahold of one of the chairs to pull out so I could sit down. But it was weird – it felt stuck to the floor. I couldn't get it to budge. I couldn't be bothered hassling with it, so I slumped down in a chair near the stove instead, a few feet away from the table, off to my parents' right. They didn't even look over at me, which I thought was rude of them.

'Did you hear what Mrs Meyer had to say about that loan you and Bill got from Mr Hoyomoto's firm?' my mother asked my father, taking a bite of the chocolate cake Amanda and Mrs Parish and I had talked about at length.

'No,' my father replied, lighting up a cigar and leaning back in his chair. 'But I imagine she said something about us helping the Japanese buy the world out from under us.'

He looked tired, as did my mother, but they both looked good. They were dressed to the hilt, and they were a handsome couple. My father was of medium height, solid, with shoulders that could ram down a door. He radiated strength and masculinity. He didn't smile often, but he wasn't a cold man. He was just too busy to smile. There was too much building to be done. He had closely clipped rust-coloured hair, a tan, and small, sharp blue eyes.

My mother bore him scant resemblance, except that she also was attractive. She was tall and sleek, quick and loose. Her wide, thick-lipped mouth and her immaculately conceived black hair were her prizes. At present she had on a long black dress slit up the side to reveal one of her smooth white legs. It was odd she was eating cake that late. She usually took such good care of herself. In fact, taking care of herself took up so much of her time that she couldn't take quite as good care of us. But she loved my father, and she also loved her children. It was just a shame that she loved us all in a way she had learned from her therapist.

'She didn't say it in those words,' my mother replied, her voice cracking slightly as if it were being electrically interfered with. 'But you'd think you were selling secrets to the Russians from the tone she took. Really, she's nothing but a pain in the ass.'

'Her husband's not a bad fellow, though,' my father said, blowing a cloud of smoke towards the ceiling. It was a strange cloud. It had that *stuff* in it, that mysterious haze that could have been a super-refined blend of smoke and gas and water all rolled into one.

'Oh, Ted,' my mother said, putting down her cake fork and waving her hand. 'He's adorable, absolutely wonderful. I can't imagine how he's stayed with that shrew so long.'

'I almost threw out that cake,' I said.

'He's a good man,' my father said.

'He's too good for her,' my mother said. 'But you know, I heard from Wendy that Colleen Meyer's got six wells down in Texas.'

'Ted told me only three of them are pumping,' my father said.

'Three pumping wells can make up for a lot of character flaws,' my mother said.

'Hello,' I said. 'It's me. I'm here, waiting patiently to have my presence acknowledged.'

They continued to ignore me. I couldn't understand it.

Then the phone rang. My mother stood up and walked over and picked it up, carrying her cake with her. But just before she answered it, she said something really weird.

'That's probably Shari,' she said.

'Huh?' I said.

My mother lifted the handset to her ear. She was smiling. She was tired, but her life was in order. She had a big house, a rich, hard-working husband, great clothes, far-out-jewellery, one wonderful son, and one OK daughter.

'Hello,' she said. 'Yes, this is she. Who is this, please?'

My mother listened for several seconds, and as she did so, her hand holding the cake plate began to shake. But her smile didn't vanish immediately. It underwent a metamorphosis instead, slowly tightening at the edges, bit by bit, until soon it could not be confused for a smile at all. She dropped the plate holding the cake. It shattered on the tiles. Her mouth twisted into a horrible grimace. My father and I both jumped up.

'What is it?' my father asked.

'It's Shari,' she whispered, slowly putting down the phone and sagging back against the counter. My father grabbed her at the waist, steadying her.

'What's happened?' he demanded, anxious now.

'Yeah, what's going on?' I asked, coming over to them.

'Shari,' my mother whispered, closing her eyes and shaking her head.

'What?' I asked. 'What's wrong?'

Still holding on to my mother, my father snapped up the phone. 'This is Mr Cooper,' he said. 'Who is this?'

His face paled as he listened. 'Will she be all right?' he asked after a minute. 'What do you mean?' He paused, listened some more, biting his lower lip all the while, something I had never seen him do before in my life. 'You don't know?' he asked finally. 'Why don't you know? I see, I see. Yes, I know where that is. Yes, we'll be there shortly.'

My father didn't thank whoever had called. He just hung up the phone and hugged my mother, who was close to collapsing in his arms.

'Hey,' I said, beginning to get emotional. 'Would someone please tell me what the hell is going on?'

They ignored me. Yet that was not it. They didn't hear me. Something terrible must have happened, I thought, that they could get into such a state that they blocked me out altogether. I reached out for my father's arm.

'Dad, please,' I said. 'I need to know, too.'

I might as well have not been in the room. My father helped my mother over to the table, sat her in the chair, and took her hands in his. 'We don't know yet, Christine,' he said.

My mother kept shaking her head, her eyes closed. 'It's no good,' she whispered. 'It was too far. Oh, God. Shari.'

'I have to go get Jim,' he said, letting go of her.

'Yeah, go get Jimmy,' I said, nodding vigorously. But my mother suddenly opened her eyes and grabbed my father's arm.

'No, we can't tell him,' she said. 'Leave him alone.'

My father shook his head. 'I have to get him.' He leaned over and kissed her on the top of her head as she squeezed her eyes shut again. 'The three of us should be together.'

'Aren't there four of us?' I asked. Obviously, something dreadful had happened, but there was a note of bitterness in my question. Jimmy had always been their favourite. I had never been jealous of him, but I had never felt that parents should have favourites, especially their own.

My father left. My mother cradled her head in her arms on the table. She wasn't crying, but she was having a hard time breathing. I sat beside her and put my hand on top of her head, my resentment of a moment ago disappearing.

'It'll be all right, Mom,' I said.

She sat up suddenly and stared right at me, her mouth hanging open slightly, and I was mildly relieved that I had at last made some impression on her. But when she kept staring at me and didn't speak, my relief quickly changed to something quite different. A splinter of fear began to form deep inside me – a faint fear, true, but a cold one.

Something was not right, I told myself. Not right by a million miles. I prayed Jimmy would come quick and make it all right.

My brother appeared a minute later. He was suffering, however, from the same problem as my parents. He was so shook up that he had totally blotted me out of his awareness. He was not as pale as my father, nor was he trembling as my mother was. His symptoms were more subtle, worse in a way. His eyes – those warm, friendly blue eyes – were vacant. Even as he crossed the kitchen and hugged my mother, they remained blank.

'Jimmy!' I cried. But he didn't hear me. I thought he couldn't even see me.

They were all going to a hospital of some kind. I had got that much from my father's remarks. They were hardly dressed for it. My father had on a wrinkled black tux, my mother a tired evening gown. Jimmy had pulled on a pair of blue jeans and a white sweatshirt, but he had forgotten his shoes and socks. As I followed him out to the car, I said something about it being chilly. I could have been talking to myself.

So far the night had abounded with extraordinary events. Yet nothing had prepared me for what happened when I reached the front door. In keeping with recent developments, Jimmy ignored the fact that I was behind him and opened and closed the door without giving me a chance to get outside. Naturally, I tried to open the door myself.

But I couldn't.

The doorknob wouldn't turn. I twisted it as hard as I could, clockwise and counterclockwise, but still it wouldn't budge. It seemed to be not only stuck but somehow *different*. As I shifted my hold to try again, the difference hit me like a bucket of ice water.

The doorknob and my hand were not connecting. I was touching it, I knew, but it was as if an extremely fine barrier was preventing me from having any effect on it. Oh, was I confused. To touch something and not to have it respond to your touch. I stepped back and waited for my father to open the door for me. There seemed nothing else to do. He came by a few seconds later, leading my mother by the shoulder, and I managed to slip outside in front of them.

Jimmy was already in his car. He sat hunched over the steering wheel, with the engine running, staring straight ahead. He didn't have a red Ferrari like me. He had a white Ford station wagon, and he was paying for it with the money he earned working for the telephone company. My father helped my mother into the front seat of the Ford, fastening her seat belt for her. She was holding a handkerchief to her face now, and I believe she was weeping quietly. I hopped in the backseat when my father opened the rear door on the passenger side. I wasn't about to wrestle with another door. It was amazing, I thought as I settled in the seat behind Jimmy, that I had not bumped my father as I squeezed past him.

But I wasn't in the mood to be amazed. I was suffering from the worst kind of fear – fear of unknown origin. No one in the car was speaking, and I chose to remain silent. I sat by the window and stared up at the sky, at the stars. Never before had I found them so numerous, so bright and varied in colour. But it was the red ones that drew my attention. There was something about them that filled me with dread. I kept expecting them to suddenly swell and drown out the others. They were dark red, like dripping candles seen through blood-smeared glass.

I recognised the hospital – Newport Memorial. It was located on a low hill only a couple of blocks from the beach, a fifteen-storey cube. I had taken Jo to the emergency ward there the summer before when she had slipped on the rocks on the Newport jetty and cut her knee open. The nurses and doctor had been nice. As Jimmy parked near the emergency entrance, I wondered who we could possibly be going to see. My grandfather – my mother's father – had a bad heart. My father's brother had also been having serious stomach ulcers. Climbing out of the car with the others, I prayed it wasn't family.

We went inside, and I was surprised when my nose didn't react to the hospital's medicinal smell; ordinarily, the odour of alcohol and drugs made me cringe. But I smelled nothing, although I continued to see things I knew I shouldn't be seeing. The stuff in the air had not gone away, and now, walking with my family towards the front desk, I noticed threads of shadow weaving through the film, growing and fading in front of me, almost as though the shadows were alive and seeking me. I didn't want them to touch me; I was afraid they'd hurt me.

My mother and father went to talk to the nurse on duty while Jimmy stopped at a drinking fountain in the hallway leading to the examination rooms. I went with him. He didn't appear to be thirsty. He just ran the water up high for a few seconds, without leaning over for a sip, and then thrust his hands in his pockets and stared at the floor.

'Jimmy,' I said. 'Why won't you talk to me? Why won't you even look at me?'

He ignored me, and in desperation I reached out to grab his arm, to scream his name so loudly that they would hear it on the top floors of the building. But I choked on the word.

For an instant, my fingers appeared to go through the material in his sweatshirt. To go right *into* his arm. I recoiled in horror.

Jimmy rejoined my parents. The woman at the desk picked up a phone and requested a doctor somebody. The young white-coated gentleman appeared within seconds; it seemed he had been waiting for us. I would have tried to say hello to him had I not still been in shock over my hands' newfound powers of penetration. He spoke quietly to my dad for a few seconds, and then we were off.

I expected the doctor to lead us to one of the examination rooms, or perhaps to the critical care ward. But he immediately whisked us into an elevator and pushed the bottom button. The doors riffled shut. My father turned to the guy in confusion.

'Why are we going down?' he asked.

'I told you, I'm just an intern,' the young man said. 'Dr Leeds is in charge of the case.' He added, almost ashamed, 'I'd rather you saved your questions for him.'

'But what's in the basement?' my father asked. And then, more reluctantly: 'Is she all right?'

The intern spoke to the elevator wall. 'Ask Dr Leeds.'

Downstairs, we walked along a short, narrow hall that

dead-ended in twin green metal doors. They opened from the inside just before we reached them. A white-haired man appeared and clasped my father's hand. He looked like a kindly old country doctor. I could imagine the twinkle in his eyes as he handed a little girl patient a lollipop and told her that if she took her medicine like a big girl, she would be outside and playing with her friends in no time. But now the doctor was not smiling.

The intern nodded and left.

The white and black letters on the doors said: MORGUE.

'Mr and Mrs Cooper,' the elderly gentleman said. 'I'm Dr Leeds. I'm afraid I have bad news for you.'

'How is she?' my father asked. 'Is she going to be all right?'

'No, she's not.' Dr Leeds let go of my father's hand and looked him straight in the eye. 'She's dead.'

'Who's dead?' I asked.

It must have been a stupid question. The rest of my family knew the individual's name. My father paled again, much worse than he had in the kitchen when he had picked up the phone. My mother literally doubled over in grief. Jimmy had to grab her to keep her from passing out. I couldn't bear it. I had to turn away. When I looked back a few seconds later, my mother had somehow managed to straighten herself up, although she was crying openly now.

'I want to see her,' she said.

Dr Leeds looked concerned. 'Later would be better.'

'No,' my mother said, wiping her damp cheek. 'Now.'

'Honey, please,' my father said, reaching out to take her from Jimmy. My mother would have none of it.

'I'm seeing her!' she cried, brushing off both Jimmy and my father. 'I *have* to see her.' Then she suddenly stopped, clenching her eyes shut, her whole being shaking. 'My baby.'

Her baby? I said to myself. My mother didn't have a baby. She didn't even like babies.

'Would it be possible to see her?' my father asked.

'She fell four storeys, headfirst, on to a cement sidewalk,' Dr Leeds said reluctantly.

'You just can't take her,' my mother pleaded pitifully, her head bowed. 'Jim, don't let him take your sister.'

Your sister? I thought miserably.

'But *I'm* his sister,' I whispered.

My father and Dr Leeds exchanged uneasy glances. Jimmy stepped forward. His eyes were still vacant, but there was a trace of life around his mouth, a flicker of strength.

'It'll be hard for us to see what happened,' he said quietly. 'We know that. But I think it could be harder for us to have to think what happened, without seeing her. If you know what I mean?'

Dr Leeds considered a moment. 'All right,' he said finally, turning towards the green metal doors. 'Give me a few minutes.'

While waiting with my family in the bleak hallway, I started to get a funny feeling. I was already scared and confused, but this new feeling was worse. My cold splinter of fear had grown long and sharp in the last half-hour. Now it was like an icy blade that was threatening to cut my sanity in half and leave me floundering in darkness for eternity. Yes, eternity – that was the element that hit me then. Something terrible had happened, I realised, and whatever it was, it was for ever.

The deduction wasn't that clever.

'Morgue,' I whispered aloud to myself, to no one.

Dr Leeds reappeared approximately five minutes later and led my family through the double green doors. Apparently everyone had gone home for the night; there were only the five of us in the morgue. And maybe, I thought with growing understanding, there were fewer.

Off to the right was an open square room with rows of lockers. Only they weren't lockers. I'd seen enough police shows. They were the cubicles in which they stashed the stiffs.

Off to the left was a white-tiled wall. In the middle were three tables. The centre one was occupied. There was a person there, a short dead person, lying under a thin white sheet. Dr Leeds stepped to the head of the table. The rest of us followed. We had asked for it, and now we had to take it.

Dr Leeds slowly pulled down the sheet. He appeared to be starting at the head. The first thing we saw, however, was not a head; it was a green towel, and it was stained dark and wet. The doctor had obviously just wrapped the towel around the girl's hair. I could tell it was a girl. The conversation on the other side of the green doors had made that clear enough, and a lock of her dark-blonde hair had peeped out from beneath the towel. There was no blood on the hair, on those particular strands, but it didn't require a great deal of imagination to see that the rest of her hair must be a disaster.

It was, of course, silly of me to wonder what kind of shampoo it would take to clean that hair when it was clear that the entire top of the girl's skull had been crushed to a pulp.

Even before Dr Leeds folded down the sheet further and revealed the girl's face – washed clean of blood – I knew what we would see. I knew that hair. I had fought with it all my life, and now it would rest in peace for ever, along with that face.

A moment later Dr Leeds folded down the sheet, tucking it under her chin as if it were a blanket that could keep her warm. He stepped back. Her eyes were closed, thankfully, and although a ghastly black and blue patch had coloured her forehead and sent bruised streaks down the sides of her cheeks almost to her mouth, death had not stolen her beauty. You see, that's how I felt then, in the presence of a person who could have lit many lives with her beauty had she just been given the chance.

My father didn't move. My mother couldn't move. But Jimmy reached out and touched the girl's lips with the tip of his finger. It was fortunate his fingers strayed no higher. I remembered the long fall towards the sidewalk then, the fat red stars, the wave of hot wax covering the sky, my blood flowing over my open eyes. Maybe it had been Dr Leeds who had closed them. It was good. Better she remain a sleeping beauty, I thought. I knew if Jimmy were to open them, they would no longer be the sparkling green she had told him they were, nor even the warm brown he had thought they must be. They wouldn't be beautiful. They would only be flat and colourless.

It was me lying there. Just me.

CHAPTER 6

I have read articles describing how hard it is to accept the death of a loved one. How people often go through phases where they actually deny the person is really gone. I can imagine how difficult it must be. Yet I must say it is harder to accept one's own death.

As long as I stood in the morgue with my body, I could intellectually understand that the fall off Beth's balcony had killed me. But when my family left the room a few minutes later and I followed them out of the green doors and back down the hall, I began to have doubts. I began to get upset, angry. I couldn't be dead, I told myself. I was too young. I had too much to do. I hadn't done anything wrong. Besides, how could I be talking with myself if there was no one left to talk to? It simply made no sense that I was dead. It was illogical.

I decided I must be dreaming.

This decision didn't last long. The death state can vary in the extreme, yet it is usually much closer to the waking state than dreaming. I didn't try pinching myself or anything silly like that. I simply paused for a moment and examined my thinking process and realised I could not be unconscious.

On the other hand, that didn't mean I couldn't help believing that someone somewhere had made a terrible mistake. I tried telling my family just that after the doctor bid them a sympathetic farewell and they climbed into the elevator.

'Hey,' I said as the doors closed and we started up. 'I know you can't hear me too well for some reason for other, but you've got to listen to me. That girl in there was not me. She couldn't be me. I'm me, and I'm right here. Mom, look at me. I'm all right. Dad, that doctor's a nice guy and all that, but I swear, he's messed me up with someone else. Jimmy, you know I can't be dead. I wouldn't die on you.' I reached out and hugged my brother. My hands did not go through his flesh this time, but they did not touch him, either. I could have been trying to hug a reflection in the mirror. 'Jimmy?' I cried, pleading.

It was no use. They exited the elevator without a glance over their shoulders to make sure I had got off safely. But I continued to follow them. What else could I do? There was a handsome blond policeman waiting by the emergency front desk. He wanted to have a word with them. I chose not to listen. I went and sat on one of the chairs in the waiting room. A young couple were there with their three-year-old son, who had split his upper lip open. It didn't look serious. The child was colouring in a colouring book, and the mother and father were talking about how much fun they were going to have in Hawaii on their vacation.

A few minutes later the policeman and my family started for the exit together. I had to pull myself out of my chair to go after them. I didn't have a headache or a stomach ache or any other specific physical complaint. I just didn't feel well.

Outside, I realised dissension had entered the group. Apparently Jimmy wanted to go somewhere that the others – particularly the policeman – didn't want him to go. It took a moment for me to understand that he intended to go to Beth's place.

I got all excited at the idea. If we went to Beth's condo together, I thought, we would be able to figure out exactly what had happened. Then we could prove that I was really all right, and people would start seeing me again!

Jimmy finally got his way. The policeman agreed to take my parents home. My brother embraced my mother and father as he said goodbye. It was hard to look at my mother, even though I could see her much clearer than I had any right to in the dark parking lot. She just kept shaking, and I kept thinking that if she didn't stop soon, her heart would begin to skip beats, and she'd have a heart attack. I felt guilty as I ran away from my parents, chasing Jimmy as he jogged towards his car. But I had no difficulty climbing over the driver's seat into the passenger's seat when Jimmy opened his door. I was already getting good at it.

We were almost to Beth's house, coasting along the coast highway at a high speed, the ocean off to our left, when the worst possible thing happened. It was worse than seeing a pretty young girl lying on a cold morgue slab and realising it was me. Jimmy suddenly pulled over to the side of the road and laid his head on the steering wheel and began to cry.

I had seen my brother upset before, but I had never seen him cry. I would not have thought it possible. Oh, he wasn't so tough that I couldn't imagine him breaking down. It was just that I couldn't imagine him doing it where I could see him. That was what made it all so horrible; I was here, and he was there, and there was hardly anything separating us – nothing at all, really.

Only the entire span of an uncaring universe.

'No, Shari,' he whispered as he closed his eyes and sobbed in his clenched fingers. I tried to unclench them, to soothe him, but I could not. I couldn't because his sister was dead, and I was his sister, and it was only right that we should both grieve. It was then, finally and for ever, that I accepted the fact that my life was over.

'Yes, Jimmy,' I said and wept with him.

When we reached Beth's place, I made the mistake of letting Jimmy climb out of the car in front of me, and then, of course, I couldn't get the car door open. Fortunately, he had left the window down, and I was able to squeeze through the space. It took me a couple of minutes, however, and by then Jimmy had already entered the complex, leaving me trapped at the front gate, unable to turn the knob or ring the bell. I realised I was a ghost. I considered trying to walk through the gate. But I had a horrible fear that I'd get stuck. I just couldn't bring myself to make the attempt.

There were a couple of police cars sitting in the visitors' parking lot. As I paced the gate area waiting for someone to appear and let me in, a blue truck pulled up and parked beside them. But the driver didn't get out, and I started to become frustrated. I headed over to his truck to try to hurry him along.

He was a man on his way down in life. In his mid-forties, he had on a frumpy green sports coat and a wrinkled white shirt with a loosely knotted purple tie caught beneath his oversize belt. He needed a good meal. His thin brown hair was going grey, and his red wizened face had seen either too much sun or too much life. He looked burned out. He was lifting a pint of whisky to his lips when I tapped on his window.

'Hey, mister,' I said. 'They're talking about me in there, and I want to hear what they're saying. Let's get a move on.'

In response, he took a deep swallow and coughed. I probably would have left him right then if I hadn't noticed that he had a CB radio in his truck. It cracked to life, and he set down his bottle and flipped it off. He withdrew a handful of breath mints from his coat pocket and began to chew them down, one after another. When he was done, he picked up his pint and took another huge hit. It amazed me that such a wasted individual could afford such a nice truck.

After finally capping his bottle and stowing it under the seat, he climbed out and grabbed another handful of mints from his jacket. I followed him to the front gate. I couldn't smell his breath – I couldn't smell anything – but I doubted that he was drunk; his step was firm and direct.

He pressed the button to Beth's condo – number 413.

'This is Garrett,' he said, clearing his throat.

'Do you know Beth's family?' I asked, for all the good it did. The gate buzzed open, and I followed Garrett inside. I trailed him all the way up to the third floor. He was headed the same place I was. He walked into Beth's place without knocking.

All those who had been at the party – Daniel, Beth, Jeff, Jo and Amanda – were sitting in the living room. They looked shocked, but no one was crying. Daniel was on the loveseat with Beth. Jo and Jeff were seated in individual chairs. Amanda was alone on the couch. Standing with Jimmy in the dining room were a couple of police officers. One strode over to greet Garrett, holding out his hand.

'Hello, Lieutenant, I'm Officer Fort,' he said. 'This is my partner, Officer Dreiden. And this is the deceased's older brother, James Cooper. Have you been assigned to this case?'

'Yeah,' Garrett said, shaking his hand briefly.

This was the lieutenant who had been assigned to my case? I asked myself, horrified. I didn't even know what my case was, but I certainly didn't want a boozer put in charge of it.

'Just you?' Officer Fort asked.

'Yeah.' Garrett turned to Jimmy. 'Why don't you have a seat, son.' Jimmy did as he suggested, sitting on the couch beside solemn Amanda, who took his hand and held it in her lap. Garrett spoke to Officer Fort. 'What are we looking at here?'

Fort was cut in the same mould as the cop at the hospital: young, blond, handsome. He had, however, a high, annoying voice. He began to annoy me the moment he opened his mouth.

'It looks pretty clear-cut,' he said. 'The kids were trying to have a séance when the deceased, Shari Cooper, got upset over a couple of remarks the kids made and ran to the balcony and jumped off.'

'*What?*' I shouted, standing in the centre of the floor. 'I jumped off the balcony? I didn't jump off the balcony. I *fell* off it. I—'

I stopped. How could I have fallen? The blasted rails reached practically to my neck. I looked towards the balcony. The rails were still in place, standing straight and firm. It was funny, but it wasn't until then that I began to question how I happened to be dead.

'Shari would never have done that,' Jimmy broke in, bitter.

'Were you here when this happened?' Garrett asked.

'No,' Jimmy said. 'I was home in bed, sleeping.'

'Were the rest of these young people here?' Garrett asked Officer Fort.

'These were the only ones present.'

Garrett addressed the group. 'Does everyone agree that Shari jumped?' he asked.

'She must have,' Beth said.

'Yeah,' Daniel agreed.

'No!' I screamed.

Garrett looked at Jeff. 'Well?'

Jeff shrugged, trying to light a cigarette. He appeared as cool as usual, except he couldn't get his match to light. 'I don't know what happened.'

'You didn't see her jump?' Garrett asked.

'No.'

'I didn't, either,' Jo said. She didn't appear unusually upset, which upset me a great deal. But Jo, I had to remind myself, seldom showed anything when she was hurt or hurting.

'Did anyone see her jump?' Garrett asked. No one responded, although Amanda moved closer to Jimmy. Sighing under his breath, Garrett turned to Officer Fort. 'I want to have a talk with these kids,' he said.

'Now?'

'Yeah. Alone.'

Officer Fort didn't like the idea. 'The couple who live

here have been notified about what happened. They should be here any second.'

'So?' Garrett said. 'You and your partner go downstairs and welcome them. Tell them the place is off-limits for tonight.'

'The whole night?'

'Yeah.'

Fort glanced at his partner. 'Dreiden and I have already questioned the kids at length. Don't you want to hear our report?'

'I can't imagine there could be anything you could add to the report you've already made,' Garrett said dryly.

'Are you sure you don't want our help?'

I could not be certain, but the way Fort held Garrett's eye as he spoke made me feel that Fort believed Garrett incapable of handling the situation, that Fort might in fact be aware of Garrett's drinking problem. But since Fort had already classified me as a suicide, I wasn't inclined to favour him over Garrett.

'Yeah,' Garrett said, obviously growing tired of the sameness of the questions. He made a gesture of dismissal towards the door. The two uniformed policemen left reluctantly.

'Can I stay?' Jimmy asked.

'That'll be fine,' Garrett said. Then he spoke to the

group. 'I know all of you have had a bad night. Try to relax for a few minutes while I take a quick look around.'

Garrett disappeared into the hall. Nobody spoke for a long while. Finally, Daniel asked nervously, 'What's he looking for?'

'Evidence that Shari didn't jump,' Jo said.

'She didn't jump,' Jimmy said softly.

That killed the conversation right there. Amanda stroked Jimmy's hand. I had to look away. I had tried to do the same thing in the car on the ride over.

When Garrett reappeared, he took a chair from the dining table and placed it at the end of the living room, sitting down and pulling a pen and notepad from his coat. I was just glad he didn't pull out a bottle. Yet I was having to revise my initial impression of him. His blue eyes were bloodshot, true, but they were also sharp. As he scanned the group, I didn't believe he missed much. Except me, of course, and I could have told him a thing or two.

'We have a simple floor plan here,' he began. 'We have a living room, with attached dining area, a kitchen, and a balcony. We have two master bedrooms. The one at the end of the hall has its own separate balcony, which faces south, down the coast. The other bedroom leads directly on to the west-facing balcony and faces the ocean. Tell me, when Shari ran from here, did she go through the kitchen or the first bedroom?'

'The kitchen,' Jo said.

Garrett apparently wanted to get that point out of the way before anything else. He leaned back in his chair, crossing his legs and resting the tip of his unpolished black right shoe a fraction of an inch from the edge of Beth's beautiful glass coffee table and a foot above the red wax stain on the floor. They had put the candle away.

'Tell me what happened,' he said to Jo.

'Me?' Jo asked.

'Yes, you,' Garrett said. 'Please.'

Jo didn't hesitate. 'We were trying to talk to the spirits. We were using Shari as a subject. She was lying on the floor here near the table. We were trying to put her in a trance by talking about her as if she had crossed over.'

'Come again?' Garrett said.

'We were pretending she was dead,' Jo said. 'It's a common method of putting people in a state where they can channel. We had her pretty deep, I thought, when she suddenly jumped up and ran out on to the balcony.'

'You say *we*,' Garrett said, obviously wondering if this was a normal teenage activity. 'Wasn't one of you leading this thing?'

'Yes, I was.' Jo said.

112

'While you were putting her into her *trance*,' Garrett said, 'what kind of suggestions did you make?'

'Like I said,' Jo replied, 'we were acting like she was dead, saying how much we were going to miss her and stuff like that.'

'You didn't by any chance make any suggestion as to *how* she had died?' Garrett asked.

'No,' Jo said, surprised at the question.

'Did she say anything while she was in her trance?'

'Not really,' Jo said.

'She did say something,' Daniel broke in.

'What?' Garrett asked.

Daniel glanced at Beth. 'I don't remember,' he said.

'She said she was a ghost,' Jeff said.

'That's right,' Jo said, nodding.

'Anything else?' Garrett asked.

'No.' Jo glanced around the room. 'I don't think so.'

'Why did she suddenly leap up?' Garrett asked.

'I'm not sure,' Jo said. 'I think she got scared.'

'Did she say anything when she jumped up?' Garrett asked. 'Was anything said to her?'

'Yes,' Jo said. 'Jeff asked her – that's Jeff there – asked her why she had stopped. Then I told her she shouldn't have jumped up. Like I said, she looked scared. Amanda asked her what was the matter. Shari said it was nothing.

113

Then she ran out to the balcony.'

'And jumped?' Garrett asked. 'She jumped right away?'

'Oh, no,' Jo said.

'How long was she on the balcony before she jumped?'

'A few minutes,' Jo said.

Garrett frowned. 'Did anyone leave the living room during this time?'

Now Jo hesitated. 'We all did.'

Garrett sat up and clicked down the point of his ballpoint pen. 'Who was the first one to leave the living room after Shari?'

'I was,' Amanda said quietly, speaking for the first time. Garrett glanced over at her and stopped. I don't know why. Maybe it was her beauty. Maybe it was her sorrowful eyes. Then again, Garrett could not have known that Amanda was often grave.

'What's your name?' he asked.

'Amanda Parish.'

'How long after Shari left did you leave?'

'A couple of minutes.'

Garrett jotted down a note in his pad. 'Where did you go?'

'I went into Beth's bedroom.'

'The bedroom at this end of the hall? The one that leads to the west balcony?'

'Yes,' Amanda said. 'I had to go to the bathroom.'

'Did you see Shari on the balcony before you went into the bathroom?'

'No.'

'Do you recall if the sliding door that leads on to the balcony was open or closed?'

'No.'

'How long were you in the bathroom?'

'A few minutes.'

'What did you do when you left the bathroom?'

'I returned to the living room.'

'Who was there?'

'No one. At first. Then Jeff came in from the hall.'

Garrett paused and then scanned the room again. I waved to him, but he didn't wave back. 'Who left the living room after Amanda?' he asked.

'I did,' Jeff said, a lit cigarette in his hand.

'What's your last name, Jeff?'

'Nichols.'

'How long after Amanda left the living room did you leave?'

'A minute or so.'

Garrett made another note in his pad. 'Tell me about it.'

'I had to go to the bathroom,' Jeff said. 'I went into

Beth's bedroom, but there was already someone in there. So I went into the bedroom at the end of the hall and used that bathroom instead.'

'Did you see Shari on the balcony when you went into Beth's bedroom?'

'Yeah.'

'You're sure it was her and not Amanda?'

'Yeah, it was Shari.'

'What was she doing?'

'Standing by the rail, looking out at the ocean.'

'Anything else?'

'No.'

'Was the sliding glass door open or closed?'

'It was closed.'

'Was it locked?'

'I don't know. I didn't try opening it.'

'Could there have been anyone else on the balcony besides Shari?'

'I doubt it.'

'How close did you get to the door?'

Jeff took a puff of his cigarette. 'Maybe ten feet.'

'Did you have a clear view of the entire balcony?'

Jeff hesitated. 'No.'

'What portion of the balcony couldn't you see?'

Jeff considered a moment. 'The area behind the wall

between the kitchen and the bedroom.'

'How did you know there was someone in the bathroom?'

Jeff shrugged. 'The door was closed; the light was on.'

'It was you who was in there, right?' Garrett asked Amanda.

'Yes,' she said, her hand on Jimmy's knee.

Garrett turned his attention back to Jeff. 'How long were you in the bathroom in the master bedroom?'

'A couple of minutes. Then I came back into the living room.'

'Who was in the living room at that point?'

'Amanda.'

'What was she doing?'

'Sitting on the couch, looking at a magazine.'

'Who left the living room after Jeff?' Garrett asked the group.

'Beth did,' Daniel said. He glanced over at his big-breasted object of desire. He had to shake her. 'Beth?'

'Yes, we were good friends,' Beth said suddenly, blinking. Garrett uncrossed his legs and leaned towards her.

'You were a good friend of Shari's?' he asked.

'Yes,' she said. Studying her closer, I realised she must have been crying before Garrett and I had arrived. Good girl, I thought. But she was still a slut.

'What is your full name, Beth?'

'Elizabeth Palmone.'

'How long after Jeff left the living room did you leave?'

'Not long.'

'How long?' Garrett asked.

'Less than a minute.'

'Where did you go?'

'Into my bedroom.'

'Did you see Jeff or Amanda in there?'

'No.'

'Did you see Jeff leaving your room?'

'No.'

'Did you notice Amanda in the bathroom?'

'No. I mean, I noticed there was someone in the bathroom. But I didn't know who it was.'

'What did you do in the bedroom?'

'Nothing.'

'Did you see Shari on the balcony?'

'No.'

'You're sure?'

'Yes.' Her eyes strayed to Daniel. 'I went out on the balcony. I didn't see her. She wasn't there. Right, Jo?'

'Right,' Jo said.

'Wait a second, Beth,' Garrett said. 'Jo was on the balcony when you stepped outside?'

'Yes,' Beth said. 'I think.'

'Was she or wasn't she?'

'It was dark.' Beth was confused. 'I think she was.'

'How long were you in your bedroom before you went outside?'

'A little while.'

Garrett leaned forward even more. His next question was to be the important one, I knew. 'Was the door to the balcony open or closed when you went outside?' he asked.

'It was closed.'

'Was it locked?'

'Yes,' Beth said. 'It locks when you close it.'

'And when it's locked, you can't get back in from the outside, right?'

'No. Unless you come in through the kitchen.'

'Does that door also lock when you close it?'

'Yes.'

Garrett nodded to himself and made a note in his pad. 'Who left the living room after Beth?'

'I did,' Jo said.

'What's your full name, Jo?'

'Joanne Foulton.' She added, 'I was Shari's best friend.'

'How long after Beth left the living room did you leave?'

'A few seconds. I went through the kitchen to the

balcony. I wanted to see about Shari, make sure she was all right.'

'Why did you take so long to go after her?'

'I wanted to give her a few minutes to settle down.'

'Did you by any chance tell the others to leave her alone for a few minutes?'

Jo paused. 'Yes.'

'What did you all do after Shari ran off and before you started to leave the living room?'

'Nothing really,' Jo answered. 'Amanda picked up the candle and then went to the bathroom. Jeff went after her. Dan helped me turn on the lights and straighten the furniture. I flipped on the stereo.'

'You turned on the music? How loud?'

'Medium volume.'

'When you started for the balcony, did you leave Dan in the living room?' Garrett asked.

'We left the living room at the same time.'

'Did you see Shari on the balcony?'

'No. I only saw Beth.'

'Beth was there before you?'

'Yes.'

'You're absolutely sure?'

'Yes.'

'Was Dan?'

'No. But he walked out a few seconds after I did. He came out of the bedroom and put his arm around Beth.'

'Did he have to slide the door open? Was it shut?'

'I think so, but I couldn't swear on it.'

'Who was the first one to see Shari lying below?'

'I was,' Daniel said, uneasy.

'What is your full name, Dan?'

'Daniel Heard. I didn't kill her.'

Garrett smiled. It was not a particularly handsome smile. He looked as if he was out of practice. 'Why do you say that?'

'Because I didn't.'

'What was your relationship with Shari?'

'She was a friend of mine.'

'Oh, Christ,' I muttered, disgusted.

'She was your girlfriend,' Jo said sharply. I was surprised Jimmy hadn't said it. But Jimmy was sinking, I realised, down deep inside. He hadn't spoken in a while. I was glad, in a way, that Amanda was there for him to hold on to.

'I didn't know I was investigating a murder here,' Garrett said slowly, watching Daniel carefully. 'If I believed that, I should have first advised you of your rights.' He leaned back in his chair. 'Have I made a mistake, Dan?'

121

'I don't know. No. I think Shari jumped.'

'You think she was suicidal?' Garrett asked.

'Well, no. I wouldn't say that.'

'But you're saying she killed herself?'

Daniel shifted uncomfortably. 'I'm not the only one.'

'*Were* you her boyfriend?'

'Yeah, sort of. We were about to break up, though.'

'Why?'

'No particular reason. I wanted to date other girls.'

'Did she know this?'

'No,' Jo broke in.

'She did,' Daniel said. 'I had told her.' He looked down at his sweaty palms. 'But I still liked her. She was a good kid.'

'I was too hot a babe for you,' I grumbled. 'You liar.'

'What did you do when you left the living room?' Garrett asked.

'I went into Beth's bedroom,' Daniel said.

'Was Amanda still in the bathroom?'

'Yes.'

'Could you hear her in there?'

'I could hear the water running.'

'Was the door leading on to the balcony open or closed?'

'It was closed.'

'Was Beth on the balcony?'

122

'Yes.'

'What was she doing?'

'Nothing.'

'Nothing?'

'She was just standing there, looking out.'

'She wasn't by any chance looking down?'

'I don't think so.'

'When did you notice Jo on the balcony?'

'The second I stepped outside.'

'Was Jo looking down?'

'No.'

'Why did you look down?'

'I just did.'

'How long were you out there before you did so?'

'Not long.'

'What did you see?'

Daniel bit his lower lip. 'Shari.'

'You knew right away it was her?'

'Yeah.'

'What did you do? When you saw her?'

'I told Beth and Jo. Then Jo went and got Jeff and Amanda. Then we called for the paramedics.'

'Before you called the paramedics, before you saw Shari, did you notice Amanda leaving the bathroom?'

'Yes.'

'You're absolutely sure?'

'I noticed her in the bedroom behind me, yeah.'

'Jo,' Garrett said. 'Were Amanda and Jeff both in the living room when you went to get them?'

'Yes. They were sitting on the couch together.'

'Listening to the music?'

'No,' Jo said. 'The music was off.'

'Who turned it off?' Garrett asked.

'I did,' Amanda said. 'It was giving me a headache.'

Garrett stopped his barrage of questions for a full minute to study his notes. The gang watched and waited without making a peep.

'Let me sum this up,' he said finally. 'And if I've made a mistake anywhere, let me know.' He straightened himself up in his chair. 'Shari jumped up from the floor and ran to the balcony. A couple of minutes later Amanda went into Beth's bedroom. She didn't see Shari on the balcony. She didn't know if the door leading to the balcony was open or closed. She went into the bathroom. A minute later Jeff came into the bedroom. He noticed Shari on the balcony. He also noticed that the bathroom light was on and the bathroom door was closed. He definitely saw that the door to the balcony was shut, although he wasn't sure if it was locked from the inside. He left Beth's bedroom for the master bedroom, where he stayed in the bathroom for a couple of minutes. Less than a minute after Jeff left the living room, Beth entered her bedroom. She stayed there for a little while doing nothing.

'She noticed that there was someone in the bathroom and that the door to the balcony was locked. She didn't see Shari on the balcony, however. Not even when she unlocked the sliding glass door and stepped out on to the balcony. But she did see Jo on the balcony, even though she wasn't sure if Jo had been there before she was or not. And it's feasible that Jo did reach the balcony before Beth. It, in fact, appears likely, because Jo left the living room only seconds after Beth did. But whereas Beth dawdled in her bedroom before stepping on to the balcony, Jo went straight from the living room to the balcony.'

'Beth was out there before me,' Jo interrupted.

Garrett nodded thoughtfully. 'We have a bit of a problem here. If Jo and Dan left the living room only a few seconds after Beth, and Beth hung out in her bedroom for a little while before going out on the balcony, then Dan should have caught up with Beth while she was still in her bedroom.' Garrett turned to Daniel and Beth. 'Well?'

'Jo and I didn't leave that soon after Beth,' Daniel said. 'It was more like a minute.'

'Maybe half a minute,' Jo said.

'Did I see you in the bedroom?' Beth asked Daniel.

'No.' Daniel shook his head. 'No.'

'Why did you put your arm around Beth when you did catch up with her on the balcony?' Garrett asked Daniel.

'We're friends,' Daniel said quickly.

'Are you good friends?' Garrett asked.

'Pretty good.'

'Tell him about the Jacuzzi, Amanda,' I shouted.

But Amanda was not telling.

'Do you two date?' Garrett asked.

'No,' Daniel and Beth said simultaneously.

Garrett found the coherence mildly amusing. But he frowned as he rechecked his notepad. 'It seems to me that Shari must have jumped after Jeff entered the bedroom but before Beth did. Do the rest of you agree?'

Everyone, with the exception of Jimmy and Amanda, nodded. Jimmy didn't look like he was doing much of anything except trying to breathe and stop thinking. But Amanda spoke up.

'Do you think that one of us pushed Shari from the balcony?' she asked.

'Why do you ask?' Garrett said, and he might have been toying with her a bit, not knowing he had picked the wrong person.

'Because you keep asking us so many questions.'

Garrett shrugged. 'It's my job.'

'I see,' Amanda said evenly.

Garrett held her eyes a moment. He might have been admiring their cool beauty. I don't know. He certainly couldn't have suspected her of foul play. Unless he also suspected her of the ability to be in two places at once. He addressed the group.

'I have only one more question, and then I'll let you all go.' He paused. 'Did any of you hear Shari scream?'

No one did, and I couldn't remember if I had. Like I said, screaming wasn't supposed to be cool. I probably hadn't made a sound. I hadn't had a chance. Four storeys is not that long a fall, and whoever had pushed me had taken me by surprise.

Whoever had pushed me?

Getting my head burst open must have slowed me down a step. It wasn't until that moment that I realised I had been murdered. It really pissed me off. Especially because I didn't know who had done it. Oh, I can't tell you how mad I got. I was seeing things.

Actually, I *was* seeing things. There was the stuff in the air, of course, and now it had traces of colour throbbing on and off, in complex crystalline patterns, deep within its depths. Yet it was so faint, I could not be absolutely sure I wasn't imagining it. But even that concern made me crack a bitter smile. A ghost worried that she was imagining things. It was funny in a sick sort of way.

Everybody got up to leave. Garrett called downstairs and learned that Beth's parents had arrived. He told them, and Beth, that he was placing the condo off-limits for the night while he evaluated the situation. Officer Fort came on the line and expressed the belief that Garrett was putting Beth's family through unnecessary hardship. Garrett didn't seem to care. In some ways he appeared a hard man.

He must have had a soft side, though. Jimmy and Amanda were the last two to leave, and when my brother stopped to speak to the lieutenant near the door, Garrett didn't brush him off.

'My sister didn't kill herself,' Jimmy said.

'You two were close?' Garrett asked.

'Yes. She wouldn't have killed herself. It's not possible.'

Garrett was listening. 'Did she have any enemies among those present tonight?'

Jimmy glanced at Amanda, pained. 'I don't think so.'

'There was no reason anyone here would have wanted to kill Shari,' Amanda said.

'Was there enough reason for her to kill herself?' Garrett asked Amanda.

'Excellent question,' I observed.

Amanda took Jimmy's arm. 'No,' she said.

Garrett nodded and put his hand on Jimmy's shoulder. 'Try to get some rest, son. The truth has a habit of emerging in time. I'll do what I can from my side.'

Amanda and Jimmy left. I hoped she was driving him home. I didn't consider following them. I wanted to see exactly what Garrett had cooking on his side.

The first thing Garrett did when he was alone was take down a bottle of Scotch from the liquor cabinet.

'Come on, Garrett!' I shouted at him as he plopped down on his chair in the living room and poured a stiff one into a dirty glass he'd swiped from the coffee table. 'Gimme a break. You're on duty.'

Garrett didn't give a damn. He finished his drink in three burning swallows and poured another. This one he nursed. I doubt he would have enjoyed it nearly so much had he been able to see me pacing back and forth across the floor in front of him. Actually, he probably wouldn't have seen me had he been able to see me. His eyes had settled on the red wax stain on the floor. At least, that was what I thought he was staring at. But then he suddenly set his glass and bottle aside and got down on his hands and knees near the couch. I knelt beside him.

'What is it?' I asked.

There was a dust of fine orange chalk on the carpet.

Garrett touched the stuff and then held it up to his eyes, rubbing it between his fingers, feeling its consistency. I thought maybe he was on to something and started to get excited, but then he rubbed the chalk off on his trouser leg and reached for his glass again.

He didn't get back in gear for another half-hour. By then the bottle was half empty, and he had definitely slowed down. He began to stroll around the condo, wandering from one room to the next, seemingly in a random fashion. He ended up on the balcony, hanging over the rail. He had to be drunk by now, I figured, and I was concerned he was going to fall and kill himself. Then again, if he did, I could have told him to his face what I thought of his investigative preparations.

He did look around a bit while he was out there, and then he stumbled back inside and plopped down on the floor beside his bottle. Now he'd finish it, I thought to myself. But he didn't touch the Scotch. He pulled out his notepad instead and began to draw a diagram. I stood behind him as he worked. He could have been an architect; he was good at proportions. Yet when he was done, I failed to see the point of it all. He had not put down everybody's position at the moment I had supposedly jumped. He had just marked my place. And I didn't understand the dotted lines that he had sketched

in, crisscrossing behind me on the balcony.

Garrett decided to call it a night. The clock in the living room read four in the morning. I followed him out and into the elevator down to the ground floor. He looked pretty fried; I was worried about him driving home in his truck. My concern was not purely altruistic. I figured if he was all I had, then he'd better stay alive.

He did not, however, head straight to his truck once we were outside. He strolled instead over to the cement walkway that ran beneath Beth's balcony. I followed with great reluctance. The police had roped off the spot and had wiped up most of the blood. But I could still see the wide, dark, lopsided memento my plunge had left on the ground. I began to feel sick.

'Hey, Garrett, let's go,' I said. 'This was just a place to land. It's not important.'

He didn't share my opinion. He stared for a long time up at the balcony, and it seemed to me he was trying to picture my fall. Then he did something very strange; he actually sat on the ground beside the stain on the concrete. He pulled out his wallet. There was a picture of a girl my age inside. She had dark hair, sharp features – we didn't look alike. She was probably a shade more beautiful than me. Sitting alone, with me by his side, the picture in his hand, Garrett's face visibly sagged.

I figured whoever she was, she must also be dead.

I didn't know what to do. I felt too shaky to try to console him. And I knew it would be a waste of time. I sat down across from him on the other side of the stain.

'It wouldn't be so bad for us,' I whispered, 'if only you knew we were still here.'

I didn't know how bad it could get.

Garrett sat there awhile, but eventually he put his picture away and stood up and walked away. I didn't chase after him. He was probably going home to bed. Also, although I had approached the spot with many reservations, I was finding it had a peculiar allure for me now. Twice I tried to stand and leave, but I couldn't. I felt my hand reach out and touch my lost blood. But unlike the doorknob at home or Jimmy's arm at the hospital, I did touch it. When I pulled my fingers away, they were dark and dripping. I could see it, the warm red life running out of my hand.

My surroundings began to whirl, and I had to lie down. It seemed only appropriate that I should lie on my back with my head in the centre of the mess. I was where I belonged, I thought miserably. Where it had all ended. There was the annoying lamppost off to my left, and far above I could see the balcony. But I didn't have to picture my fall as Garrett had done. I could remember it;

especially the hot wave that had come upon me at the end and washed me away.

Only now, unlike then, I began to feel pain in my head, a throbbing, skull-cracking pain. My hand instinctively tried to reach up to the top of my head. It tried, but it didn't succeed. Something kept pushing it down.

No. Some*one*.

Suddenly I was not where I had been. I was back in the hospital, in the morgue. Dr Leeds was standing above me, a glaring white light at his back. He was trying to put me in a green bag. But my right arm kept popping out. He had taken away my towel. It had been gross and disgusting, but I wished with all my heart that he had left it alone. My brains literally felt as if they were spilling out of my head.

Stuffing my arm back under the plastic, Dr Leeds pulled the fat zipper towards my face.

'No!' I shrieked in horror. I fought to pull my arms up, to kick the bag off with my feet. But I was paralysed. The zipper kept coming, past my sewn lips, over my glued eyelids. The doctor, looking down at me, sadly shook his head one last time. Then there was darkness, and he was lifting me up and shoving me into a locker. I heard the door slam shut. I felt the cold go deep within my black heart. Oh, Lord, yes, it was black then. It was the abyss I had glimpsed as I had lain on the floor at the party.

But darkness inside, outside – it is not so different as the living might believe. In the next instant I was back on the messy walkway, the balcony above me. Only now there was something standing up there.

It was my first glimpse of the Shadow.

It bore no resemblance to a human being, and yet, from the start, it reminded me of a person. There was no reason it should have. Its shape and colour were difficult to comprehend. It seemed a dark cloud caught in a state of flux between a solid and a vapour. It also appeared to be a part of the surroundings, a dam of some sort on the plasma that continued to flow through my new world. Or perhaps, I thought, it was a scar on the world. It was painful to behold.

It was watching me.

I got up very slowly and began to back away from it. It shifted as I moved, following me. I couldn't see its eyes, but I could feel them on me – cruel and penetrating. The thing didn't like me. I didn't like it. When the concrete walkway came to an end and the asphalt parking lot began, I ran.

It ran after me.

Someone had left the gate open. I dashed out of the complex, down a short road, and on to the deserted coast highway. I could see no one – no cars, no lights, no signs of life anywhere. I had a monster on my tail and no one around to help. Many times, when I was a child, I'd had a nightmare in which I tried to flee from a hungry creature with scales, claws and dripping teeth. I had awakened in a cold sweat, crying for my mother. Sometimes she would come to my bed and comfort me. But other times she wouldn't hear me, and there'd be no comfort, and no sleep, until the sun came up.

I knew it was hopeless, but as I raced across the highway and on to the sand towards the vast ocean, I called for her once more.

'Mother!'

It was a hundred feet behind me, and in the next moment it was on top of me. I had run out of room. I'd run straight to the water's edge, boxing myself in. I turned to face it, to plead for mercy, but I couldn't bear to look at it. Without looking, I knew there could be nothing more horrible than what it had planned for me.

It stopped several feet from me. For several seconds it appeared to study me, and I could feel wave upon wave of loathing radiate from it like dark swells in a poison ocean. And what made it so utterly terrible was that it *knew* me. It had reason to hate me. It reached out a distorted hand to touch me.

'No!' I shrieked, turning and fleeing into the water.

I was no saint. I couldn't walk on water. I began to go down, but still it pursued me. 'Mother!' I cried. 'Save me!'

'Shari.'

I heard my name. I opened my eyes. It was dark. I was home, in bed with my mother. She lay with her back to me, and I was holding on to her, trying to. I couldn't see her face, but I could hear her crying. I could feel her heart breaking. I tried to squeeze her tightly.

'I'm here, Mom. I'm here. Please don't cry.'

There was a pause, and then, when she said my name next, it was as if she had heard me. 'Shari?'

'Yes!' I cried. 'It's me! I'm here! I'm here! I never left!'

She didn't respond, not directly. But she did stop crying, and soon she was asleep. And so I also slept, holding on to her as best I could, and swearing to myself that I would never, ever let go.

CHAPTER 7

I awoke to a sunny day. My mother was gone. So was her bedroom. I had moved again. I was at Amanda's house. I jumped up from the bed on which I was lying. I still had on the green trousers and yellow blouse I had worn to Beth's party. They were wrinkled, as if I had in fact slept in them, and I felt greatly relieved. It was not as though I had forgotten what had happened the previous night, but I had a sudden rush of confidence that it couldn't have *really* happened. People died all the time, I realised, but it was simply too ridiculous to think I could have been so unfortunate.

My confidence lasted long enough for me to walk into the living room. Mrs Parish, dressed in mourning black, was sitting on the couch holding a rosary.

'Hello, Mrs Parish,' I said, flipping a spunky wave at her.

Nothing. Not even a puzzled glance in my direction. I

plopped down in the chair across from her. 'Damn,' I said. Apparently, dying was one condition a good night's sleep couldn't remedy.

'You better finish your breakfast,' Mrs Parish said to Amanda. 'They'll be here any minute.'

Amanda, wearing a long grey dress that matched her wide grey eyes, was seated at the dining-room table, a bowl of oatmeal in front of her. The table, in fact the whole place, was fairly undistinguished. There wasn't a piece of furniture one couldn't have found at the Goodwill.

'I'm not very hungry,' Amanda said.

'You'll need your strength,' Mrs Parish said, although it was clear from her shaking hands that it was she who needed the strength. 'Please eat.'

'All right,' Amanda said, spooning down another soggy bite. 'Where's the service going to be?'

'At the chapel at the cemetery,' Mrs Parish said.

'Now hold on a second,' I said. 'I just died. I'm not ready for any funeral. I'm not ready to—'

Why say it? Who was ever ready to be put in the ground?

But there was still a scheduling problem here. No one was buried the day after they died. The only logical explanation was that I had slept away several days. My, I thought, how time flies when one splits open one's skull.

'Will it be a Catholic service?' Amanda asked.

'I don't know. I don't think so.'

'You might not want to bring your rosary. They only use those at Catholic masses.'

Mrs Parish looked down at her string of tiny black beads. 'I can pray quietly,' she whispered, squeezing her eyes shut.

'What?'

Mrs Parish looked up. 'Nothing, honey. Are you almost done? They should be here soon.'

'I'm almost done,' Amanda said, nodding patiently.

'How are you feeling?'

'Fine.'

'You're remembering to take care of yourself?'

'I'm fine, Mother.'

'Good,' Mrs Parish said weakly. 'That's good.'

Jo and her mother, Mrs Foulton, arrived shortly afterwards. I felt honoured that they were all going to my funeral in the same car since they seldom did anything together. Mrs Foulton had on a black dress – somehow it still looked like a nurse's uniform – but Jo was wearing orange trousers and an orange blouse. It was incredible. Who would wear orange to a best friend's funeral?

'This isn't Halloween, for God's sake,' I told her, insulted.

Amanda set her bowl of half-finished oatmeal in the sink and headed to her room for her bag. Jo went with her. Mrs Foulton sat beside Mrs Parish on the couch. Neither looked as if she had been getting much sleep lately. But Mrs Foulton clearly had no intention of showing any weakness.

'You've got to get a handle on yourself,' she said to her sister, pulling out a cigarette and a Bic lighter. 'This is going to be hard enough on the girls.'

Mrs Parish nodded, bunching up her rosary in her hand. 'I know,' she said.

'How's Amanda taking it?'

'I thought I heard her crying last night.' Mrs Parish took a breath. 'How's Jo?'

'She doesn't say a word.'

'Have you tried to talk to her about it?'

Mrs Foulton lit her cigarette and exhaled a large cloud of smoke. 'I don't want to talk about it. She's gone. It's done.'

Mrs Parish looked at her. 'How can you say that?'

'It's true.'

Mrs Parish held her eye. 'You're not going to forget her.'

Mrs Foulton went to snap at her sister but then thought better of it. She ground out her cigarette, lowering her eyes and voice. 'No, I don't suppose I ever will forget.'

The girls reappeared. We went outside and climbed into Mrs Foulton's Nissan. I sat in the back between Jo and Amanda. The sky was a sparkling blue, and the sun was cloaked in a dazzling aura of purple. That was another thing – I could stare right at the sun and not hurt my eyes. Mrs Foulton lit another cigarette and started the car. Cruising down the road, the breeze through the open windows didn't mess my hair one tiny bit.

The cemetery was not very close to my house. My parents had lived in another neighbourhood earlier. I suppose they had purchased a couple of local plots back when things were cheaper. In other words, I was being stuck in a plot they had one day planned on using for themselves. That was fine with me. I didn't intend spending a lot of time underground.

But I felt a morbid curiosity as we drove through the flower-lined cemetery gates and started up the grassy hill along the narrow winding black road that led to the chapel. I leaned over Amanda and stared out the window. I was looking for other ghosts, but I couldn't find any, not even a little white Casper to go for a walk with. I began to feel lonely.

Part of the reason I had never been much of a churchgoer when I was alive was the minister of our church – the Reverend Theodore Smith. He wasn't an old-school fire-and-brimstone preacher; he was just straight, so straight you could line up your wallpaper next to him. He was one of those rare men you just knew had never been to bed with a woman. He was about thirty-five and by no means bad looking, but the only suits he wore were the ones his father had left him in his will. He was always talking about Jesus. You would have thought they were old friends. He could have bored any empty pew. But I wasn't surprised that he was there to host my funeral. I bet he figured this was one service I couldn't walk out on.

I was in for a big disappointment when I walked into the chapel with Jo and Amanda and their moms. Besides seeing Reverend Smith up front, I discovered that few kids from school had bothered to come. At first I figured we must be early, but the service started almost immediately, and there were no latecomers. I couldn't understand it. I had gone to Hazzard High for four years. I hadn't been on the cheerleader squad or anything, but I had got around. I had been invited to every damn party there was, and, all told, there couldn't have been more than a dozen kids present.

Then it hit me. Everyone thought I had committed suicide. It angered me for a minute that that should make any difference, and then I started to feel a bit better. If

143

they'd known I'd been murdered, I told myself, they would have had to turn people away at the gate. I probably would have got my picture on the front page of the paper.

My casket rested at the altar on a wooden table. Black and shiny, with gold trim and smart angles, I supposed it would do. As long as they kept it closed. I was relieved to see I wasn't on display.

My family was sitting up front. I didn't want to sit near them; I didn't think I could handle it. Amanda and Jo and Mrs Foulton, however, headed straight for them. Fortunately, Mrs Parish decided to stay in the back where she could say her rosaries in peace. I sat beside her. Beth and Daniel were three rows up from us. If they hadn't come together, they would probably be leaving together. It was only fair, I supposed. A girl wasn't much good to a guy without a body. Of course, he mustn't have been that crazy about me when I had a body. He must have been wondering how he could get rid of me without hurting my feelings.

I wondered if he had killed me. I didn't see Jeff Nichols anywhere, and I wondered about a lot of things.

Reverend Smith stepped to the podium.

'I would like to welcome everyone to this service on behalf of Mr and Mrs Cooper, and their son, James

Cooper,' he said in his smooth, sympathetic voice. 'We are gathered here today to pay our final respects to a wonderful young lady – Shari Cooper. It warms my heart to see how many of her friends have taken the time to remember her. She was, in all truth, a very special person. I knew her well . . .'

'You didn't even know what colour eyes I had,' I muttered, already tuning him out. My gaze wandered to the pew across from me. There was a guy about my age sitting there who looked familiar, but I couldn't place him. His clothes made me laugh. He was wearing baggy white shorts and a red T-shirt. To my funeral? At least he'd come, I thought. He must be someone from school who had loved me from afar. I wished I knew who he was.

Mrs Parish had tuned the reverend out as well. She was praying: ten Hail Marys preceded by an Our Father and followed by a Glory Be to the Father. I knew the prayers. I had even said a few of them during my days on earth. But I doubt I had ever said them as Mrs Parish was now – with feeling. She was whispering softly, but I found, as I turned my attention her way, that I could hear her clearly, better even than the reverend, who had a loud voice, not to mention a microphone.

There was something about her praying that began to charm me in a special way. I didn't understand it. Mrs

Parish was crushed. Her fingers trembled as she slipped from one bead to the next. Yet, as I listened, I began to feel lighter. I would go so far as to say I felt a thrill of joy. The weird plasma in the air began to shimmer with a cool silver light. It was faint, true, but it was there, beyond question. I wondered if it was coming out of Mrs Parish. I wanted the light to keep coming. I began to become quite engrossed in it. I closed my eyes, but still I could see it – better, in fact. My mind began to drift with the words without actually listening to them. The meaning was unimportant, I began to realise. All that mattered was that they were being said with love. The light increased and seemed to encompass me. As the brilliance intensified, so did my peace. It was the first peace I had felt in a long time.

And then it stopped, and it was like a mountain crushing down on my soul. I opened my eyes. The light was gone. The service was over. I couldn't believe it. We had just got there! It should have taken at least an hour to remember how wonderful I had been. What about my favourite song – 'Stairway to Heaven'? Jo could have played it on her acoustic guitar. What about my closest friends getting up and saying a few words about how much they were going to miss me? I wanted to be remembered!

People began to file out. I had no choice but to follow. A hearse was brought around front for the coffin. I stood on the chapel steps and wondered what had gone wrong with time. Every time I closed my eyes, the hands on the clock would spin forward.

I rode to the gravesite in the hearse. It seemed the thing to do. But I sat in the front with the driver, not in the back with the black box. That was how I had begun to think of it now, a prison they would lock my body in beneath the ground while my spirit wandered alone and forsaken on the surface. I had begun to feel sad again and lonely, terribly lonely.

We lost a few people on the short trip out to the lawns, about half, actually. I couldn't blame them. They had things to do. And what the hell, Shari had been a nice girl, but she hadn't been that nice. Oh, it was awful. It was true. I had done nothing in my life that was worth remembering. Why should they remember me? I watched them unload the coffin and set it on the ground next to a pile of brown dirt and a black hole.

They had another short service. Reverend Smith read a few verses from the Bible. They were nice, but they were nothing; he just read them because he was supposed to read them. Daniel stood next to Beth and held her hand. Mrs Parish and Mrs Foulton stood next to each other and behind their daughters. Out of the group, only Mrs Parish was weeping.

My mom and dad were also there, of course, and Jimmy. They looked as if time had been moving slowly for them, as if they had no more tears to shed. They held individual white roses. I liked roses; orange ones for parties and red ones for love. White ones were OK, too, I guessed. They set them on the top of the coffin at the reverend's bidding. Then the minister closed his Bible. There was a note of finality in the way he did it. People began to walk away.

The last person to leave was Jimmy. He knelt for a moment by the coffin and placed his hands palms down on the shiny black surface as if he were trying to touch me one last time. But I was standing behind him, beyond reach.

Finally, he left, and it was only minutes later that the grave diggers appeared. They seemed to be in a hurry to get me in the ground. They came in a truck with concrete liners and ropes and pulleys. They also brought shovels. They sealed my coffin up so it would be safe from robbers and perverts, but not so safe, I thought, that it would be beyond the reach of the slimy creatures that lived deep in the soil. After they had lowered me into the ground, they began to throw shovel after shovel of dark moist earth on top of me.

'No!' I pleaded irrationally, panicking, trying to grab their arms, to stop them. 'You can't do this to me! I was just getting started! I was going to do all kinds of neat stuff! Please don't cover me up! People will forget that I'm here!'

They buried me quickly. Eighteen years to become the person I had become and thirty minutes to disappear for ever. They threw their equipment in the back of their truck and drove away, leaving me alone and crying on top of a pile of unsettled earth that probably wouldn't give up my bones until the day the world came to an end.

'Oh, God, help me,' I wept. 'Please help me.'

I don't know how long I sat there before I noticed the pair of sandalled feet in front of me. I glanced up. It was the boy from the chapel with the baggy white shorts and the red T-shirt. I had been happy to see him before, but now I resented the fact that he hadn't even brought a flower to lay on my grave.

'Go to hell,' I told him, looking back down.

'We're already there, wouldn't you say, Shari?'

My head snapped up. I didn't understand how I could have failed to recognise him before. 'Peter,' I whispered.

CHAPTER 8

My relief in that moment was wondrous. It was as glorious as my sorrow had been horrible. I don't remember jumping up and stretching out my arms, but I do remember how sweet it felt to hug him, to *feel* him and know that he could feel me. I think I held him for quite a long while before I let go. I was afraid he'd disappear.

'Peter,' I said again, shaking my head in amazement as I finally stepped back. He looked great, and I don't mean that he looked great for someone who had been dead a couple of years. He was as I remembered him from biology class: thin and wiry, his blond hair thick and curly, his broad smile wide and wild. That was one thing I had missed so much about Peter when he died: the mischievous way his mouth would twist up whenever he told me something that he swore was the absolute truth and which in most cases was a complete fabrication.

He had eyes as blue as my brother's but even more clear; they shone in the bright sun, although his head cast no shadow.

'You remember,' he said, pleased.

'Of course I remember! God, this is incredible. I never thought I'd see you again. How are you?'

'All right. How are you?'

'Great,' I said. Then I made a face and giggled. 'Well, I'm OK, considering that I'm dead.'

He nodded and spoke softly. 'I know.' Then he smiled again, but it, too, was soft. 'It's good to see you, Shari.'

'Yeah? Thanks. It's great to see you,' I laughed, gesturing to the pile of dirt at our feet. 'So here we are. At my funeral!'

'Yeah.'

'Some place to get together, huh? How was yours? Did you go?'

'Yeah. It was pretty good.'

'That's good.' I hadn't gone to his funeral. I had stayed home and cried. In fact, I had never gone to a funeral before, and had Peter not shown up, I would have regretted attending my own. I surveyed the cemetery. We were alone now, just us and the tombstones. It seemed much more peaceful than before. 'So there is life after death, after all,' I said. 'It's hard to believe.'

'For some people.'

'Is that true?'

He shrugged, and the gesture reminded me of his brother. 'It can be.'

'No. I mean, did I screw up by not believing, or what?'

He shook his head. 'Not at all.'

'That's a relief,' I said, and I meant it. 'So what's the deal? Is there really a God?'

'Sure.'

I brightened. 'That's neat! Where is he? Can I see him?'

'He?'

'You mean he's a *she*?' I said. 'Oh, wow, that's far-out. What's she like?'

'God isn't what we used to think he was like when we were alive, Shari. He isn't a he or a she.'

'Is he an *it*?' I asked.

Peter laughed. 'These are deep questions, and I don't have a lot of deep answers for you. From what I've been able to tell, everything's much simpler than we used to think. It's so simple you can't even talk about it. God just is. He exists. He is everything. He is us. We are him.' Peter turned away and looked over the green lawn. I could not remember where he had been buried, but I doubted it had been in the same cemetery. He added, 'And that's all I know.'

152

I thought a moment. 'Why are you here?'

'To help you.' A note of seriousness entered his voice. 'As long as you want my help.'

'Oh, I do,' I said.

'Good.'

The dirt at my feet caught my eye. I hadn't forgotten what lay beneath it. 'What I mean is, why are you here *now*?'

'And not before?'

I nodded reluctantly. 'Yeah.'

His expression softened, and he reached out and rubbed my shoulder. 'It was hard for you, wasn't it?'

I didn't feel the tears coming. They were just there, falling silent and invisible to the ground. I wanted to fall, too, into his arms again. But I hadn't known him *that* well. We had never kissed. We had never gone out. I wiped at my cheek, unsure if it was damp or not.

'It was hard,' I said.

Peter hastily took back his hand, almost as if he were ashamed. 'I'm sorry, Shari. I couldn't come earlier.'

'I understand. Well, actually, I don't understand. Why couldn't you come?'

'You hadn't asked for help,' he said.

'You mean, since I've been dead, all I've had to do was ask for help and I would have got it?'

'Yes.'

'But I didn't know that. Why didn't someone tell me?'

'You didn't ask,' he said.

'But—'

'It says in the Bible, Shari, if you knock, the door shall be opened.'

'Since when did you start reading the Bible?' I asked.

'I haven't actually been reading it. But your minister read that line during your service.'

I had been crying a second ago, and now I burst out laughing. 'That's the most ridiculous thing I ever heard!'

'It's the absolute truth,' he said.

'What a crazy system,' I said, not sure if I believed him. Then I remembered how I had cried to my mother for help when the monster had tried to eat me, and how I had been immediately transported to the safety of her bed. I peered at him curiously. 'Why is it you were sent to help me?'

'I told you.'

'Why you in particular?'

He hesitated. 'I was available.'

'*Who* sent you?'

The question amused him. He tugged at his red T-shirt. 'I don't suppose I look like a messenger of God.'

'Damn right, you don't. Why are you dressed that way?'

'This is what I was wearing when I died.'

'You died riding your motorcycle,' I said.

'It was a warm night.'

'We don't get a change of clothing?'

'Soon you'll be able to wear whatever you want.' He stepped past me then, walking to the edge of the hill where I had been buried, looking up at the sun and its glorious purple halo. At least, I thought he was looking at the sun. When I came up at his side, I realised he had closed his eyes and that the light playing over his face had nothing to do with sunlight. There was a faint silvery lustre to his skin, and it seemed to brighten as he stood there – listening, perhaps, to some internal voice.

'Peter?'

'You can't stay here,' he said.

'Where should we go?'

He opened his eyes, stared at me. 'You know where to go.'

'Where?' I asked.

'Where you started to go when you were in the chapel.'

I was confused. 'Where was that?'

'When Mrs Parish was praying,' he said.

'But I didn't go anywhere then.' I paused. 'Do you mean the light? I have to go into that light?'

'Exactly.'

'How do you know? Did God tell you just now?'

'No,' he said. 'I read about it in the *Enquirer*.'

I socked him. 'Peter!'

He grabbed my hand, stopping me, trying to be serious in spite of his laughter. 'I mean it, Shari. You mustn't stay here.'

'But what am I supposed to do? I didn't have a rosary with me when I died. And I hardly remember those prayers.'

'The rosary and prayers are not as important as where you put your attention. Put your attention on the light, and the light will come.'

'How do I do that?'

'You just have to want to do it, that's all.' He began to sit down, gesturing for me to do likewise. 'It's very simple.'

I sat so close to him that our knees touched. And I suddenly began to feel uneasy and was at a loss to explain why. I remembered the serenity of the light in the chapel. If Peter was going to lead me into it, I reasoned, I should be happy.

Then I thought of Jo and the party. The trance.

'You're not going to give me suggestions, are you?' I asked.

'No. The desire to be with the light must be from your side.'

'But do I have to close my eyes?'

156

'You may close your eyes, if you wish,' he said. 'But it isn't necessary.'

'Are you coming with me?' I asked.

'This is between you and the light. I'm just here to point you in the right direction.' He smiled and reached over and patted me on the back. 'Don't worry, Shari. Soon you're going to be happier than you can imagine.'

'Will I know who killed me?'

He hesitated. 'Does that matter?'

'Yes! I want to know who did it.'

'Why?' he asked.

'What do you mean, why? If someone killed you, wouldn't you want to know who had done it?'

'Not really,' he said.

'That's only because you've been dead for a while. Believe me, if you had just been snuffed out, you'd want to know who the murderer was. Now, tell me the truth — will I know who killed me?'

'I don't know.'

'What do you mean, you don't know?'

'I don't,' he said.

'Is there someone who does?'

Peter looked uncomfortable. 'Shari, you're dead. You had a nice go of it on Earth, but now it's time to move on.'

'Exactly where am I moving on to? Heaven?'

'Heaven is a word the living use to describe a place. Over here, places do not exist, not as they existed for you when you were alive. Have you noticed since you've been dead that sometimes you'll be in one spot, and then suddenly you'll be in another?'

'Yeah.'

He nodded. 'Again, it's a question of where your attention is. Put your mind on your house, and you'll be back home. Put it on the light, and the light will be with you.'

'But what about my family? They think I'm dead.'

'You are dead,' he said.

'Yes, I know. But they don't know what death means.'

'That's not unusual.'

'But it is unusual to have your family think you killed yourself when you didn't.' I paused. 'They all must think I was crazy.'

'They don't,' he said.

'They do. Did you see how many kids from school came to my funeral?' I sighed. 'I bet you had ten times as many.'

'Neither of us is running for student office.'

'If I go into the light, can I still come back here and snoop around?'

'I don't think you'll want to do that.'

'But could I?' I insisted.

'Didn't the police assign someone to investigate your death?'

'Yeah, but the guy's a drunk!'

'He's not that bad.'

I stopped. 'You know Garrett?'

Peter hesitated. 'I've seen him around.'

'Were you there when he was interrogating the group?'

He looked down. 'Yes.'

'What were you doing there?'

'Hanging out.'

'Were you at the party?'

Peter obviously wished he had not made the slip about the lieutenant. 'Some of the time,' he replied carefully.

'Why were you at the party?'

'I like parties.'

The cool air of coincidence touched me. 'Were you there because you knew I was going to die?' I asked.

He glanced up, not at me but towards the north end of the cemetery, where a residential street ran alongside the sloping green lawns. Two little girls were riding their bikes on the sidewalk, laughing together. They looked like sisters.

'That's an interesting question,' he said.

'Yeah, it is,' I said, thoughtful. 'I'm not sure why, but I

took his response to mean yes. I remembered Jeff's question at the party concerning destiny. 'Was I meant to die that night?'

He nodded. 'Nothing happens by accident. We are born with so many breaths. When they're used up, we die. Nothing can stop it.'

'Nothing?'

'Nothing.'

I tried to digest the concept. I couldn't say it made it any easier for me to accept what had happened. In fact, I think it depressed me further. 'Are you sure about that?' I asked.

My doubt made him smile. 'The girl falls off a balcony and she turns into a philosopher.'

'Come on.'

'I would rather talk about baseball,' he said.

'I hate baseball.'

'Did you know that running head-on into that truck at sixty miles an hour didn't slow my fastball one bit?'

'Peter, please.'

He saw how serious I was. 'I've already told you, Shari, I can't answer these kinds of questions, not to your satisfaction. I say you were destined to die that night, and from everything I've seen since I've got over here, I know that to be true. But I also know you have free will. You are totally in charge of your destiny. You did not have to go to the party last Friday.'

'But if I hadn't gone, I'd still be alive. You're contradicting yourself.'

'That is the trouble with these discussions. Let me try an analogy. Say you took out a bank loan. Being a person of your word, from that point on, it's predetermined you will pay it back. But how fast you pay it back is up to you. You can take eighty years, or eighteen. So you have both: destiny and free will. Life is like that. And death.'

'But this stupid bank foreclosed on my house!'

He smiled. 'You must have exceeded your credit limit. Don't worry, this is just an analogy. You're in debt to no one. Words explain so little. You have a chance to go into the light. That will mean much more to you than anything I can say.' He touched me again on the shoulder. He had beautiful hands, large and strong, perfect for a big-league pitcher. I had only been kidding him. I had loved baseball, especially watching him play. 'Do you have any other questions before we say goodbye?' he asked.

I sat upright. 'You're not coming with me?'

'I can't.'

'Why can't you?' I asked, and I almost choked on the words. I don't think I could have told Peter how much it had meant to me to see him again.

He looked back towards the children on the bicycles. For mortals, they would have already been out of sight, but with us, they were still crystal clear.

'I have a responsibility,' he said. 'There are others like you who, when they die, wander around lost and confused, unaware that they are dead.'

'And you help them?'

'I try.'

'Do you need another helper?'

My offer startled him. He shook his head. 'You cannot stay here, Shari. You must go on.'

'But why? What's the hurry?' It might be kind of fun, I thought, helping out other novice ghosts like myself. I would definitely advise them to stay away from morgues. 'I'm not getting any older,' I said.

'That makes no difference. You are *supposed* to go on.'

'Who says? Don't I have free will?'

'Yes, but . . .'

'Then I decided to stay. And my decision must be destined.'

'How so?' he asked.

'Because I just made it. Look, I want to find out who killed me. I want to clear my name.'

'You can't clear your name. Even if you did figure out who killed you, you wouldn't be able to communicate the

162

information to the living.'

I had forgotten about that. 'Is there no way to get through to them?'

'No,' he said.

'Are you sure?'

He shook his head again. 'Shari, you've got to leave it to the police. They're better equipped to deal with the situation.'

'I told you, Garrett's a drunk.'

'Yes, but he has an advantage over you. He's alive.'

'I would think dead people would make better spies,' I said, remembering how my mother had twice seemed to hear me, in the kitchen immediately after the hospital had called and, even more distinctly, in her bedroom when I had tried to comfort her. There must be a thread that connects us to the living, I thought. There had to be a way to talk to them. 'Why are you so anxious to get rid of me?' I asked.

'I'm not anxious to get rid of you.'

'Do you have a girlfriend over here? Some big-bosomed wench from the Middle Ages, maybe? I bet she doesn't know about women's liberation. I'd like to meet her.'

He wasn't laughing. 'It's dangerous for you to stay.'

I stopped my teasing. 'Why?'

He was watching me. 'You know why.'

163

Sitting on the grass in the bright sun with a friend by my side, it might have been possible to forget the creature on the balcony. But I was never going to forget, I knew. 'What was it?'

'The Shadow,' he said.

'The what?'

He closed his eyes and lowered his head. The thing scared him. 'It's the most awful thing.'

'Is it like a devil?'

'It can't be . . .' He opened his eyes, staring down at the grass, I had never seen him this way before. He was as pale as a ghost, and that was no joke. 'Yes, it's like that. It's evil.'

'If it's evil, why did God make it?'

'I don't know.'

'Is there just one of them?'

He turned towards me. 'Listen, Shari, you mustn't give it the chance to catch up with you. You must leave here.'

'What would it do to me?'

'Imprison you.'

'How?' I asked.

'I can't explain. That's just what it does.'

'Can't you protect me from it?'

'No,' he said.

'How do you protect yourself from it?'

164

'I avoid it. And that's not easy.'

'But wouldn't the two of us be safer together?'

He went to argue with me some more when he suddenly stopped. I didn't know what was happening. He closed his eyes as he had done before. It was almost as if he were meditating. Only this time his face didn't brighten. I let him be. When he finally did open his eyes, he looked down at his open left hand. He had been a southpaw; he had pitched left-handed. He had been so good.

'I didn't know,' he said.

'You didn't know what?'

'That you were going to die that night.'

'You didn't see who did it?'

'No. I left the party a few minutes before it happened.'

'Oh,' I said.

'You won't go on?'

The Shadow had scared me more than death itself, but there was Jimmy still grieving alone and a murderer walking free. Plus there was Peter. He continued to study his open palm. I thought to put my hand in it and tell him that I wanted his company as much as I wanted my name cleared. But I didn't. It was not to be, I guessed. A lot of things aren't.

'No,' I said.

He closed his hand into a fist and gently pounded the grass beside his knee, bending back not a single blade of grass. 'You're making a mistake,' he said.

'We'll see.'

He raised his head, and I was relieved to see him smile. He was giving up, at least for now. He offered me his hand. 'I guess we're partners again,' he said, referring to the days when we were lab partners in biology.

'There is no wench from the Middle Ages?'

'No such luck.'

CHAPTER 9

We didn't leave the cemetery right away. We had to decide how we were going to conduct our investigation. I started out by asking Peter if he could read people's minds. He thought it was a weird question.

'Of course not,' he said. 'I'm not psychic.'

'I was just asking. I figured it would make our work a lot easier if you could.'

'I can't.'

'All right,' I said. 'So what should we do now?'

'Who at the party do you feel was capable of murder?'

'No one.'

'We're off to a great start,' he said.

'But if I had to choose someone, it would be Amanda.'

'Why? She seems like a nice, soft-spoken girl.'

'She's too soft-spoken. I haven't trusted her from the day she started going out with my brother.'

He chuckled. 'Do I detect a hint of jealousy here?'

'No. Well, maybe. But I think that girl's hiding something.'

'When did you start thinking that?' he asked.

'I've always thought that.'

'But if she is the one, then she only just killed you a few days ago. What could she have been hiding before?'

'I don't know,' I said.

'We should review where Garrett had everybody when you went over the balcony.'

'All right.' Something struck me. 'How come I didn't see you in the condo when he was doing his questioning?'

'You're easy to hide from,' he said.

'I am?'

'You've always been that way.' He thought a moment. 'Wasn't Amanda supposed to be in the bathroom when you died?'

'Yeah,' I agreed reluctantly. 'When your brother came into Beth's bedroom, I was still on the balcony. Wait! What if she came out of the bathroom after Jeff left, shoved me off the balcony, and then re-entered the bathroom before Beth came into the bedroom?'

'She would have had to have moved extremely quickly.'

'But it's possible,' I said.

'It's unlikely. Beth said she left the living room less than a minute after Jeff. Besides, you haven't given me a single reason why Amanda would have wanted you dead.'

'Let's look at Dan, then. Amanda said he was fooling around with Beth in the Jacuzzi. He had a motive to knock me off.'

'A slim one,' Peter said. 'Dan only had to break up with you if he wanted to date Beth. He didn't have to kill you.'

'But I had humiliated Dan.'

'What did you do?'

I hesitated. 'It's a long story.' A disturbing idea occurred to me. 'Peter?'

'What?'

'Since you've been dead, how much have you been hanging out with us guys, you know, who were still alive?'

He smiled. 'Are you asking if I ever spied on you while you were taking a shower?'

I would have blushed had I real blood in my veins. 'No.'

'I did once.'

'What? You didn't!'

'Just once,' he said, giggling.

'When? Was it last summer? Did I have a tan?'

'I don't remember.'

'You don't remember! How did I look?'

'Fine.'

'*Fine?* What does that mean?'

He continued to laugh. 'You looked great.'

I hit him. 'You're disgusting.'

'I was curious.'

'Why did you choose me? Or did you go around peeking through curtains all over the city? I bet you did. I bet you still do. And here you were trying to give me the impression you're a guardian angel.'

'You were the first one I checked out,' he said.

'And I suppose I should be flattered?'

'Yeah.'

I thought a minute and decided I *was* flattered. Of course, I thought, I couldn't let him know that. 'I hope you weren't disappointed,' I said.

'I found the entire experience spiritually exhilarating.' He stood and began to pace in front of me at the edge of the grassy bluff, returning to business. 'Dan may be the last person we can pin your murder on. He was one of the last people to leave the living room, and he didn't come out on to the balcony until after Jo and Beth were already there.'

'He could have been on the balcony before Jo got there and then gone inside before coming back outside.'

'But he left the living room at the same time as Jo,' Peter said. 'He wouldn't have had time to kill you before Jo got to the balcony. Also, Beth would have had to have been in cahoots with him.'

'Then what about Beth herself? Jo said Beth was on the balcony before her.'

Peter nodded. 'From the point of view of timing, Beth has to be considered the number one suspect. But what about a motive? So she had the hots for your boyfriend. That's not a good enough reason to kill you.'

'But Beth was acting weird that night. After Jo used the magnet on her, she looked spaced out. Peter, when exactly did you leave the party?'

'I told you. A few minutes before you died.'

'What was the last thing you saw? Did you see the seance?'

He stopped his pacing. 'What seance?'

'When Jo was hypnotising me,' I said.

'I caught some of that.'

'Why did you suddenly leave?'

'It was getting late,' he said.

'But you don't have to sleep. Do you?'

'Not exactly. But I do rest sometimes.'

'Why did you leave?'

He shrugged. 'I just did.'

'Well, I don't know what was wrong with Beth. Do you?'

'How would I know?'

'I don't know.' Something was bothering him. I think I knew what it was. There was no sense avoiding the matter. 'Peter? What about Jeff?'

'He didn't kill you.'

'He says he saw me on the balcony. But when Beth came into the bedroom, she said I was gone.'

'It wasn't my brother. He couldn't harm a fly.'

'He didn't like me,' I said.

'Why do you say that?'

'I could tell.'

'He wouldn't have had time to kill you before Beth appeared.'

'It doesn't take a whole lot of time to shove someone in the back.' Peter didn't say anything. 'Why didn't your brother like me?' I asked.

'Shari, as far as I know, when I was alive, Jeff had nothing against you.'

'All right. I believe you.'

'What about Jo?' he asked.

I had to laugh. 'Jo's my best friend.'

'Did you trust her?'

'What kind of question is that? Of course I trusted her. Anyway, she didn't get to the balcony until after Beth.'

'Beth thought Jo was there before her,' Peter said.

'Beth didn't know what she was talking about.'

'You shouldn't automatically eliminate Jo.'

'You shouldn't automatically eliminate Jeff,' I snapped. Dying obviously hadn't improved my disposition. I felt ashamed. 'I'm sorry,' I muttered.

He nodded. 'So am I. It's no fun dissecting your friends.'

'And your family,' I said.

'Yeah.'

'Are we making any progress?' I asked.

'Who knows?'

'God must. Can't you give him a call?'

Peter smiled. 'Did you notice how Garrett drew those crisscrossing lines behind your position on the balcony?'

'You saw those too?' I asked.

'I was peering over your shoulder when you were peering over his. Do you know what those lines meant?'

'No.'

'Garrett's considering the possibility that someone was standing at your back on the balcony in the one spot that wouldn't have been visible from the centre of Beth's bedroom.'

'Amanda,' I whispered.

'It would seem that she could have been behind you even when Jeff was in Beth's bedroom.'

173

'It must have been her!'

Peter shook his head. 'It would seem so on the surface, but let's look at it a little closer. Jeff said the sliding glass door to the balcony was closed when he went into the bedroom. Garrett made it clear that when you close that door, you lock it. Amanda would have had no way to push you off the balcony and then get back inside, unless she went through the kitchen, where Beth and Jo and Dan would have seen her. Amanda *must* have been in the bathroom. Dan noticed her at his back when he was on the balcony, and when Jeff came back into the living room, Amanda was there.'

'So we've determined it couldn't have been Dan or Amanda?'

'Maybe.' Peter glanced up at the kaleidoscope sun. 'What if it wasn't someone at the party?'

'You mean someone from the outside might have murdered me?'

'No. We may be too caught up on the idea of someone. What if two people were involved? Or three? And they arranged their stories for Garrett so that the facts we're taking for granted might be completely false.'

My jaw dropped. 'What if it was *all* of them?'

'Then we're really in trouble.'

* * *

We decided the best course of action would be for us to try to pick up clues by following my friends around for a few days. A ghost can't do much else, really – or so Peter said. Yet I was secretly determined to explore any imaginable way to make contact with the living.

We were leaving the cemetery when Peter remarked that it was time for my first lesson in spirit transportation.

'We don't use cars on this side of the fence,' he said.

'What do you use?'

He tapped his head. 'Our minds. But let's go over to the park before I show you what to do.'

He didn't say it, but he meant he wanted to get me away from my burial plot. The whole time we had talked, my eyes had strayed to the mound of fresh brown dirt. Like the spot where I had died, it held a perverse allure for me. I couldn't help thinking how my body would decompose beneath the earth. I wished I had been cremated and my ashes thrown into the ocean.

The park was across the street from the cemetery. The two girls we had seen earlier had set aside their bikes and were playing on the swings. Peter steered me towards a bench beneath a shady tree.

'We're going to perform a little experiment,' he said when we were comfortably seated. 'First, close your eyes.' I did so. 'Now, picture to yourself the courtyard at

Hazzard High. Think of how the benches surround the snackbar area. Think of the buildings and the trees, the people we know who go to school there. Then say to yourself—'

'There's no place like home,' I muttered, giggling and thinking of Dorothy in *The Wizard of Oz*.

He laughed with me, but only for a moment. 'Keep your eyes closed, Shari. Think to yourself: I want to be there. I want to be at school. You mustn't try to concentrate on the desire. You simply want to have it, quietly, innocently. Now, go ahead. Do it for a minute or so.'

I did as he requested. At the end of the minute, I opened my eyes and asked, 'How am I doing?'

'You're still here.'

'This is supposed to teleport me to school?'

'It's the way I get around,' Peter said. 'You've done it yourself, remember? Close your eyes, try again. But don't try too hard. Just picture the school and imagine yourself there. We have plenty of time.'

'Indeed we do.'

I worked at it for half an hour, and I would have to say that was one of my problems; I couldn't help trying. Finally, I opened my eyes. 'I can't see this working,' I said.

'That's why it isn't.'

'Thank you, Yoda. Feel the force, Luke.'

He smiled. '*Star Wars*. Good. Do you remember Peter Pan?'

I began to shake my head. 'I'm not flying. No way.'

He bounced up. 'Anybody can fly, even the living. There are yogis in India who float from one mountaintop to another. I've seen them. But it's easier when you don't have a physical body. Watch this.'

Taking an extraordinary leap upward, Peter crossed his legs lotus-style in midair and hovered a half-dozen feet above my head. 'Christ,' I whispered.

'Just Saint Peter, please. See how easy it is? Come on up.'

'I can't. I can't get into a full lotus.'

'How your legs are crossed is unimportant. All that matters is that you understand you can do it and that you have no fear of hurting yourself. Let's fly, Shari Poppins.'

'*Can* I hurt myself?' I asked.

'That's impossible at this point. Now jump up.'

I jumped. I didn't go very high, and I landed quickly. I tried it again, trying to pretend I was light as a feather. It didn't work. 'Can't I hold on to you like Lois Lane did in *Superman*?' I asked.

'No. Your lead-foot mentality would make me sink.'

'Why do I have to *learn* to do this?'

'You are not learning to do it. You're unlearning the belief that you *can't* do it. Try again, without trying.'

It's hard not to try when you're trying not to. I couldn't get off the ground, not even far enough to break Hazzard High's high-jump record. Peter finally floated down to my side.

'It'll come in time,' he said.

'I feel that if I had a broom I could pretend better.'

'I could get you one if you think it would help.'

'Really? Where?' I asked.

'I could make you one.'

'How?'

He gestured to the stuff in the air, which I had begun to forget about. 'When you were alive,' he said, 'you were in a realm of matter. There's matter here, too, but it is of a finer nature and more easily manipulated. All I have to do is put my attention on a broom and the ether around us will generate one.'

'Could you make me some new clothes?'

'Sure.'

'Could you change the colour of my eyes?' I asked.

'Yeah.'

'My body?'

'What's wrong with your body?'

'I didn't think anything was wrong with it until

someone told me it was *fine*.'

He laughed. 'Would you like bigger breasts?'

'No, I'd like— What colour are my eyes?'

'Green. Why?'

'You are a saint.' I hugged him. 'Never mind, I'm satisfied with the way I look. And forget about the broom. I was never into witches like Jo.'

'You'll have to walk,' he warned, sounding like the good witch in *The Wizard of Oz*.

'Can't I hitch rides?'

'If you get through the car doors.' He pointed to the tree. 'Walk through that trunk.'

'No way. There're bugs beneath the bark. Hey, that's something I wanted to ask you about. How come I touch things, but don't really touch them?'

'Because you're dead.'

'Yes, we've already covered that. What I mean is, my feet are touching the ground right now. The ground is supporting me. How come I don't just sink into it?'

'Because you *expect* the ground to support you,' Peter said. 'It's all in your mind.' He paused. 'Since you died, has a part of your body passed through anything physical?'

'Yeah. When I tried to grab Jimmy at the hospital, my hand went right through his arm.'

Peter nodded. 'You were probably desperate at the time, and dropped your psychological inhibitions. The point is you've already seen that it can be done.' He gestured to the bench. 'Walk through that.'

'All right.' I had finally decided it was time to stop messing around. I strode towards the bench as if it wasn't there. I was furious when I cracked my shin on the wood. 'Ouch!' I cried, bending over in pain.

'It only hurts because you think it hurts.'

'Would you shut up! It hurts! I don't care why it hurts!'

'Imagine that it doesn't,' he said.

'I'd rather have an aspirin and a glass of water.'

Because I was bent over and rubbing my poor leg, I didn't see any flash and glitter. Maybe there wasn't any. The next thing I knew, he was handing me an aspirin and a glass of water.

'Swallow it, and let's get out of here,' he said.

CHAPTER 10

We took the bus. The doors opened automatically. We didn't have to worry about correct change. I was thankful for small favours. We had to catch a couple of connections to get to my neighbourhood. The last bus we got on was jammed. I stood with several people while Peter sat on a cute blonde's lap.

'Pervert,' I said

'You think sex is dirty. You have a dirty mind.'

'I think sex is fine between two consenting *living* adults.'

'What about between two dead adolescents?' he asked.

I just laughed. I didn't believe he was serious.

Daniel's house was closer to the bus stop than my own. I told Peter I wanted to check on my old beau. A window around the side was open. Peter had to help me up. He didn't need any help. As I turned around inside, he was already heading from the kitchen into the living room.

181

There were voices. Big Beth and Spam.

They were making out on the couch. Daniel had his hand under her blouse. She was undoing his belt. They were both groaning. Peter stood above them shaking his head.

'And you're not even cold in your grave,' he said.

'Peter,' I moaned, deeply hurt. He was by my side instantly.

'I'm sorry. That was tactless.' He put his arm around my waist. 'Are you OK?'

'I think I'm going to be sick.'

'No, you're definitely not going to do that. Let's go in the kitchen.'

'I want to leave!'

'Not yet. This might get interesting. I mean, as far as your case is concerned. Come on.'

We sat at the kitchen table. I could still hear them in the next room. I stared at the apples in the fruit bowl and wished I could stuff one down each of their throats. 'I thought he cared about me,' I whispered.

'You get used to it,' Peter said.

'No.'

'Forget him. He was trash.'

I chuckled sadly. 'Your brother said he was an asshole.'

'He's a smart guy.'

'Yeah. If he was so smart, what was he doing with Beth?'

'Well,' Peter said, peeking around the corner of the kitchen into the living room. 'I suppose he had a couple of good reasons.'

Someone knocked at the front door. We jumped up, but not nearly so fast as Daniel and Beth. They were busy pulling themselves together when we re-entered the living room.

'Just a minute!' Beth called.

'Shh! This is my house,' Daniel said. 'Just a minute!'

Peter peeked out the window. 'We're in luck, Shari. It's Garrett. He's caught them red-handed.'

'He's a couple of minutes early,' I growled.

The kids finally got themselves presentable and answered the door. Garrett was not wearing his frumpy green sports coat, but his unironed black shirt was a questionable improvement. He looked as if he had spent the night with his head bent over a toilet. He needed a shave in the worst way.

'May I come in?' he asked Daniel.

'I don't know.' Daniel glanced at Beth. 'This is sort of a bad time.'

'I bet,' Garrett said, stepping inside anyway. 'Are your folks home?'

'No,' Daniel said.

'Good.' He took out the notepad he had brought to Beth's condo. 'I'd like to ask you two a couple of questions.' He gestured to the couch. 'Have a seat.'

Daniel and Beth sat down. Garrett pulled up a footstool. 'Did you go to the funeral?' he asked.

'Yes,' Daniel said.

'It was sad,' Beth said.

'They usually are.' Garrett coughed as he clicked open his ballpoint pen. 'Did either of you push Shari off the balcony?'

Daniel gave a ridiculous smile. 'What?'

'Did you kill your girlfriend?'

'She jumped,' Beth said.

'Did you see her jump?' Garrett asked.

'No,' Beth said.

'I didn't push her,' Daniel said. 'Jo can tell you that.'

'She wouldn't tell me if she stood by and let you push her,' Garrett said.

Daniel stopped smiling. 'I don't believe, sir, that we have to answer your questions.'

'You do have the right to remain silent,' Garrett agreed.

Daniel nodded self-righteously. 'I know my rights.'

'But that's only if you've been arrested. I'll have to arrest you if you want to remain silent.'

'I love this cop,' Peter said.

'Shh,' I said.

Daniel and Beth exchanged uneasy glances. 'We didn't kill her,' Beth said. 'What else can we tell you?'

'Was Jo on the balcony before you?' Garrett asked her.

'She says she got there after me,' Beth said.

'What do you say?'

'I don't know. I told you, it was dark.'

'It wasn't that dark. The balcony's not that big. What was the matter with you that night, Beth? Were you drunk?'

'She doesn't drink,' Daniel said.

'I'm asking her,' Garrett said.

Beth put her hands to her mouth and grimaced. 'I don't know what was wrong with me.'

Garrett leaned forward. 'Were you mad at Shari?'

'No.'

'Why not?'

'Because . . . s-she was my friend,' Beth stammered.

'How could she be your friend when she was going out with your boyfriend?' Garrett asked.

'Dan wasn't my boyfriend.'

'Is he your boyfriend now?'

'No,' Daniel interrupted.

'No,' Beth echoed weakly.

Garrett turned to Daniel. 'When you were on the balcony, did you see Amanda come out of the bathroom? Please try to remember as best you can, or I might have to arrest you.'

'I saw her.'

'Are you positive?'

'Yes.'

Garrett closed his notepad and stood. 'That's all for now.'

Daniel's fear turned to anger. 'Why are you hassling us like this? You have no right.'

Garrett stared down at him for a moment – way down; he appeared to be studying Daniel's feet. Then his eyes flickered upward, and he reached over and plucked something from Daniel's shirt pocket before Daniel could stop him.

It was an unopened condom.

'What's this for?' he asked.

'It's none of your goddam business,' Daniel snapped.

Garrett tossed the condom into Daniel's lap. 'You may think you're practising safe sex, son.' He smiled and put his notepad away. 'But you're not even close.'

Garrett left. Peter wanted to go after him.

'He's probably going to question the others,' Peter told me. 'We can ride in the back of his truck and not have to worry about the buses. Come on.'

'No. I want to see what these two have to say.'

'They're just going to have sex.' Peter paused. 'I suppose we could stay.'

They did not have sex. The instant Garrett was out the door, Beth burst out crying. Daniel tried to comfort her.

'He was just bluffing,' Daniel said. 'He's not going to arrest us.' He put his hands on the back of her neck as she wept into the couch cushion. 'Hey, babe. I'm here. It's all right.'

She sat up suddenly, throwing off his hands. 'I shouldn't be here! We shouldn't be together!'

'Why not? You said you liked me.'

Beth gave him an incredulous look. 'Dan, Shari's dead. We just buried her.' She glanced around, obviously confused about how she had come to be where she was. She stood. 'I've got to get out of here.'

Daniel tried to stop her. 'I'm upset, too. You know, she was *my* girlfriend.'

'If she was your girlfriend, why are you trying to make like you hardly knew her?'

'That's not true.'

'Let me go. It is.' She went to shove him away and then stopped. Looking at his face, her own changed. The ding-dong expression vanished. 'It is true,' she said, a note of regret in her voice.

Beth left. Daniel let her.

'Shari,' Peter said. 'We have to get into Garrett's truck.'

'Just a second,' I said. Daniel just stood there staring at the closed door before finally trudging upstairs to his bedroom. I went with him. Peter remained behind. Plopping down on his bed, Daniel opened a drawer in his nightstand and took out a picture of me in my white prom dress. My corsage was huge, as big as my smile. He had pinned it on me only a couple of hours before the picture had been taken. He had told me how beautiful I was, and that night he had been beautiful.

Now he looked old.

'Shari,' he said, biting his lower lip. I had to move closer. I couldn't believe what I was seeing. They were tears.

I might have taken pleasure in them or even wept with him. But he didn't give me a chance. A second later he hurled my picture against the far wall, breaking the glass. Then he buried his face in his pillow, and all I could hear was his heavy breathing.

'Catch you later,' I said.

Downstairs, Peter hurried me out the window. We hopped into the back of Garrett's truck as he pulled away, heading in the opposite direction from Beth. Garrett did not fail to note Beth's hasty departure.

'I heard something break?' Peter asked.

'It was nothing,' I said.

Garrett went to Jeff Nichol's place next, Peter's old house. I could tell that's where we were headed a couple of blocks before we got there. I had an eye on Peter, but he appeared undisturbed by our destination.

'I never asked you,' I said. 'What was it like when you died?'

'What do you mean?'

'Did you know you were dead?'

'Oh, yeah,' Peter said. 'I didn't black out like you did. I was on my motorbike one moment with the wind in my face, and the next thing I knew, I was standing on the road beside my body and a huge semi.' He shrugged. 'There was a lot of blood. I knew it was over.'

'It was the truck driver's fault, wasn't it?'

'No.'

'That's what I read in the papers.'

'It was my fault.'

'Really? What happened?' I asked.

'I was careless.'

'Did someone meet you on this side and help you along?'

'I was worse than you,' he said.

'What do you mean?'

He smiled faintly but refused to elaborate.

Jeff was out front, working on his motorcycle. The love of fast machines obviously ran in the family. Jeff had grease on his hands, a cigarette in his mouth, and a half-finished six-pack sitting beside a ratchet set. He hardly glanced up as Garrett climbed out of his truck and walked towards him.

'Busy?' Garrett asked.

'I suppose.'

'Can I have a beer?'

Now Jeff looked at Garrett. He set down his tools and handed Garrett a can. 'It's not cold,' he warned.

'That's all right, I'm on duty,' Garrett said, popping the beer and taking a deep drink. 'Thanks. I wanted to ask you a couple of questions.'

'I have nothing to add to what I said the other night.'

'You like beer, Jeff?'

'Yeah. Do you?'

'I like whisky.' Garrett finished his can and set it beside Jeff's pile on the cement driveway. The Nicholses were fairly well off. Their house was roughly the size of my own. Jeff appeared to be the only one home. Garrett pulled out his notepad. 'Were you drinking the night of the party?' he asked.

'Yeah.'

'How much did you have to drink?'

'I wasn't drunk,' Jeff said.

'How much?'

'Two or three cans.'

'Following the seance, why did you try to go to the bathroom in Beth's bedroom when you had just seen Amanda go in there?'

'Beats me.'

'You can do better than that,' Garrett said.

'I had to take a leak. I just went in there. I didn't give it a lot of thought. Want another beer?'

'No. When you were in Beth's bedroom, did you hear anything that would indicate Amanda was actually in there?'

'I don't know. Maybe,' Jeff said.

'Could you be more specific?'

'I thought I heard water running.'

'What was your relationship with Shari?'

'I didn't have one,' Jeff said.

'Weren't you friends?' Garrett asked.

'No.'

'Did you dislike her?'

'Not really.'

'Would you say she was suicidal?'

'I told you, I hardly knew her.'

'What is your relationship with Beth?'

'I used to go out with her,' Jeff said.

'When did you stop going out with her?'

'The night of the party.'

'Why?' Garrett asked.

'It started to get old.'

'What is your relationship with Joanne Foulton?'

'We're friends.'

'Have you ever dated?'

'No,' Jeff said.

'Might you in the future?'

'I doubt it.'

'What's your sign, Jeff?'

'Huh?'

'Your astrological sign. What is it?'

'I'm a Scorpio.'

'You don't strike me as the type who'd be into astrology.'

'I'm not,' Jeff said.

'How did you know what sign you were? Did Joanne tell you?'

Jeff hesitated. 'That's right,' he said flatly.

The phone inside the garage rang. Jeff went to get it. I tagged along and pressed my ear to the receiver as he answered it. Garrett stayed in the driveway.

'Hi, Jeff, this is Jo. Am I calling at a bad time?'

'Sort of,' Jeff said.

'I won't keep you. I just wanted to tell you that I'd like you to come over to my house tonight at ten o'clock.'

'What for?'

'You'll see when you get here, but it's important.'

'I can't make it,' Jeff said.

'It has to do with Shari. The group's going to be here.'

Jeff glanced at Garrett. 'Can't make it.'

'Come on, Jeff. Please? It really is important.'

'I'll think about it.'

Jo paused. 'All right. I hope you come.'

Jeff set down the phone and returned to Garrett and his bike. He picked up his ratchet. 'Finished with your questions?' he asked.

'Just about,' Garrett said. 'Who was that?'

'Some girl.'

Garrett gestured to Jeff's greasy white sneakers. 'Are those the shoes you wore to the party?'

'Maybe.'

'Are you sure you didn't have on black shoes?'

'I don't remember.'

Garrett put away his notepad. 'Those sneakers are a mess. I doubt Beth would have let you into her place with them on.' He turned to leave. 'Take it easy, son.'

'You, too, Lieutenant.'

Peter and I climbed into the back of Garrett's truck again. Garrett started the engine, and we were on our way. It had to be close to seven; the sun was nearing the horizon. I couldn't get over how the breeze was not messing up my hair.

'Who was on the phone?' Peter asked.

'Jo. She wanted Jeff to go over there tonight. She said the gang would be there. It's supposed to be about me.'

'We'll have to stop by,' Peter said.

'You bet. What did you think of Jeff?'

'He didn't do it, Shari.'

'But he was so evasive.'

'That's just the way he is.'

'Why do you think Garrett asked Jeff about his shoes?'

'I was wondering that myself,' Peter said.

I soon regretted hitching a ride on the truck. Garrett left our neighbourhood and got on the freeway. He headed west, towards downtown LA. Peter told me I could jump off any time I wanted, but my shin still hurt from the park bench.

We got off the freeway in a crummy part of town. It was dark by then. Garrett stopped at the first liquor store we came to. He bought himself a pint of whisky and drank half of it before he left the parking lot.

'I think we should get off now,' I said as Garrett restarted the truck.

'I wouldn't worry about him crashing,' Peter said.

'I am worried. I don't want to be late to Jo's get-together.'

'I won't be late. I can always just pop over.'

'Lucky you. What do you think Garrett's doing in this sleazy part of town?'

'He's probably going to buy drugs,' Peter said.

For a while I thought maybe Peter *was* psychic. Garrett rode several blocks north to Sunset Boulevard, to the bad end of Hollywood, where the porn shops and hookers carved out their existence. Garrett could have been searching for a pusher. He parked on a side street a hundred yards off the big boulevard and reached for a pair of binoculars. I noticed again the telescopic vision I'd had at the cemetery; I was able to follow Garrett's magnified gaze without effort. He was studying a tall, pasty white dude leaning against a streetlight. The guy looked like a threat to young girls everywhere. He had on tight black leather trousers and an orange Day-Glo shirt. A thin gold chain circled his shaved head.

'He wasn't at the party, was he, Shari?' Peter asked.

'Hardly. What's Garrett doing?'

'Let's wait and see.'

A half-hour later, I began to fret. I could see Garrett's watch through the rear window. It was just past eight-thirty. 'We have to go,' I complained.

'Not yet,' Peter said, gesturing to the dude on the corner as Garrett simultaneously leaned forward inside the truck. Someone was approaching. 'Look at her. Wow.'

The girl had long straight black hair and a cute heart-shaped mouth. Her face was bony, her dark eyes set deep and wide. She needed a decent meal; she was thin as a rail. Yet her dress was conservative: a longish grey skirt and a freshly pressed white blouse. I understood Peter's wow – she was beautiful.

'I know her,' I said.

'She was at the party?' Peter asked.

'Would you shut up.' She was several years older, but it was definitely the girl in the picture Garrett carried in his wallet. I cringed as she embraced the slime on the corner. 'What could she be doing with him?' I asked. 'Is he her pimp?'

'I doubt it,' Peter said. 'She doesn't have the hooker look. But she could be an addict. The guy could be her connection. How do you know her?'

'I've seen her before.'

'I hope Garrett invites her for a ride in his truck.'

Garrett, however, did not make his presence known. He continued to follow the couple until the slime ball kissed the girl on the neck and slipped a plastic Baggie holding white powder into her hand. Then Garrett lowered his binoculars and leaned his head back on the seat, reaching for what was left of his bottle.

'It's his daughter,' I said, understanding at last. The couple parted company, heading in opposite directions along the boulevard.

'Are you serious?' Peter asked. 'A cop with an addict for a daughter? Sounds like TV. Hey, where are you going?'

'I want to follow her,' I said, leaping out of the truck.

'If you insist,' Peter said, catching up with me in the blink of an eye.

The girl did not go far before she turned into a discount motel half a block off Sunset. The place was not only run-down, the stuff that clung to its walls was choked with the threads of shadows I had first seen in the hospital. Only these threads were thicker and twisted at sharp angles like a form of astral barbed wire.

'What is that?' I asked, pointing.

'Pain,' Peter said.

'Is that what people mean by bad vibes?'

'Most definitely.'

'Can it hurt us?' I asked.

'If we let it.'

We followed the girl into the lobby. The guy at the desk nodded to her as she strode by. Her room was on the second floor. She opened it with a silver key she took from her black boot. Surprisingly, inside it was fairly neat. The sheets on the bed were clean, and the paint on the walls was a fresh blue. But the threads of darkness were now rope thick. I kept thinking they would cut me if I bumped against them.

I don't know what I hoped to discover. She was in the room less than a minute when she got out the plastic bag of powder, a syringe, a spoon, and a rubber tourniquet on the stand beside her bed. It was sickening to watch. She set a portion of the powder into the spoon and mixed it with water. Then she pulled out a lighter and ran the flame beneath the solution. I had to turn away a minute later when she steered the needle towards her vein.

'Why don't we leave?' Peter asked.

I nodded weakly. 'All right.' But the girl had closed the door as she came in. I had to go out the window. As I peered into the night with Peter and tried to estimate what the fall to the pavement would do to my supposedly invincible legs, I noticed the girl staring at me with wide, dilated pupils.

'Hi,' I said.

'Hi,' she whispered.

I jumped so high I almost hit my head on the ceiling. 'Peter, she can see me!'

He was not impressed. 'Sometimes, when the living are in an altered state of consciousness, they can glimpse the realm we're in.'

'Are you serious? Why should a drug give someone special powers?' The girl continued to stare at me with her weird, unblinking blue eyes.

'It is hardly a power,' Peter said. 'At best, drugs can give a peek at where we are. They never give people an insight into the higher realms you would now be enjoying had you followed my advice this morning. They often do the opposite, opening the mind to dark levels, to madness.'

'I want to talk to her,' I said.

'Why? She's stoned. You'll be late to Jo's meeting.'

'Just a sec.' I strode to the bed, where the girl now lay stretched out. Her head followed me as I moved.

'Hi,' she said again.

'Listen,' I said, sitting beside her. 'You're blowing it. You're a great-looking girl. This is no life for you. You're messing up your dad's life as well. He's drinking himself into the grave because of you. He's so screwed up he can't find the person who murdered me.'

'Murder,' she mumbled.

'Careful,' Peter said. 'Don't give her any ideas.'

I stood. 'We're going to have another talk, you and me,' I told her. 'As soon as I figure out what you need to hear.'

The jump to the pavement didn't slow me down a beat. We rode a fire truck back to the freeway, where we caught an ice-cream truck heading east. We didn't exactly get invited into the front seat. The freeway rushed beneath us, and Peter laughed at me for hugging the brightly lit cherry snowcone on top.

CHAPTER II

Jimmy and Amanda were sitting in Jimmy's station wagon at the end of Jo's driveway when we arrived. I told Peter to go on ahead while I eavesdropped on their conversation. I did it without feeling a twinge of guilt. That's one good thing about being a ghost. When all you can do is watch and listen, you feel you should be allowed to watch and listen to everything.

Amanda had her arm around Jimmy's shoulder, and that annoyed me. Here she wouldn't even return his calls, I thought, and I die and now she's in love. It was sort of a ridiculous thought. Actually, I was happy she was taking good care of him. He looked pretty messed up. He had his window down, and I stood by his side as they talked.

'I don't know,' Jimmy was saying. 'Maybe I should have stayed home. I wasn't invited.'

'Jo won't mind you coming,' Amanda said.

'I guess not.'

'Are you worried about your mom?'

'I probably shouldn't have left her alone,' Jimmy said.

'We can always go back.'

'We're here. We may as well see what Jo wants.' He glanced towards the house, shaking his head. 'Someone in there—'

'What?'

'Nothing.'

Amanda knew what he meant. Jimmy thought my murderer must be in the house. She let it pass. 'Are your parents still thinking of going away tomorrow?' she asked.

'Yeah. My dad wants to get my mom out of the house.'

'Are you going to go?' Amanda asked.

'I haven't decided.'

She kissed him on the cheek. 'If you don't, I'll come over to see you.'

He looked at her. 'I'll be lousy company.'

She smiled. 'I don't mind.'

They got out of his car and walked towards the house. They almost bumped into Mrs Foulton coming out the front door. She had on her nurse's uniform and was in her usual hurry.

'I didn't know everyone was coming over,' she said, and

I immediately understood why Jo had set the meeting for ten o'clock and not earlier – she had thought her mother would already be at work. 'What's up?' she asked.

'Jo just said to come,' Amanda replied. 'She said it was important.'

'Yeah, well, she thinks everything she does is important,' Mrs Foulton said, turning to Jimmy. 'How are your parents?'

'Not good,' Jimmy said.

Mrs Foulton nodded sympathetically. 'I thought that service was never going to end. That minister read practically the whole Bible. I wish that – that he hadn't done that.' She had been on the verge of saying something else. Jimmy was making her nervous. She fussed over Amanda's hair, brushing it away from her eyes. Amanda was her favourite niece. 'Your mother just called,' she said. 'She was looking for you.'

Amanda took Jimmy's arm. 'Really?'

Mrs Foulton's uneasiness increased, for no apparent reason. 'She wanted to know when you would be home.'

'I'll call her,' Amanda said.

'I'm really sorry about Shari,' she said to Jimmy, leaving in a hurry.

I followed Jimmy and Amanda into the house. I had never seen the place so clean. Everyone was in the living room. I was surprised to see Jeff – he was lounging on the couch with Jo. Beth and Daniel were not close to each other; they were sitting stiffly in chairs and avoiding each other's eyes.

'What's Jo want?' I asked Peter, who was planted cross-legged on top of the TV.

'She's been waiting for everyone to get here,' Peter said. 'But as soon as her mother stepped outside the door, she went for her Ouija board.'

'Oh my,' I said, interested. 'Do those things really work?'

'What do you mean?'

'Can we talk to them through it?'

He shrugged. 'They can work. Sometimes.'

'I guess you're all wondering why I invited you here,' Jo said as Jimmy and Amanda took a seat on the floor. Jo had finally put on her black dress – better late than never, I supposed. The Ouija board rested on the coffee table at her knees. Jeff gestured to it and snorted.

'You want to use that thing again,' he said, annoyed. 'You should have told us. We wouldn't have come.'

If the remark hurt her, Jo showed no sign of it. 'I know this may seem like the wrong time,' she said. 'God knows this has been an awful day. But think back to the party just before Shari jumped up and ran to the balcony. Something remarkable happened. I think we contacted Peter.'

Jeff took a deep drag on his cigarette and ground it out. I wouldn't have been surprised to see him leave. Yet he said nothing, nor did he move to get up. I turned to Peter.

'Is that true?' I asked.

He spoke reluctantly. 'Yes.'

I grabbed him. 'You used *my* body to talk to them?'

'Yes.'

'But that's – that's obscene!'

'You volunteered to act as a channel.'

'But I didn't know it was real!'

Peter was embarrassed. 'I know, Shari, and I'm sorry. I just wanted the chance to talk to my brother.'

I refused to accept his apology. I was furious with him, and I wasn't even sure why. But I was a hypocrite. I was wondering if it could be done again.

'It was just Shari talking,' Daniel said.

'It was more than that,' Jo said. 'I can't be the only one who thinks this way. What do you say, Amanda?'

'I hardly knew Peter,' she said.

'How about you, Beth?' Jo asked, sounding less sure of herself.

Beth didn't answer immediately. I remembered that Peter used to talk to her frequently – probably out of respect for her big breasts.

'There was something in Shari's voice,' Beth said finally, confused. 'It gave me gooseflesh.'

'Why?' Jeff asked sharply, sitting up.

'It sounded like him,' Beth said. 'I mean, it sounded like Shari, but also like Peter, using Shari's voice.'

'She's smarter than she looks,' I said, scowling at Peter.

'You knew Peter best of all,' Jo said to Jeff. '*Did it* sound like him?'

He began to snap at her. He was mad. But he was also confused. He pulled out another cigarette. 'If you want to use the board, then let's do it and get it over with,' he growled.

'Excuse me,' Jimmy said, breaking in. 'I'm missing something here. Why do you want to do this now? Tonight?'

'I want to talk to Shari,' Jo said. She raised her hand when the group started to protest. 'What happened at the party makes me feel it's possible. I don't think she's left yet. I've read a lot on this subject. It's normal for someone who has recently passed over to hang around for several days. We must try to contact her before she leaves.'

'That's my girl,' I said.

'Don't get carried away,' Peter warned.

'But Jo knows what she's talking about,' I said.

Peter was unconvinced. 'She has some knowledge. But a little knowledge is often dangerous.'

'But can we talk to them?' I insisted.

'Let's see,' Peter said.

'But Peter has been dead two years,' Daniel said. 'How did we get ahold of him?'

'Sometimes people have reasons to stay,' Jo said.

'Showers they have to attend,' I agreed.

'I don't believe any of this,' Daniel said.

There followed an uncomfortable silence. Except for Jo, I doubted any of them honestly believed they could communicate with either Peter or me. Yet I also realised even before they took their vote that most of them probably felt that if there was one chance in a thousand it wouldn't hurt to try. It both excited and depressed me to see from Jimmy's expression that he was willing to give it a try. He had never been into such nonsense, and it didn't matter now that it might not be nonsense; it just hurt to see how desperate he had become.

Jo called for a vote. Daniel was the only one who was opposed. The others went along. They moved to the kitchen table. Jo lit a candle and turned down the lights, handing Jimmy a paper and pencil to keep notes. That surprised me, since he had obviously been closer to me than anybody. Perhaps Jo felt he was too upset to act as a medium, I thought. Jimmy did not appear to mind his role. The Ouija board was placed in the centre of the table, and Jo instructed everyone to lightly rest the fingertips of one hand on the planchette. Daniel continued to be stubborn.

'I'd rather watch,' he said.

'And I'd rather you joined us,' Jo said. 'I want the same group mind we had at the party.'

'The same what?' Beth asked.

'It won't hurt you,' Jo told Daniel.

He finally gave in. I strode back to Peter, who was still on top of the TV. 'I am getting tired of your vagueness,' I said.

'Why don't we see what they come up with on their own before we interfere,' he said.

'They won't come up with anything. How do we interfere?'

Peter stood. 'You have to put your hands inside their hands.'

'*Inside?* I can't do that.'

'You could if you really wanted to,' Peter said.

'Come in here,' I said, taking him by the arm. The session was already under way. The planchette was coasting wildly over the board beneath their fingers. Jo was the only one who had two hands on the plastic indicator. Jeff still had a cigarette dangling from his mouth.

'Who's there?' Jo asked.

'Peter and Shari,' I said loudly.

The planchette continued to roll in meaningless circles. 'Who's doing this?' Daniel asked.

'I'm not,' Amanda said.

'You're making it move,' Daniel accused Jo.

'Shh,' Beth said.

'Give it a few minutes,' Jo said. She asked again, 'Who's there?'

The indicator looped over the letters for a minute more before beginning to swing in an arc between yes and no. It was amazing how fast it moved.

'Is anybody there?' Jo asked. 'Shari?'

'They'll quit soon if we don't answer,' I said to Peter, beginning to panic. 'Do something!'

'You can do it, if you must,' Peter said. 'Blend your hands in with theirs. If they don't resist, you should be able to steer the indicator where you want.'

'I can't,' I said. 'You saw what happened when I tried to walk through the bench. If I put my flesh inside theirs . . .' I shuddered at the thought. 'I might start bleeding.'

'You don't have any blood,' Peter said.

'This is stupid,' Daniel remarked.

'Why aren't you helping me?' I pleaded.

Peter looked me straight in the face. 'It's what I've been trying to tell you all along. The dead shouldn't mingle with the living. It only leads to problems.'

'But you mingled,' I said in a cold voice. 'More than once. Why did Beth feel so weird when Jo used the magnet on her? Was it because you merged your legs with hers? Was it because you were *inside* her?'

Peter hesitated, then nodded. 'You're very perceptive. I used to think that even when we were both alive.'

'Please answer if you can, Shari,' Jo said as the planchette swung back and forth like a dead man at the end of a short rope.

'Then it's true,' I said.

'Yes,' Peter said.

It made little sense, but it was only then, when I no longer trusted him, and when I ached because of it, that I realised how much he meant to me. 'Did what you do have anything to do with how I died?' I asked, so softly that even a ghost might not have heard.

'I don't think so, Shari.' He lowered his head. 'I don't know for sure, but I really don't think so.'

'I'm getting a headache,' Beth said.

'We should stop,' Daniel said.

'Do it,' I ordered Peter, pointing to the board. 'I think you owe me.'

Peter sighed and moved to the table, standing between Jo and Jeff. As he plunged his hands into the others, I felt my guts heave, even though I probably didn't have any of those, either. Yet it was fascinating to watch. Faint blue sparks flickered in the places where his fingers moved in and out of the group's. He directed the planchette towards the happy-face sun in the corner of the board.

It followed his direction.

'Something's happening,' Jo said, excited.

'Who's doing this?' Danicl asked.

'Shut up,' Jeff said, taking his cigarette from his mouth and grinding it out in the glass tray that held the candle. It was a green candle this time, but on my side of the mirror the flame looked more silvery than orange, more like ice than fire. The indicator stopped above the sun. I stepped to Peter's side.

'Who's there?' Jo asked.

'Spell my name,' I told him.

'I'll try,' he said.

'It's coming,' Jo said. 'S—H—E—R—'

'No!' I shouted. 'Goddammit, Peter! It's Shari with an *a*.'

'How should I know?'

211

'It was on my tombstone, for Christ's sake,' I said.

'Your tombstone isn't up yet,' Peter said.

'In biology, the whole stupid year we were partners, it was written in big block letters on my lab notebook!'

'What's wrong?' Jimmy asked, clenching his pencil tightly.

'It's stopped,' Jo said.

'Start over,' I said. 'No, finish it. Then spell out your name.'

'We have to concentrate harder,' Jo said.

'Oh, no,' Peter said.

'What?' I asked.

'When they strain, they block me out,' Peter said, shifting his hands so that they overlapped as many living fingers as possible. The faint blue sparks brightened and took on a purple tinge. The planchette began to move again. 'Something's wrong,' he muttered.

'Are you being blocked?' I asked.

'I don't—' Peter began.

'P—E—T—E—R,' Jo spelled out loud.

'It's working,' I said.

Peter frowned, started to speak, then stopped.

'Peter,' Jo said. 'Is that you?'

The planchette swung to yes.

'Is Shari there?' Jo asked.

The planchette circled the yes.

Jo smiled. 'I told you guys.'

'We could be making this happen,' Jeff said, doubtful.

'Tell them hello for me,' I said, excited. 'Tell them I'm all right and that I didn't kill myself.'

'This is real,' Jo said.

'I don't know,' Peter said, still frowning.

'You do it!' I said.

'Ask how Shari is,' Jimmy said, his eyes big.

'Shari,' Jo said. 'Are you all right?'

The planchette went to no.

'Peter!' I cried.

'It's not me,' he said.

'What's wrong with her?' Jimmy asked.

'We have to be careful how we phrase our questions,' Jo said. 'Naturally, as far as we're concerned, she's not all right. She's dead.'

'Ask if Shari and Peter are together,' Jimmy said.

'We've already asked that,' Daniel said, and there could have been a twinge of jealousy in his voice. 'It said yeah.'

'Ask again,' Jeff said.

'Shari,' Jo said. 'Is Peter there with you?'

The planchette glided to yes.

'Good,' I said.

'No,' Peter said.

'What is it?' I said. 'Don't stop.'

Peter took his hands out of the others, put them back in, trying, so it seemed, to get a better grip on the situation. 'There is another force at work here,' he said.

'Where are you?' Jeff asked directly, bypassing Jo.

'T—O—G—E—T—H—E—R,' Jo spelled out.

'Good,' I said. 'Tell them we're happy.'

'Where are you together?' Jeff asked. 'Is it a place?'

The planchette went to no.

'Where?' Jeff insisted.

'B—U—R—N—I—N—G,' Jo said and winced. 'What?'

'Burning,' Jimmy said softly, staring at the candle.

'No!' I yelled at Peter. 'Stop it!'

Peter did not respond. He was struggling with the planchette. Tiny sparks cracked at the tips of his fingers – I could hear them as well as see them. But the indicator kept moving.

'H—E—L—L,' Jo said slowly.

'Hell,' Beth whispered. 'Burning in hell.'

I should not have exploded at Peter right then. I could see he was having trouble directing the planchette. I knew he would not have wilfully tried to hurt either me or Jimmy. I suppose his admission of having used my body was still bothering me. Also, when I saw Jimmy, his face pinched and withdrawn, suddenly stand and run from the room, I lost all control.

'You bastard!' I yelled. 'Look what you've done!'

'I didn't write that,' he protested, removing his hands from the planchette. As if it had become too hot to touch, the others did likewise. Amanda pushed away from the table and went after my brother.

'Don't suicides always go to hell?' Daniel asked.

'My brother didn't kill himself,' Jeff said to Jo, disgusted, knocking the board off the table, almost knocking the burning candle on to the floor.

'I'm sorry,' Jo said miserably.

'You did it on purpose!' I screamed at Peter.

'No,' he said.

Jimmy was already out of the house. Amanda had her hand on the front door as I turned after her. She slammed the door shut behind her. Fortunately, it bounced open, and I was able to get outside. I followed her down the driveway. Jimmy wasn't in his car. Amanda searched up and down the dark street but couldn't find him. She didn't have my magical eyes. I could see him running fast beneath the shadows of the oak branches that hung like tired arms over the deserted sidewalk. I knew how foolish he could be when he was upset, and I feared for his safety. I went after him.

But I never reached him.

The faster I chased my brother, the slower I appeared to move, and the greater my anxiety became. I was trapped in the nightmare again where I was fleeing from the monster with the scales, claws and dripping teeth. Only now the monster was in front of me.

It came out of my brother. One instant my eyes were focused on the clear outline of Jimmy's back, and the next the outline blurred into a whirling vortex of dust and pain. A pair of gaping green holes in place of eyes peered at me from deep inside it.

It was the Shadow.

I stopped dead on the street. Yes, I was dead in this arena, it seemed to say to me, while it was very much alive. It was still strong and powerful while I was only a shadow of my former self. It was hungry, and I was easy pickings.

I turned to flee but tripped over a mound of unsettled earth that shouldn't have been there. I landed in a terrible place. The sidewalk was gone. I was back in the cemetery, my hands buried in the mud that covered my dead body. I raised my head and glanced over my shoulder to see if my assailant had followed me in my leap through space. But the cemetery was empty. I saw only a rectangular tombstone standing tall at the foot of my grave: SHARI ANN COOPER.

My name was carved on the top in red block letters. The stone shone a faint purple, and as I watched, it began to clear, like a mirror as the dust is wiped away. I stood, brushing off the dirt that I imagined would have stained my trousers if I'd fallen wearing real trousers. I knew my tombstone couldn't be up yet, not the night after my funeral, but more than anything else I had encountered since I had gone over the balcony, the stone looked real to me.

It continued to clear, to brighten with the purple light, and my name began to dissolve. It was a mirror. I could see myself in it. I couldn't look away. I looked as I had the hour before the party when I had stood half dressed before the mirror in my bedroom with my broken brush in my right hand. And I had thought I had problems then.

Then I began to change. I started to get younger. I looked as I had when I entered high school, my hair long and straight, braces on my crooked teeth. The image held for only a moment; the march back through time continued. Suddenly, I was twelve years old, skinny, and tan as a deer from a summer of swimming in the Gulf of Mexico at my uncle's house in Mississippi. Then I was only five years old and had a joyful gleam in my eyes that I would lose the following year when I entered school.

The years rocketed quickly backward until I was a healthy pink baby sleeping in a white crib. Here the picture froze, inviting my inspection. I leaned closer. A hand was entering the scene from the side. It was a big hand, with red nails as long and sharp as claws. It grabbed my infant form. I screamed.

It was a trap. The light of the mirror died. The tombstone vanished. The Shadow stood in its place. It had a hand out to grab me. I screamed and turned and fled.

'*It's awful. It's the most awful thing.*'

I remembered Peter's warning as I ran down the hill from where I had been buried, and my fear was a knife in my heart. Leaping over a tombstone, I tripped on the steep hill and went sprawling, striking my nose hard on the ground. A bolt of pain exploded in my head. The sound of the Shadow's slobbering breath filled my ears. I scampered to my feet, my lungs burning on the ethereal night air. It was getting closer.

'Peter!' I cried. 'Help me!'

He did not appear. I knew I had to get out of the cemetery. If the Shadow caught me in this wasteland of memories and grief, I knew it would drag me under the earth and imprison me in my coffin, where I would be forced to watch the rot of my body for the next hundred years. It knew what frightened me most.

I didn't pause to ask myself how we understood each other's minds so well.

I got as far as the fence that surrounded the cemetery. The black poles and bars that made up the barrier were tall and slippery, crowned at the top with a row of spikes that would have made the most adventurous young lad decide on another place to play. I leaped up and caught hold of a narrow bar a few feet above my head. For several seconds I struggled to pull myself up, my feet thrashing uselessly against the smooth metal. Then I lost my grip and fell into a rose bush ripe with petals of red and thorns of pain. They only cut me because my mind let them, Peter would have said, but they cut me nevertheless.

'Shari.'

The word came out like the hiss of a snake as the Shadow halted approximately ten yards from the fence and held out its hand to me. It wasn't an ordinary hand with fingers and a thumb. It didn't even have claws. The hand was more a force that the Shadow wielded to draw me towards it. It was not actually something I saw – more something I sensed. I should have been repulsed – and I was – but I was also drawn to it. Slowly I pulled myself out of the thorns and took a tentative step in the direction of the dark being. Another appendage appeared out of its other side, and the Shadow's pull on me grew stronger. Then I looked up into those eyes again, those pale, bottomless green pits into madness, and I retreated, horrified, pressing my back against the metal poles. I told myself that I was a spirit, that I could slip through the fence and vanish on the wind. It didn't work. The poles remained firm against my flesh. The Shadow took another step towards me.

'Hello,' a voice said above me. My head shot up. Peter was relaxing on the top of the spikes.

'Help me up, it's coming!' I shouted.

'What?'

I gestured to the Shadow, which was now less than fifteen feet away. Peter stared at it for several seconds without making a move. I wondered if he had frozen in fright, then dismissed the idea. His expression was relaxed, although slightly puzzled. It was almost as if he couldn't see it.

'Hurry!' I cried, holding up my arm.

'Of course,' he said, suddenly reaching down and gripping my hand. He pulled me up without effort. I didn't wait to be lowered gently on to the other side. I jumped and then ran, not looking back.

Peter caught up with me in the park across the street,

where he had tried to teach me to fly. I was a trembling wreck by then, but I was still running.

'Shari,' he said, trying to stop me.

'We've got to keep going,' I said, shaking him off.

'It's gone.'

'We've got to get out of here!'

'Shari!' He grabbed me. 'It's gone.'

I glanced back towards the cemetery. There was nothing, not as far as I could see. 'Are you sure?'

'Yes. It's all right,' he said. 'You're safe.'

'Oh, Peter,' I moaned, collapsing against his chest.

He led me to the same bench we had sat on before. I don't know how long we sat there with me shivering in his arms. I couldn't get a grip on my fear, and I think it was because I didn't know what was causing it. There was the Shadow, of course, but what was the Shadow? Peter had called it a devil, but only because I had suggested the word. Why had he chosen the name he had? I wanted to ask but was afraid of the answer I would get. It seemed to know my thoughts, I remembered, and vice versa.

A shadow – that no sun had ever cast.

I didn't want to know whose shadow it was.

Peter was talking about escaping into the light again.

'When you least expect it, Shari, it will come after you. You've got to give up trying to find your murderer. You've got to go on. You don't know what you're risking. It's more than your life now.'

I raised my head and looked around the park. There wasn't a soul around, not a sound in the air. I wished I could say I felt at peace. 'You saw Jimmy's face as he ran out of the room,' I said.

'I didn't tell them that we were burning in—'

'I know,' I interrupted quietly. 'I shouldn't have said what I did. Can you forgive me?'

'Sure.' He was so neat.

'But Peter, what happened? What went wrong?'

He shook his head. 'I don't know. It started out all right, but then the indicator just went out of control.'

'You mentioned that there seemed to be another force at work. Could there have been another spirit in the room that we were unaware of?'

'I doubt it.'

'But it is possible?' I asked.

'Yes.'

'Is it also possible that a member of the group was purposely manipulating the indicator?'

He had thought of that, of course. He was no dummy. But he didn't want to encourage any line of reasoning that would make me continue my investigation. 'If someone was writing what he or she wanted,' he said, 'that does not necessarily mean that he or she was the one who killed you.'

'But to spell what they did – that person would have to hate me.' I nodded to myself. 'It was one of them.'

'So what? Everyone's fingers were on the indicator, and you haven't eliminated a single suspect.' He leaned close. 'Shari, please, listen to me. You could close your eyes right now and in a minute be in bliss.'

I got emotional. 'How can I be in bliss when my murderer is walking free? How can I leave my brother thinking I'm in hell? Why can't you see that I can't leave?'

'Because Jimmy can't see you. He can't hear you. He can't feel you. As far as he's concerned, you're already gone.'

I shook my head. 'There must be some way to get through to them.'

'There isn't.'

'But what if we found a psychic? Could we communicate with one of them?'

'No.'

'They can't all be phonies. Are they?'

He sighed. 'There are people who can tap into our realm – without the aid of drugs. There are even some alive on the earth today whose minds can reach to the infinite. But these people are rare. They are not found at

223

your local psychic fairs reading palms. As a rule, they never display their powers.'

'But if these people are so enlightened, wouldn't they want to help me?'

'They would help you by instructing you to listen to me and leave the problems of the living to the living. Jimmy is alive, Shari, and your death – terrible as it was – is simply something that he has to go through in his life.' Peter paused, his eyes raised to the sky, to the many-coloured stars and pulsating nebula that the living would never see. 'Jeff had to go through the same thing.'

'It must have been terrible for him,' I said, thinking how terrible it had been for me when Peter had died. Indeed, with his next question, I could have told him exactly how difficult it had been. I don't know why I didn't.

'Did anyone close to you ever die?' he asked.

'My aunt Clara. She was my father's sister. She helped raise me.' I smiled at the memory. 'When I was a kid, I saw more of her than I did my mom. She was crazy but such a sweetheart. She used to feed me a diet of soda and cookies. She figured if that's what kids liked best, then it must be good for them.' I stopped smiling. 'I was fourteen when she died. She got cancer. One day she was fine, and the next . . .' I gestured helplessly. 'It went right through her body like poison.'

'You must have missed her an awful lot.'

Was he trying to tell me I could see her if I would go into the light? I might have asked if the 'Big Idea' hadn't hit me a few seconds later.

'That's strange you should say that,' I began. 'I didn't, not really. I don't know why. It might have been because of these dreams I started to have of her not long after she died, where she would talk to me and tell me that she was—' My voice didn't just trail off. It got caught in my throat. Then it exploded. 'Peter!'

I startled him. 'What's wrong?'

'That's it!'

'What's it?'

'My aunt used to talk to me in my dreams! I can talk to Jimmy in his!' I jumped up. 'Let's get back to my place.'

'How?'

'I don't care how. We'll take another fire engine if we have to.'

'No. How are you going to get inside his dreams?'

I sat back down. 'I don't suppose there's a book lying around here that I could read on the subject?'

'If there is, I haven't seen it,' he said.

I studied him. 'Have you done it?'

'Done what?'

'Don't play dumb. And please tell me the truth. Please?'

He took a breath, which had to be an act of desperation for a dead person. 'Yes.'

'Did it work?'

'Sort of,' he said.

'Come on. Were you able to get through when you did it?'

'Did Jeff strike you as someone I had got through to?'

'No,' I said, disappointed. 'Why didn't it work?'

'Because people have to be asleep for you to get into their dreams. And when they're asleep, they're – asleep. They don't know what's going on. Worse, they forget almost everything you tell them the instant they wake up.'

'Almost everything?' I asked, grasping at straws.

He nodded reluctantly. 'You saw with your aunt that you can sometimes remember certain things.'

'You think she was really talking to me? That's amazing.'

'Someone in your position shouldn't be amazed by anything.'

'How do you get into a dream?' I asked.

He stood. 'It's not hard. You'll figure it out, if you must.' He checked his watch. I hadn't noticed before that he was wearing one. It blew my mind that it worked. I mean, where did he buy his batteries? 'I have to go,' he said.

I scurried to my feet. 'Where to? Aren't you going to come with me?'

'I can't.'

'Why not?' I demanded.

'Finding out who killed you is one thing, but I'm not supposed to help you try to communicate with the living. It's against the rules.'

'Whose rules? God's?'

'Mine,' he said.

'You helped me at the seance.'

'And see where that got the two of us.' He began to walk away. 'Catch you later. Don't get lost in anybody's nightmare.'

'Peter!'

I don't remember blinking. I don't think ghosts do blink. Just the same, he was gone.

CHAPTER 12

I had a hard time getting back to my neighbourhood. It was late, and there weren't many trucks on the road that I could catch a ride with. At least not many going my way. I waited at a couple of big intersections and did manage to get aboard a flatbed, but it ended up turning away from the coast, and I had to wait till it stopped at a light to hop off. If anything, my paranoia about hurting myself was increasing. Finally, though, I found a truck that took me practically to my doorstep. It was a dump truck. I had to sit in the back with the garbage. It was fortunate my nose was no longer working on the terrestrial plane.

I had no difficulty entering my house. The front door was wide open. My father was loading a couple of suitcases into his white Cadillac, which was parked in the driveway. My bright-red Ferrari must still be in the garage,

I thought sadly. I remembered Jimmy's remark to Amanda about my parents going away for a few days. I followed my dad back into the house, getting out of the way before he could close the door on me. I didn't need my nose to tell he had been drinking. His face had that puffy red look that took a solid bout with the bottle to develop. The uncapped quart of expensive Scotch sitting on the kitchen table did more than reinforce my suspicion.

My mother was holding a tiny blue pill as my dad sat down at the table beside her. A prescription bottle stood beside the toaster. My mom had on a baggy nightgown she might have worn eighteen years ago when she was pregnant with me. The whole situation could not have been more depressing.

'We can leave first thing in the morning,' my dad said, refilling a shot glass. 'I figure we'll head north.'

'Why north?' my mom asked wearily, her jawbone visible as she swallowed her pill with the aid of a glass of water. I would not have believed anyone could lose so much weight in so few days. I doubted that she'd eaten a thing since her last bite of the chocolate cake I had wanted to throw out.

'Do you want to head south?' my dad asked. 'That's fine with me. We could drive all the way to Acapulco if you'd like.'

My mother smiled faintly. 'Remember when we went there a couple of summers ago and Shari made us stay three extra days because she had a crush on that lifeguard?'

I hadn't realised my parents knew about my infatuation with the handsome twenty-five-year-old Mexican who had watched over our hotel swimming pool. I should have been embarrassed, but I wasn't. I was glad they'd had some knowledge of my personal life. My father nodded and tilted his shot glass to his lips.

'She had a lot of love in her,' he said.

'I wonder if that young man is still working there?'

'Probably not.'

My mother put a hand to her head, massaging her temple, losing whatever smile she had. 'Maybe we should go north.'

My father swallowed his whisky. 'All right,' he said.

I couldn't stand it. I had to get out of the kitchen. I went searching for Jimmy. I was surprised to find him at the top of the stairs kissing Amanda good night outside my bedroom door. She was sleeping over. She was going to sleep in my bed!

'Try to get some rest,' she said as they parted. She had on a plain white bathrobe. Had it been one of mine, I think I would have freaked out altogether. 'We'll have a good day tomorrow together,' she said.

Jimmy wore blue jeans, no shirt. He was developing a slouch. He looked like he could have used a shot of Scotch. 'What should we do?' he asked.

Amanda smiled and ruffled his hair. 'It doesn't matter.'

Jimmy looked past his girlfriend, into my room. 'We shouldn't have gone to that meeting.'

She hugged him. 'It was stupid. Forget about it. Someone there probably made it say those things.'

He jumped slightly at the suggestion. He held her at arm's length. 'Do you honestly think one of them killed her, Amanda?'

She lowered her eyes. 'Please don't ask me that, Jimmy.'

Jimmy, I thought. Only I called him that.

I went back downstairs. I had to wait for Jimmy to fall asleep. The door to the garage lay slightly ajar. The light was on. Sucking in my breath, I squeezed through. Someone had rolled down the window on the driver's side of my Ferrari. I climbed inside and rested my hands on the steering wheel. My birthday present. Some people would have given their right arm for a car like this. Well, I thought, I had certainly paid my fair share.

I must have dozed. It was a bad habit that I had probably carried with me to the grave; I had always loved a nap.

When I came to, it was dark. I had a moment of panic when I thought I had been locked in the garage for the weekend. But the door to the house, I quickly saw, was open farther than before. I climbed out of the Ferrari and went inside. The clock in the kitchen said almost two-fifteen.

Upstairs, Jimmy's door was the only one not closed all the way. I counted my blessings. If it had been shut, I would have been out of business for the night. With the rest of for ever ahead of me, I shouldn't have been concerned about wasting one night. Yet I was, and it wasn't just because I was worried that the Shadow would get to me before I could communicate with my brother. I just had this feeling that I had to hurry.

Dreams were not my expertise. I knew that people's eyelids fluttered when they had them and that they supposedly aided in the release of stress. That was it. I certainly didn't know how to climb into one. Jimmy was sleeping on his back, the sheet tangled around his waist, his chest bare. Sitting on the bed by his side, I silently cursed Peter for deserting me in my hour of need. I had no idea what to do next. Yet Peter had said I should be able to figure it out. I decided to experiment. I reached out and touched Jimmy's hands.

The brush of mental dullness caught me by surprise.

It was not strong, and it stopped the instant I let go of Jimmy, but it gave me a rush of hope. I assumed it must have been caused by a partial merger with Jimmy's unconscious mind. I couldn't think of another explanation. I sat back to wait for his eyelids to begin to flutter. I figured he should be in the midst of a full-fledged dream before I made a determined effort to say hello.

A half-hour must have gone by before his long black lashes began to twitch. I immediately reached for his hands. The wave of dullness returned, but this time it was mixed with a sinking sensation. The feeling was far from pleasant. Internally, I could sense Jimmy's presence, although he seemed light-years away. I was caught between two universes, split in two, and the desire to be whole again wrenched at my heart. His world was so painful!

But I refused to let go. I wanted to get closer to him. I wanted to pull him up. Instinctively, I moved my hands up his arms towards his face, and the light-years changed to miles, and then to mere feet. Spreading my fingers over the crown of his head, I glimpsed him wandering lost along an endless corridor of shadows, and I felt the same weight on top of my chest that I had on the floor of Beth's condo when my so-called friends had tried to bury me before my time. The bedroom vanished. The new background was thick with smoke and dust, devoid of colour or definition. He was dressed in black. His eyes were open. He was looking at me. No, he was looking for me. And he couldn't find me. Tears ran over his sunken cheeks, and then fell, mingling with the pale clouds that dogged his weary feet.

'Jimmy,' I called to him. 'I'm here, Jimmy. Over here.'

He didn't look up. There was a veil between us made impenetrable by his sorrow. I didn't want to let go, but I had to. I simply could not bear it! I felt for my invisible hands and yanked them upward.

I landed face down across his chest as he turned uneasily in his bed.

'Oh, Jimmy,' I whispered, brushing his cheek and kissing him goodbye. Maybe we were still partially connected. I could feel the dampness of his skin, and it was no dream.

There was a window downstairs in the laundry room that had been left open. I used it to climb outside. It was almost a relief, I thought, that my parents had closed their door. I doubted that I could stand to be that close again to grief caused by me.

But I was frustrated by what little I had accomplished. I did not leave the vicinity of my house right away.

Crossing the backyard, I noticed another window open. It was on the second storey, and it led to my bedroom. A peek behind Amanda's cool grey eyes, I thought, might be educational.

I needed a ladder. I really needed to get my ghostly wings flapping. I had to settle on a network of ivy and the frail wooden framework it entwined to help me up the side of the wall. Being the psychologically inhibited ghost that I was, I expected my support to break beneath my feet with each upward step I took. It was with a sigh of relief that I climbed through the window and plopped down on the floor.

Amanda was sleeping snug and secure beneath the quilt Mrs Parish had knitted for me on my fifteenth birthday. She looked so beautiful with her long black hair spread over my pillow that I couldn't help but feel disgusted.

I waited for a half-hour for her eyelids to flutter, as I had with Jimmy, but the best her gorgeous lashes would do was bat every now and then. I finally decided to grab her head and just go for it.

My awareness began to alter. It was different this time. There was no crushing grief, no sudden change of location. Slowly, almost imperceptibly, the room around me was overlaid with the faint image of a flat grey landscape riddled with thousands of narrow poles that reached high into the sky. As I held tight to Amanda's forehead, the image grew in clarity and depth, and I began to realise that the poles were actually tall steel needles. They glittered bright and hot beneath the light of an unseen sun. There was no feeling associated with the scene. It was simply there, although Amanda was not. I understood I was seeing the landscape through her eyes, despite the fact that I was still aware of the dimensions of my bedroom.

One by one, gigantic bubbles of air began to form at the tips of the needles, breaking off and drifting into a hard white sky towards a long translucent pipe, which floated miles above the ground, stretching out of sight in both directions. Flowing with a dark pulsating liquid, the pipe appeared to draw the bubbles towards it. But even though the bubbles bounced harmlessly off the side of the pipe, I sensed they were anxious to get inside it and flow with the liquid.

I wondered if there was a particular significance for Amanda in the scene, and why, no matter where I looked, there wasn't a trace of colour.

The image started to fade a few minutes later, and a wave of drowsiness began to overcome me. I let go of Amanda's forehead. The night was getting on, I thought.

I had other dreams to walk. I stood and turned towards the window. I did not kiss her goodbye.

My next stop was Daniel's house. A Hell's Angel unknowingly gave me a ride most of the way there on the back of his Harley-Davidson. The dude was most gracious. He knew Jimi Hendrix's songs word for word and sang several for my personal entertainment. He had a pretty good voice.

The open kitchen window I had used that afternoon to walk in on Daniel and Beth's sexual sinning was still available. I hoisted myself inside without difficulty and headed upstairs. Daniel had his door shut, however. I was about to leave when his mom got up for a drink of water and stopped to have a peek in at him. I'm sure she would have been shocked to know she had just let her offspring's supposed love into his bed. But I did not enter the room without first checking that there was an open window I could jump out of in the event she closed the door on me – which she ended up doing.

Daniel lay in the centre of his bed with his arms and legs wrapped around a big stuffed teddy bear. I laughed, thinking the poor boy must be in desperate need of affection. As I made my way towards his bed, his eyelids were twitching. I didn't wait. I grabbed his head and dived in.

I probably should have gone slower. His bedroom instantly vanished and was replaced by his dream bedroom. This one had a naked blonde with Beth's chest and my face lounging on a circular waterbed. A silver tray stocked with caviar and champagne sat beside it. Hundreds of lights were on, and the ceiling was all mirrored. Better to see you with, my dear, I thought. Or was it Daniel saying it in response to the girl's question? He stood to the side of the bed with his mouth hanging open and his eyes wide. He had on a full wet suit and flippers.

If only I'd brought Freud along for the ride.

'I love you, Danny Boy,' the girl on the bed crooned, shifting provocatively on top of the satin sheets. It pissed me off that she sounded just like Beth. I mean, if he was going to steal my mouth, why didn't he take my voice as well? The guy was disloyal to the core – as well as being a pervert. He flapped his flippers on the red velvet floor like a fish in heat.

'I love you, Marsha,' he said, excited.

'Who the hell is Marsha?' I asked.

He heard me. He looked over and almost fainted. 'Shari,' he said. 'What are you doing here?'

I strode towards him. 'What am I doing here? I'm your girlfriend!' I pointed to the bed. 'What's she doing here?'

'Who?'

'Her!'

He put his hands to his mouth and began to bite his nails, his teeth chattering as if he were a cartoon character. 'I don't know,' he mumbled.

'Get rid of her,' I ordered. 'And take off that stupid suit. You look like a senile penguin.'

He turned to Marsha. 'Could you come back later?'

'Later?' I yelled. 'You cheating bastard! Here, I'll tell her myself. Miss, get your tight ass out of this room and never come back.'

She took the hint. She gathered up her clothes – they were all over the floor; he had probably torn them off her – and hurried from the room. Daniel sat down on the edge of the bed and began to pull off his flippers.

'Gee, Shari,' he said. 'I didn't know you were coming over.'

'Who's Marsha?' I demanded, sitting beside him. He had really fixed the place up since he had been awake. Besides the velvet carpet and the mirrors, there was a plush lavender loveseat near the closet and a swirling blue Jacuzzi in the corner. There was, in fact, colour everywhere, like in an ordinary dream.

'She's a cousin of mine visiting from Florida,' he said.

'Did you have sex with her?'

He looked guilty. 'We took a shower together once.'

'You took a shower with your cousin! Were you going with me at the time?'

He hesitated. 'No.'

'Liar!'

'I wasn't.'

'Then what are you doing with her now?'

He appeared confused. He couldn't get his stupid flipper off. It looked like it had melted on his toes. He finally gave up on it and put his foot back down. 'Shari, you're supposed to be dead.'

Here was my big chance. 'How did I die?' I asked.

He scratched his head like a cartoon character, his nails on his scalp sounding like files rubbing against wood. It was getting to be too much. 'I don't remember,' he said.

Just my luck, his subconscious was as dumb as his conscious state. Yet he had told me something. If he'd murdered me, he wouldn't have forgotten. 'Somebody killed me,' I said.

He suddenly snapped his fingers. I couldn't believe it when I actually *saw* an exclamation point zoom off the top of his hand. 'I know what happened!' he said. 'You jumped off the balcony!'

'No, I didn't!'

'Yes, you did!'

'I did not!'

'I saw you!'

I froze. 'You saw me jump?' I asked softly.

His face fell. 'You were lying in a puddle of blood.'

'But before that, what did you see?'

He lowered his head between his knees. He was having trouble breathing. He began to cry. 'Oh, Shari. Your head. Oh, God.'

'Dan! Tell me, what happened?'

'Crushed. Splattered. Oh, Jesus.'

'What did I do!?' I screamed, reaching out and grabbing his hands. And as I did so, his eyes swung towards me, and a look of pure horror filled his face. For an instant I saw everything from his perspective. I saw the girl I had found lying on the table in the morgue, minus the green towel that had hidden the worst of the damage. Had I a meal in my stomach and a stomach in my body, I would have vomited.

Then I was back in his bedroom, his *real* bedroom, sitting by his side in the dark as he stirred restlessly in a nightmare I knew intimately. I had accidentally removed my hands from his head. Perhaps it was just as well. I touched my own head gingerly, drawing small comfort from the fact that it appeared to be all in one piece.

241

Shaken, I stood and ran to the window. I had to get out of that room.

Jo's was my next stop. I walked the whole way there, hoping the exercise would calm me down, quiet my fears. It didn't help a bit.

Jo's mom, Mrs Foulton, was sitting on the front porch in the dark smoking a cigarette. She was probably just off work; she had on her uniform. I estimated the time at about four-thirty. The sun would be coming up soon.

A newspaper lay across Mrs Foulton's lap. I could read it without a light, even though she couldn't. The paper was a couple of days old. She had it open to page three. There was a picture of me in the upper right-hand corner beneath the headline, 'HIGH SCHOOL SENIOR JUMPS TO HER DEATH'. They'd plucked the photo right out of my junior year annual. I looked all right.

I sat in a chair beside Mrs Foulton and noticed she was using her cigarette for more than just smoking. Between puffs, she would hold it close to the picture. Either she wanted to burn out my eyes, or else she was trying to get a better look at me. Remembering back to the indifferent tone she had taken with Mrs Parish before my funeral, I wondered why she would bother one way or the other.

Her hands were trembling slightly, yet her face

betrayed no emotion. After a while she ground out her cigarette and went inside, leaving the paper on the porch chair. Naturally, I followed her.

Mrs Foulton went straight to bed. She didn't even bother to remove her uniform; she just lay on top of the sheets and closed her eyes. I reasoned that she had to return to the hospital in a few hours. Because she hadn't been at the party and couldn't possibly have pushed me from the balcony – if I had, in fact, been pushed – I didn't try to probe her dreams.

Jo's door was wide open, which struck me as unusual. Jo normally guarded her privacy vigorously. Entering the room, I found her sleeping with her blanket thrown off, her head buried under her pillow. I had to wait for several minutes until she turned to get even a glimpse of her head. But as I let my fingertips brush close to her hair, I almost passed out. Yet Jo had to be dreaming, I thought; her eyelids were twitching violently. Moving cautiously, I gently touched the top of her head with my right hand.

I was not cautious enough.

I fainted and began to dream myself . . .

The parlour was dimly lit. Dull buff-coloured curtains had taken the place of the walls, and if I'd looked up I knew I wouldn't have cared to see the ceiling. The furniture was Victorian, old and splintered, and the forlorn statues that haunted the four corners were dismembered remnants from forgotten places. At the far end of the room, propped up in an overstuffed rocking chair in front of a large crystal ball, sat the witch.

It was Jo, clothed in a stained and ragged black gown, an ancient Jo of many wrinkles and aching bones, who had seen the best years of her life wither away with the burden of the knowledge that she had lost everything of value in her youth. Her expression was a mask of deep secrets, but I recognised it for the lie it was and was not afraid. She knew nothing of significance. She didn't even remember my name, although I remembered her clearly. She raised a bony finger and bid me approach. I was there to have my fortune read.

'Have a seat, child,' she said in a tired voice, making an effort at a smile but coming up short. I sat before her on a low brown stool. Two squat red candles stood on either side of her crystal ball, their smoky flames watching each other through a prism of polished glass. The woman regarded me with flat hazel eyes. 'What concerns you?' she asked.

I had the question prepared and already knew its answer – it was part of a play. 'I want to know if I will live a long and happy life,' I said.

She thought it was a silly question for one as young as myself. She leaned towards me, and now she smiled. 'Yes.'

'You're sure?'

'Yes, child, you have no need to worry.' She held out her left hand. 'Ten dollars, please.'

'Look in your crystal ball,' I said.

'It is not necessary. I can see your destiny in your face.'

'But I *want* you to.'

She cocked her head to the side. 'What is your name?'

'My name is not important,' I said, doing my best not to sound rude. I gestured to her ball, feeling my confidence grow. 'I've heard your magic is very powerful.'

She withdrew her money-seeking hand and nodded. 'You have heard correctly.'

'Friends of mine said you told them exactly what was going to happen to them. And it happened.'

'Who are these people?' she asked.

'Just friends. They had great respect for you. You told one of them he would live to an old age and be miserable all his life. And he did.'

She started to get suspicious. 'But you are young. How is it that you have old friends?'

I shrugged. 'I get around. I've met many interesting people. I once knew this extraordinary girl. She was in a state of pure joy all the time.' I added, 'Pure bliss. She came to you for a reading.'

The old lady sat back uneasily. 'I remember no such person.'

'I can understand how you might have forgotten. Actually, she wasn't that happy. She was as miserable as my other friend. I think you were a little off on her reading. Are you sure you don't remember seeing her?'

'No.'

'You gave her a nickname,' I said.

'What nickname?'

'It was – oh, I've forgotten. It doesn't matter.' I pointed to the glass ball again. 'Please, tell me my fortune.'

'I've already told you.'

'But you haven't looked in the crystal. Come on, I'll pay you double. Twenty dollars.'

She was undecided. Twenty dollars was obviously a lot of money to her. 'Why did all your friends come to see me?'

'They didn't. You came to them.'

'Tell me some of their names,' she said.

'What for? They're all dead now.'

'How did they die?' she asked.

'You know. You told them how they would die. They were old like you are. They died of old age.'

She clasped her hands together to keep them from

shaking and glanced down at the dry and cracked flesh of her fingers. She was beginning to remember. 'Who are you?' she whispered.

I smiled. 'A friend.'

She closed her eyes. 'I've never met you before.'

'Look in the crystal.' I put my hand over hers and squeezed gently. 'I'll pay triple.'

'What do you want to know?' There was fear in her voice.

'How I'm going to die.' I squeezed harder. 'Open your eyes, old woman. Look in the crystal.'

She looked. She had to. I moved my grip on her frail hands to the top of her brittle skull and forced her to look. I was through playing with her. I lowered my gaze and peered through the other side, seeing her lifeless hazel eyes, poor imitations of my clear green eyes, and her tired parched mouth, pressed to the surface of the ball so tightly that I wondered if she were able to breathe, if I wasn't in fact smothering her. I wanted to kill her right then, but I also realised that it would be a mistake to do so before I learned what I had come for. I loosened my grip on her head slightly, expecting her to pull her lips off the glass and catch her breath.

It didn't happen that way.

Things started to get confused. Suddenly, I couldn't tell

what I was holding on to. I worried that I had shifted my hands too far forward. The rough scalp of sparse hair had disappeared beneath my fingers. Now I was touching glass.

I was holding on to the crystal ball.

The old woman was inside it.

She was dead. I had killed her. A long time ago. She was dead and now decayed beyond recognition. Staring into the glass, I saw a white skull that a swarm of insects could have picked clean. But the top of the skull was badly cracked, and somehow that didn't fit. Jo had never been shoved off a balcony. It was I who had died that way.

All of a sudden, I was very afraid and in terrible pain. I couldn't get my hands off the damn ball. Somehow, the candles had become attached to the side of the glass, heating the crystal to an intolerable level, and the flesh of my fingers was melting and sticking, and no matter how hard I pulled, I couldn't get them off.

I began to scream.

I still didn't know how bad it could get.

What happened next – it wasn't good. I began to lurch about the parlour, trying to knock the crystal ball with the old woman's skull inside it out of my dissolving hands. It was almost, but not quite, like burning in hell. To be there, I thought, I would have had to be *inside* the ball.

I should never have considered the possibility.

It happened next. I don't know who put me inside. I guess it was myself. Events were unfolding with perverse irony. People had always said that Jo and I looked like sisters. And when I had peered through the crystal ball and seen the old face on the other side, it had been like looking into another mirror. I had seen myself as I would have appeared if I'd lived to an old age.

I hadn't lived, though, and my dream wasn't an ordinary dream a mortal girl could have survived with her sanity intact. I found myself careening wildly around the parlour, surrounded by flames, with my hands locked on top of my cracked skull. The dance went on for ever and a moment. I heard devils applauding.

Then I heard Jo cry out to her mother.

I came to on the floor beside Jo's bed. A bundle of typed sheets lay scattered around my knees, the pages of Peter's story about the girl who could videotape the future. They had been sitting in a neat pile on Jo's nightstand when I entered the room. Jo must have knocked them down. It couldn't have been me; I was no poltergeist, and besides, my hands were clamped to the top of my head. I practically had to prise them loose. I thanked God I was awake.

Jo was sitting up in bed crying. Her mother was by her side, holding on to her. Jo was close to hysterics.

'Shari says I killed her!' she raved. 'She blames me for pushing her off the balcony! But I didn't, Mom. I swear I didn't!'

'Jo.'

'She thinks I murdered her!'

'Shh, honey, no.' Mrs Foulton hugged her daughter to her chest. 'Shari was your friend. She couldn't blame you.'

'She does! She came back to tell me she does! She grabbed my head and tried to stick me in a crystal ball! It was horrible! There was a skull grinning at me, and I was burning!'

'Jo, it was only a bad dream.'

'No, it was real! She was really here! I kept telling her, I didn't kill you! I didn't kill you! I told her a thousand times! Why wouldn't she listen to me?' Her head collapsed on her mother's shoulder, and she moaned softly. 'I wouldn't have hurt her for anything. I loved her.'

Mrs Foulton held her at arm's length, staring into her face. Jo was not calming down. Her nightgown was soaked with sweat. I kept waiting for Mrs Foulton to say something, to reassure Jo some more. But in the end, all she did was hug her daughter again and say, 'You were the lucky one. She knew how you felt.'

My guilt was a miserable thing. I understood more clearly why Peter had insisted I leave the living alone. I was becoming a nightmare for all of them. I don't know how I could have suspected Jo.

But if she hadn't killed me, if none of them had killed me, then that must mean I had . . .

I couldn't say it; I couldn't even think it.

I was standing to leave, to jump out the open window headfirst if that would have helped to get away from it all, when I heard a desperate cry. It came to me through my mind, not my ears. It was still loud and clear.

'Shari! Help me! It's after me!'

It was Peter.

CHAPTER 13

I found him four blocks away, cowering at the end of an alley behind a trash can. His call had led me to him like a cosmic homing beacon. I had run the whole way. But when he saw me, he waved frantically for me to stand back.

'Don't move,' he cried.

I froze, knowing he must be talking about the Shadow. Yet I saw nothing. Even more important, I sensed nothing. Always before, the Shadow had announced its arrival by filling me with dread. 'Where is it?' I whispered.

He nodded in the direction of a green garbage bin that stood between us against a grimy brick wall, his eyes wide with fright. I could actually hear his rapid breathing.

But there was nothing there.

'Peter?' I said.

He put his finger to his lips to silence me and began to

creep towards the wall that blocked the rear of the alley. He obviously was going to try to make a run for it, and this was a guy who could beam himself to the top of the Himalayas at a moment's notice.

He was halfway up the wall when I grabbed his foot. That was a mistake. Letting out a yelp, he kicked me in the face and scampered over the wall out of sight. I went after him, clearing the wall with far more ease than he had.

'Peter!' I cried.

It took me less than a block to catch up with him. It amazed me; in real life he could have easily outrun me. And as an experienced dead person, he had far more powers to draw on than I had. It was as if he was suddenly handicapped.

'Would you stop!' I said, grabbing hold of him in much the same way he had grabbed me after my flight from the cemetery. He fought me off.

'It's coming.'

'No,' I said.

'We've got to keep going!'

I had said the very same words. Leaping on to his back, I tried to slow him down. 'There's nothing there!' I yelled.

He threw me off, and I landed on my butt on top of a manhole cover. But a glance over his shoulder made him pause. 'Where is it?'

'God knows,' I replied. He continued to search the street for a full minute. Finally, though, he drew in a deep breath and relaxed.

'It's gone,' he said.

'It was never there,' I said.

He looked down at me. 'How would you know?'

'I knew before. What gives?'

He turned away. 'Never mind.'

I jumped up. 'No, tell me. Why is it I couldn't see it just now? And why couldn't you see it in the cemetery?'

He stopped. 'You don't want to know.'

'Why do you call it the Shadow? Is there a different one for each of us?'

He closed his eyes briefly at my question, and I believed it scared him almost as much as the thing he imagined had been chasing him. 'Yes,' he said finally.

I let go of his arm and sat down on the kerb. We were near the corner of Baker and Third. A memory of the place tugged at a corner of my mind, but I forced it back. I had more pressing concerns. 'What is it?' I asked.

He sat beside me. He wouldn't look at me, only up at the sky. It was as if he wished he could get up there and far from all earthly concerns. Although the sun couldn't have been far away, the stars were very bright, the colours pretty.

'It is the worst thing we could ever have to face,' he said. 'It is ourselves.'

'I don't understand.'

He smiled at the remark, a weary smile; he could have been running from it since the day he died. 'I would give you a long, involved explanation if I knew one, Shari. Maybe it would cover up what I don't understand, or how I lied to you about it in the first place.'

'Peter?'

He kept his focus upward. 'There is a different Shadow for each of us. While we live in the world, it is with us all the time. It colours our thoughts, how we feel, how we see others, and even how others see us. But it is not different from us. It is a part of us. It is with us from birth. We simply add to it as we grow. It is the product of our experience on earth. It is the sum of our thoughts and feelings.'

'Then why is it so horrible?' I asked.

'It is not horrible in and of itself. It is only horrible to the person it belongs to. When you come face to face with it, you see yourself as you really are.'

'But I wasn't that rotten a person while I was alive.' I thought of what Daniel had started to tell me before the memory of my cracked head had made him sick. 'Was I?'

'No, you were fine. But like most people, you refused

to accept yourself as fine. In the presence of the Shadow, any judgement you hold against yourself is magnified a millionfold.'

'Is that why I felt such hatred from it when it was near?'

'Yes,' he said.

'But you've said that if I go into the light, I will escape from it. How can I escape from myself?'

'You've asked a question that has many answers. Even though the Shadow is you, it is not all of you. It is not what you would call the soul. The true soul is never tainted by what you think or do. When you enter the light, you leave the Shadow behind. Imagine – how could you possibly enjoy the joy of heaven carrying such a burden with you?'

'I just leave it behind? Where does it go?'

'Nowhere,' he said.

'What does it do?'

'It waits for you to return for it.'

'You mean, I pick it up again when I'm reborn?' I asked. 'Like reincarnation?'

'We need not bring religion into this. Reincarnation is a model mortals use to explain the unexplainable. Heaven is another model. Who is to say which is more accurate? As I told you before, reality is so simple there is nothing that can be said about it. But if you wish, you can imagine that the Shadow does wait for your return and that it does remember everything that has gone before and that it doesn't let you accept yourself as perfect until *you* let it. There is truth in that. That is why a child usually cries as soon as it's born. With its first breath, the Shadow returns.'

'But knowing all this, why does it still terrify you?'

He lowered his eyes from the sky towards the ground. 'You saw for yourself, Shari, in the cemetery. The fear it brings is not something you can reason away. It is just there, and you have to run from it.'

'Has it ever caught you?'

He looked at me. 'No.'

'Then how can you know what would happen if it did?'

'I don't.'

'So it might not imprison me? It might do nothing to me?'

He shook his head. 'It would do something.'

'Why do you stay here, on earth, where it can keep chasing you?'

'I can't— it's my job.'

'What job is that?' I asked. 'I haven't seen you rush off to smooth anybody's crossing since you've been with me. Tell me the truth, Peter, are you here because of me?'

He stared at me oddly for a moment. Then he rested

his head in his hands. 'No.'

'Why, then?'

'I can't tell you why.'

He sounded so sad; I didn't have the heart to press him. I switched to a more cheerful subject. 'What about suicide?'

His head shot up. 'What?'

'Suicide, you know, when you kill yourself. I've been in a few of my friends' heads since I saw you last.' My voice began to crack. 'I don't think any of them killed me. Maybe everybody's right. Maybe I jumped, Peter.'

'Shari, that's ridiculous.'

I had been holding back the tears since I had run from Daniel's bedroom. Now they burst from my eyes like cold rain. 'It's not. You said yourself you weren't there when I died. You don't know what I did. I don't know what I did! I was upset. I ran to the balcony. All I remember is thinking how good it would be if I could fly over the ocean and disappear for ever.' I nodded to myself. 'I must have jumped.'

'That's not possible.'

I hung my head low. A spider was walking towards my foot. I moved my shoe to kill him. Then I decided to let him live. For all it mattered. I couldn't have hurt it had I jumped up and down on it a hundred times. I had no say in anything any more. 'It is more than possible,' I muttered. 'It is likely.'

'Garrett doesn't think so.'

I got up. 'Garrett's just doing his job. I was wrong about him. He's a good detective. And if he hasn't been able to find my murderer by now, then it's because there isn't one.'

'You didn't jump, Shari.'

'You keep saying that. How do you know?'

He looked at me again in that odd way he had a few seconds ago. But this time a faint smile played across his lips. I couldn't understand the reason for it, or for his next remark. 'I was glad when I got you for my lab partner in biology.'

'You wouldn't have been so glad had you known your partner was a loony.' I turned away. 'I've got to go.'

He stood quickly. 'Where are you going?'

'To see what it can tell me about myself.'

'Your Shadow?' He grabbed my shoulders from behind. 'No, Shari. You don't know what will happen.'

I didn't fight him. I just let myself fall back against his chest. I took him by surprise, but then he wrapped his arms around me, and I was able to hold his hands in mine close to my heart. I could feel it beating still, and I was happy for that. For a few moments we stood together in the middle of the silent street, and I remembered back to the week before the prom my sophomore year, when I had purposely bumped into Peter in the hallways at every opportunity. I had been trying to suggest to him that if he needed a date for the dance, I was available. But he hadn't asked me. He hadn't asked anybody. I had stayed home that night and read a book. He had probably gone for a ride on his motorcycle.

I realised what had been bothering me about our location.

'You died right here, didn't you?' I asked.

'Yes.' He tightened his hold on me and rested his chin on the back of my head. 'It was my fault.'

I released his hands and let his arms fall by my side. 'I've got to know if it was *my* fault.'

'It wasn't,' he said, a soft plea in his voice.

'We'll see.' I turned and faced him. I was scared, but I joked for his benefit. 'I hope it doesn't have my bad breath.'

'You never had bad breath, Shari.'

'How would you know?' I kissed him quickly on the lips. 'You never got a chance to know.' I stepped back. 'Goodbye, Peter. Don't try to follow me.'

I walked briskly up the road towards Beth's place. He let me go. I felt as if I was hurrying to my death.

CHAPTER 14

The gate to the condominium complex was closed. I didn't bother waiting for someone to come along and open it for me. A tree hung over the brick wall that circled the estates. I was becoming quite adept at climbing and was inside fast as a cat.

The stain of blood from my head had been scrubbed off the walkway that ran under Beth's balcony. At least a mortal might have thought so. But I could still detect signs of my demise. Kneeling, I touched a finger to the dried particles of blood that had fallen between the tiny imperfections in the cement. And unlike anything else in my realm, I could *really* touch them and feel the life that had once sparked within and which had now grown cold.

I looked up. I half expected to find the Shadow standing on the balcony four storeys above. It was on that spot, after all, that it had first shown itself. But

261

it wasn't there now, and I was more relieved than disappointed. But I vowed not to leave until it came to me. An idea popped into my mind that I believed might hasten its arrival. It was sort of a sick idea; it might have sprung from the same desire that drove criminals to return to the scenes of their worst crimes.

What if I got up on the balcony?

I stood and ran my hand through my hair.

I felt drawn.

The entrance was locked tight, and I didn't have the proper identification card to buzz my way inside. But Beth's place, I reminded myself, had the best view in the complex; the top floor and the roof were not that far apart, and there was a flight of emergency stairs on the south side of the building. Jogging around the side of the condos, I ran up those steps as far as I could and then went a little farther; a rain drain helped me on to the roof. Except for the part about the nine lives, Catgirl was doing well.

Adobe tile covered the roof, sun-baked Spanish clay. As I walked above the sleeping city, I noted the hint of colour in the eastern sky off to my right. Just then something about the flaking orange dust that coated the tiles troubled me. But I could not pinpoint the source of my disquiet.

The slant of the roof was mild; I was in no danger of falling as I knelt at the edge of the tiles above the accursed balcony. The Shadow had yet to put in an appearance, and this time I sent a prayer of thanks heavenward. It struck me as insane that I was going to such lengths to embrace something that I was hoping with all my heart to avoid.

It surprised me how easily I was able to lower myself over the side and swing on to the wooden rail that guarded the edge of the balcony. The upraised ends of the tiles made excellent handholds – a child could have held on to them.

The sliding glass doors to the kitchen and Beth's bedroom were both locked. I didn't know what to do with myself. I had reached my destination, and I had nowhere to go. I paced the balcony back and forth. The eastern glow took on a yellow tint.

It was half an hour later, and I was on the verge of leaving in spite of my vow, when I suddenly saw my nemesis kneeling beside the stain on the walkway four storeys below. What was left of my dried blood looked more alive and darker with the Shadow beside it. Now the gook was literally boiling up from the concrete. As I watched in horror, the Shadow leaned over and put its head into the cauldron. I didn't want to believe it was licking the blood up. Yet when it raised its head and looked up at me, the walkway was clear.

'Oh, God,' I whispered.

Dawn was near, and the eastern light was playing havoc with the Shadow's form. It was no longer an insubstantial cloud of revolving darkness. Yet, if anything, it had moved farther away from a human semblance. Strange colours sparked and cracked from its depths like electrical shorts on a logic circuit gone mad with emotion. It was deep, this thing that was supposed to be me. But not with wisdom or love. Only with life, crazy and fearful as that always was. It had drunk of my blood because it craved my life. It raised a hand and beckoned for me to come to it.

'Shari.'

My name – it might have known a thousand things to call me by, although I would have remembered none of them. I understood what it wanted, however. It was quite clear.

It wanted me to jump.

It was promising to catch me.

The night of the party, the doors had been unlocked behind me but only in a physical sense. I had closed another door for ever when I had run frightened and upset from the others. My death might have been destined, but not so the reputation of failure I had left behind with my supposed suicide. At least, that was what I imagined the Shadow was trying to say with its challenge. I could hear it clearly in my mind. Now that I thought about it, it was, and always had been, a part of my thoughts.

Suddenly, I felt no fear.

I climbed up on to the rail and jumped.

I didn't fall. Not right away. That was for the end, I was told. The sun was coming up. The only place to start was at the beginning.

The world vanished, and a baby cried

My skin cringed at the dreadful cold. My eyes winced under the harsh white light. I was being taken from my warm, wet home, and I didn't like it. Big grubby hands pulled me through the air. Rough material scraped my face clean. No wonder I was crying.

But then I was set beside a soft face. A gentle mat of hair touched me. Sweet words sounded in my ears. This was my home, I realised, talking to me. I decided maybe I could stay for a while. This was my mother.

I went to sleep happy.

Later, I awoke, and my mother was gone. But it was OK. I opened my eyes and looked around. Everything was a white blur, but it was still neat to have eyes and be able to see through them. I sniffed the air. I had a nose, too, and that was good.

I wondered when I would get to be with my mother again.

I went back to sleep.

I awoke moving through the air in the hands of a huge white person. My nose did not like this huge person. This huge person's smell made breathing difficult. Nor did my ankle like the way in which the huge person was tugging at a plastic band snapped around it. When the band slid off, I was glad.

The huge person set me down in a warm white box similar to the one I had just been in. But I knew it was not the same box; it smelled different, and besides, there was another baby in it. I knew it was a baby because it looked like me, and I was a baby.

The baby was crying. The huge person was pulling on the poor thing's ankle band, too. I began to cry in sympathy. And then I cried in pain as the huge person began to put the other baby's ankle tape around my leg. It didn't quite fit; I must have had fatter ankles. Even when the huge person finally got it on and carried the other crying baby away, the band continued to cut into my poor leg. I cried myself to sleep.

When I awoke, another huge white person was carrying me through the air to see my mother. The band had stopped hurting. This huge person smelled nice. I knew where I was going because the huge person was telling me. I understood telling and talking. I did a little of it myself as we flew down the hall, but I did not think the huge person understood me or even heard me. These huge people were going to take some getting used to.

Then something very scary happened. The huge person gave me to another huge person who was not dressed in white and told me that she was my mother. But this huge person did not smell like my mother. She didn't have her soft hair. She didn't even look like her! What was wrong with that huge person in white? She had made a mistake. Where was my mother?

I began to cry. I cried and cried, and the huge person who was not my mother didn't know how to stop me from crying.

I never did find my mother. Not for a long, long time.

But I grew older. I saw it all. I did more than see. I lived it all, quickly, at light speed, but also completely. Down to the last tiny detail, I went through everything Shari Cooper did. I grew to know the people she called mother and father but who I knew were not her parents. Through Shari Cooper, inside her, I met the boy named Jimmy and

267

loved him, clung to him. And he loved me back, and even though he was not my brother, he was just as good, if not better, than any brother. He was so good I didn't want to share him with anybody. It made me uneasy when I had to. It sometimes made me angry.

Or it did that to Shari. I just watched and listened. I was the silent witness. Occasionally, though, I tried to raise my voice and speak in silence. I tried the day Shari Cooper met her real mother and Jimmy's real sister, but by then she was too old and couldn't hear what I was saying. Too confused to listen to me, who was inside her, but also apart from her. Who was more than the Shadow that had taken hold of her as she had come from the womb. Who loved her more than life itself and who would stay with her even when her life was over.

It was I who watched her as she stood on the dark balcony and stared out over the wide ocean in those last moments.

But even I did not see who lifted her up and pushed her forward. I saw only through her eyes and knew only what she knew. But I knew it better. I knew she would never have willingly given up her life, not without a fight or for anything less than a great purpose.

Shari Cooper – I knew her greatness.

CHAPTER 15

The sun was touching the western horizon when I came to. It was going down. The day had passed me by, as fast as my life. I sat up and rubbed the top of my head. I was lying in the spot where I had died. My bloodstain was now gone for good. I had not lived through my first fall, but I had survived my second.

I was confused.

I remembered most of what the Shadow had shown me. I knew I had not committed suicide. There were, however, several crucial incidents that would not come into focus. Worse, I could not review what I had seen from the perspective of the person who had watched the review. Yet *I* had been that person, only I wasn't who I thought I was. I was the somebody else, I realised, who always watched me.

The realisation didn't help much. I decided to ignore

the heavy stuff for the time being and just deal with the facts.

I was somebody else's child.

No wonder I had never got along with my mother.

But who did I belong to?

Peter was coming up the walkway towards me, wearing his usual baggy white shorts, red T-shirt and sandals. I jumped to my feet.

'Peter! The most amazing thing just happened to me!'

'What?' he asked anxiously.

His tone surprised me. 'What's wrong?' I asked.

'What's wrong? I followed you here to this complex and saw you jump off a balcony and fall four storeys headfirst on to a concrete sidewalk and not wake up for twelve hours, and you ask me what's wrong?'

'But I'm a ghost. You've been telling me since we met that I can't hurt myself.'

His face darkened. 'I couldn't get to you. I tried to, but something kept pushing me back.' He lowered his voice. 'Did you see it?'

'Yeah. We had an intimate get-together.'

'What?'

I glanced at the setting sun. 'Never mind. It's getting late. We've got to get out of here. We have to go see Mrs Parish.'

'Why?'

I could almost touch the answer, only I think I was reaching with the wrong hand. 'I'm not sure,' I said.

We rode on a variety of interesting vehicles to the Parishes': van tops, car hoods, the backs of skateboards, anything going our way. We made good time. There was still light left in the sky when we reached the lower-middle-class neighbourhood where Amanda and her mom lived. Peeking through the curtains, we could see Mrs Parish sitting inside and sewing. Unfortunately, she had the place locked up tight. There wasn't even a window cracked that I could slip through.

'What if we go down the chimney?' I asked Peter.

'Like Santa Claus?'

'Yeah.' The idea appealed to me. Until I studied the roof. 'Wait, she doesn't have a chimney.'

'Why don't you close your eyes and imagine yourself inside?' Peter asked.

'That's not going to work.'

'It won't with—' Peter began.

'With my attitude, yeah, yeah – heard you the first time. All right, I'll give it a shot. What do I do?'

'Just do as I said, and don't be afraid.'

'Afraid of what? That I'll get stuck in a stucco wall?

That I'll rematerialise with a vase on top of my neck instead of a head? What's there to be afraid of?'

Peter sighed. 'Don't even bother.'

I pointed up the street. 'Look, Jo's mom's coming over to visit her sister. She'll let us in.'

One might have thought the timing very lucky. That is, until Mrs Foulton parked a few houses down the block from Mrs Parish's place and proceeded to smoke half a carton of cigarettes. Well, maybe not quite that many. But it was dark when she finally emerged from her car and walked towards her sister's front door. She looked stressed. She hadn't even had a window rolled down the whole time she had been in the car.

'There's one huge person I'm glad I can't smell,' I said to Peter as we followed Mrs Foulton up the steps.

'One *what*?' Peter asked.

'She – I'm not sure what. Let's get inside.'

Mrs Parish let her sister in, and the two of them sat at the kitchen table. Mrs Foulton lit another cigarette. Mrs Parish poured them both coffee.

'This is an unexpected surprise,' Mrs Parish said.

'Cut the crap,' Mrs Foulton replied. 'Where's Amanda?'

'She's out for the evening.'

'Where is she?'

Mrs Parish set down her coffee cup, her face worn

and tired but her eyes steady. 'It sounds like you already know.'

'As a matter of fact, I do. Amanda called me from the Coopers' house. She's spending the night. And I've heard Jimmy's parents have gone out of town. What do you think of that?'

'Amanda knows what's right and wrong.'

'Christ, you are stupid.' Mrs Foulton leaned forward. 'You may have raised her Catholic, but she doesn't have a drop of your bleeding religious fervour in her veins.'

'Don't talk that way.'

'I'll talk as I please. What penance do your priests prescribe for incest?'

'No!' I cried, understanding at last.

'What are they talking about?' Peter demanded.

I shook my head miserably. 'This can't be.'

Mrs Parish also shook her head, not as shocked as me, perhaps, but every bit as sad. 'You know she doesn't have any idea.'

'I wonder,' Mrs Foulton said.

Mrs Parish showed anger. 'You have no right to come into my house and say such things.'

Mrs Foulton ground out the cigarette she had just lit. 'Don't I? You had no right to ruin my marriage!'

Mrs Parish started to speak, thought better of it, and

273

took a sip of her coffee instead. 'I've paid for what I did wrong,' she said finally, softly, glancing out the window. 'We've both paid.'

Mrs Foulton sat back in her chair and closed her eyes, trying to control her anger and her grief. A tear slipped by, however, and was halfway down her cheek before she wiped it away. Reopening her eyes, she stared down at her trembling hands as if the tear had tainted them. I noticed then the nicotine stains on her fingertips, and I remembered them, from so long ago. 'Who was worse?' she asked. 'You or me?'

'You,' Mrs Parish said without hesitation. 'I made a mistake in love. You made one out of hate.' Mrs Parish studied her sister. 'Do you still hate me?'

'No.'

Mrs Parish raised a surprised eyebrow. 'When did you stop?'

'Last week.'

Mrs Parish reached across the table and squeezed her sister's hand. 'You do miss her, don't you?'

Mrs Foulton nodded. 'So does Jo. She woke up last night crying about Shari. I wanted to tell her who her best friend had been.' She shrugged and reached for her lighter. 'But it only would have made her feel worse.'

'Maybe. Maybe not.'

It was Mrs Foulton's turn to study her sister. 'When did you stop hating me?'

Mrs Parish sighed. 'A long time ago. But also a long time after you told me what you had done.'

Mrs Foulton struck her lighter. 'Do Catholics really believe that people can go to hell?'

'Some do.'

'Do you?' Mrs Foulton asked.

'No,' she answered simply.

'No matter what they've done?'

Mrs Parish nodded. 'No matter what.'

Mrs Foulton closed the cap on the flame and set the lighter on the table. 'I never hear from him,' she said.

'David?'

'Yeah. Do you?'

'No,' Mrs Parish said.

'Do you ever hear from Mark?'

'Never.'

David had been Mr Foulton. Mark had been Mr Parish.

'Tell me what they're talking about,' Peter said again.

'Amanda and me,' I said. I had to sit down on the couch in the living room. Peter came and sat by my side. He took my hand.

'What does it mean, Shari?'

I wanted to cry. I had cried over lesser things in my life,

and in my death. The calmness of my voice as I answered his question sounded forced. Yet I did feel a peculiar sense of satisfaction mixed with my sorrow, a sense of having finally arrived. They were discussing something a part of me had always known.

'Jo once told me the reason Mrs Foulton didn't like Mrs Parish was because Mrs Parish had had an affair with Mr Foulton,' I said. 'At the time, I thought Jo was kidding me. But she must have been serious. Mrs Parish and Mr Foulton must have wrecked both their marriages.'

'What does that have to do with you?' Peter asked.

'Mrs Parish is my mother.'

'*What?*'

'Mr Foulton is my father. Jo is my half-sister.' I had to put a hand to my head. 'Amanda is Jimmy's sister.'

'That's insane,' Peter said.

'No, it's logical,' I said. 'Mr Foulton had an affair with Mrs Parish, and she got pregnant with me. But Mrs Foulton found out about it. Maybe they told her, I don't know. Mrs Foulton was working as a nurse at the hospital where I was born. Imagine how she must have felt when she looked at her sister's child and knew it was her husband's child.'

'But how can you know all this?' Peter asked.

'Because I was there! Trust me, the Shadow showed it

all to me. When I was only a day old, Mrs Foulton exchanged the identification tag on my ankle with Amanda's. Don't you see? Amanda's birthday is the day before mine. No! It's the day *after* mine. Mrs Foulton switched us in our incubators.'

Peter shook his head. 'That's not logical. No one could swap babies like that and get away with it. You don't look anything like Amanda.'

'I don't now. I did then. I had dark hair as a baby. We would both have the same blue eyes. We were both only a few hours old! You've been to a hospital. It's hard to tell one baby from another. Besides, for all we know, the only time our mothers saw us before the switch was made was while they were under the influence of pain medication.'

'But Amanda is your brother's girlfriend.'

'That's why they're talking about incest! That's why they're so worried!' I stopped my raving. I let go of Peter's hand. I didn't want to let go of the most important person in my life, but I had to say it. 'He's not my brother.'

'Hold on a sec,' Peter said. 'What exactly did you see when you were with your Shadow?'

My lower lip quivered. 'We don't need what I saw. Think how much Amanda and Jimmy look alike. They both have the same beautiful black hair. They have similar eyes.' I stopped, struck with a cold realisation. 'They're both colour-blind!'

'I never knew Jimmy was colour-blind.'

'I didn't either,' I said. 'But he could never tell what colour my eyes were. Amanda couldn't tell either. And when I was in their dreams, everything was black and white. It makes sense. Colour-blindness is hereditary.'

'Colour-blindness is rare among females,' Peter said.

'It doesn't matter. Some girls are colour-blind. And there's one other thing. When I was running from the Shadow the first time, I called out to my mother for help.'

'So?'

'I assumed I was teleported to my mother's bedroom. It was pitch-black in the room when I materialised beside her. I couldn't see clearly. But I could tell there was no one else in the room, which doesn't make sense. Where was my dad?'

'He might not have come to bed yet,' Peter said.

'That's possible. But when I finally did wake up, three days later, I wasn't at home. I was here. In fact, I was lying on Mrs Parish's bed. Peter, she's got to be my mother. I've always loved her as one.'

Peter appeared doubtful and confused.

The front doorbell rang.

Mrs Parish went to answer it. Peter stood and peered out the window. 'It's Garrett,' he said. 'I wonder what he wants.'

'Hello,' he said when Mrs Parish opened the front door. He held his badge out. 'I don't believe we've met, but Amanda must have told you about me. I'm in charge of the investigation into Shari Cooper's death.' He offered his hand. 'The name's Garrett. May I come in for a few minutes?'

Mrs Parish shook his hand and glanced uncertainly over her shoulder. 'I do have company at the moment.'

Garrett poked his head in the door. He had on the same clothes he'd worn when we'd met. 'Ah, Mrs Foulton,' he said, slipping his badge back into his coat pocket. 'Your sister. I wanted to have a talk with her, too. I would appreciate it greatly if I could speak with you both. I promise to be brief.'

'Fine,' Mrs Parish said, coming to a decision, opening the door farther. 'Jan, this is the police officer who spoke to our kids the night of the accident.'

Mrs Foulton gave him a cordial welcome, and the three of them sat at the table together with fresh cups of coffee. I expected Garrett to launch into a barrage of questions concerning Jo and Amanda. But once he learned Amanda was not present, he appeared happy enough to relax in his seat, talk about the weather, and enjoy the coffee. He drank three cups of the latter at a truly remarkable speed. One might have thought he was trying to sober up, but he didn't seem the least bit drunk.

'What's going on?' I asked. 'He's not doing anything.'

'He's here for a purpose,' Peter said, watching him.

A minute later Garrett made an unusual comment. 'You know, Mrs Parish, I'm no stranger to this neighbourhood. I used to live around the block on Willow.'

'Really? Which house?'

'The one at the end of the block with the fence. I think I had the same floor plan as you do.' He stood suddenly. 'Do you have two bedrooms and one and a half bathrooms?'

Mrs Parish got up. 'We have two full bathrooms here.'

'Do any of the bedrooms have a huge closet?' Garrett asked. 'I had one of those at my place. Loved the design of that house.'

'The master bedroom's closet is plenty big,' Mrs Parish said. 'That's my daughter's room. I'd be happy to show it to you.'

Garrett smiled, showing a trace of discomfort. 'Maybe I should go myself. I'm afraid all that coffee I drank has gone straight to my bladder. If you ladies will excuse me for a minute.'

280

'There's a bathroom in the hall,' Mrs Parish said.

Garrett waved aside her suggestion as he turned and started off. 'I'd like to see if Amanda's room is the same room as mine.'

'He wants to go in her bedroom,' Peter said.

I nodded as Mrs Parish sat back down. 'And he wants to be alone,' I said. 'Let's follow him.'

We barely got into the room before he closed the door. He didn't even bother with the bathroom. He flipped on the light and quickly scanned the grey carpet. Then he strode to the closet door and flung it open, getting down on his knees and examining the soles of the three pairs of shoes that sat beneath the hems of Amanda's clothes. He didn't appear to find what he was looking for. Staying on his knees, with his nose in the carpet, he turned and carefully made his way across the floor to the bed. There he pulled up the corner of the bedspread.

A pair of white Nike tennis shoes lay under the boxspring.

'He's studied everybody's shoes that he's talked to,' Peter said, thoughtful.

Garrett picked up one shoe and turned it over, tracing the sole with the tip of his finger. A fine orange chalk caught at the edge of his nail. I recognised the colour.

I had seen it on the roof of Beth's condo.

281

'Wait a second,' Peter said. 'Isn't that the chalk Garrett found on the carpet in Beth's living room?'

'That bitch,' I swore. 'She pushed me off the balcony and then went over the roof!'

Garrett didn't have to hear me. He knew what was what. He must have suspected such a scenario from the beginning; that was why he had drawn the crisscrossing lines on his diagram between the wall that separated the kitchen from the bedroom, a few feet behind where I had been on the balcony. He stood and carried one shoe into the bathroom. He wrapped it in wads of toilet paper.

'He's preserving the evidence,' Peter said.

'That bitch,' I said again, my fury knowing no bounds.

'But why would she kill you?' Peter asked.

When Garrett had the shoe completely covered, he took it to the window and threw it into a bush at the side of the house. Then he straightened the bed – leaving the other shoe where he had found it – and returned to the living room. He was an amazing actor. He looked as natural as ever. But he made no move to rejoin the ladies at the table for more coffee.

'That room could have been mine,' he said. 'I guess that's how it is with tract houses, and I mean that as a compliment.' He smiled. 'Go into a neighbour's around here, and you can always find the bathroom.' He took a step towards the door. 'I promised to be brief, and now I must go. Thanks for your time.'

'Nice meeting you,' Mrs Foulton called out, a bit puzzled.

'Let me see you out,' Mrs Parish said, hurrying to the door.

'Do you know when Amanda will be back tonight?' he asked casually as he stepped on to the porch with Peter and me.

'She's spending the night at a friend's,' Mrs Parish said.

'With Joanne?' he asked.

Mrs Parish hesitated. 'No. She's at another friend's.'

He glanced at his watch. 'I'd like to talk to her tonight if possible. I have a couple of small questions I'm sure she could clear up for me. Would you know where I can reach her?'

He asked the question with an air of complete nonchalance, but Mrs Parish was suddenly alert. He was inquiring about her daughter, she must have realised, and policemen did not normally spend a lot of time investigating suicides. Despite what she knew, she must have still thought of Amanda as her child. Mrs Foulton had probably told her the truth too late, when Amanda was hers for good or bad.

'No, I'm afraid not,' she said.

He caught her eye. 'She wouldn't, by any chance, be at her boyfriend's house?'

She did not flinch. 'No. They've gone out of town for the week.'

'I see.' He handed her his card. 'Well, please have Amanda give me a call at this number when you see her. Thanks again for the coffee.'

Mrs Parish smiled tightly. 'It was nice of you to stop by.'

She had no sooner closed the door than Garrett dashed for the side of the house. He reappeared a moment later with the shoe in his hand and ran to his truck. Pulling open the door, he put a foot up on the floor near the clutch, took out his notepad, and grabbed his cell phone.

'He's dialling my number!' I exclaimed.

'Mrs Parish didn't fool him,' Peter said. He added a moment later, 'He's getting a busy signal.'

'We have call standby on our phone,' I said, my anxiety growing in leaps and bounds. 'You never get a busy signal unless the phone's off the hook.'

Garrett threw down the phone and reached for his cb. 'Ten-forty, this is Garrett,' he said into the receiver.

'Ten-forty, over,' a voice cracked with static.

'Code sixteen. Send the two nearest available units to three-four-two-nine Clemens. Cross streets Adams and James. Repeat, code sixteen. This is an emergency. Locate and restrain Amanda Parish. Over?'

'Ten-forty, copy. Two units to three-four-two-nine Clemens. Code sixteen. Restrain Amanda Parish. Over.'

'Out,' Garrett said, hanging up the receiver and climbing in.

'Quick, let's get in the back,' Peter said.

'No!' I cried. 'It's twenty minutes to my house from here. We've got to get there now!'

'Jim's in no danger,' Peter said. 'Amanda won't hurt him.'

'She killed me! She's crazy! God knows what she could do!'

Garrett started his truck.

'If you don't go with Garrett, you'll be stuck,' Peter said.

I couldn't think. I had to go by my gut feelings. I knew Peter was wrong. Alone with that witch, Jimmy was in grave danger. It was almost as if God himself was telling me that my brother needed me. Garrett began to pull away.

'Oh no,' I moaned.

Peter touched my arm. 'If you're worried, Shari, I can beam myself there and return in a few minutes and tell you what's happening.'

'No! I have to go with you!'

Garrett laid down rubber as he raced up the street. He was worried, too.

'Why?' Peter said.

'I don't know why!' I shouted. 'Look, I have a mental block against ending up as part of a piece of furniture, all right, but I think I can fly. I was never afraid to go up in planes. What do I do?'

'Did you ever see the Superman movies?'

'Yeah, all of them. I saw *Supergirl*, too.'

'Good. Just recognise the fact that you are Supergirl. You can do anything, and nothing can be done to you. Your arms can propel you on the breeze faster than any set of wings. Close your eyes, Shari, and let yourself float into the air. Don't concentrate, don't strain. Simply desire the ability. It is easier to fly than it is to walk.'

I closed my eyes and did as he suggested. Nothing appeared to happen. 'It's not working,' I complained a minute later.

'Open your eyes, Shari,' he said.

I did so. I almost gagged. I was ten feet off the ground!

'You're safe,' Peter said quickly, floating up by my side. 'You're not going to fall, and even if you do, you won't get hurt. Trust me. Trust yourself. Look around you. See, you can fly.'

'Do I have to flap my arms to get going?' I asked, shaking my hands in the air like a tar-soaked pelican.

'Does Supergirl?'

'No.' I raised my arms over my head and held them firm. 'Let's haul ass,' I said. 'Warp eight.'

CHAPTER 16

My anxiety ruined my first experience of flying, and that was a pity. It should have been a glorious moment. We rose up rapidly to about a thousand feet and then turned towards my street and let rip. Direction and speed seemed to be purely a function of will, and my desire to get there was overpowering. We flew like mad witches on burning brooms. The houses and yards raced beneath us in a blur. I felt no wind in my face, only the fear in my heart.

One thing I did notice, however, was that the city looked much brighter from high up than it did on the ground. I was reminded of the time I had returned to Southern California on a night flight, how easy it had been to identify the cars moving in slow motion up and down the square map of roads, to spot the miniature people walking the paper-thin sidewalks and even tell what colour clothes they wore. Yet now plasmatic auras of violet and red drenched the neighbourhood, shifting lazily from one end of the rainbow to the other as the thoughts and feelings of those beneath us waxed and waned over the spectrum of love and hate.

Even from high above, I could feel Amanda's hate. Or perhaps it was another dimension of my Shadow, my own hate for her closing in on me. Despite all I had learned and seen, I wished to God someone would choke her to death so I could get ahold of her and choke her some more.

I saw the smoke pouring out of my chimney from far off. It made no sense. It was summertime.

My window was open. We swooped into my room like gods of vengeance. But we had sacrificed our thunderbolts for wings when we died. We were here, but so what? What could a thousand angry ghosts do against one insane mortal?

We found Jimmy downstairs in the living room with Amanda.

They had a regular blaze going in the fireplace. The lights were all off. It looked as if Amanda had had Jimmy carry in half my family's winter supply of logs from out back. They were lounging together on the cream carpet in front of the flames, with Amanda sitting up on her knees and Jimmy resting on his back on a bundle of brown pillows. They appeared tired but relaxed.

They had on white bathrobes, nothing else.

'He looks like he's doing all right,' Peter said.

'No,' I said, pointing to a partially eaten chocolate cake and a largely empty bottle of red wine resting on the nearby coffee table. 'She's been feeding him that junk.'

'So what?' Peter asked.

'He's diabetic. She knows that. I don't like this.'

'Don't panic. Garrett will be here in a few minutes.'

We didn't have to listen long to learn that a few minutes would be too long.

'Would you like some more cake, Jimmy?' Amanda asked, reaching for the big knife near the dessert tray.

'No, I better not,' Jimmy said, his voice drowsy. 'I'll get sick.'

Amanda made a long face. 'That's not saying much for my baking, is it?'

He smiled and reached up to touch her long hair. 'You're so beautiful.'

She continued to hold the knife in her hand. 'But you can't eat me.'

'Oh, I don't know,' Jimmy said. 'I could try.'

'Are you sure you don't want another piece? It'll go to waste.'

Jimmy let go of her hair and put his hand over his

tummy and groaned. 'I'm sure. How come you don't have some more? You hardly touched that piece you cut.'

'I never eat cake. It has a bad effect on me. The last time I ate cake was the time Shari made me.'

Jimmy blinked. 'When was that?'

'The night of the party.'

'But why does cake have a bad effect on you?' he asked.

Amanda slowly set down the knife and turned and faced the fire. 'For the same reason it bothers you.'

Jimmy stared at her profile, which must have been difficult for him; his eyelids were half closed. 'You know I'm diabetic?'

'Yes.'

'How do you know?' Jimmy asked.

'Shari told me,' Amanda said.

'She did?'

Amanda nodded. 'But I knew anyway. I could read the signs.'

'You're diabetic too?' Jimmy asked, confused.

'Yes.' Amanda tugged softly on the ends of her hair, her face warm in the glow of the fire. 'We have that in common.'

'She never told me.' He was dumbfounded. 'Why did you tell her?'

'She caught me giving myself a shot of insulin,' Amanda said. 'She tried to pretend like she didn't know what I was doing, but she did. She knew all kinds of stuff.' Amanda shrugged. 'I went along with it. For as long as I could.'

'But I didn't know,' I cried. 'Peter, she's wrong.'

'Shh,' Peter cautioned. He was getting worried.

'She never told me,' Jimmy repeated.

'She would have,' Amanda whispered.

'What?' Jimmy asked.

Amanda turned towards him. 'She was a funny girl, Shari. She and Jo. They used to give people nicknames. Do you know what Shari used to call my mother?'

'Mother Mary. She didn't mean anything by it.'

'Oh, I thought it was a perfect name. Mother was always saying the rosary. Did you know she would sometimes pray in the middle of the night? Mother would think I was asleep, but I could hear her right through the wall. Praising the Blessed Virgin and asking God to forgive her for her sins.' Amanda chuckled softly. 'Her sins and mine. I used to listen to her sometimes. I told you that I'm a virgin, didn't I, Jimmy?'

My brother shifted uneasily, sluggishly. Amanda had probably tricked him into drinking most of the wine. I hated to think what his blood sugar level must be. 'The way I feel right now,' he said, yawning, 'I think you'll still be one tomorrow.' Jimmy sat up with effort. 'It's late. We should get to bed.'

'It's only ten o'clock,' Amanda said.

'I have to get up for work tomorrow.'

Amanda put her hands on his chest and gently pushed him back down. 'No you don't,' she said sweetly. 'You're not going anywhere.'

'She's going to hurt him,' I moaned.

There was evil in the room. A perceptive mortal might have sensed it, but I could see it. The astral barbed wire from the addict's den was growing in the ether, hanging from the rafters like red and black celebration threads strung for a party in hell.

'Garrett's coming,' Peter said, dropping all pretence that the situation was not critical. He could see the blossoming decadent products of Amanda's mind as well as I could.

Jimmy smiled. 'Is that so? Who's going to stop me?'

In response, Amanda kissed him long and deep on the lips, her bathrobe breaking open partway at the top. She was definitely naked beneath. 'I am,' she said when she finally pulled back. 'I'm going to keep you awake as long as I like, and then I'm going to put you to sleep with a bang.'

'Sounds dangerous,' Jimmy said, getting interested but yawning again.

Amanda moved back on her knees. 'You're tired because you didn't take your medicine this evening. You don't have to be embarrassed. I take insulin, too, remember?' She tossed her head as if she had just been struck with a brilliant idea. 'Hey, let me give you your shot. And you can give me mine.'

'Peter,' I cried. 'Do something.'

Jimmy pushed himself up on his elbow. 'Are you serious?'

'Sure. And then you'll have the strength to make love to me. Would you like to make love to me, Jimmy?'

He nodded as he sat up farther, even though he couldn't stop yawning. 'Yeah, but I'm bushed. I don't want a shot. I need rest. I haven't been sleeping well the last few days.'

Amanda became very still. 'Have you been dreaming of her?'

'Shari? Yeah.' It broke my heart to see him glance at the flames at the mention of my name. 'I dreamed about her last night.'

'So did I,' Amanda said. 'I dreamed we were blowing bubbles. But she kept trying to burst mine. It made me mad.'

'Shari wouldn't have done that.'

'She was doing it.'

Jimmy gave her a puzzled look. 'Shari liked you, Amanda.'

Amanda lowered her head. 'No she didn't. She didn't like me seeing you. She tried to keep us apart. She thought our relationship was – wrong. She was going to tell you, I know she was. She was just waiting for the right time.'

'She was the one who introduced us,' Jimmy said.

'She didn't know we were going to fall in love.'

Jimmy forgot about his poor dead sister for a moment. He brightened. 'You never said that before.'

Amanda smiled sadly. 'That I love you? Couldn't you tell?'

Jimmy reached out and took her hand as it rested in her lap. 'I wanted to think you did, but I wasn't sure. Especially when you stopped returning my calls.'

'My mom didn't always give me your messages.'

'Was that all there was to it?' Jimmy asked gently.

Amanda bit her lower lip. 'No. The main reason was because of what I heard my mother saying.'

'When?'

'Late at night, when she was praying. I told you. I thought I had to stay away. And I tried, too, but I couldn't.'

'What did she say?' Jimmy asked.

Amanda raised her head and stared him in the eye.

'That we were related.'

Jimmy chuckled. 'Really?'

Amanda stared at him a moment longer and then slowly nodded. 'I'm glad you don't care. I don't. I remember a line I once read in a poem. It said, "Love knows no reason." That's how I feel about you. That I would do anything for you. Anything to keep you for myself.'

Jimmy was amazed. 'Have you always felt this way?'

'Yes. I can't even imagine your being with anyone else.' Amanda took his hand and kissed his knuckles. 'Especially her.'

Jimmy wasn't sure he had heard correctly. 'Who?'

Amanda's eyes lingered on that portion of his arm not covered by his sleeve. 'I can see your needle marks,' she said, which was a lie. I couldn't see anything. 'I wouldn't leave marks like those.'

The smoke from the fire seemed to back up in the chimney and choke the room. Jimmy took hold of her chin and looked longingly into her cold, clear grey eyes, noticing, perhaps, the way her rosy lips trembled at his touch, but failing completely to see the spiked halo that spun like a sticky cobweb from the core of her black-widow heart.

'You know I love you,' he said.

She smiled faintly. 'More than anyone?'

'Yes.'

'You trust me?'

'Yes,' he said.

'Then let me do it,' Amanda said.

'What?'

'Let me give you your shot. And then you can give me one.'

'Do you need insulin?' Jimmy asked, obviously not keen on the idea. 'Have you tested your sugar level?'

She leaned closer, enclosing him in her claws. 'I need it. You need it. We can make love afterwards. Then we can sleep.'

'But why?' Jimmy began. Amanda put her finger to his lips.

'Because I want to do it,' she said. 'Please?'

Jimmy thought a moment and then shrugged. 'All right.'

'Where is Garrett?' I cried.

Peter checked his watch. It had a luminous dial. 'He could be as long as another ten minutes.'

Amanda kissed Jimmy quickly and stood up and walked from the room. Leaving Peter with Jimmy, I went after her. She headed upstairs to the hall bathroom, where I had unknowingly caught her sticking herself before the party. There she retrieved three syringes and one vial of insulin from Jimmy's refrigerated supplies. Going back down the stairs, I tried tripping her, but she didn't care.

'Bitch,' I swore at her.

In the flickering shadows outside the door to the steaming living room and the crackling fire, Amanda poked a needle into the vial. Like most diabetics, Jimmy took two forms of insulin: regular and long-lasting. Regular acted far more quickly, and it was that kind Amanda held in her hand. It was the medication of choice to rid a diabetic of sugar blues. But whereas Jimmy's normal dosage was ten units, Amanda filled the hundred-unit syringe to the hilt.

'What will that do to your brother if she gets it in his bloodstream?' Peter asked, rejoining me and watching Amanda's secret preparations.

'It could send him into insulin shock,' I said, unable to stand the tension.

'But could he survive it?' Peter insisted.

'Yes. But even if it just puts him to sleep, that's no good. The girl's nuts!'

'How long till it takes effect?'

'It requires half an hour for its effect to peak,' I said. 'But he'll be out in less than fifteen minutes.'

'Still, time is on his side,' Peter said.

'Time is never on your side when you're alive,' I said.

Amanda stuffed the loaded syringe into her bathrobe

pocket and strode into the living room. The bad black vibes were alive and hungry and everywhere to be seen. Jimmy continued to lie on the pillows by the fire. He had his eyes closed and only half opened them as his true love knelt by his side.

'I'm thirsty,' he muttered.

'Your pancreas is probably freaking out,' Amanda said, the two empty syringes and the half-filled vial clearly visible in her hands. 'You need this.'

'I don't know,' he mumbled, yawning and rolling over. 'I just want to sleep.'

Amanda put her left hand on his right ankle, setting down the insulin and unused syringes and carefully slipping the full needle from her pocket. 'Let me take care of you, and then you can rest,' she said.

Jimmy suddenly sat up. Amanda deftly dropped the needle back into her pocket. He nodded to the unopened syringes lying on the rug near the fireplace bricks. 'Maybe I should test myself first.'

'We can estimate your dosage,' Amanda said.

He was doubtful. 'You use synthetic, right?'

'Yes. In the evenings, I usually take ten units of regular. How about you? The same?'

Jimmy yawned and nodded wearily. 'All right, let's do it.'

'Turn over,' she said.

'What?'

'I'll give it to you in your backside like a nurse.' She smiled at his discomfort. 'Don't be embarrassed, Jimmy.'

'I usually just do it in my arm.'

'Your arms are all sore.' She picked up one of the opened syringes and gestured for him to turn over. 'It'll just take a sec, and then you can do me in the same spot.'

Amanda was convincing. Jimmy lay down on his belly and closed his eyes. Yet she made no move to pull up his robe. 'If it will make you feel any better,' she said, undergoing an abrupt change of tone, 'I can put it in your leg.'

'That would be fine,' Jimmy muttered.

'Or your foot,' she said, setting down the empty needle and picking up his right foot. Once again, she removed the loaded syringe from her pocket.

'Won't that hurt?' he asked.

'You'll hardly feel it,' Amanda promised.

'Be careful not to hit a vein,' Jimmy said.

'Peter!' I cried. 'She's going to put it in his vein!'

'What will that do?' Peter asked.

'The insulin will go straight into his bloodstream! He'll be out in minutes!'

I had guessed Amanda's plan well. Quickly and smoothly, she pinched the skin around the big vein closest to his ankle and slid the needle home. Jimmy's eyelids barely flickered. It took Amanda only a few seconds to empty the syringe. Then she gathered together all the needles, plus the insulin vial, and put them in her pocket. She patted him on the rump as she stood.

'Rest there a minute,' Amanda said.

'What about you?' Jimmy asked.

'I have to go to the bathroom,' she said.

'Watch him,' I told Peter as I chased after her.

Amanda returned to the bathroom upstairs and put away both the unused needles and the tiny bottle of insulin. Yet she left the opened needle in her pocket, even though it was now drained. I could not imagine what she wanted it for.

Amanda stopped to wash her face before she left the bathroom. I stood to her left and watched her in the mirror as I had done the previous Friday night when I had been admiring her beauty.

'Please don't do anything else to him,' I pleaded.

Amanda dried her face and put out the light.

Jimmy was sitting up on the pillows when she re-entered the living room. 'I don't feel so good,' he mumbled.

Amanda strode to the pile of wood to the left of the fireplace. 'You'll feel better in a few minutes,' she said.

Jimmy frowned in her direction. 'What are you doing?'

Amanda picked up a log. 'Keeping the fire going.'

'Don't. I'm hot.' His head swayed atop his shoulders, and he raised a hand to steady it. 'What's happening?'

Amanda threw the log into the fire. The sparks cracked like cheap fireworks. She came and knelt by his side and placed what might have been a cool palm over his sweaty forehead. 'You poor darling,' she said. 'Can I get you something to drink?'

'No.' He bent over. 'I feel like I'm going to be sick.'

'That's the insulin,' Amanda said. 'I gave you a hundred units.'

He sat up and winced. '*What?*'

Amanda sat back on her knees. She looked sad. 'Mrs Foulton called me earlier. She's over at my mother's house right now. They're discussing us. They don't want me seeing you any more.'

'What are you talking about?'

'I thought it would stop with Shari. I thought they would leave us alone. But they're not going to.'

Something darker than sickness touched Jimmy's face. Too late, he was beginning to get the message. 'Why do you bring up Shari?'

Amanda looked to the fire and appeared to go blank for a few seconds. When she spoke next, it was with a peculiar mixture of bitterness and confusion, a small girl

302

mad at a world suddenly grown big and complex.

'When I decided to go to the party,' she said, 'I didn't know what I wanted. I thought maybe I would talk to Shari about us, bring it out in the open and get it over with. I didn't want to, though. Then she kept me from having my shot when I needed it. She forced me to eat cake. It made me feel weird – I shouldn't have had a second piece. I could hardly think. Then, at the party, there was this magnet that you could ask questions. I asked about us, and it said that our love was real. It said that I should protect it. The magnet told me I had to take control of my own destiny.' Amanda lowered her head, her pale face disappearing behind the fall of her long hair. 'But what I did, I did on the spur of the moment.'

I glanced at Peter, silently asking if he knew what she was talking about in regard to the magnet answers. He quickly shook his head.

'What did you do?' Jimmy whispered. He was having trouble breathing. Sweat no longer merely dampened his forehead; it poured off his brow and into his eyes. Amanda raised her head, and her arm, too, and gestured to the richly furnished living room.

'I grew up in a slum,' she said, her tone harsh. 'She grew up in a mansion. She was given everything she wanted: new cars, new clothes. I had to take the bus to school and wear hand-me-downs. She was spoiled rotten. Do you know my own mother had to make her bed for her? She should burn in hell!'

'The message on the Ouija board,' Peter gasped.

Jimmy sagged forward and had to throw out an arm to keep from landing face-first in the carpet. 'What did you do to my sister?'

Amanda was suddenly concerned. 'Are you still sick?'

'What did you do?' he demanded.

Amanda smiled. 'Nothing. Your sister's fine.'

Jimmy swallowed thickly. 'You killed Shari.'

Amanda nodded. 'I did push her off the balcony. She deserved it. She was standing there and thinking mean thoughts about me. I pushed her, and then I climbed on to the roof and went over to the fire escape and came back in Beth's front door. I thought I had blown it, that everyone would know. But I was lucky. When I came back into the bathroom, Dan saw me and thought I had just come out of the bathroom.' Amanda's face softened, and she touched Jimmy on the shoulder as he huddled before her in the throes of his insulin fit. 'I know you liked her, but she really was no good. She wasn't even your sister.'

He fought it but was unable to stop from toppling over on to his side. He glared up at her with glazed eyes.

'You're crazy.'

She looked hurt. 'No, I'm not. I had good reason to do it. And *I* am your sister.' She leaned over to give him a kiss. 'If I can't have you, no one's going to have you.'

Then she jolted upright, blood on her face.

He had bitten her on the lip.

'Go to hell,' he gasped, his eyes falling shut.

Amanda stared at him for a long time after he had lapsed into unconsciousness, the blood trickling over her chin in a steady stream. 'Yes,' she said finally.

Still, I didn't know how bad it could get.

Amanda put more logs on the fire. Then she took out the empty syringe and drew back the plunger, filling it full of air.

'She's going to put a bubble in his vein!' I groaned.

'That will give him a heart attack,' Peter said grimly. 'Or a stroke. I'm surprised she didn't shoot him with the bubble with the first shot. But maybe she didn't want him to have to suffer.'

I looked at Peter. 'You have to stop her.'

He sighed. 'I can't.'

'Go into her body. Make her put the bubble in her own vein.'

Peter was shocked. 'That would be murder.'

I gestured to Jimmy sprawled before the sacrificial

flames. 'This is murder. What you do would be justice.'

Amanda kissed Jimmy on the forehead and picked up his arm.

'She would resist me,' Peter said.

'Resist her back,' I said.

'I can't make her commit suicide!' Peter cried.

Amanda rolled up the sleeve of Jimmy's bathrobe.

'And you can't let Jimmy die!' I yelled.

His face filled with dread, Peter bowed his head. I was quite prepared for him to say again that he couldn't interfere. But then he suddenly stepped forward and went into Amanda.

Amanda paused. Had she been able to see what I could see, she would have got out of the room while the going was good. The phenomenon was similar to when Peter had overlapped his hands with the others during the seance, only a dozen times more intense. Most of Peter had vanished; I could catch only a faint glimpse of his face through the thousand miniature geysers that had erupted like psychedelic discharges over every square inch of Amanda's body. The girl knew something was wrong. She raised her arm and peered at the syringe in her hand.

The point of the needle bent towards her eyes.

Amanda jumped to her feet. She tried, but she couldn't

drop the syringe. Peter, I supposed, did not have the control to aim for a tiny vein. I didn't mind, as long as he kept her occupied until Garrett arrived. Amanda twisted around the living room like an epileptic caught in a fit, the blood from her torn lip splattering the lapels of her white robe, screaming for help. It was a wonderful sight.

Then she stopped in midstride. Peter reappeared by her side, staring anxiously into the dark doorway at the north end of the living room.

'It's coming,' he said.

'What?' I demanded.

'My Shadow.'

Amanda shook herself, still holding on to the needle, and turned towards Jimmy. I jumped to Peter's side and grabbed hold of him. 'You can't run,' I said.

'It's coming,' he said, panicking.

Amanda knelt by Jimmy's side. Pulling back the plunger, she refilled the syringe with deadly air.

'It's not as bad as you think,' I said. 'I faced it.'

'It wouldn't be the same for me,' Peter said, throwing off my hold.

'You can't leave till you kill her!' I yelled.

'I can't kill again!' he yelled back.

I stopped. Even Amanda paused in the middle of her evil deed. She was wiping the blood from her mouth. She

307

had everything ready; she just wanted to kiss Jimmy goodbye. 'When did you kill someone?' I asked Peter.

He pressed his arm over his eyes and sucked in a deep breath as if he were about to shout. But all that came out was a shameful whimper. 'I crossed the lane in front of that truck on purpose,' he said. 'I killed myself.'

Amanda touched her bloody lips to Jimmy's sleeping mouth.

'That's not possible,' I said, echoing his words to me about my own conviction of suicide.

He nodded miserably. 'It's not something I'm likely to forget.' He turned to go. 'It's not something my Shadow will ever forgive.'

Amanda reached for Jimmy's arm, searching for a vein.

'But we need you, Peter,' I pleaded.

His gaze strayed again to the dark doorway, and he trembled. 'I can't, it's too close,' he said.

Amanda squeezed the flesh on the inside of Jimmy's elbow.

'All right,' I said, my voice empty. 'Leave, if you feel you must.'

He looked at me with pain in his eyes. 'I'm sorry.'

I turned my back on him and stepped towards my brother. 'So am I,' I replied, and I heard the disgust in my tone, even though I did not want him to hear it.

There followed another pause, in both realities. Amanda had found the desired vein and was pressing the tip of the needle to it. But she couldn't stop looking at Jimmy's face. Peter, it seemed, couldn't stop looking at me; I could feel his eyes on the back of my head.

'I love you,' Amanda told Jimmy.

'Shari,' Peter said. 'I love—'

He didn't finish. It wasn't the time for confessions of the heart, he must have realised. He went by in a flash towards my brother. Unfortunately, he had waited too long. Before he could re-enter Amanda's body, something came through the dark doorway at the north end of the living room. I couldn't see it as I could my own Shadow, but I could sense its movements. Peter only had time to throw a single terrified glance in its direction before it crossed the room and was upon him.

He crumpled to the floor precisely as Amanda stabbed Jimmy with the needle and began to depress the plunger.

I had previous information about the dangers of air in the bloodstream. A relative was a registered nurse and had once explained how careful RNs had to be when giving people injections to clear away any bubbles from the medicated solutions. She had added, however, that if the system could quickly break down a large bubble into a number of tiny ones, then the person would most likely survive.

It gave me an idea. And if I could fly, I thought, I should be able to do anything.

I dived *into* the air in the syringe.

I don't know how I did it. Once again, the power must have simply come to me because I wanted it badly enough.

I saw little before I was thrust into Jimmy's body: a blur of curving plastic walls, the vague shape of a gargantuan thumb, the distorted flames of the fireplace blazing before my microscopic vision like a sun gone nova. Then there was the motion of powerful winds, and I was riding a wild and pulsing current of liquid night.

Yet not everything was dark for me inside Jimmy's vein. Outside the window of the air bubble, I detected huge spheres of tumbling tissue chasing me along an endless tunnel of blood. Even more remarkable was the sound, a pounding thunder that grew so rapidly in volume and force that I feared it would drown out my mind. A fool could have recognised it – the beating of Jimmy's heart – and I was racing towards it with the speed of an angel.

A dark angel.

The thunder skipped as I plunged into a spacious chamber of churning blood. It skipped twice, three times, and then it halted altogether and everything was silent.

Dead silence. The bubble had caused Jimmy's heart to stop.

A golden light began to dawn in the strange night.

A realm of beauty and bliss unfolded.

It was Jimmy's dream. I remembered.

'We were in a strange place. It was like a world inside a flower. I know that sounds weird, but I don't know how else to describe it. Everything was glowing. We were on a wide open space, like a field. And you were dressed exactly as you are now, in those slacks and that blouse. You had a balloon in your hand that you were trying to blow up. No, you had blown it up partway, and you wanted me to blow it up the rest of the way. You tried to give it to me. You had tied a string to it. But I didn't catch the string right or something, and it got away. We watched it float way up in the sky. Then you began to cry.'

It was all true. It was a miracle. We were on a field that stretched almost to infinity, to the borders of an all-encompassing lotus that sent a thrill through every particle of my being at the sight of it. A brilliant-white light shone in the sky, radiating a peace and joy beyond understanding. It was the light Peter had spoken of. It was all-knowing. It knew our situation. Yet it was not there to interfere. It was merely there to observe. It was the silent witness of the movie of my life finally

311

uncloaked. Jimmy turned to me and smiled.

'This is nice,' he said.

I had on my green trousers and yellow blouse. Jimmy was wearing his white bathrobe. The balloon I held in my right hand at the end of a thin string was not the brown Jimmy had told me after he had awakened from his dream, but red. And he had been wrong about me wanting to blow it up farther. I wanted to pop the balloon. It was the bubble that had stopped his heart.

Still, it was impossible not to be happy. The field we stood on was like a living jewel.

'Yes,' I said. 'It's beautiful.'

Jimmy took more notice of me. 'Shari,' he said, puzzled. 'What's going on? You're supposed to be dead.'

'I am dead,' I said. 'But being dead isn't like people think it is. Anyway, I can't go into that now or you'll die.' I pulled down the balloon and tried to pop it in my hands. Unfortunately, it had a surface as firm as steel. 'Oh no.'

'What's wrong?' he asked.

'This is an air bubble that Amanda put into your bloodstream. It has to be broken up.'

His eyes widened. 'That's right. She was trying to kill me. Did she succeed?'

'Not yet, I don't think,' I said, continuing to wrestle

with the balloon. 'Your heart's only been stopped a few seconds.'

Jimmy gazed about the glass field, and his concern quickly receded. 'But it's so peaceful here. And that light's so nice. I want to stay. I want to die.'

'No,' I said firmly. 'You have to live.'

'Why?'

'Because you're young and beautiful. You're wonderful. The world needs you. Mom and Dad need you. If you die, it'll break their hearts.'

'But I want to talk to you,' he said. 'I miss you.'

'I miss you, too. But you have to live a long life. And then, when you're done, you can be with me.'

'Where is this place? Are we in heaven?'

'No, we're in . . .' I began, hesitating, wanting to say we were in his heart, before deciding we might be talking about the same thing. 'Yes, this is heaven.'

'I'm glad you made it here,' he said.

'So am I.' It occurred to me then that because the bubble was in his heart, it might be better if *he* tried to pop the balloon. But when I started to give it to him, it began to slide from my grasp. It was only the warning of his dream that enabled me to react quickly enough to pull it back in.

There was slippery gook on the palms of both my

hands. It was like black chimney soot. Jimmy had a little on his hands, too, I saw a moment later, although not nearly as much as myself.

'What is this stuff?' he asked, brushing with his fingers. Neither of us could get it off. It was the only stain in our entire world of light. We had brought it with us, I realised. The light itself must have helped me with the realisation. When I spoke next, I did so with the certainty that I spoke the truth.

'It's hate,' I said. 'We've got to get rid of it. We have to forgive Amanda in order to be able to burst the balloon.'

'That bitch. She pushed you off the balcony.'

'So she did. But what's done is done. I see that now, Jimmy. I really do. Don't you see?'

'But she murdered you,' he protested.

'Amanda is sick. She needs your help.' I added, 'Besides, she told you the truth. She is your sister.'

He raised an eyebrow. 'You can't be serious.'

I nodded. 'I'm afraid I am.'

'Oh no.' He shook his head. 'I knew I should have gone away with Mom and Dad.'

I had to laugh at his discomfort. And it has been said there is nothing more forgiving than a hearty laugh. When I looked down, my hands were clean; so were his. Jimmy had never been one to hold a grudge for more than two minutes. I estimated that was how long his heart had been stopped. We were running out of time. I handed him the balloon, and he held on to it.

'Pop it,' I said. 'It's the bubble in your heart. It's killing you.'

'Will I remember any of this?' he asked, worried.

'I don't know,' I replied, my voice faltering as a tear ran down my cheek. 'It doesn't matter. You will always remember me. And I will remember you. You were the best brother a girl could've had.' I started to hug him goodbye and found I couldn't budge from my place. Neither of us could move, and it was getting late. 'Pop it, Jimmy,' I said. 'Live. Be happy. Be happy for me.'

'You know, Shari . . .' He began to squeeze the balloon in his fingers. But he didn't get a chance to finish the sentence. I didn't get a chance to hear it. The golden lotus exploded with a flash of a thunderbolt. It was not, however, real thunder that I heard. It was the beating of his heart.

CHAPTER 17

I reappeared standing beside Jimmy. He was still lying on his back on the pillows. Only now he was coughing. He was alive!

For the time being. Amanda had scattered logs across the carpet and was transforming the living room into a furnace of flame and smoke. A funeral pyre for both of them. She really was off her nut. She had the needle in her hand and was going to put a big balloon in her own vein. Fine, go ahead, I thought, before I remembered my promise to forgive her. Ten seconds, and I was already forgetting.

Someone was hammering on the front door.

Amanda had the needle up to her skin. The someone at the door was going to be too late to save her.

I crossed the room in one leap and jumped inside her. It was weird. It was like having a physical body

316

again, only one that didn't fit. I felt so *thick*. I decided not to worry about it. I whipped my right arm upward and flexed my palm open. Amanda did the same and dropped her needle on the floor. She was bending over to search for it, coughing her blessed lungs out, when the front door burst open.

'What the hell,' Garrett shouted, running into the room.

Amanda dashed behind her barrier of burning logs. I got out of her quick. 'You can't have me!' she screamed.

'Honey,' Garrett said, hurrying to Jimmy's side and grabbing him by the wrists. 'I don't want you.'

Garrett dragged Jimmy away. Amanda appeared to be set on going to an agonising end until a spark landed on her bare foot. Letting out a silly cry, she ran after Garrett. I loved it.

Peter lay where he had fallen. Following Garrett's lead, I took hold of his arms and pulled him out into the night air. I was surprised at how light he felt, forgetting for a moment that he didn't weigh anything at all.

The house survived. Two black and white units arrived on Garrett's tail, and the policemen were quick to gather the front and backyard hoses and get water on the flames. A fire engine appeared shortly afterward. They had paramedics with them. Jimmy got plenty of attention. He sat propped up beside Garrett on the neighbour's front lawn while a medical man pressed an oxygen mask to his face. Leaving Peter still unconscious but out of the way of the stampede, I walked over to check on him.

'How's he doing, doc?' Garrett asked, concerned.

'I'm not a doctor,' the man replied. 'But he appears to be doing fine.'

'I can breathe,' Jimmy said, pushing away the face mask. The excess insulin in his blood was not affecting him as much as it should have. I could only believe the light had somehow detoxified him.

The paramedic put down the oxygen. 'Then breathe,' he said. 'But you're still going to the hospital.'

'No, I'm not,' Jimmy said. 'I feel fine.'

'What did she do to you?' Garrett asked.

Jimmy's voice hardened. 'She killed Shari. She pushed her off the balcony. She tried to kill me. She shot me up with too much insulin and knocked me out. Then she put an air bubble in my vein.'

'If she knocked you out with insulin,' the paramedic said, reaching for an instrument that resembled the tool Jimmy used to check his blood sugar, 'how do you know what she put in your vein?'

I crossed my fingers *and* made the sign of the cross waiting for Jimmy's response. But I was in for a disappointment.

318

'I don't know,' he said after a moment's hesitation.

'We're going to keep him in the hospital overnight,' the paramedic told Garrett.

'Oh, no,' Jimmy muttered.

Garrett slapped Jimmy on the side. 'Son, remind me someday that I've got to introduce you to some nice girls.'

Satisfied that Jimmy was in good hands, I returned to where I had deposited Peter. The flashing lights of police cars bathed the surrounding houses. The whole neighbourhood had poured out to watch the spectacle. Her white robe gross with bloodstains, Amanda stood pale and bent in the custody of a police officer.

Peter had not moved an inch. Kneeling by his side, I shook him gently. 'Peter? Can you hear me? Wake up, it's Shari.'

He stirred and opened his eyes. 'Where am I?' he mumbled.

'It's not Newport Memorial, and I'm sad to say you didn't make it.' I helped him up. 'How do you feel?'

'Embarrassed,' he said. 'How's Jimmy?'

'Fine. Everything's fine. Why are you embarrassed? You stayed. That took guts. Believe me, I know.'

He wouldn't look at me. 'I lied to you.'

I sat by his side and put an arm around his shoulder. 'What happened?' I asked.

He was ashamed. 'I committed suicide.'

'I don't believe it.'

'Believe it. I was out on my bike, driving like a maniac, when I saw this truck coming at me the other way. I jerked my bike into its path.'

He was serious. 'But *why*?' I asked.

He shrugged. 'I'm not sure. It was a number of things. Everybody at school was ecstatic about how I'd pitched Hazzard to the city championship. But what they didn't know was that the coach pressured me into starting the last four playoff games. I let him pressure me. Anyway, I blew out my arm, tore my rotary cuff. I wasn't going to pitch again.'

'*That's* why you ended your life?'

'No. There's more. It's complicated. I was depressed.'

'Why?' I asked.

'I was lonely.'

'But you had lots of friends. You had me.'

He looked at me. 'You heard what I said before the Shadow arrived?'

'Yes. You were going to say you loved me, right?'

Ordinarily, he would have snorted at my nerve. Now he just nodded. 'I've always been crazy about you.'

I laughed. 'You are so dumb. I was crazy about you!'

He shook his head. 'Don't, Shari.'

'I'm telling you the truth! Why didn't you ask me out?'

'You wouldn't have gone out with me.'

'I would have given my right arm to go out with you! God, I'm so angry at you! We could have had so much fun together!' I sighed. 'And I wouldn't have had to suffer so when you died.'

'You suffered?' he asked in disbelief.

'Of course I did. I never got over losing you.'

'But you didn't even go to my funeral.'

'Because I was too upset. I stayed home and cried for days.'

He stared at me strangely. 'Are you serious?'

'Yes! I loved you! I love you now! When you found me in the cemetery after they buried me, it was the happiest day of my life. I mean, it was great! You didn't have to kill yourself over me.'

'I didn't do it just because of you.'

'Oh. All right. What else was the matter?'

'I was curious,' he said.

'You were *what*?'

'I was curious to see what it was like on the other side. Jo showed you some of my stories. I was obsessed with death. It was an unhealthy obsession.'

'I should say.'

'There was something else. This is hard to explain.

Remember when we were in the park and trying to figure out who killed you? Remember how I kept insisting we needed a motive?'

'Yes,' I said.

'I should have known better. Did you hear what Amanda said in the house? She had all these reasons for what she did, but when it came right down to it, she did it on the spur of the moment.'

'Are you saying you pulled in front of the truck on the spur of the moment?'

'It sounds strange, but it's true.'

'That's dumb,' I repeated.

'I can't argue with you.'

'Did this have anything to do with why Jeff dislikes me?'

'He knew I cared for you,' Peter said. 'But he thought you were a tease. I'm not sure, but from watching him the last couple of years, I sometimes got the impression he blames you for what happened that night.'

'Did he think you hit the truck on purpose?'

'No. He thinks that I had reasons for living dangerously. But that's not quite the same thing.'

'And that I was one of those reasons?'

'Yes,' Peter said. 'Does that bother you?'

'No. I understand.'

322

'I'm glad. He's a great guy.'

'I have another question for you,' I said. 'Why did you put me in your story?'

'That wasn't you,' he said.

'You used my middle name – Ann.'

'I didn't know that was your middle name.'

'That's right,' I said. 'You don't even know how to spell my first name. OK, let's back up a sec. You were driving along, and you decided to add some excitement to your life by dying. What happened next?'

'I realised I had made a terrible mistake.'

'Is there a penalty over here for committing suicide?'

'Yes. Remember I told you I knew you couldn't have killed yourself?'

'Yes,' I said.

'The reason I knew was because you have the opportunity to go into the light.' He paused. 'I haven't had that opportunity.'

I wrinkled up my face. 'Why?'

'Until all the years my life *should* have lasted have gone by, I have to stay on earth. I am earthbound.'

'Who bound you? Who told you this?'

'Those are the rules,' he said.

'That's B.S. Peter, I've been in the light. I went into it when Jimmy's heart stopped. And I can tell you from personal experience that it wouldn't hand out penalties. It can't – it's too nice. It's completely non-judgemental. The reason you're stuck here is because you're keeping yourself here. You're feeling guilty.'

'Wouldn't you?' he asked. 'I threw away my life. It was only by blind luck that I didn't kill the driver of the truck.'

'Yes, I would feel guilty. But not for the rest of eternity. Who told you that you have to stay?'

'Other ghosts in my predicament,' he said.

'Oh, swell, go to the man on death row for advice about your trial. They're obviously as screwed up as you are.'

'I am not screwed up,' he said indignantly.

'Yes you are. Here you give me all these boring lectures on how anything is possible, and you don't even know how to knock on the door to ask to be let in. And another thing, if you haven't been in the light, how can you know anything about it?'

'I didn't lie to you about everything. I really have helped many people that have just crossed over. Dozens of times I've seen what happens when the light comes over an individual, the joy they experience, the peace – even before they leave.'

'But you've only watched, Peter. Tell me, have you ever tried to go on?'

That got him. 'No,' he said.

'See? Tell me another thing. What happened when your Shadow caught you?'

'My whole life passed before me.'

'And?' I asked.

'And what?'

'Was it so horrible? Were you such a bad guy? The Peter I remember couldn't do enough for people.'

'The Peter you remember wasn't the real Peter.'

I stood and spoke to the sky. 'Listen to this guy – Mr Suffering Servant himself!' I kicked Peter in the shin, and I honestly believe he felt it – he winced. 'Stay here, then. Go play with your other unhappy ghosts. Spend the rest of eternity peeking in at girls in the shower. I don't care. I have better things to do with my time.'

He raised his head. 'I didn't peek at you in the shower.'

'You said you did.'

'I was kidding,' he said. 'I left before you took off all your clothes.'

'All my clothes? How much did I have off?'

'Ah, your top,' he said.

'How did I look?'

'I told you, fine. Great.'

'Why did you leave at all?' I asked. 'I thought you were lusting after me.'

'I didn't say that.'

'Crazy about me, love me, lusting after me – it's all the same thing.'

'I didn't peek at you in the shower.'

'Why not?' I asked, feeling mildly insulted.

'That would have been unethical.'

'Ah-ha!' I exclaimed, pointing a finger at his nose. 'That's your problem. You think sex is dirty. You have a dirty mind. No wonder you can't get into the light.'

He took hold of my finger. He surprised me when he pulled it down and gently kissed the back of my hand. 'I can get in,' he said quietly.

I took a step back at his change in tone. 'Did I convince you that easily?' I asked, surprised.

Peter stood and put his hands in his pockets. We had almost forgotten the commotion going on around us. The fire was out, although smoke continued to pour from the front door and the side windows. My dad would probably have to replace the downstairs furniture and carpeting. I wasn't worried; he could afford it. Slowly, in twos and threes, the neighbours were returning to their homes, probably thinking those Coopers were crazy.

'You did the most for me when you made me stay and face the Shadow,' Peter said. 'I'm not afraid of it any more. I don't have to keep running. It helps that I was able to talk about it right now. I guess I've finally accepted what I did. And what you said just now, yeah, it makes good sense. I can go on, I think, as long as I can go with you.'

He paused. 'You were serious about liking me?'

'*Loving* you,' I corrected, squeezing up against him. 'But don't make me out to sound like a soul winner, all right? It's not what I want out of this relationship.'

'What do you want, Shari?'

I thought a moment. 'Kisses. Two years' worth.'

He grinned. 'For that, you'll have to take off your top.'

Later, we rode to the hospital in the back of the ambulance with Jimmy. Garrett was also there, and that was good. I put my arm around the detective and gave him a big hug. Maybe he felt it, I don't know. He belched.

'I owe this man,' I said.

'He saved your brother's life,' Peter agreed.

'He also saved my reputation. There's got to be something I can do for him.'

'Shari.'

'I'm going to give it some thought,' I insisted, calling over to my brother, who was sitting with a wary eye on the paramedic. 'Hey, Jimmy, what do you say?'

Others might have disagreed, but I believe what happened next meant Jimmy remembered a portion of our talk in the golden lotus. At my remark, he turned to Garrett and finished the sentence the popping of the red balloon had interrupted.

'You know,' he said, 'Shari was the best sister a guy could've had.'

I burst out crying, I was so happy.

EPILOGUE

Peter and I did not leave immediately. I wanted to see what happened after all the excitement died down. I also wanted to offer what help I could to smooth out what I believed was going to be a rough period for those I loved.

The truth about Amanda's biological parents came out. It was, I suppose, inevitable. Yet Mrs Foulton's full involvement in the switch of infants was never brought to light. Mrs Foulton and Mrs Parish got together and led the authorities to believe that they had 'felt' for many years that some 'mistake' had been made long ago at the hospital. It was amazing how vague they were about what this mistake was, and even more amazing that the police didn't haul them both over the coals. It may have been because nobody was pressing any charges.

The police did, however, take a print of Amanda's feet and mine – lifted from inside one of my shoes – and compared them to the ones in the hospital's files. This verified that the mistake had indeed been very real. I was worried about how my parents would react when they learned that their pretend daughter had been murdered by their real daughter. My concerns proved to be groundless. They were both so elated to have a daughter again that they went out and hired the best lawyer in town to defend Amanda for killing me!

It is a strange universe.

Amanda got off light – she was sentenced to five years of state-supervised psychiatric care. I guess the judge figured she had been subjected to psychological pressures of a most unusual nature. I didn't mind; I felt no need for vengeance. Nor did Jimmy. He provided Amanda with moral support throughout the course of the trial. He never, however, let himself get caught alone with her again. He was a nice guy, but he wasn't stupid.

Two days after the red balloon and the big fire, I had my picture on the front page of Los Angeles's two biggest papers: 'HIGH SCHOOL SENIOR'S SUICIDE TURNS OUT TO BE MURDER' and 'SHARI COOPER DIDN'T JUMP.' I liked the sound of the second one the best. The latter headline was also above a colour picture of me – not a black and white – and everybody in town got a chance to enjoy my sparkling green eyes.

The gang – Jo, Jeff, Daniel and Beth – got together at Beth's condo shortly after the articles came out to discuss how they knew all along that I wasn't the jumping kind. I just listened and laughed. Especially when Beth slapped Daniel across the face for trying to grab her breast after Jo and Jeff had left holding hands and cuddling.

But through all this, I fretted over Mrs Parish the most. She had, in a sense, lost not one but two daughters. I would like to say her quiet strength allowed her to accept Amanda's crime with a sense of equanimity. Regrettably, besides being strange, the universe is often hard. Mrs Parish suffered terribly with Amanda's trial. One consolation, however, was that my mother bore no malice towards Mrs Parish for not having brought the mix-up to light sooner. Quite the contrary, she supported and encouraged Mrs Parish at every opportunity. I was proud of my mother, finally proud to call her Mom, even though she no longer was.

In the end, Mrs Parish did gain a measure of peace. I am happy to report that I had a hand in it. For many nights after Amanda was arrested, I would visit Mrs Parish in her dreams and tell her that I was doing well and that I held no grudge against Amanda. For a while it seemed my interludes did no good and that she would remember nothing upon waking. But then one afternoon when she was sewing in her living room and I was sitting by her side and listening to the melody she was humming, she suddenly put down her needle and thread and stared off into empty space.

'Shari,' she said. 'If you're there, if you can hear me, I want to tell you something that I almost told you a thousand times while you were alive. Finding you again after losing you all those years was wonderful. It was the best thing that ever happened to me. It brought me so much joy, I thought I would never again ask God for anything, because he had given me everything. And I kept that promise, until right now. You see, I have to ask him one more thing, to tell you this, that I loved you as much as any mother loved a child. You were always my daughter.'

Then she went completely still for a moment and smiled, and there was the same light on her face that I had seen in the church above her head when she had prayed for me. 'Thank you,' she whispered. 'So it is done, I've heard you, too, Shari. Don't worry about me, I'll be fine.'

And from then on, she was much better.

But I still had my debt to Garrett to repay and, more important, the desire to do something for him. I thought about the problem a long time, and finally a solution came to me.

Peter helped me implement it. He showed me how to alter my form at will and acted as my accomplice. Together we journeyed to the seedy motel room where Garrett's daughter spent her miserable nights.

I returned as a radiant angel of light. My hair was long and golden. I had eyes of emeralds and a beautiful silver robe. I spent a long time getting my translucent wings to shimmer with a celestial glow. A fine sight I made standing beside Peter.

He played a devil, and it was hard to look at him and not cringe. His mouth was a chopping maw of pointed green teeth, his hide a red and purple map of dragon scales. He had short, squat reptilian legs and took particular delight in drooling dark clots of blood and poking me with his huge black pitchfork.

We waited in the closet of the motel room for the girl to shoot up with her drugs. After my recent bad experiences with needles, it was difficult for me to watch. But Peter was encouraging. He made an excellent devil.

'This is going to be fun,' he slobbered with glee as we trooped out of the closet. The girl lay sprawled in her underwear on the bed, deep in the spell of her narcotic, her pupils dilated. But she blinked at the sight of us. She knew we were there, though I'm sure she couldn't have guessed why.

We were going to fight over her soul.

'Let me eat her alive!' Peter cried, jumping towards the bed with his pitchfork held high. 'Let me chew off her fingers – one through five!'

Garrett's daughter recoiled against the bedstand, her nails going to her mouth, her face turning white. I leaped in front of Peter and held my arms and wings out wide. 'You cannot have her!' I cried. 'Not while she lives!'

Peter halted and snorted like a fiend. 'She will be dead soon! With all the drugs she takes, she will die in this very room!' He tried to squirm around me. 'Then I will come for her! I will peel off her skin and wear it like fur!'

I barred his way. 'She might not die! She might turn away from her evil ways!'

Peter laughed uproariously. 'She will never change! She is already in my cage! Soon I will carve her dry! I will lick her bones and make her cry!'

'You cannot do this!' I said.

'Let me have her tonight!' He fought to get by me. 'Let me have a bite!'

'Stop him,' the girl pleaded, shaking like a leaf.

'I can't,' I said, looking over my shoulder and through

my wing, barely holding Peter at bay. 'I cannot stop him without your help, child. If you die on drugs, he will come for you.'

'A leg!' Peter chortled. 'Give me her legs! They taste so good with sausage and eggs!'

'Please,' the girl cried.

'Leave here,' I told her in as clear and urgent a tone as I could muster. 'Go to your father. Only your father can keep this devil away.'

'I must have an eye!' Peter howled. 'A soggy eye for my sandwich of ham and rye!'

The girl nodded frantically. 'I will go.'

'You must promise me,' I said. 'I can do nothing for you without your promise.'

'An ear!' Peter yelped. 'An ear to mix in my salty beer!'

The girl tried to grab my hand and kiss it. 'I promise.'

Peter stopped his struggling and took a step back, falling silent. I laid my hands atop her thick black hair. She was very pretty.

'You are stronger than you know,' I said. 'You will be able to keep your promise.' I leaned over and kissed her on the forehead. 'Close your eyes now, child, and be at peace. All is well. Tomorrow you will return to your father's house and start a new life.'

The girl did as I requested and lay back on her bed.

Peter and I hurried out the door. (I had no trouble walking through them nowadays.)

'We scared the hell out of her,' Peter said. 'It might work.'

'What was the deal with the rhymes?' I asked.

'Devils always speak in rhymes.'

'How do you know?' I asked. 'Have you ever met any?'

'No. But I read about it in the *Enquirer*.'

The girl did return home to Garrett. In fact, she called him the next morning, and he drove across town to pick her up. She tried to tell him about her vision. He nodded in understanding and told her to get into the truck. These days they're living together in a tidy house with a white picket fence and two-car garage. They're driving each other crazy. But at least she's no longer tripping, and he has stopped drinking. I'd say they're happy.

I'm happy. Peter and I are going to be leaving soon. The light is waiting. The sun is rising. It really is rising. Jimmy hasn't got over his bad habit of leaving his computer on, and he is still sleepwalking. He will probably be waking up soon, and I'm sure he's going to be tired. He has never spent an entire night typing at the speed of a supernatural being. He has never spent so long with a ghost sitting, not beside him, but *inside* him.

It was Jimmy who unknowingly wrote this story. I merely provided the inspiration.

I am going to miss my brother, but he is getting on with his life. The wonder he experienced when we stood together inside his heart has not left him, even if he does not consciously remember it. I watch him even now, through the images that flash behind his fluttering eyelids. And I know he dreams of me, of everything I have gone through since I last bid him farewell on my way to Beth's party. His touch lightens as he types this happy ending. Mrs Parish is not the only one who knows I'm doing well.

If you who read this story are really there, then it means my brother did not accidentally erase this computer disk I store my words on. It means that my last wish has been granted.

In the beginning, I called myself a ghost and said this was because I was dead. But those were Peter's words that I borrowed when he tried to communicate with his brother using my body. Even though Peter is a fine writer, I think he could have put it better.

I am not dead. Death does not exist. I am alive! That is the purpose of this tale, to let everyone know that they do go on and that they don't need to be afraid, as I was afraid.

Yet I also have a selfish reason for wanting my story told. I was young when I died. I didn't have a chance to make my mark in the world. I didn't do anything unique, nothing that will change the course of history. But I wasn't a bad girl. I don't want to be forgotten.

I want people to remember me.

THE
RETURN

PART 1

For all the Wanderers of the world.
May they one day remember where they came from.

CHAPTER 1

Jean Rodrigues did not want to become her mother. A not quite forty-year-old woman with five kids, a dead husband lost to booze, working sixty hours a week at a coffee shop just to pay the rent on a run-down house in the wrong part of town and to put food in the mouths of children who could not have cared less about her. Most of the time Jean couldn't give a damn, not about school or work or even about herself. Yet sometimes she'd watch her mother as the woman got dressed for work, the lines of ruined dreams on her weary face, and Jean would feel sorry for her. She'd think, There must be something that would make my mother smile. There must be more to life than what I see waiting for me. Yet Jean could never see that 'more', and so she seldom smiled herself.

Jean Rodrigues was eighteen years old and it was two weeks before her high school graduation. Her father had been Mexican, pure Aztec – at least that's what she was told. Her memories of him were few; he had died of pneumonia and heart failure while she was still in first grade. Her mother – she wasn't positive what her mother was. Half Hispanic, a quarter Italian, two-thirds the rest of the world. The numbers and genes never added up. Jean supposed the same was true for her. But Jean knew she looked good, no matter what her gene pool or how broke she was. Her long dark hair was her glory. She wore it unadorned and straight down to her butt and washed it every night with a herbal shampoo – one of the few luxuries she allowed herself. Her face was strong; relatives said she took after her father. Her nose was big, but since her mouth was as well, the flaw only enhanced her beauty. She may have had her father's fearless expression, but she had her mother's body. They were both voluptuous. Her looks were one of the things Jean felt good about. There were so few things.

That evening was a warm Friday. If Jean had read the papers closely and had an excellent memory, she would have remembered it was exactly fifty-two Fridays after the death of another eighteen-year-old in another section of Los Angeles, a certain Shari Cooper. Like Shari of a year ago, Jean was in her bathroom preparing to spend Friday night at a birthday party for a friend. Her friend was

342

Lenny Mandez. Jean had been dating Lenny for about three months and had a special surprise for him tonight. It was so special that she wondered if she should let him know about it on a night reserved for celebration. She was six weeks pregnant with his kid.

My mother got pregnant with me when she was eighteen. The same sad story, all over again. I don't want to become my mother.

Jean knew why she was pregnant, besides the obvious reason that she'd had sex. Six weeks earlier when Lenny and she had made love, their condom had broken. And there they were being so responsible, practising safe sex and all. She'd been a fool to believe all that hype, she thought. The only hundred per cent safe sex was between Barbie and Ken, and she'd heard rumours they weren't doing it any more. What made it worse was that she wasn't sure if Lenny knew how badly things had misfired that night. She worried that he might think the kid belonged to someone else. But it wasn't a huge worry – Lenny was cool – not as huge as the kid growing inside her. She didn't know what to do. She didn't want to think about it, so she planned to get loaded that night.

Jean was brushing her hair when the car horn outside startled her, although she'd been waiting for it to sound. Her best friend, Carol Dazmin, was driving her to the party. Jean did not have a car. She did work after school and most weekends at a Subway Sandwich but only to supplement her mother's meagre income and to buy clothes and pot. Not for a car. Jean smoked pot practically every day; it was the only thing that made the clocks on the walls at school fun to watch. Carol got loaded with her, too, but spent her days staring at the other girls. Carol was a lesbian, but she never hit on Jean or anything and it was OK. In fact, Carol was another of the few things in Jean's life that could be called positive. Carol was one of the kindest and funniest people Jean had ever met.

At the sound of the horn, Jean jerked her hand the wrong way and ended up breaking the handle off her brush with it right in her hair. Even if she'd possessed a perfect memory and had read every paper in town, Jean wouldn't have known that Shari Cooper had broken brushes regularly. Jean stared at the plastic handle in her hand before pulling the clump of bristles from her hair. She had never broken a brush before.

Jean left the bathroom and walked into the living room. It was getting dark, but her younger stepbrothers and -sisters were still outside playing, even four-year-old Teddy. The only one Jean really felt close to was Teddy; the world had yet to ruin him. As for the rest, she didn't care if they ever came inside. Her mother had crashed on the couch in front of an old 'Star Trek' rerun on TV. Jean had no interest in science fiction or anything to do with space. She would just as soon the government spent the money on nuclear bombs.

'Hey, *Mamá*,' Jean said softly, staring down at her mother. 'I'm knocked up. Knocked up and dropped down.'

Her mother stirred. Her hair was already grey; she couldn't be bothered dyeing it. She had on green coffee-stained pants, a white blouse she had worn the past two days. Her lipstick was a cheap colour; it looked as if she'd put it on in front of a dusty windshield rather than a clean mirror. Most of all she looked tired. She had to be up at four to be at work on time. Jean felt that somehow she was standing before a mirror as she studied her.

Her mother yawned. 'Did you say something, Jean?'

Jean hesitated. She'd have to tell her sometime. Or would she? Maybe Lenny would talk her into an abortion. Or perhaps he'd just take her out and shoot her. There were all kinds of possibilities, when she thought about it.

'No,' Jean said. 'I'm going out.'

Her mother opened her eyes. 'Where are you going?'

'Lenny's having a party. It's at his house.'

'Will his parents be there?'

'His parents are dead, Mom. I told you that.'

'Well, who will be there? Just you kids and a cloud of smoke?'

Jean acted bored. 'Mom, nothing like that's going to happen.'

Her mother snorted. 'Yeah, like it doesn't happen every day. What do you take me for, *mija*? One of your teachers at school?'

'I don't know.'

'What time are you coming home?'

'Midnight, maybe a little later.'

'Don't you have work tomorrow?'

'Yeah. I'll be there. Do I ever miss?'

Her mother shook her head. 'I don't know what you do any more, Jean. Except that you don't stay around here much. What's this Lenny like? Have I met him?'

'You met him last week.'

She scratched her head. 'He wasn't that black fella, was he?'

'Mom! He's the same colour as you and me. He's a great guy. I like him. It's his birthday tonight.'

Her mother nodded. She liked birthdays. They were next to All Saints days in her book. 'What'd you get him?' her mother asked.

Jean had passed the two-minute-get-your-ass-in-gear mark. Carol honked again. Jean stepped towards the door, saying, 'I got him something special. I'll tell you about it later. Don't worry if I'm a little late.'

'If you don't come home, I'll worry,' her mother called after her.

Jean opened the door and stepped outside the house, the same house she'd lived in all her life. She drew in a deep breath of smog. North and south, east and west, her neighbourhood was in the throes of a holocaust. Had been since the word *ghetto* was first used.

'I wouldn't,' Jean muttered under her breath.

Carol had made herself up, much more than Jean had. Carol had on a tight black leather skirt, a long-sleeved red blouse, fake silver and gold chains. Jean wore blue jeans and a yellow shirt. Carol was not butch; she liked to attract the girls as a girl. Jean knew Carol's fantasy, Darlene Sanchez, would be at the party. Jean also knew Carol was wasting her time on Darlene, who needed guys the way a smoking car needs a quart of oil.

But Darlene was not in a romantic mood these days. Her boyfriend, Sporty Quinones, had been gunned down near the projects in a drive-by only two weeks ago. Lenny had been with him at the time, but hadn't been hurt. Sporty had taken three shots in the chest and bled to death in Lenny's hands. At the funeral Darlene had not been silent in her mourning; there was too much fire in her blood. Even as they lowered Sporty into the ground, she shouted for vengeance. That was the trouble with drive-by hits; they were just guns poked out of dark windows. The killers didn't leave cards. Darlene said she knew who did it. Lenny didn't know how; he said he didn't even see the car. The whole thing confused Jean. She didn't know what the hell the guys were doing so close to the projects in the middle of the night. That was like walking into a sewer pipe and asking not to get dirtied. She missed Sporty as well; he had been a good friend. If it hadn't been for Lenny, she might have gone out with him. They had fooled around a little at some boring party just before Lenny and she got together.

'Guess what?' Carol said as Jean climbed into the car. Carol had a ten-year-old red Camaro that had once been hit by a school bus. It sounded like a tank under enemy fire, but it always started, which was the important thing.

'What?' Jean said, closing the car door.

'You have to guess.' Carol put the car in gear and they rolled forward.

'I don't want to guess.'

'I got asked out today.'

'Who asked you out?' Jean asked.

'You know the guy with the Russian accent at the McDonald's on Herald?'

'That guy? His face is scarred.'

Carol giggled; she often did. Her lips were glossy, her eyelids neon. She was skinny as a wire plugged into a shorted socket. She had a lot of energy. She could eat two Big Macs with fries at lunch break and still do situps in PE an hour later. She was pure Hispanic but wore so much white powder that she looked as if she were auditioning for a circus clown.

'What do you think?' Carol asked.

'About his scars?'

'No! About him asking me out. He knows I'm a lesbian, and he still wants to go out with me. Doesn't that make him some kind of pervert?'

'No. I bet he thinks he can turn you on. Are you going out with him?'

'I don't know. I told him to come to the party tonight. Do you think he'll come?'

'Why do you keep asking me questions like that? I don't even know the guy.'

Carol nodded excitedly. 'I hope he comes. It might make Darlene jealous.'

'I wouldn't count on it.'

Carol lost her smile. 'Don't you think she likes me –

just a little? And don't say you can't answer because you don't know her.'

'Yes. I think Darlene likes you. I just don't think she wants to sleep with you. God, Carol, the girl is a complete horn dog. She's slept with just about every guy at school.'

'Yeah. But she's just suffered a major personal loss. That can sometimes shake up a person's sexuality. I heard that on *Oprah*. There was a woman on there who didn't become a lesbian until her husband's head was cut off by a helicopter blade.'

Jean groaned. 'Oh, brother.'

'What is it?'

'I need some *mota*. Do you have a joint?'

'At home, not with me. But there'll be plenty of stuff at the party. Can't you wait?'

'I suppose.'

'What's bothering you, Jean? You look like you're worried about your sexuality.'

'I'm pregnant.'

'*Qué?*'

'I'm pregnant.'

Carol almost rammed the back of a bus. 'Wow! That's big. Whose is it?'

Jean was disgusted. 'What do you mean, whose is

350

it? It's Lenny's. He's my boyfriend. What kind of question is that?'

'I was just asking. I just wanted to be sure. Wow. What are you going to do?'

'I don't know. What do you think I should do?'

'I don't know. Get rid of it.'

Jean shook her head. 'Just like that? I don't know if I can do that.'

'Have you told him?'

'I was thinking of telling him tonight.'

'That should liven up his party.'

'Shut up. Maybe I'll tell him later. I haven't even told my mom yet.'

'Don't tell your mom. She won't let you go out any more.'

'I'll think about it,' Jean said.

'What did you get Lenny for his birthday? I got him a book.'

'What kind of book?'

'I don't know. It had a scary cover on it. Does Lenny like scary stuff?'

'I don't think he's read a book in his life. I don't know if he can read.'

Carol laughed. 'I was thinking the same thing! I was thinking this is the stupidest present I could possibly buy him! That's why I bought it. What did you get him?'

'Nothing so far. Let's stop at the music store. Maybe I can buy him a CD.'

Carol settled back down. She reached over and touched Jean on the leg. Her voice came out gentle. Jean knew Carol was not as insensitive as she liked to pretend.

'If you do keep the baby, then we could all play with it,' she said. 'It might not be so bad. It might even be fun.'

Jean sighed. 'Nothing's fun any more.'

CHAPTER 2

Lenny Mandez had a hilltop home with a view. Unfortunately, the house rested on a weed-choked plot of land between a slum and a ghetto. The surrounding area was covered with aged oil wells that creaked so badly in the middle of the night it sounded as if the house were under attack from an army of arthritic robots. The latest earthquake had actually made some of his neighbours' homes stand up straighter. The whole area looked as if it had been thrown together for the express purpose of violating every code in the book. Lenny's home had two bedrooms for the cockroaches and a bathroom for the real nasty creatures. Still, it wasn't a bad place to have a party, Jean thought, as long as there was enough booze and dope. Fortunately, that was never a problem with Lenny. Intoxicants followed him the way ants beat a path to the food across his kitchen floor.

Lenny Mandez was twenty, but if his age was measured by mileage rather than years, he was ready for retirement. He had joined his first gang while walking home from kindergarten. He was in juvenile hall for stealing a car he didn't know how to drive when he was thirteen. But that two-year stint inside sobered him some, and Lenny returned to public school and graduated from high school last year. He had a full-time job now, working as a mechanic at a gas station owned by an uncle. He owed allegiance to no particular gang, but had friends in all the wrong places and made as much money dealing drugs as he did tuning engines. Jean knew he was trouble, she was no fool, but she took solace in the fact that he didn't like being a pusher, any more than he liked the idea of returning to prison. He told her that he was trying to change, and she could see that he was. He took a couple of night classes at the city college – general ed stuff. He didn't know what he wanted to do with his life any more than she did. They had that in common, at least.

She had met him through the late Sporty Quinones, who, at the age of twenty, had still been trying to get a high school diploma. They had been introduced in the middle of the street, literally, and for a moment, when she'd looked into his dark eyes, she forgot about the oncoming cars. There was passion in his eyes, she sensed, as well as danger. She wondered if that's what it took to turn her on – the possibility of a bad end. He had a great body; she had seen a few in her day. He had heavy muscles, generous lips and wore his straight black hair long on to his shoulders. He had taken a hip tone with her. 'Hey, baby, I heard about you. Heard you were hot. What do you say we get together tonight?' Of course she had told him where to stick it, and he had laughed, reverting to a more subdued tone, which she was to learn was more normal for him. He had taken her to the movies that night, and they had necked so hard in the back row they had turned a PG Disney film into a hard R erotic mystery. That was what she liked most about Lenny – the mystery. Even after six weeks of dating, she still had no idea what he was thinking. At Sporty's funeral, as his best friend was lowered into the ground, he hadn't changed the expression on his face. He could have been staring at the sky for all the emotion he showed.

Jean ended up getting Lenny a Snoop Dogg CD, which he slipped into the player as soon as she and Carol arrived at his house, and cranked up the volume. Jean assumed that meant he liked it even though she hadn't had a chance to wrap it. He gave her a quick kiss and handed her a beer and she sat on the couch in the living room with a bunch of people she hardly knew and the party moved forward as they always did. There was alcohol, pot, music, laughter and cursing. She and Carol cornered a hookah loaded with Colombian Gold near the start of the festivities and each took four hits so deep into their lungs that they could feel their brain cells leaving on the sweet cloud of smoke as they exhaled. They both began to laugh and didn't stop until they remembered they had nothing to laugh about, which was an hour later. So the first part of the party passed painlessly.

Even though Jean got loaded regularly, marijuana often had an undesirable side effect on her psychology. The moment her high began to falter, her mood sometimes plunged, so rapidly that she felt as if she were sinking into a black well. In other words, the pot bummed her out as surely as it made her laugh, and this was one of those unfortunate times when, after an hour of giggling, she felt close to tears. But since she seldom cried, and never in front of other people, she just got real quiet and tried not to think. She didn't want to know she was in a place she didn't want to be with people she didn't care about and who didn't care about her. That her whole life was headed in the wrong direction and that it wasn't going to change because that was just the way the world was. That she was pregnant and didn't want a baby and didn't want to have an abortion and didn't want to end up like her mother. It was this last thought, spinning around in her head, that caused her the most grief. And the weird thing was, her mother was one of the few people in her life she actually respected.

Come midnight, though, when the party began to thin out, and the dope began to filter from her bloodstream, her depression lifted sufficiently so that she was able to talk again. At the time she happened to be sitting on the end of Lenny's bed watching as Darlene Sanchez used the cracked mirror precariously attached to the top of Lenny's chest of drawers to replait a few loose braids. Darlene was Hispanic, but wanted to be black; a formidable task, to be sure, since she was naturally whiter than Carol after make-up. Sporty Quinones had been Darlene's first non-African-American boyfriend, a fact that was somewhat at odds with her reputation of having slept with most of the juniors and seniors in the school. But who was counting, colours or numbers. Darlene was hot, no debating that.

'How are you feeling, girl?' Darlene asked, gazing at her in the mirror.

'I'm all right,' Jean said.

'You looked like hell all night.'

'Thanks a lot.'

'No, I mean your mood.' Darlene lifted a few strands of hair above her head and, in the blink of an eye, braided them. Her braids made her look pretty scary when she wore them just right. Her long painted fingernails were just as bad. They reminded Jean of razors dipped in blood. Darlene added, 'You look like someone just died.'

Jean realised she had a can of beer in her hand and took a sip. 'Someone just did.'

Darlene acted pissed. 'Great! You had to bring that up. I'm here to have a good time, and you have to talk about Sporty.'

'I wasn't talking about him.' Jean shrugged. 'In this town someone dies practically every hour.'

'Yeah, right. God, what a downer you are.'

Jean burped. 'Sorry.'

Darlene waved her hand. 'It doesn't matter. I don't mind talking about him. We're going to talk about him later anyway. We're going to have a little meeting when the party's over, Lenny and I. You should stay for it.'

'What kind of meeting?' Jean asked.

'You'll see.'

'I came with Carol. Can she be there?'

Darlene seemed exasperated. She could change her expression quicker than most people inhaled. 'That girl. She doesn't know what she is. Do you know what she said to me this evening?'

'I can guess.'

358

'She said, "You know, Darlene, there are two sides to everything. You don't know what belongs on front until you check the behind." Can you believe she said that to me?'

'I don't even know what it means.'

'It means, dope head, that she's still trying to get in my pants. Lenny tells me you're straight as an arrow. How can you have a dyke as a best friend?'

'It's easy. She's not a dyke to me. She's a great girl.'

Darlene paused. 'Have you two ever done it?'

'Done what?'

'Had sex, for godssakes! Have you?'

'No. Carol's not interested in me that way.'

'What is she interested in then?'

'She's my friend. She needs friends as much as straight people. Maybe more. Maybe you should try being her friend rather than always badmouthing her.'

'Maybe she should quit hitting on me first,' Darlene said.

'She's not hitting on you. She's just flirting with you. You should be flattered.'

'I'm not. She makes me nervous. She makes me feel like I might be a *joto* and not know it.'

'Maybe you are a *joto*, Darlene.' Jean allowed herself a rare smile. 'Anybody who goes around with a head looking like a snake fest has got to have something wrong with her.'

Darlene laughed. 'Hell, you're probably right.' She finished with her hair and turned around. 'How do I look?'

'Am I the right person to ask? I just told you. You look great.'

'Thanks. You want to go get something to eat?'

'You mean, leave the party?' Jean asked.

'Yeah, I mean leave the party. You can't eat any of the rot in Lenny's refrigerator. We can hit the Jack-in-the-Box down the street and be back in twenty minutes.'

Jean shook her head. 'You go ahead. I don't feel very hungry.'

Darlene sat on the bed beside her friend, concerned. 'Really, are you all right, Jean?'

Jean shrugged. 'Yeah, I'm just tired.'

'Are you and Lenny getting on all right?'

'Yeah.' Jean paused. 'I think so. Do you know something I don't?'

Darlene hesitated. 'No.' She stood quickly. 'I'll be back soon. Remember that meeting. I want you there.'

'I won't be there unless Carol's there. She's my ride home.'

'Aren't you going to spend the night with Lenny? It is his birthday, after all.'

'No,' Jean said. 'My mother would freak.'

Darlene seemed to think for a moment, then nodded. 'That's what mothers are for.'

Darlene left. Jean continued to sit on the edge of the bed and sip her beer. She studied herself in the mirror. It was only then she remembered the dream she'd had that morning. It had been wonderful yet simple, painful to wake from. She dreamed she was floating above her house and that just a few blocks away she could see a colourful amusement park, the rainbow of shimmering lights illumining her insides as much as the neighbourhood. The feelings of the dream had been more important than the actual events. She knew that if she would just fly over there, she could enter that place of constant fun and excitement. Where there were people who cared and things to do that meant something. And in the dream she was being given that choice, to leave her house, her life, and never return. Why had she awakened? She sure as hell hadn't said no to the offer. Now the memory of the dream made her sad. Made her sad that it was gone, for ever.

After some time Lenny entered his bedroom. He had on his black leather jacket; he seldom took it off, even on nights as warm as this. His long black hair was pulled back in a ponytail. They had talked little all night.

Conversation wasn't big with either of them. They were better just sitting and watching a movie together, or smoking a joint, or making love. She had assumed they'd have sex tonight since, as Darlene said, it was his birthday. But now she had to wonder if she could talk herself into the right mood. Lenny sat on the bed beside her and leaned over to give her a kiss. She kissed him back – sort of. He sensed her lack of enthusiasm and drew away.

'What's wrong?' he asked.

'Nothing.' She touched his leg. 'How are you doing?'

'Good. Great party, huh?'

'Yeah. That was great dope. Where did you get it?'

He shrugged. 'The usual sources. Where did Darlene go?'

'To Jack-in-the-Box. She was hungry.'

'We have pizza in the living room,' Lenny said.

Jean forced a smile. 'It's on the living room floor. I think Darlene worries about hygiene.'

Lenny chuckled; it sounded forced as well. 'Then I don't know what she was doing with Sporty. That guy had equipment that needed to be machined to get clean.'

'Was he that bad?'

Lenny paused and stared at her. 'I don't know. He just told me so many stories.'

'About so many girls?'

Lenny nodded. 'Yeah. You must have seen how he carried on at school?'

'Yeah, he got around some, I guess. When Darlene wasn't around.'

'But they weren't going out that long,' Lenny said.

'Really? I thought it was a few months.'

Lenny continued to watch her. 'Something's bothering you, Jean. What is it?'

She lowered her head. 'Well, there is something I wanted to tell you. I should have told you earlier, but I was afraid. But I don't know if this is the right time, either.'

Lenny sucked in a deep breath and became still. She sensed his rigidity more than saw it because she continued to keep her head low. Finally he let the breath out.

'Yes?' he said softly.

'I'm pregnant.'

The two words seemed to float out of her mouth and into a vacuum. The room became a bowl sitting on some troll's table, and they were breakfast. She raised her head and saw that Lenny had closed his eyes. A vein pulsed on his forehead. It looked as if it might pop if the pressure wasn't released soon. She wanted to say something to make him feel better like I'll get rid of it or maybe the test kit was wrong. But she doubted he would have heard her at that moment. His mind seemed to have fled to a place where there were no words. Finally, though, he opened his eyes and looked at her. His expression was strangely blank.

'Are you sure?' he asked softly.

'Yes.' She paused. 'I'm sorry. Lousy birthday present, huh?'

'I've had better. What do you want to do?'

'I don't know. What do you want to do?'

'It's up to you.'

'No, it's up to both of us.' She felt a painful lump in her throat. She had taken her hand off his leg, and she wanted to put it back, to hug him, maybe kiss him again. But they were like two strangers sitting in a cheap motel room. At least that was how the two people in the cracked mirror looked. Jean regretted having started the conversation in front of their reflections. It made her feel more lost. How did she really feel about Lenny? She had told him she loved him; he had told her the same. But those were just words. She didn't believe she could love him because she didn't know what love was. She didn't even know if there was such a thing, if it wasn't all hype. She added, 'We can keep it or we can get rid of it. I'm not going to force it on you.'

'How much does an abortion cost?' he asked.

'Three hundred dollars. About.'

He smiled thinly and shook his head. 'That's *mucha lana*. You were raised Catholic. Could you go through with an abortion?'

She sighed. 'I don't know.' His next question caught her off guard.

'What do you think he'd look like?' he asked.

She hesitated. '*Bueno*. Like the two of us. But it might be a she, you know.'

'Have you ever seen pictures of me when I was a baby?'

'No. You haven't shown me any.' She paused. 'I'd like to see some.'

'No, you wouldn't. I looked awful. But maybe he would look – better.' He stood and eyed the door. 'Let's talk about this later when no one's around. Right now I have to enjoy my twentieth birthday party. It's the only one I'm ever going to have.'

'*Lo siento*, I'm sorry,' she said again.

'Don't be sorry,' he said as he left the room.

Ninety minutes later Jean was sitting in the living room with Lenny, Carol and Darlene. After Lenny had left her, Jean had fallen back on the bed and passed out for an hour. She hadn't dreamed, only entered a black void where there was no sound or feeling and slept the sleep of the dead. She didn't even know who she was when she awakened in the dark. The disorientation had lingered. Who had turned off the bedroom light? She didn't know and it didn't matter.

The four of them were the only ones left at the party. Jean sat on the couch with Lenny. Carol was on the floor, acting bored. Her Russian boyfriend had never shown. Darlene, as usual, paced. Darlene wanted revenge, she wanted blood. Her little meeting was about planning a hit on Sporty's murderers, specifically on Juan Chiato. Juan was the biggest drug dealer at their high school, although he hadn't been to class in ten years. He was twenty-one years old, high up in the Red Blades, one of the most vicious of the inner-city gangs. Jean knew Juan by sight; she had met him twice at Lenny's house. He'd been leaving as she went in. Out of necessity, Lenny said he occasionally had to deal with Juan, although Lenny clearly did not like to be in the same room as Juan, who was known for his violent temper. But Juan had direct contact with Colombian drug lords and practically set the price of cocaine in their neighbourhood. His face was badly scarred from knife fights. Jean thought he looked like one of Satan's first lieutenants. She hadn't known

Sporty was connected to Juan, but she supposed she'd been mistaken.

'Let me tell you why I know it was Juan,' Darlene said as she strode back and forth in front of them, a cigarette in her hand. 'The week before Sporty died, he told me about a deal he had going with Juan. You didn't know about it, Lenny. Sporty told me Juan had sworn him to secrecy. Anyway, Sporty told me about it because he could never keep his mouth shut when he was drunk. It had nothing to do with drugs. Juan had stolen a truckload of Levi's jeans. He had slipped on to a freight company's lot with a gun and put the barrel to the security guard's head and driven away with the trailer. He wanted to use Sporty to sell the jeans to certain stores. Sporty was game. The commission looked good, and he thought dealing with store owners would be a lot more pleasant than the jerks that hung around Juan. But what he didn't know was that Juan was just using him. The stores he sent Sporty to paid protection to the Bald Caps. You know them?'

Lenny nodded. '*Cierto*. They're a small gang, but they control much of downtown, especially around the convention centre and the skyscrapers. Why did Juan want to piss them off?'

'I asked Sporty that,' Darlene said. 'He thought maybe Juan was trying to set something up between the Red

Blades and the Bald Caps. Juan was trying to move up in the Blades, and he was impatient. He wanted some action that he could lead, show the others how strong he was. He wanted a fight. He sent Sporty out, not to sell jeans, but to start a war with the Bald Caps. Right away Sporty ran into trouble. The Caps cornered him and threatened to cut out his heart for daring to enter their territory. They stole his van full of jeans. Sporty went running back to Juan and told him what had happened, but Juan didn't want to hear about it. He gave Sporty an ultimatum – either he got the jeans back or *he* was going to cut out his heart. Sporty yelled at him, said he had just been set up. Then Sporty made a big mistake. He told Juan he was thinking of going to the police to tell them the whole story.'

'No,' Lenny said, shaking his head. 'He wouldn't have been that *estúpido*.'

Darlene paused in her pacing. 'Sporty was pretty stupid sometimes. I can say that because I loved him. I asked him how Juan reacted, and he said Juan didn't say anything, which we all know is not the best response to get from a bloodthirsty sonofabitch like Juan Chiato. I tell you, Sporty was scared. He had a right to be scared.' Darlene nodded, her eyes burning. 'That all happened four weeks ago, and now look what's happened. Sporty's

368

dead. Juan killed him, there's no doubt about it. We have to kill the bastard.'

The room was silent for a full minute. Jean didn't know what to say. It did sound like Juan was probably the culprit, but who in his right mind would take revenge against someone who had a whole gang at his back? The Red Blades would re-earn their name hunting down and slaughtering whoever touched Juan. And if they just happened to murder a few who were only guilty by indirect association, then so much the better. Jean regretted having asked if Carol could stay for the meeting. Sitting on the floor against the wall, Carol looked full of regrets. Darlene must have been loaded to be talking about such things so openly. Yet she appeared in full command of her senses. It was Lenny who spoke first, and Jean was surprised when he didn't dismiss Darlene's proposal outright.

'I can't understand why Sporty didn't tell me he was having trouble with Juan,' he said. 'He should have come to me right away, before he tried to sell any jeans. I would have told him to stay as far away as he could from the guy.'

'He wanted to make his own mark,' Darlene said. 'He wanted to make his own money. Sporty got tired of living in your shadow and wanted to do something about it.'

Lenny shifted uncomfortably. 'He picked a bad way to go about it.'

'We've already established that he wasn't the most intelligent guy on the planet,' Carol said.

'Shut up,' Darlene said. 'I can say those things, but you can't. You didn't love him.'

Carol made a face. 'I hardly knew him.'

'Let's say, for the sake of argument, that it was Juan,' Lenny said. 'If we want him dead, we have to do it ourselves. Anyone else will talk to someone else. And if we do kill him, it's got to look like someone else did it. Because the second Juan's Blade buddies find his body, they're going to guess it was either Darlene or me who was behind it because we were Sporty's best friends.'

'I hope you're not suggesting that it has to look like an accident,' Carol said.

Lenny shook his head impatiently. 'If Juan has a dozen bullets in him, it can't look like an accident.'

'We could run him over,' Darlene suggested.

'It might be better to blow him up,' Lenny said. 'The less left, the better.'

Jean felt compelled to speak. 'Wait a second. What are we talking about here? Sporty's dead and that's terrible. But we can't avenge his death, *especially* if it was Juan who killed him. His gang will know who did it no matter how you plan it. They'll kill us all.'

'Why would they kill you?' Lenny asked, an odd note in his voice.

'Because I was Sporty's friend, too,' Jean said, annoyed at the question. 'Because I'm here with you guys talking about this foolish plan. You can't go up against someone that's high up in a gang. It's just not done. You know that, Lenny. Why are you even listening to Darlene?'

Lenny held her eye before answering, his face dark. He hadn't appreciated her remarks. 'Because I was his friend. A real friend doesn't do nothing after his friend's gunned down. I was there. He died in my arms.'

Jean returned his stare. When angered, few people intimidated her. 'What were you two doing at the projects so late at night?' she asked. 'So close to Juan's home ground?'

Lenny didn't blink. 'I didn't know about Sporty's problems with Juan. I said that already.'

'But that doesn't answer my question,' Jean said. 'At night that piece of turf is a death zone.'

'No one's asking you to be involved, Jean,' Darlene said bitterly. 'I just thought since Sporty always told me what a great girl you were that you'd want to be in on the payback.'

'What payback is that going to be?' Jean asked, her

voice hot. 'Kill Juan and live in fear every second until they come for us? And who's to say they'll simply shoot us? They might torture us first. You heard about what happened to that teenage bookie that the police found on Main? During the autopsy they found a pillowcase in his stomach. Do you know how scared someone has to be to swallow a pillowcase? Oh, and did I forget to mention that his throat had been cut from ear to ear? That was down on Main, Darlene – Red Blade territory, Juan's playing ground.'

'Was it a *whole* pillowcase?' Carol asked.

'Oh, would you shut up,' Jean said this time.

Darlene glared at Jean. 'I thought you were more than a chicken bitch. I guess I was wrong.'

Jean turned to Lenny, her boyfriend, the father of her unborn child. He still hadn't answered her original question. Earlier she had been right to think of him as a stranger. Looking at his dark, cold mask-like face, she hardly recognised him. And to think, she had made love to him only two days before on this very couch. No, she had had sex with him – there was a difference.

'How can you let her talk to me that way?' she asked. 'This is your house. Kick her out. You know she's talking crap. You know this whole meeting is insane.'

Lenny took his time answering. Something on the floor

between his legs had him fascinated. It must have been the dirt because that was all that was there. The heavy burdens on his attention – the filth and her request. Finally he spoke, his head still down.

'You just didn't care about him the way we did. You can't understand.' He shrugged, adding, 'We can't let Juan get away with it.'

Jean jumped up from the sofa, feeling the blood suffuse her face. 'I cared about him more than any of you know! I knew him before any of you knew him! But he's dead, and it's really sad, but why do we have to die with him? Why do we even have to talk about killing people?' Her throat choked with emotion; her voice came out cracked. 'Why do we even have to live like this?'

Jean didn't wait for an answer to her painful questions. She ran from the living room, into the bedroom and out on to Lenny's balcony. The platform was a haphazard affair, a collection of splintered planks thrown on top of a randomly spaced group of termite-zapped wooden stilts. Yet the drop to the ground was substantial: thirty feet straight down. Jean heard the boards of the railing creak as she leaned against them. The view was pretty at least, if you liked smelly oil wells and run-down houses that doubled as fear-infested fortresses. The downtown skyscrapers were visible, far in the distance; dark towers with dots of light in a bleary haze of pollutants. Really, Jean thought, it was all the same no matter which direction she turned. It wasn't a city, it was a dying monster. She wanted it to die. She wanted the big bombs to fall, the red mushroom clouds to form. She didn't know why she had argued so passionately for life when she felt so little life in her heart. It was ironic that ever since the seed of a new human being had started growing in her body she had felt more and more like ending it all. Not suicide, no, but something close to it. Something like a contract that could be entered into without serious penalties. Not a devil's contract certainly, more like a person-to-person handshake and a pat on the back and an understanding that it was OK. That it would be all right.

I did the best I could, God, but it wasn't good enough. But I don't hate you and I don't hate myself. I just don't know what the hell I'm doing. Help, please, help me.

Standing on the creaky balcony, time passed for Jean Rodrigues.

How much time, she didn't know.

But somewhere in the sand at the bottom of Jean Rodrigues's fallen hourglass, the colours of the night-time city altered. The dull yellows turned to blues and the sober reds to fresh greens. The intensity of the light grew as well, as one after another tiny candles were lit in dark corners above homes that had never been built and atop skyscrapers that would never fall. The shift was subtle at first, and she didn't know it was even happening to her until she suddenly found herself staring out upon a landscape bathed in pulsing light. It was only then that she realised she was back in her dream, being given the chance again to lift up her arms and fly, over the wall and into the land where the wishes and the wisher were one. It was a chance she was not going to pass up twice. There, she thought eagerly, there, make me immortal.

Happy at last, still leaning against the railing, she lifted her arms.

But Jean did not fly; the human body could not. The floor of the balcony abruptly vanished from beneath her feet and she fell instead. Headfirst towards a ground that took for ever to reach. Yet the plunge was not terrifying, as Shari Cooper's fall from a balcony one year earlier had been. The contract was signed and sealed. It wasn't suicide but an accident. Or at the very least someone else's fault. There would be no penalty for Jean Rodrigues. There would be no more pain.

CHAPTER 3

Floating downstream in a boat on a river, you can see only a little way in front of you, a little way behind, the nearby shore, and if you're lucky and the river isn't lined with trees, maybe a far-off field or house. But if you go up in a plane and look down at the river, you can see the entire course of the waterway. You can see where it began, and you know where it will end. In a sense, the aerial view is like being given a vision of the future, at least as far as the life of the river is concerned.

Death is a vision that never dies. I am supposed to be dead, but I experience the entirety of my life as if it were all happening at once. I float above the river of personality that was once Shari Ann Cooper. I know her, I am her, but I am something else now as well, something blissful. Even as I poke into the dark corners of my life, my joy does not leave me. It is separate from personalities and events. My joy is what I am and has no name.

I did many things in my eighteen years on planet Earth. I was born. I learned to walk, to talk, to laugh and to sing. I learned to cry as well, and I chased boys. I even got laid once. I was popular. My junior year, mine was voted the best smile in the whole high school. But few of the things that I considered important on Earth interest me now. As I view the whole of my life, a seemingly insignificant event holds my attention. I was sixteen years old. There was a girl in my biology class who was deaf, not a crime in itself, but she was homely as well. Those were two big strikes against her with my friends, and two strikes were completely unforgivable in those days. No one ever talked to her – I didn't either – or even thought about her, except occasionally to wonder why she wasn't in a special school. It never occurred to me that she might be a brave soul trying to live a normal life despite her handicap.

There was one day, though, as I was leaving biology class after the bell had rung, that I noticed the girl was having trouble finding her glasses. On top of everything else she couldn't see well and I knew that she would sometimes remove her glasses while the teacher talked and just sit with her eyes closed, trying, so it seemed to me, to absorb the lesson by osmosis. I didn't know at the time that someone had swiped her glasses, but I did know she was going to have a hard time making it to her next class without them. I walked over and gently tapped her on the shoulder. I scared her, made her jump, and immediately felt bad about it. But she smiled quickly at me after she'd recovered and squinted. I wasn't sure how much of me she could see.

'Hi,' I said. 'Can I help you?'

She leaned forward, closer to my mouth, and gestured for me to repeat myself. I realised she was reading my lips. I put my face right in front of hers and asked my question again. This time she nodded vigorously. She gestured that she couldn't find her glasses and if I would help her look for them. I didn't have to look long to realise someone must have taken them. I mean, it wasn't like there were a lot of hiding places on a school desk. I placed my face in front of hers again.

'Lost,' I said. 'Gone. Stolen. I will help you.'

The news seemed to take her aback, but only for a moment. She nodded, collected her books and stood up. She offered me her arm; clearly I would have to touch her to help lead her to her next class. I didn't mind, although at that time – that week I think it was – it was something of a taboo to touch anyone of the same sex. In fact, I was happy to help her. Very happy I had finally stopped to speak to her.

Her name was Candice, but she said to call her Candy in her uninflected, flat speech. I helped her around for the next two days while she waited for new glasses to arrive. We never did find out what happened to the original pair. During that time I learned to sign quite a few words. We became friends, and I learned something else as well – that life was good even when it was hard. That hidden beauty was much greater than physical beauty. Candy could not hear our teachers; she could hardly see them. But she taught me more than any of them had. I was sad the day I heard she would be coming to school no more. She had ended up returning to a special school for deaf kids, after all. I missed her.

But what I didn't know at the time was that from the moment the thought occurred to me to help Candy, and all the time I was with her, tidal waves of light and energy rolled from me and spread out over the entire universe, to the farthest planet circling the loneliest star in the most distant galaxy. I touched that much. But I could only see these waves as I reviewed my life when my life was over. My good grades, my good looks – none of that had mattered. None of it had affected the creation, but my simple act of service and kindness had been like a miracle. And the strange thing was that I had helped Candy only because I wanted to. Because, for once, I had stopped thinking of myself and thought only of someone else. As I watched the beginning and the middle and the end of the river of Shari Cooper, I could see then the answer to one of our age-old riddles. Does love survive? Yes, I thought, somewhere in some place it is saved and made sacred. I had not known how much love Candy had given to me, and how much I had given to her.

I had known nothing.

'Good,' a voice said.

I opened my eyes and found myself sitting on a grassy bank on a sunny day beside a gently flowing stream. The still air was warm, fragrant, radiant with light and good feelings. In the distance were trees, snow-capped mountains, but no houses, no roads. I was in paradise but I wasn't alone. Beside me sat an extraordinary man.

He appeared to be thirty years old. He had an austere face, hollow cheeks, deepset blue eyes, a soft smile. It was difficult to specify his race. His skin was a deep coppery colour; he could have been an ancient Egyptian priest come to life before me. Perhaps he was, I thought. He wore a blue silk robe. I had on the same clothes I had died in: green pants and a yellow blouse. I was going to have to change one of these days, I thought. My surroundings were pervaded by peace, but the man's aura was even more tranquil. I had no memory of seeing him before, yet I felt as if I had known him a long time. His smile widened at my thought.

'Very good, Shari,' he said. Like his smile, his voice was soft, yet it carried great authority behind it. He was not someone with whom I would have argued.

I smiled. 'Can you read my mind?'

'Yes. Do you want me to stop?'

'It doesn't matter. You were with me as I reviewed my life. I felt you.'

'Yes. How do you feel about how you did?'

'Like a fool.'

'That's a good way to feel. Only a fool can get into heaven.'

'Is that where we are? Did I make it?'

'I joke with you. All this you see is just a thought. You created this place because you still feel the need to occupy a certain space and time. People usually carry that habit with them when they cross over. It is to be expected; it is fine. But you don't need to talk to me with a body. When you feel comfortable, you may drop it.'

I rubbed my legs with my open palms. They felt the same as they had on Earth. 'I'm still sort of used to this body.' I paused, troubled. 'But I suppose it's really back on Earth rotting in a grave somewhere.'

'Is that real, Shari? After all you have experienced, would you say that any part of you could rot?'

I frowned. 'I'm not sure I understand. I do know I have a soul and that it survived death. I learned that the hard way. But my body died. It's still on Earth. I saw them bury it. I went to my own funeral.'

'I was there.'

'Really? You should have introduced yourself. What is your name? Do you have one?'

'You may call me by a name.' He considered. 'Call me the Rishi. Rishi means "seer". When I was in a physical body, people often called me that.'

'So you've been on Earth?'

'Yes. We're on Earth now, Shari.'

I was amazed. I looked around. 'Are we in Switzerland?'

He laughed softly. 'We are in another dimension of Earth. But these concepts – distance, space, time – they have no meaning for you now, unless you give them meaning. You're free of those limitations. You can be on any world in the universe just by wishing it.'

His words made me smile. 'How is Peter? Where is he?'

'Not far. You'll see him soon.'

'Good. I mean, don't get me wrong, I like being here with you, but I want to know why you're here with me.

What our relationship is.' I stopped. 'Am I asking too many questions?'

'I'm here to take your questions. When people first cross over, they often go through a question-and-answer period like this. But understand that not all your questions can be answered with words. Our relationship is a beautiful thing. We are, ultimately, the same person, the same being. But if that is too abstract a concept for you, then think of a huge oversoul made up of many souls. Throughout many lives on many worlds, these different souls learn and grow. Each life is like a day in class, and as you know, some people do better in class than others, but all will graduate if they keep going.' He paused. 'We are a part of the same oversoul, Shari.'

'But you've already graduated?' I asked.

'Yes.'

'To where? To what?'

He gestured around him. 'To all that is. To God if you like. I see your surprise, but it is so. Yes, I am with God now as I speak to you. I see you as my Goddess.' He reached over and touched my hand, his fingers warm, soothing. 'You are very dear to me, Shari.'

I felt so loved then I began to cry. He was like my big brother Jimmy. Or my father even, my real father, whom I had never known. I realised then that even when I had been alive he had been with me, just out of sight, helping me, guiding me. It meant so much to me to be able to see him again with my eyes. I felt as if finally I had come home. I clasped his hand in mine.

'Will you stay with me?' I asked.

'Yes. Always I am with you.'

I laughed, I felt so foolish for weeping. 'Wow. Who would have thought it would be like this?'

'That you would die and end up in Switzerland with an ancient Egyptian priest?' he asked with a twinkle in his eye. 'I was in Egypt a long time ago as people *on* Earth measure time. I am there now. I teach beside the pyramids. People call me Master.'

I was fascinated that he could be in many places at the same time, even as he lived outside of time. 'What do you teach?' I asked.

'Hmm. Big question. I will give a short answer.' He considered for a moment. 'The teachings of a Master appear different in different times. The needs of the time and the place vary. When you were alive few would have said the words of Buddha matched those of Krishna or Jesus. But in essence they all said the same thing – that there is one God and that we are all part of him. That it is important to realise this great truth while we are on Earth. But over time the message becomes distorted.

People take God out of man and put him up in an imaginary heaven, where he is of no use to anyone. Or else they found a religion based on the worship of a particular Master. Yet Buddha never founded Buddhism. Christ never founded Christianity. Krishna hardly spoke about religion at all. He was too busy dancing and playing his flute. He was too ecstatic to be dogmatic. I am very happy now as I speak to my followers in ancient Egypt. But I know a short time after I vanish from their view they will begin to squabble over what I really said and what I really meant. Even now they quarrel amongst themselves. I have to laugh – it is natural that a Master should speak from his level of consciousness but that his followers should hear the words at their level. A long time ago, as mortals are fond of saying, the Rishi was also worshipped as the only son of God. But we all deserve that title, don't you think?'

I nodded. 'How about saying "the daughter of God"?'

'Very good. You understand, I am not saying religion is bad. Where it turns men and women inward and helps them realise that they are as great as the creator who created them, that there is an ocean of love and silence deep within the heart, then it is useful. But where it divides people against one another, where one person is led to believe he is saved and another is damned, or where it leads a person to think that true happiness will be found only in an afterlife, then it is harmful. Each life on Earth is very precious. I called each one a day in class, but if you are wise, if you go deep inside, you can go all the way to the goal in just one life.' He paused. 'It's a wonderful thing to be alive.'

I sat up with a start. 'That's a line from the story that I wrote before I left.'

'I know.'

'Did you help me write that story?'

'Yes. And it has not been lost. Your brother saved it. He read it and believes it to be true. It means much to him. He keeps it safe.'

There were tears in my eyes again. 'That was my last wish before I left. To be remembered. How is Jimmy?'

'He's fine. He thinks about you often.'

I dabbed at my eyes. 'What I wouldn't give to see him again, to tell him I'm all right.' I stopped and shook my head. 'Here I am in paradise with you and I'm still complaining. I guess I'll never learn. I can't see him until he dies and I don't want him to die until he's an old man. I guess I'll have to wait.'

The Rishi took his hand back. He stared at me with his beautiful eyes – the colour of limitless sky. I sensed the joy behind them, but also the power of eternity. I knew I was safe in his company, yet something in his expression made me shiver. He was as gentle as an angel, but I sensed he could also be as firm as a king. I was still in class, I realised. He was the teacher. It was wise to listen to him.

'You don't have to wait,' he said.

'What do you mean? I thought you said Jimmy was fine?'

'He is. But you can go back.'

'To Earth? To a physical body? So soon? Will I be born as a baby?'

'No. You can, if you want, become what we call a Wanderer. You can enter the body of an eighteen year old girl.'

I had never heard of such an idea. 'Is that legal? I mean, what will happen to the girl? Won't she go running to the nearest priest for an exorcist to get me out of her?'

'She will leave the body altogether. She'll be fine. She's already made this choice. At night, when she sleeps, her soul converses with me. She feels she is going nowhere in her life. She wants to give you another chance. Her leaving is purely her choice. It is always that way.' He paused. 'She'll be with me.'

'Who is this girl?' I asked.

'Her name is Jean Rodrigues. If you wish, that will soon be your name.'

CHAPTER 4

The first sensation Jean Rodrigues felt was of pressure, as if she were under a thousand feet of water. Every square inch of her skin was being smothered. She wanted to cry out, to shove the water away, but was unable to make a sound or move. For a while she struggled in a black place, then she felt a prick of something cold and sharp, and her struggling ceased, at least for a little while.

Time went by, jumbled moments of consciousness and unconsciousness. Next, she heard voices. They seemed to come from far off, and she listened to them for what could have been hours before realising that they belonged to her mother and Carol. She could make no sense of the words except to realise that they both sounded worried. She was about to doze off again, when someone shook her roughly. She moved to push the person away; she really didn't want to wake up yet. But she couldn't find her hand so she opened her eyes instead. Her mother was standing over her with bloodshot eyes. It looked as if her mother hadn't slept in a long time. Jean wondered where the hell she was.

'*Mamá*,' she said softly.

Her mother glanced at someone to the side. '*Gracias a Dios*, she's awake,' she said.

That someone came into view. It was Carol. She also looked exhausted. 'How do you feel, Jean?' Carol asked, concerned.

'Tired.' She coughed weakly. 'Thirsty. Where am I?'

Her mother thrust her hand out and then held a glass of water to Jean's lips. 'Sip this. You'll feel better.'

Jean did as she was told. She realised her lips were badly parched, bleeding even. The water went down cool and delicious. Her heart pounded at the back of her skull Her head did not hurt so much as it felt as if it were being steadily squeezed by a clamp. She swallowed and gestured for her mother to take away the glass. Her vision went beyond them, to the hallway beyond the open door. She saw nurses walking back and forth. She was in a hospital, she thought.

'What happened?' she asked.

Her mother and Carol looked at each other as if deciding how much to tell her. 'There was an accident,' her mother finally said.

'Lenny's bedroom balcony collapsed,' Carol added.

'You fell down the hill and hit your head and broke a few ribs,' her mother continued. 'But now that you're awake, you're going to be all right. But I have to say you gave us quite a scare for a couple of days there.'

'A couple of days?' Jean whispered. 'What day is it?'

'It's Monday morning,' her mother said. 'You've been unconscious this whole time.' Her eyes dampened as she leaned over and hugged her daughter gently. Jean had to stifle a groan. Her right side was extraordinarily sensitive. She wondered if the *few* broken ribs really meant her whole side was caved in. Clearly, to be unconscious as long as she had been, she must have suffered a serious concussion. Her mother added, 'My poor girl.'

Jean patted her mother's head. 'Don't worry, *Mamá*, I feel better than I probably look. I'll be out of here in no time. How're my brothers and sisters doing?'

Her mother sat up and smiled. 'Why, that's sweet of you to ask, since you're the one who needs special attention right now. They're fine. I'll call them and tell them you're awake.' She stood. 'In fact, I'll go tell the doctor. I think he'll want to examine you.'

Jean smiled. 'Is he cute? Did he examine me while I was asleep?'

Carol and her mother chuckled; they seemed so relieved. 'He couldn't keep his hands off you,' Carol said.

Her mother stepped toward the door. 'I'll be back in a few minutes. Try sipping a little more water, Jean. Carol, maybe you can help her.'

'*Cierto*, Mrs Rodrigues,' Carol said.

'*Mamá*,' Jean said. 'Has Lenny been by to see me?'

Her mother hesitated at the door. Again she and Carol exchanged looks. 'Yes,' her mother said. 'He's been by.'

'Could you call him as well?' Jean said. 'Tell him I'd like some flowers and chocolates and an immediate visit.'

Her mother lowered her head and nodded. 'I will.' She went to leave.

'*Mamá*,' Jean said.

Her mother paused once more. 'Yes?'

'*Te amo*,' Jean said.

Her mother had to take a breath. The words had caught her by surprise. Again her eyes dampened – no, this time they spilled over and tears ran down her cheeks. 'My,' she said, touching her heart. 'I haven't heard that in a long time. I love you, too, Jean. I'll be back as soon as I can.'

When she was gone, Jean gestured for Carol to help her sit up. Carol picked a remote control off the nightstand. 'This will make the top half of the bed move up,' Carol

391

said. 'That way you won't have to bend so much. Ready?'

'Yes,' Jean said. Carol pushed the button and the top of the bed moved her into a sitting position. The shift in the blood supply in her body brought a wave of new aches and pains. It felt as if her right knee was pretty screwed up as well; there was, in fact, a thick bandage wrapped around her right leg from the top of her calf to halfway up her thigh. An IV ran into the back of her left hand. But she didn't feel any bandages on her ribs beneath her wrinkled green hospital gown. She wondered what had become of her clothes. Carol carefully sat on the bed beside her. Jean offered her her right hand and Carol took it.

'You really had us scared,' Carol said.

'Have you been here a lot?' Jean asked.

'Most of the time. To tell you the truth, the doctor didn't know if you were going to wake up or not. Not until early this morning.'

'He could tell then?'

'*Sí*. Don't ask me how. It was only this morning they moved you out of intensive care. You should have seen yourself yesterday and the day before. You had a ton of tubes and wires hooked up to your body.'

'Sounds kinky.' Jean considered. 'What's the deal with Lenny?'

'What are you talking about?'

'What you and my mother are afraid to talk about. I saw the looks you gave each other when I asked about him. What's going on? Why isn't he here?'

Carol sighed; she was trapped. 'Jean, what do you remember about last Friday night?'

Jean frowned. 'Everything, I think, up until I fell. I remember we had that stupid fight about whether to waste Juan or not. Then I ran out on to the balcony. I remember staring out over the city.' She paused. 'And the fireworks.'

'What fireworks?'

'There weren't any fireworks?'

Carol laughed. 'You must have seen those after you fell.'

'No. I remember – just before I fell – the whole city was lit up with coloured lights. And I felt so happy.' She stopped and shook her head. 'But you're right, they couldn't have been fireworks. Who would be setting them off in the middle of the night?' She studied Carol. Her friend had yet to answer her question. 'You tell me what happened last Friday. Where were you when I fell?'

'I was in my car, on my way home.'

'What? You left Lenny's house without me?'

Carol shrugged. 'Lenny told me to go. Jean, don't look

393

at me that way. You were out on that balcony for so long. It didn't look like you were ever coming back in.'

'How long is *so long*?'

'More than half an hour.'

'I wasn't out there that long. No way.'

'Yes, you were. I came up behind you and called your name and you ignored me. You were out there at least thirty minutes when I left the house.'

'Was Darlene still there when you left?'

'Yes.' Carol thought for a moment. 'It might have been Darlene who said I should go, instead of Lenny. Yeah, I think it was her.'

'And you just did what she said without talking to me first?'

'I told you, I tried to get your attention but you weren't answering. I figured you wanted to be alone. Or at least alone with Lenny.'

'This is too weird. What does Lenny say happened?'

Carol hesitated. 'I don't know. I haven't talked to him.'

'Why not?'

Carol averted her eyes. 'I don't know how to tell you this. Lenny was on the balcony when you fell. He fell with you. He's in this hospital right now, but he's in worse shape than you.'

Jean could feel her heart pound. 'How worse?'

Carol's eyes filled. 'He broke his back in the fall. It looks like he's paralysed from the waist down.'

'Oh, God,' Jean whispered. She thought of Lenny's beautiful body, his powerful legs – now as good as dead. How could this have happened? Why did the balcony suddenly collapse? Carol was shaking her head.

'I'm sorry,' she said. 'I wasn't trying to keep the truth from you. It's just that your mother didn't think we should tell you when you woke up. She wanted to wait until you were stronger.'

'I understand,' Jean said softly, staring at the far wall, seeing only wheelchairs and impassable stairways, boredom and despair for Lenny. He was so active – how would he be able to live? She added, 'Is there anything else you want to tell me? That you were afraid to tell me?'

Carol raised her head and nodded. 'There is one other thing. The fall was rough on you. While you were unconscious, you began to bleed, you know, down there. You lost the *bebé*, Jean.'

Jean blinked. 'What baby?'

'*Your* baby. You were pregnant, remember?'

Jean couldn't keep up with the barrage of information. It was true she could remember buying and taking the pregnancy test, and failing it. She could also remember telling Carol about it. Yet, at the same time, she had trouble accepting the fact that she had indeed been pregnant. Like it was something that could not possibly have happened to her, not under ordinary circumstances. But there was no arguing with the facts. Strangely, she felt neither relief nor a sense of loss that the baby was gone. She simply felt nothing, as if the whole matter had been someone else's problem.

'Does my mother know I was pregnant?' Jean asked.

'Yes. The doctor told her, after your miscarriage. She took it well. She didn't freak out or anything.'

'*Bueno*. Anything else?'

Carol smiled sadly. 'No. Except that I'm glad you're awake and feeling better.'

Jean patted Carol's hand. 'You're a good friend. Thank you for staying with me while I was out. I won't forget that.'

Carol did a double take. 'I've never heard you talk that way before.'

'Talk what way?'

'I don't know, just the way you're talking. You sound nicer than usual.'

Jean nodded. 'Maybe the fall did me some good.'

Her mother returned with Dr Snapple, who must have changed his name to his favourite drink because there

396

was no disguising the fact that he had been born in the Middle East. Dr Snapple had a thick accent and a face so dark he could have been conceived staring into the sun. He was a big man with fingers as thick as Cuban cigars. Jean didn't find him attractive but competent, preferable for a physician. Dr Snapple asked her a few questions about how she felt and did a number of tests involving her vision. The results seemed to satisfy him, but when he touched her right side and the back of her head she groaned. Not mentioning her miscarriage, he explained that her concussion and broken ribs would take time to heal, that there was no magic procedure to speed her recovery. At the same time, he said she was to stay in the hospital for at least two more days, possibly three or four. Jean fretted over the cost. She had no insurance.

'Why can't I go home now?' she asked. 'If you can't do anything for me?'

'Because you have been unconscious for over two days,' he said. 'Who's to say you might not slip back into a coma? We have to keep you for observation.'

'But I won't go back into a coma,' Jean said. 'It's not possible.'

Dr Snapple was amused. 'Since when did you develop the ability to see inside your own brain?'

Jean was annoyed. She knew her mother was too

proud to accept help from the state. 'I don't need to see inside my head to know how I feel. *Mamá*, I shouldn't stay here, you know. How are we going to pay for it?'

Her mother was staring at her. 'You're worried about that? You're not worried about yourself?'

'Of course I'm worried about the money,' Jean said. 'We don't have any.'

Her mother smiled faintly. 'Don't worry, Jean, we'll find a way.' She glanced at Dr Snapple. 'Thank you, Doctor. I'll make sure she stays here, and in bed.'

Dr Snapple left and a few minutes later Carol excused herself. For a moment Jean was alone with her mother. It was obvious to Jean that her mother had suffered terribly while she had been unconscious, and that the poor woman didn't know what to say or do now that the worst was over. Jean didn't know if anything had to be said. She just held her mother's hand and smiled at her, and after a while her mother seemed to feel better. Her mother kissed her goodbye and promised to come that evening, after work. She also warned Jean about staying in bed.

The moment she was gone, Jean got up. She lasted all of five seconds before a wave of dizziness made her sit down quickly. All right, she thought, her brain had to get used to gravity again. Taking several deep breaths, she got up slowly, then sat back down before she could fall over.

She did this a few times and eventually was able to stand without feeling as if she were strapped to a Ferris wheel. Her side hurt awfully, as did her right knee. She wondered what she had looked like when they found her. She hadn't heard Lenny come up behind her on the balcony. Not that she could remember, anyway.

Jean knew she wouldn't rest until she saw him.

She limped across the room and found her clothes in the closet. The hospital dry cleaning service hadn't been by since Friday. She saw instantly how much she had bled. Her jeans and top were both stained dark red. She didn't know what to do. The green hospital gown she wore was draughty; she didn't want to go strolling down the halls with her ass hanging out, although she thought she had a very nice ass. Indeed, glancing over her shoulder at her bare behind, she was pleased to see she was still curvaceous even after her special coma diet.

Jean searched the closet for a robe but didn't find one. She was about to give up and return to bed when she noticed a door in the corner opposite the closet, one that didn't appear to lead into the hallway. Cracking it open a couple of inches she discovered – big surprise – that it led into an adjoining room. Her neighbour was a seventy-year-old white woman with a snore like Fred Flintstone's and a wardrobe the equal of Elizabeth Taylor's. The woman had so many clothes jammed in her closet it was as if she planned to attend numerous costume balls on the other side in case she failed to check out of the hospital. Jean took one glance at the woman stretched out on the bed and figured the woman would never know if she was missing a dress or not.

And so, not many minutes later, wearing a long print gown that she wouldn't have been caught dead in under other circumstances, Jean went searching for Lenny. She sneaked out of her wing without difficulty, but by the time she reached the hospital lobby she had to sit down to rest. She couldn't decide which hurt worse, her head, her leg, or her side. All together, though, it was one nasty ache. Yet the strange thing was that the pain bothered her only as far as her body was concerned. It didn't depress her *inside* that she was injured. She accepted it so well she actually surprised herself.

When she was sufficiently recovered, Jean strolled up to a woman at the reception area. She did her best to appear of sound body and mind but the huge bandage around her head was not something she could make vanish with witty conversation. To make matters worse, the bandage was even stained with blood. But the elderly woman behind the counter didn't seem to notice. She looked up as Jean approached.

'Can I help you, miss?' she asked.

'Yes,' Jean said. 'My brother, Lenny Mandez, is staying in this hospital. He broke his back last Friday. Could you please tell me his floor and room number?'

The woman put a hand to her mouth. 'The poor dear. Is he going to be all right?'

Jean had to swallow before answering. She wondered what it would be like to see him. She reminded herself that she mustn't break down. 'I hope so.'

The woman turned to her computer. 'How do you spell that last name?'

Jean gave her the name letter by letter. She thought it wiser to act like Lenny's sister rather than his girlfriend because surely he was still in intensive care and there might be restrictions as far as visitors were concerned. Indeed, a moment later the woman confirmed her suspicion that he was not in a normal room.

'He's on the eighth floor, Room Nine,' the woman said. 'That's a restricted area. You might have to show ID to get in.'

'No problem,' Jean said. 'Thanks for your help.'

'You look like you've been in an accident yourself,' the woman observed.

'Yeah, I fell off a balcony.'

'You were lucky you weren't killed.'

Jean felt a cold wave, goose bumps all over. Had someone just walked over her grave? Felt like it. 'Yeah,' she muttered.

Room Nine turned out to be many small adjoining cubicles hooked up by wires and computers to a central nurses' station. One thing they didn't worry about in intensive care was people's privacy, Jean thought. The area was thick with the smell of alcohol and pain. The moment Jean walked in, she had to sit down. Her head throbbed. A young nurse who looked like a nun came over to check on her. Jean assured the nurse she was fine and explained how she was there to see her brother. The woman recognised Lenny's name. She didn't ask for ID Jean was helped into the last cubicle on the left and left alone with her boyfriend.

He was not a pretty sight, and it broke her heart because he had been such a pretty boy. Surprisingly, he was not in a body cast but held rigidly in place by a combination of plastic rods and screws and clamps. His bed, it was clear, was capable of rotating so that his body could be turned. Jean suspected it was necessary to circulate his blood and keep him from getting bed sores. He had no marks on his face, no wounds to any part of the front of his body, although she could see the edge of the large bandage on his back. Still, he looked like death itself. His skin was pasty white, as if a vampire on a binge got hold of him. His eyes were closed; he appeared to be asleep.

'Lenny,' she whispered, her voice shaky.

He opened his eyes, but didn't look over at her, staring at the ceiling instead. 'Jean,' he said softly.

She moved to his side, went to take his hand, then thought better of it. The simple fear of touching him hurt her as much as anything had so far. It must have hurt him as well; he looked at her with such wounded eyes it was all she could do to not burst out crying. She remembered a dog she had had as a child. He had looked at her the same way right after being struck by a car, right before he died.

"*Ola*,' she said.

"*Ola*,' he said. 'How are you?'

'Fine.' She touched her bandage. 'Just bumped my head is all.'

'Yesterday they told me you were in a coma.'

'That was yesterday.' She paused. 'How's your back?'

He smiled bitterly. 'I don't know. I can't feel it.'

'What can you feel?'

He closed his eyes. 'I can use my hands and arms. I don't know what else works.'

She reached over and gently touched his big toe. He

had on underwear, nothing else, but there was a vaporiser steaming in the corner and the cubicle was warm and humid.

'Can you feel that?' she asked.

'Feel what?' His eyes remained closed.

She took her hand away, the weight on her chest heavier than the one on her head. 'Nothing. Lenny. Look at me, please, I need to talk to you.'

He opened his eyes. 'What do you want to talk about?'

She fretted with her hands and had to make herself stop. 'You're going to get better.'

His voice was flat. 'No, I'm not. The doctor says my spinal cord's been severed. It won't heal, they never do. I'm crippled for life. I'm screwed, that's a simple fact. So don't stand there with that little bump on your head and tell me I'm going to get better.'

Her throat choked with grief. 'I'm sorry.'

He turned his head the other way. 'I don't want your sympathy.'

'What do you want?'

'To be left alone. Get out of here and don't come back.'

Finally her tears came; she couldn't stop them. 'You don't mean that.'

He turned his head back in her direction. His eyes were red, with anger as well as pain. 'But I do, Jean. I can't stand to see you walking around while I'm stuck here in this bed.'

'Damn you!' she yelled. 'That's not fair! Just because I'm not paralysed I can't be your girlfriend any more?'

'My *girlfriend*?' he said sarcastically. 'How can I have a girlfriend? I can't even control when I have to go to the bathroom any more, never mind have sex. I'm no good to you. I'm no good to anybody.'

'I don't care what you can and can't do. All that matters is that you're alive.' She dared to touch his hand. 'I mean it, I'm not going to leave you. We can work on you getting better together. And if you're unable to make a full recovery, then we'll work on that as well.'

He looked down where she touched him. His eyes seemed to soften. 'I can feel that,' he whispered.

She nodded eagerly. '*Bueno*.'

Unfortunately, the softness only went so deep. He shut his eyes and turned away again. 'I have to sleep, Jean. I'm very tired.'

She leaned over and kissed his hand. 'I'll be back,' she said.

He did not respond. He needed time, she told herself as she left the cubicle. Time and love. She couldn't remember having ever loved him so much.

CHAPTER 5

The Rishi walked with me beside the stream. I still found it hard to understand how I had created the paradise we were enjoying when I had never imagined a scene so beautiful. The flowers that bloomed beside the water were like none found on Earth – or at least the Earth I knew – so many different colours and shapes. The joy of existence, of walking with this great being, was like a constant stream of gladness inside my chest, as clear and sweet as the water at our feet. I questioned him about Wanderers.

'Were there any on Earth that I knew personally?' I asked.

'You met many as Shari Cooper. But you weren't close to any.'

'How about in history? Were any famous people Wanderers?'

'That is a perceptive question. The answer is yes, many well-known people were Wanderers. To be a Wanderer is a great honour as well as a great sacrifice. A soul has to be highly evolved in order to bypass the birth process. Because a Wanderer enters into a developed physical body, he – or she; sex is, of course, not an issue here – carries more of the knowledge of the spiritual plane with him to Earth. Always, he returns to the physical plane with a particular mission, and because he radiates so much soul energy, he often succeeds. By nature, Wanderers are charismatic, intelligent, loving. People are attracted to them. They want to be with them.'

'Have you ever been a Wanderer?'

The Rishi smiled. 'I wander all over the place.'

'Will you ever return to Earth again?'

'I am on Earth now.'

'I mean, somewhere in the time frame that I understand to be modern society?'

'Perhaps. It is up to God.'

'Does he talk to you? I mean, like I am talking to you now?'

'God is an unbounded ocean of light and consciousness. I float in that ocean on whatever current or wave arises. I go with that, it is my joy to do so. I talk to God when I talk to you. I see God when I see the trees.

407

I feel God when I touch my head. Who is there to talk to but myself?' The Rishi chuckled. 'I'm sorry, I don't know how to answer your question.'

I smiled. 'It doesn't matter. Your answer was beautiful. Tell me some of the famous people on Earth who were Wanderers?'

'They're often hard to spot, but they do have one quality that makes them stand out from others. At one point in their lives they all undergo a huge change of heart and awareness. That, of course, is when the new soul enters the body. Einstein was an example. From a young age he was intelligent, but not the genius he became when the Wanderer who brought the theory of relativity to Earth arrived. That was his mission, to bring that knowledge.'

'But wasn't the atomic bomb developed as a result of his theories?'

'Yes. His knowledge was insightful. But it is up to mankind to decide what to do with such knowledge. The theories themselves were neither good nor bad.'

'Who was another example of a Wanderer?'

'Martin Luther King. I think his purpose must be obvious to you. But this will surprise you – Malcom X was also a Wanderer.'

'Him? But wasn't he a bigot?'

'He was many things while on Earth. Can any man or woman be defined by one word? But the Malcolm X whom history will remember entered while he was in jail. Immediately there was a huge change in his outlook. He became interested in religious matters. Many Wanderers go through this phase because in your society, religion is seen as the main source of spirituality, although, in reality, that is a great misunderstanding. But as I said, religion has its purpose and Malcolm X became deeply religious. He was extremely charismatic. He drew people by the thousands.'

'But wasn't he a black Muslim? Didn't he hate white people?'

'You just came from a predominantly Judeo-Christian society. Both Judaism and Christianity are fine religions, as are Islam, Buddhism and Hinduism. One is not better than the other, no matter what the priests and ministers and rabbis would have you believe. Where religion awakens divine love, it is useful. Where it narrows the mind with dogma, it is harmful. And it is true that Malcolm X spent much of his adult life trying to separate Caucasians from African-Americans. But we must come back to what his mission as a Wanderer was. He came to give pride to people of colour. At the time many African-Americans, particularly young males, felt a certain helplessness as far as dealing with society. Malcolm X showed them how to be proud and strong.'

'But doesn't pride divide people?'

'It can. But it was a necessary step for that segment of population *at that time*. You cannot let go of pride until you've first had it. Malcolm X stirred things up – that was his purpose. You cannot judge people such as him. You cannot judge anybody.'

'But if he was a Wanderer, why was he assassinated? Why didn't he have divine protection?'

'He had divine protection. But when a Wanderer is finished with his mission, he often leaves suddenly. Either in a blaze of bullets or quietly.'

'Was Malcolm X happy when he got over here?'

'He did not accomplish everything he set out to accomplish. He was used by others, and his mission was distorted. But that happens. He had no regrets. Regret is the most useless of all emotions.'

'I'm confused. You speak as if when he entered the body he didn't know he was a Wanderer?'

'That is correct. Few Wanderers realise what they are while in a physical body, at least consciously. But deep inside they know they are on Earth for a reason. They usually move towards their particular mission spontaneously.'

'Will I realise that I'm a Wanderer?'

'It's possible. It's up to you. You have free will.'

'What will my mission be?'

'I speak of missions because it gives you some understanding of why you would want to return. But in reality there is only one mission – to realise divine love. To awaken that divine love in others. But different people do that in different ways, and they don't have to be Wanderers to inspire others. Every man and woman born into a physical body on Earth has a mission. Your particular one will be to inspire the often forgotten segment of the poor Hispanic community. Jean Rodrigues is Hispanic and poor. As her, you will write stories that millions of people will read. They will not necessarily be spiritual stories. They can be about space ships or aliens or dragons or ordinary people. The topic does not matter. But the spirituality will be in your stories because it's inside you. It will flow into your words. People will read your stories and without understanding why, yearn for something greater. And because you are a young Hispanic woman, you will also serve as a role model for other young people like Jean Rodrigues.'

I smiled. 'I always wanted to be a writer. But where will I get my ideas? Will I have a muse?'

The Rishi smiled. 'You will be inspired, don't worry.

But perhaps you can write a story about where you get your ideas. I imagine it would be very popular.'

'This is great. I couldn't ask for a better job. I loved writing that story about what happened to me when I died. Do you think I'll be able to find my brother and get my story published?'

He regarded me fondly. 'It's possible.'

'What does that look mean? You know something I don't. Will I find Jimmy?'

'Yes.'

I clapped my hands together. 'Great! Will I recognise him as my brother?'

'That is up to you.'

I stopped walking. 'But I have to know him. Can't you help me out here?'

The Rishi was amused. 'I am always helping you, Shari.'

'I know that. I appreciate that. But what can I do after I get in Jean's physical body to make it more likely that I will remember that I'm a Wanderer?'

'You can learn to enjoy silence.'

'Come again? Do I have to learn to shut up?'

He laughed. 'No. That would not be possible, or natural, for you. You can talk all you want. But sometime during your busy life you will want to sit in meditation.'

'But I don't know how to meditate. Can you teach me now before I return?'

'I will teach you. But you must be taught again while you're in the physical body. You must be taught by a Master. That is very important. There is a new consciousness entering your society, new ideas. Many people call this New Age information. Much of it is useful. Much of it is confusing. The New Age movement speaks of many of the same things I speak of, but there are major differences between what I tell you and what you will find in most New Age books. I will go over these differences with you. Even if you don't remember them consciously while you're in the body, you will have a sense for what is true and that sense will guide you on your path. You will even write about the things I tell you now.'

'I can't imagine that a story about a dragon could bring out any profound truths.'

'It all depends on the dragon, Shari. Listen attentively to these points. Meditation is never an act of mood making. Pure silence, pure consciousness, the eternal side of your nature – it is beyond thought. You cannot talk yourself into it. It comes by grace and by grace alone. But what is grace? How do you make it come? That is where a Master is important. Many in the New Age movement are too anxious to throw off all authority. They say that no one can teach anything, that it is all inside the student. And that is true to a certain extent. On the other hand, to uncover what is inside you must bow at the feet of someone who has already discovered that great treasure. I use the word *bow* carefully. Because until a person is ready to humble himself and admit that he doesn't know, then he can learn nothing of value. It takes great humility to even approach a Master. These are things the New Age movement sometimes forgets.'

'The whole eighteen years I was on Earth, I never saw a Master.'

'This time you will. They will begin to appear in the world at this time. They teach techniques: meditation, certain kinds of breathing, physical exercises. But a technique only points towards the goal. It is not the goal itself. It is like a branch on a tree at night-time. You can say to a friend, "Follow the way that branch points and you will see the most wonderful star." The branch gives direction, but it is not the same as the star. The branch is made of wood, the star is pure energy. Or say you want to eat a bowl of cereal. To do that you need the technique of using a spoon: how to hold it, which end to put in the bowl, how it goes up and into your mouth. The spoon is crucial, but it is the cereal you want. The cereal is the grace. Grace flows from a Master. It has to flow because he embodies that divine love.'

'I wish I had been on Earth with you in Egypt,' I said.

'You were. You are. You are with me there as much as you are with me now.'

I shook my head. 'Let's stick to one time frame, please, or I just end up confused.'

'If you wish. But sometimes a Master is purposely confusing. He destroys preconceived ideas and beliefs. Always, though, he gives an aspirant a spiritual practice. That is very necessary to do even though many on the physical plane don't think so. They say, "The time is changing and all will be taken care of." They don't want to do any practice. And they are right, to a certain extent. The time is changing. That is why so many Wanderers are beginning to appear on Earth – to help prepare for this change. Mankind is entering a new age where spirituality will dominate. But many fear this change. They have heard about the disasters that are to come. Many so-called prophets say the majority of the world will be wiped out. That is not true. The world has an insurance policy. It has the Masters. There will be disasters, however, to shake things up a little. It can take a needle to remove a thorn. It can take a shaking of the Earth for people not to totally depend on the Earth, to make them look inside. You will write stories about the disasters as well. People will read them and understand that when things appear the darkest, it is a sign that dawn is near. You will write stories of enlightened dragons and aliens, and people will want to learn to meditate. Even though the coming dawn is inevitable, it is good to be awake to enjoy it. Meditation helps with that.'

'I am never going to remember all this,' I said. 'I can't remember half of what you just said.'

'It doesn't matter. I see your mind has begun to wander. That is all right – you are a Wanderer, after all.' He paused. 'You want to see Peter.'

I nodded. I knew I could hide nothing from the Rishi. 'I miss him.'

'Where would you like to see him?'

'What do you mean?'

The Rishi knelt for a moment and picked a red flower that resembled a rose. He gestured to the serene landscape. 'I told you, this is all a dream. What would you like to dream with Peter? It can be anything. It can even be that you don't know that it is a dream. Really, that is all human life is. Just a dream people choose to enter into so that they can learn something. But people take it so seriously and become afraid of their own creation. They even fear to wake up. That is the one lesson humanity most needs to learn in the coming days. That there is no reason to be afraid. That things will work out for the best. That God knows what she's doing.'

'She?'

He tapped me on the head with his flower. 'When I am with you, Shari, you are my God. What universe do you wish to create for you and Peter?'

I considered. Boy did I consider. 'It can be anything?'

'Anything.'

I blushed; I could feel the blood in my cheeks even though I was a ghost. 'Can it be an R-rated creation?'

'Yes.'

'I don't want you to watch.'

'I won't watch.'

I laughed. 'You promise?'

'I promise.' He chuckled. 'I swear it, Shari.'

I rubbed my hands together in anticipation. 'Awesome. Let the creation begin. Let there be light. Let there be boys!'

I never knew I had such a dirty mind.

Well, I may have suspected.

CHAPTER 6

Jean Rodrigues couldn't remember when she had last tied her little brother's shoes. Teddy sat above her on the kitchen table as she knelt at his feet and stared at her as if trying to remember the same thing. He was a cute four-year-old, with hair as long as a girl's and dimples. He touched the top of her head as she finished with his laces. She no longer wore her bandage, although she still suffered from a dull headache. But she couldn't complain; her ribs and knee were healed. She had been released from the hospital nine days earlier. She had just made it to her high school graduation the night before, and had been happy to be there. It was before nine on Saturday morning, two weeks after her fall.

'Is your head sore?' he asked.

She smiled and clasped his outstretched hand. 'Now that you've touched it, Teddy,. it's all better. Did you know you have magic hands?'

He blinked at her pronouncement and pulled his hands back to study them. His eyes went wide. 'What can they do?' he asked.

'They can give love. That is their special magic. Go give Mom a hug and then you go play. Here, I'll help you down.'

Jean lifted Teddy from the table and he hurried over to the sofa where their mother lounged in front of the TV. Today was their mother's only day off. Teddy gave her the briefest of hugs before dashing out the door yelling something about showing the other kids his hands. They both laughed at him. Her mother shook her head.

'You'll have that boy trying to heal all the kids on the block, Jean,' she said.

Jean sat beside her on the sofa. 'Maybe he can,' she said thoughtfully.

Her mother continued to smile. 'I don't think anyone's sick around here at the moment.'

'There's sick and there's sick,' Jean muttered.

'What do you mean?'

Jean smiled quickly. 'Nothing, just mumbling. Are you still worried about me being a candy striper? I won't go if it really upsets you.'

'I think you're still too weak to be volunteering for a

job that pays nothing.'

'But if it did pay well, I would be strong enough?'

Her mother slapped her playfully on the arm with a magazine. 'That's not what I mean and you know it. You should rest while you have the chance. Why did you tell the nurses you were coming in anyway? Is it so that you can see Lenny? You can see him without working.'

'I do want to be close to Lenny, that's true. But I volunteered because when I was in the hospital I saw a lot of patients who weren't getting any attention because the nurses are too overworked.' Jean shrugged. 'I don't want to sound like a saint. I just want to help out.'

Her mother stared at her. 'But you do sound different.'

Jean started to deny it, but only nodded. 'Carol said the same thing. But I don't feel any different since the accident, except for my constant headache.'

Her mother continued to watch her. 'I don't believe that. You seem freer in a way. You don't walk around like you have the weight of the world on your shoulders.'

'I never used to do that.'

'Yes, you did. You were always *triste*.'

Jean shrugged again. 'Well, maybe I had my reasons.'

Her mother nodded. 'Do you want to talk about it?'

'About what?'

'You know. Your pregnancy.'

Jean acted shocked. 'Was I pregnant? God, those comas are amazing things. Here I slept through an immaculate conception and a miscarriage all in the same two days.'

'I was pregnant with you when I was your age,' her mother said.

Jean quieted. 'I know. I thought about that a lot.'

'Before or after you had sex with Lenny?'

Jean looked over sharply. 'Only after I failed the pregnancy test.'

'You took one of those? Where did you get one of those?'

'At the same drugstore where I bought the condoms that didn't work.' Jean shook her head. 'They're not hard to use. All you have to do is be able to pee on a stick.' Jean paused. 'Why are you asking me these questions, Mom? You must know Lenny doesn't stand a chance in hell of knocking me up again.'

'I'm sorry what happened to him. You know I mean that. I'm sure he was a fine young man.'

'He still is, Mama. Being crippled hasn't changed that. Not in my book.'

Her mother touched her arm. 'I'm going to say something harsh now, and you're not going to want to hear it. But I just want you to listen to me a second and think about it. I know Lenny is hurt and needs your help.

You should go see him and help him in any way you can. But I think it would be a mistake for you not to see the facts for what they are. Lenny's going to be crippled for the rest of his life. At best he will be able to get around in a wheelchair. You can't let yourself get any more attached to him than you already are.'

Jean spoke calmly. 'Why not?'

'I just told you why. Because he's crippled for life. You can't be with a man like that. You'll spend all your time taking care of him.'

A tear sprang into Jean's eye, but she managed to keep her expression flat. 'I like taking care of people.'

'No, you don't. You've never liked it before. You can't be with half a man.'

Jean drew in a painful breath. 'First you're worried that I was pregnant. Now you're worried I want to be with someone who can't get me pregnant. What's the deal, Mom?'

Her mother sighed. 'Maybe this is not the time to talk about this. You go see him. Do what you can for him. We'll talk later.'

Jean stood and looked down at her. 'I'll feel the same later. I love him. I didn't know that before, even when I slept with him, but I know now. Maybe my love can't heal him. Maybe I just lied to Teddy and there isn't any magic in this world. But at least my love makes him whole in my eyes. Lenny is not half a man.' She turned away. 'Now, if you'll excuse me, I think I'll wait outside for Carol. She's supposed to pick me up in a few minutes.'

Her mother sounded sad. 'I don't want to fight with you, Jean. I just want to protect you.'

Jean paused at the door. 'I know that. We're not fighting. We're just – arguing.' She opened the door. 'Have a nice day, Mama. I don't know when I'll be home.'

While waiting for Carol, Jean reflected on why those close to her were saying she had changed. There was truth in their comments. Despite Lenny's serious injury and her own wounds, she did feel lighter. Each morning she woke up anxious to start the day. Why, even the sun was brighter, the sky bluer. It was as if she had refound a childhood innocence she couldn't remember ever having enjoyed. Plus her head was filled with strange ideas she had never had before. She kept thinking of the stars and planets, dreaming of ancient civilisations, imagining vast supernatural dramas. She had begun to jot down her thoughts in a notebook, although she had no idea what she would do with them.

'What did happen that night?' she wondered aloud.

Carol arrived a few minutes later. She was on her way to a date with the Russian guy who worked at

McDonald's, the guy with the scarred face. Seemed the guy didn't have a car. Carol was dressed to kill and excitedly smoking a joint. She offered Jean a hit the moment Jean got in the car. Jean took the joint and threw it in the garbage can at the end of their driveway.

'Hey!' Carol protested. 'I just rolled that.'

'I don't want any.'

'Well, excuse me. I want it. You could have just said no and handed it back.' Carol started to get out of the car. 'I'm getting it.'

Jean grabbed her arm and smiled. 'I don't even want to have to smell it. Leave it in the can, *por favor*.'

Carol looked at her as if she were an alien creature. 'You don't want to get loaded any more? What's gotten into you?'

Jean let go of Carol and gestured to the block. 'You see this street? There's graffiti on every wall. There's garbage on every lawn. Paint is peeling from the houses. Dogs and children are running wild. This is my street, but your street is just as bad.'

'So? We live on the crappy side of town. When you get rich and famous, you can move to Malibu.'

'I don't want to move to Malibu. I want to stay in this neighbourhood because this is where I grew up. I want to clean up this place. I have given it a lot of thought. But I can't clean this place up by myself and, besides, it will just get dirty again because the minds of too many people around here are dirty. I know we get screwed in school. We have the worst teachers and the ugliest buildings. I know we get screwed at work because we're not white. But I think we're screwing ourselves with all the drugs we're taking. Look, you and I have been stoned since we were twelve. Haven't you gotten sick of it yet?'

Carol stared at her dumbfounded. 'I don't know. I guess.'

'I'm sick of it. I'm not getting loaded again, ever.'

'But you'll still smoke pot now and then, won't you?'

'Carol. I'm not taking anything. And I don't want you to, either.'

Carol was annoyed. 'Right, great. If I don't want to be Miss Purity, I can't be your friend any more. You know it, Jean, you might be nicer nowadays, but you're also turning into a royal pain in the ass.'

'I didn't say you couldn't be my friend any more. It's just that every time you light up a joint around me, I'm going to throw it away. And you won't be able to stop me 'cause I can kick your ass any day.' Jean smiled sweetly. 'But I still love you, Carol.'

Carol put the car in gear. 'Thank God for that.'

They headed for the hospital. The day was hot and

Carol's air-conditioning hadn't worked since the last ice age. Jean rolled down her window and looked at the houses she had seen every day of her life. Somehow, it was as if she were seeing them for the first time. It was true, most of them were in poor shape, but Jean could see the potential there. Everywhere she looked, she saw all kinds of possibilities.

'How long are you working at the hospital?' Carol asked.

'Three hours. That's all they'll let me with my injuries, and I had to push for those.'

'Why are you doing it?'

'So I can steal hospital drugs.'

'But you just said you don't want to get loaded any more?'

Jean laughed. '*Menso!* See what all that *mota* has done to your brain? I'm not going to steal drugs. I volunteered to work at the hospital because they need help. That's the only reason.'

Carol was impressed. 'That's neat. Maybe you'll get to give some way-cool girl or guy a shot in the ass.'

Jean couldn't stop laughing. 'They don't let candy stripers give shots. Certainly not to way-cool girls and guys.'

'Well, I don't know what they do.'

'Tell me what's happening with you? Why are you going out with a guy?'

'He's not exactly normal, you know.'

'I understand that. But he is a he. That makes him different from a girl.'

Carol giggled. 'That's true.'

'Look, are you still a lesbian or not? I just want to know for future reference. If you're not, then I can quit defending you.'

'Does it bother you to defend me?' Carol asked.

'No. It turns me on. But answer my question.'

'I don't know the answer. I just know I like this guy. But I still like girls. Maybe I'm bisexual.' Carol paused. 'Does that gross you out?'

'No,' Jean said honestly. 'It makes you complex. I like that in a boy or a girl.'

Carol nodded. 'I like to think it gives me colour.'

'Just remember that a guy can get you pregnant where a girl can't.'

'I have you to remind me of that.' Carol paused. 'Will you get to help Lenny today?'

Jean sighed. 'I don't know if I can help Lenny. I've seen him every day since I woke up, but he hardly talks to me. I keep thinking he'll feel better when the bones in his back have healed enough so he can start physical therapy.

Lying in bed all day would depress anybody.'

'When will he be able to get into a wheelchair?'

'Not for a while. Another couple of months.'

'That long?'

'At least. Where his back broke, they had to fuse the spine together. That takes time to heal.'

'Will he ever walk again?' Carol asked.

Jean hesitated. 'The traditional medical answer is no. That's the answer he's supposed to learn to accept. But I don't believe it. I can't help but think his condition is only temporary.' She shook her head. 'Maybe I'm just fooling myself.'

'I hope he gets better. Hey, have you seen Darlene lately?'

'No. She never talks to me. She never came to visit me at the hospital. What's with her?'

'I think she still plans to go after Juan,' Carol said.

'After all that's happened? You can't be serious.' Jean was thoughtful. 'I'd like to talk to her more about what happened that night Lenny and I got hurt. You know, weird as this may sound, I don't even know if she was still there when we fell.'

'I think she was,' Carol said. 'I think she's the one who called the ambulance.'

'But you're not sure?'

'No. What does Lenny say?'

'That he can't remember.'

'Do you believe him?' Carol asked.

Jean shrugged. 'I don't know why he'd lie to me.' She added, 'We can't let Darlene go after Juan. It would be a death sentence for her.'

Carol looked worried. 'Maybe for all of us.'

Carol dropped Jean off at the hospital twenty minutes later. She was going to spend the day with Scarface, and Jean assured her she could take the bus home. Actually, Jean liked riding the bus, especially since her accident. It was a good place to meet people.

Her candy-striper duties were simple: she delivered meals to patients. But even this job turned out to be complex with the elderly patients. Not one but two old women thought she was their granddaughter. At first Jean denied the relationship, but when she saw how much it meant to the women to have a visit from a granddaughter, Jean decided to play along, reminiscing about events she had no memory of and adding details the women had no minds to doubt. On the whole she had the most fun with the senior citizens and children. Really, helping people got her high, and somehow she had known it would happen.

The patient who affected her the most, though, was a teenage girl named Debra Zimmerer. She was eighteen, the same as Jean, and dying. Just before Jean delivered her food, the nurses told her that Debra had leukaemia, and they felt she wasn't going to make it. When Jean brought in her tray, she found Debra lying in bed and reading J.R.R. Tolkien's *The Lord of the Rings*, which Jean had read in the hospital. Debra was worn-out pretty, with faded brown eyes as weary as those of a sick model in an old oil painting. She was five feet five and weighed maybe eighty pounds. Jean took one look at her and felt a painful stab in her gut, but somehow she managed to smile as she set down the tray.

'Awesome book, huh?' Jean asked.

Debra set the fat book aside. 'I guess. I'm just near the beginning.'

'Keep going. It keeps getting better and better. In fact, I think it's the best story I ever read.' Jean lifted the lid off her plate. 'Would you like something to eat? I brought you chicken, but if you don't like it they have some kind of fish.'

Debra sat up weakly. 'I'm not that hungry.'

'How about something to drink? I have apple juice or orange juice or ginger ale.'

Debra nodded. 'I could drink some ginger ale.'

Jean opened the can and poured Debra a glass. Debra's voice was dry, which Jean understood to be a side effect of the morphine she took to control the pain. Debra lifted it to her lips and took a sip. The act seemed to exhaust her, and she put down the glass quickly. Jean sat on the bed beside her.

'Is there anything else I can get you?' Jean asked.

Debra coughed. 'No.'

Jean patted her on the back. 'Are you OK?'

Debra nodded and wiped at her colourless lips. 'Yes.'

Jean shook her head. 'That was a stupid question. I'm sorry, of course you're not OK.' She paused. 'I heard you have leukaemia.'

Debra watched her. 'Yes. It's a drag. What's your name?'

'Jean. You're Debra, right?'

'Yes.' Debra glanced at the book. 'Could you tell me how the story ends?'

Jean forced a smile. 'I don't want to do that. It'll spoil it for you.' Then she stopped, hearing what Debra was really asking her. It was a long story, really three books in one. Debra was not going to live long enough to finish it and she knew it. 'But if you want me to, I can. I can do it today after I finish delivering these trays.'

Debra stared at the far wall for a moment. 'How about tomorrow? That would be a good day for me.'

Jean nodded. 'I can come tomorrow evening and tell you the whole story.' She added, without even thinking about what she was going to say, 'Maybe I can tell you one of my stories as well.'

Debra was interested. 'Do you write stories?'

Jean shrugged. 'I'm only working on one so far. It's about this famous writer and her muse. Only her muse is a troll who appears out of her bedroom closet one day and demands half her royalties. I'll tell you what I have of it so far and you can tell me whether you think I should bother finishing it.'

'OK.' Debra lowered her head. 'It'll be nice to have a visitor.'

'Doesn't anyone come to see you?'

'Just my father. But I can't talk to him because he's too scared about me being sick.' Debra hesitated. 'He's afraid I'm going to die.'

Jean spoke gently. 'Are you afraid?'

Debra raised her head and wiped her nose. 'Yeah. I know it's going to happen, but I'm still scared. My doctor told me.' Again she stared at the far wall. 'I have no idea what it's going to be like.' She shrugged. 'Maybe it won't be like anything. Maybe I'll just be dead and that will be it.'

'No,' Jean said firmly. 'Your body will die but you'll go on.'

Debra smiled sadly. 'I wish I had your faith.'

It was Jean's turn to hesitate because she really didn't know what she wanted to say to the poor girl. But at the same time she felt compelled to speak, and she believed that what she would say would be the truth.

'It's not that I have faith. I just *know* that your time of death is no more important than when you change your clothes. Don't ask me how I know. I can't explain it. The main thing is, when death comes, you don't need to be afraid. That's important. Fear is the only thing that can hold you back.'

Debra listened. 'Hold you back from what?'

'From going on to more joy. It's a lot harder to be born than to die. You'll see, and when you do, you'll say to yourself, "That foolish girl in the hospital was right."'

'Are you a fool?'

'Sure. But you know, only fools get into heaven.'

Debra grinned. 'Who told you that?'

Jean stood up quickly from the bed. Debra's question had a profound effect on her. For a moment Jean felt as if there were two of her standing in the room, one visible, the other a reflection. She felt as if she should be able to glance over her shoulder and see her other half to answer Debra's question. She felt inexplicable joy even with a dying girl watching her.

'Someone wise,' Jean said softly, turning away. 'I'll see you tomorrow.'

'I hope so,' Debra said with feeling.

It was inevitable that when she finished her shift Jean would go and stand at the end of Lenny's bed and try to think of something inspiring to say. Lenny had been moved to a normal room with the motorised bed that allowed him to be rotated without the assistance of four nurses. At present, thankfully, he was lying face up and she was able to address him rather than his scarred back. Unfortunately, no words of wisdom came to her and he had yet to open his eyes despite her saying his name several times. She heard her mother's words in her mind and had to convince herself they weren't true.

'I can leave if you want me to,' Jean said finally. 'But you're going to have to tell me to leave. Otherwise I'll just stand here feeling awful. But maybe that's what you want, Lenny, I don't know.'

He opened his eyes. 'You should know by now what I want.'

Jean stepped closer, touching his bare arm. This room, like his previous one, was warmer than normal. Probably because they kept him scantily dressed to make it easier to care for him.

'What do you want?' she asked reluctantly.

'To die,' he said flatly.

There was anguish in her voice. 'No.'

'Yes.' Finally he looked at her face. 'I can't live like this. You say you love me, Jean. If you do, then help me end this.'

She clasped his right hand. 'You just have to hold on for a little while longer. Soon you'll be in a wheelchair and able to get out. I'll take you to the beach. I'll take you to the movies. You can't imagine how many great films have come out since you've been in here. I can show you—'

'You can take me,' he interrupted. 'You can show me. That's true because I can't do any of those things without you. But how long will you be there? You say for ever but we both know that's B.S. One day you'll get tired of pushing a cripple around and you'll meet some other guy and then you'll say, "I'm sorry Lenny but you know it's a tough world." Then you'll leave, and what'll I do? I'll tell you. I'll kill myself. But why should I have to wait for the day we both know is going to come? I don't want to go through the pain. I want to do it now. I want you to help me.'

Jean wept. 'I won't leave you, I swear to you.'

Lenny strained to move his head as close to hers as he

435

could. 'You can get what you want if you keep your eyes open and move fast. A bottle of sleeping pills, a dozen packaged shots of Demerol – either of these would be enough to kill me. Are you listening to me, Jean? If you don't help me you just make it harder for me. I'll have to slit my wrists. No, that will be too slow. I'll have to cut my throat. The blood will be all over the place. You'll walk in here one day and the walls will be sprayed with red and—'

'*Cállate!*' she cried.

Lenny let his head fall back. 'I'm going to do it. You know I'm going to do it.'

She sighed, her tears sprinkling his arm. 'You must have some reason to live.'

'None.'

'Don't say that.'

'I want to die today.'

'Lenny.'

'Right now.'

'Damn you! You have to give yourself time. If you can't think of a reason to live, then you have to find one. Think, Lenny, of everything and everyone in the world. Think of something you want to do. Hold on to that, at least until you get out of here.' She squeezed his hand, a desperate note in her voice. 'Can't you think of anything?'

He started to answer but then stopped, only staring at her for several seconds. His expression became strangely blank. 'Maybe,' he muttered.

She nodded. 'Good. That's a start. Hold on to that. It can make you strong.'

'Don't you want to know what it is?' he asked.

She shook her head. 'No. It doesn't matter. As long as it keeps you alive.'

Lenny sucked in a weary breath and closed his eyes.

'But the day it stops doing that, then what? Will you help me end it?'

Her head throbbed. 'Do I have to?'

'Yes. You must promise me.'

She let go of his hand, let his arm drop. 'I promise,' she whispered.

CHAPTER 7

Jean did not take the bus home after she left the hospital, but rather, to the beach, Huntington Beach, located in Orange County. It was a long ride for her, and on the way she kept asking herself why she was going there when Santa Monica Beach or Venice Beach was closer and just as nice. Indeed, she couldn't even remember when she had last entered Orange County. Yet a wave of nostalgia spread over her as the bus headed for the Huntington pier. Staring at the brightly coloured shops, she felt strangely at home, at peace even. She was glad she had hours of free time. The dull ache of her perpetual headache had eased somewhat.

Jean had forty dollars on her. The first thing she did after getting off the bus was buy herself a bathing suit, a navy-blue single-piece affair that showed her breasts and bottom to good advantage. She wanted to look sexy but she also wanted something comfortable to swim in. She also bought herself a beach bag and towel and headed for the sand with the suit on. The area immediately around the pier looked like the happening place; she found a spot in the shade of the first lifeguard station. The people around her seemed so different from those in her neighbourhood, she thought, with their rich summer attire and perfect hair. Most of the kids looked like they were riding their daddy's credit card limits. Yet, at the same time they were young and confused like everyone else she knew. She couldn't take her eyes off them. Since her accident she was always observing and watching, like a spectator at a play she had no part in.

Jean did not spend long lying on the sand. Soon she was in the water, and the motion of the waves was more than enough to wash away the stress of the last two weeks. She had always been an excellent swimmer. Her worries about Lenny and Debra fell off as she swam out three hundred yards past the first break and let herself bob up and down on the huge south swells. The air was hot, the water cool, and there wasn't a cloud in the sky. It was almost as if she swam in paradise.

Wherever I am is paradise because I am there. I am joy itself.

Where had she heard that? From a book? A teacher at

school? She couldn't remember and it didn't matter because it was true, she was that joy, and that was all that mattered. She swam farther out and felt the ocean welcome her. The blue horizon seemed to stretch to infinity and she felt as if she could keep going. She felt completely free.

Then she began to feel tired. The fatigue came on her all at once, and when she turned and saw that the beach was a half mile back, she felt a stab of anxiety. The water felt cold now. She wasn't out of the hospital that long. Her supposedly healed ribs suddenly didn't feel as if they were all knitted together. What if she cramped up? She might die. Yet it wasn't the thought of death that frightened her. It was the idea that she'd leave without completing an important task. For the first time in her life Jean felt she was on Earth for a purpose.

She slowly began to make her way back in, conserving her strength as best she could. She was halfway to the beach and experiencing exhaustion when the lifeguard boat happened by. The twenty-five-year-old-bronze god behind the wheel waved and asked if she'd like a ride to the shore. She humbled herself and gasped that she would. Once aboard, the lifeguard complimented her on her stamina and her bathing suit. But he didn't hit on her or anything. He probably rescued way-cool babes all day, she thought. His name was Ken, as in Barbie and Ken. He kind of looked like Ken.

The warm sand was a delicious treat for her weary goose-bump-covered limbs. She lay back on her towel and was out in ten seconds. She slept for an hour, and dreamed of the sun and the heavens. She flew above mankind's burning star on the back of an angel, while all worlds spun below her. Worlds of light, worlds of pain – it was all there for her to choose, the angel said. If she wished to go back.

'Go back,' Jean whispered as she awakened with a start. She sat up and looked around, feeling as if she had to start back. But not to the other side of town, to her side of town. But to another place, she thought. She stood and collected her towel and clothes. Without knowing why, almost as if in a dream, she walked north.

Two miles from the pier, on a stretch of sand where Huntington Beach ended and Bolsa Chica Beach began, a row of expensive and multi-storeyed condominiums had been erected to provide a view of Catalina on every clear day Southern California had to offer. Jean paused to stare at them. It was not their decor that drew her – if anything she thought they were something of an eyesore, with their oversize balconies protruding from their back sides like lines drawn on a blueprint by an architect on acid. She realised she had a prejudice against places she knew she'd never be able to afford. Still, the condos drew her attention, even though she didn't like them, even though they frightened her. How curious, she thought, to fear buildings she had never seen before. Yet it was as if the condos were bathed in black and red light, in memories of horror that someone had desperately tried to blot out.

'But I've never been here before,' Jean muttered to herself.

Horror can attract as well as repel. She felt herself walking towards the buildings, pulled by invisible strings that could have stretched from the ground as well as from the sky. She continued to move as if in a dream, her angel long gone, replaced by a being from a lower region who whispered silently. Maybe it was a demon, she thought. Maybe it was just someone's past that had somehow passed by without touching her. The condo on the right, in particular, drew her. It was three storeys high, like the others, but somehow it appeared taller. The roof was covered with orange clay adobe-style tiles. A metal fence surrounded the building, but the gate was open. Without asking permission, without ringing a bell, she went inside.

She went straight to the spot.

What spot? She didn't know what to call it. A stain on the ground.

Going down on her knees, she touched the dark stain on the smooth concrete and wondered what had made it? Why did it fill her with such dread? Who had died here?

Yes. That's the real question. It's a bloodstain, I can see that. Only blood permanently turns concrete dark. Only blood refuses to fade. Only blood never forgets.

Jean felt her hair slip forward over her shoulders and fall on to the stain. It was almost as if the strands of hair strained to soak up the blood that had once flowed at her knees. Soak it back into her head, deep into her brain cells, suffuse them with the life and death of that night. Whatever had happened here, she knew, had happened in the dark. It had been an act of surprise, an act of vengeance. Jean could feel all those things as she knelt there. But most of all she felt sorrow. Whoever had died here, she knew, had come to a bitter end.

Jean didn't know how long she remained by the stain. But eventually she became aware of a shadow stretching over her from above. She raised her eyes into the glare of the sun and saw a tall elderly lady in a lovely white dress. She carried a smart grey handbag in her right hand and it was obvious she had just had her hair done. Although she was as old as some of the patients Jean fed in the hospital, she was nowhere near retirement. She stood erect and her blue eyes were clear and alert.

'Can I help you, miss?' she asked in a pleasant voice.

Jean stood reluctantly. The stain repulsed her, while at the same time she was afraid to leave it. Somehow, it connected her to a part of herself she felt she should know. She wiped her palms over her knees – the heat of the concrete had slightly burned her flesh. She still had her suit on.

'No,' Jean said, realising how foolish she'd sound if she spoke of how the stain preyed on her mind. She stooped to collect her bag. 'I was just resting. I'll be on my way.'

'The way you were kneeling there,' the woman said. 'The expression on your face – I thought you knew her.'

Jean stopped. 'Knew who?'

The woman nodded to the stain. 'The girl who died here.'

Jean felt dizzy. She had to stick out her arm and hold on to a fence to support herself. 'Oh, God,' she whispered.

The woman put her hand on her arm to steady her. 'Are you all right, dear?'

Jean nodded weakly. 'Yes, I'm fine. It's just – the heat.' She straightened up as well as she could, although the world continued to wobble as if the Huntington Beach fault had just decided to try for the top of the Richter scale. She added, 'I really should be going,' and turned in the direction of the gate but didn't move.

'If you'd like a glass of lemonade before you go, I'd be happy to get you one.' The woman stuck out her hand. 'My name's Rita Wilde. I manage several of the condos on this block. Most are owner occupied but quite a few are rentals.'

Jean shook her hand. Her eyes kept straying back to the mark on the ground. 'You were the manager here when the girl died?' Jean asked.

'Yes. It happened a year ago. She was about your age.' Rita cocked her head upward. 'She fell off that balcony right above us.' Rita frowned 'She might have lived if she hadn't landed directly on her head.'

'How did she fall?'

A shadow crossed Rita's face. 'A bunch of teenagers were having a party. The parents weren't home. The girl didn't die until near the end of the party. At first everyone thought she jumped. But then the police figured out she had been shoved. It was all over the papers. You must have read about it.'

'I didn't. Not that I remember at least.' Jean nodded to the stain. 'This is from where she hit the ground?'

'Yes. I've tried a dozen times to scrub it away but it refuses to go. The poor child. She was only eighteen.'

'I'm eighteen,' Jean said quickly.

Rita smiled. 'Are you? That's a wonderful age. What I wouldn't give to be eighteen again. Can I get you that glass of lemonade now?'

'No, that's OK. I'm feeling a bit better.' Jean hesitated. 'Do you remember the girl's name?'

Rita stopped to scratch her head. 'It was something Cooper. I can't remember her first name. But I do know her parents lived near Adams. The father came by a couple of days after she died. I talked to him and he told me a little about himself.' Rita shrugged. 'I guess he just wanted to see the spot where his daughter had died. Maybe I'd do the same, I don't know.' Rita paused and studied her. 'Are you sure you weren't friends with that girl?'

Cooper, Adams. Cooper. The father. Cooper.

The words chilled Jean to the bone.

'No,' Jean said. 'I didn't know her. Why do you ask?'

It was Rita's turn to look at the stain. 'I don't know. It's just a thought I had.'

Jean began to back away. 'Thank you for your time, Rita. Have a nice day.'

'You, too, child. Enjoy yourself.'

Jean searched for a telephone booth the moment she left the complex. She found one outside on a liquor store wall a block over. There was a telephone book; she hastily

446

scanned the white pages and found sixteen Coopers. She flipped to the map at the front of the book and located Adams, studied the streets around it, then returned to the list of sixteen. Only one man, Stewart Cooper on Delaware, lived anywhere near Adams. She memorised his number and again consulted the map. From where she stood it was approximately three miles to the man's house, but she figured she would probably have to walk half that distance just to catch the bus home. She decided to pay Mr Cooper a visit.

But what are you going to say to him? I didn't know your daughter but I'm sorry she's dead. And, oh, by the way, her bloodstain really freaked me out. When my hair fell on it, I felt as if I were the one who had died. Imagine that?

Jean decided to cross that bridge when she came to it. She entered the liquor store and bought herself a tall Coke. Her walk already had her dehydrated. Taking a couple of slugs from the bottle, she set out for Adams, this time heading south, back towards the pier. She figured it would take her close to an hour to reach the Cooper residence. Plenty of time for her to figure out what the hell she was doing.

As it turned out, her estimate was overly optimistic. Between her long swim and her still healing body, she couldn't do twenty-minute miles. She was about to call a cab by the time she stumbled on to Delaware, *ninety minutes later.* Fortunately the Cooper house wasn't far up from the beach. In fact, it's just over there, she thought. The house with the white picket fence and the maple in front . . .

Wait a second! I have to check the address to know which house it is. I don't know anything about picket fences and maple trees. Hell, I couldn't tell a maple tree from an olive tree, even if it was growing maples.

That was true, she thought. But what was also true was that she recognised the house the instant she saw it. She didn't have to confirm her feeling by checking the number she'd obtained from the phone book. The Cooper house was the third house on the right. Still, as she drew closer, she did check the number against the numbers on the kerb. The perfect match brought another wave of dizziness to her already overwhelmed brain. As did the sight of the young man in the driveway loading his pickup. He was tall and handsome with dark hair and a nice build and that was cool and everything. But what was not so cool, at least not at the moment, was that he looked so familiar.

He, in fact, looked like someone she had known all her life. Yet she had never seen him before.

'He's the dead girl's brother,' she whispered to herself.

Jean walked up to him, probably looking like the overheated radiator that she felt like. His truck was loaded with a disassembled bed and a chest of drawers, plus a generous helping of wrinkled clothes and what appeared to be a PC. It didn't take a genius to realise he was moving out. He had a gold-coloured lamp in his hand when he glanced over at her. His eyes were warm and blue and yet they sent a shiver down to her toes.

'Can I help you?' he asked.

'Yes,' she mumbled. 'Which way is the beach?'

He pointed toward the large blue body of water at her back, the one with the waves and the salt in it, and the sandy beach beside it. 'It's over there,' he said.

She glanced over her shoulder. 'Oh, yeah. I have a terrible sense of direction.'

'You're not from around here?' he asked. The way he spoke, she knew he knew the answer to his own question – which he should have, because of her inner-city bad-girl accent. Yet, even though she liked him, she didn't like being categorised. She straightened up and cleared her throat.

'How can you tell?' she asked.

He shrugged and set down his lamp. 'Your voice. Your bathing suit.'

'What's wrong with my bathing suit? I just bought it. I

bought it down here.'

He paused and studied her up and down, perhaps wondering what he was getting himself into, and if it was worth it. 'There's nothing wrong with it,' he said carefully. 'It just doesn't look like the kind of suit girls around here wear.'

'Because my ass doesn't stick out?'

He smiled. 'If you like. Where are you from?'

Jean took a step closer to him. 'Guess.'

'South Central.'

'Close enough. Does that scare you?'

'Well, since it doesn't look as if you're carrying a switchblade or a gun beneath that suit, I'd have to say no.'

'I might have one in my bag. You never know.'

He gestured to his jammed truck. 'If you are going to rob me, these are all the worldly possessions I have. Take what you want, I don't care.'

Jean smiled. 'I'm not as dangerous as I look. Are you moving out or is that a stupid question?'

He nodded. 'Yeah, it's finally time to leave the nest. I found a studio apartment up on Baker. It's on the third floor. There's a pool, but the place is kind of small. But then I don't have a lot of stuff.'

'Did you move that chest of drawers by yourself?'

'Yeah.'

'I'm not impressed. That's a good way to wreck your back. Isn't any of your family home to help you?'

'There's just my mom and dad, and I want to move while they're out.' He shook his head thoughtfully. 'My mother isn't exactly crazy about me leaving.'

'Is it because you're their only child?'

He hesitated. 'Yeah. There are just the three of us.'

Jean offered her hand. 'My name's Jean Rodrigues. What's yours?'

'James Cooper.' He shook her hand. 'Pleased to meet you.'

It was weird to touch him. It was like touching a mirror, while an old friend stood behind her. 'I bet people call you Jimmy,' she said.

Her remark made him stiffen. 'Not usually. Most people just call me Jim.'

'Then that's what I'll call you.' She nodded to the truck. 'It looks like you're about ready to take this load over. I'll give you a hand if you like.'

Her offer took him aback. But then he smiled. 'That's nice of you. But you're dressed for the beach. You should just go and enjoy yourself.'

'I have an ulterior motive in wanting to help you, Jim. I took the bus over here and it'll take me two hours to get home. If I help you move your stuff, then I was thinking

451

maybe you could give me a ride home.' She added, 'You're going to need some help if your place is on the third floor.'

He raised his eyebrows at her offer. She could see he was shy, a sweet guy. By the faint lines around his eyes, she could also see that he had suffered in his life. It had to do with his sister, she knew. Yet she didn't feel this was the time to ask about her.

'Can you work in a bathing suit?' he asked finally.

'Are you afraid my breasts might pop out?'

He blushed. 'I wasn't worried about that exactly.'

'I have clothes in my bag here, along with my forty-four Magnum.' She paused. 'I would like to help you.'

He watched her. 'Why, Jean?'

She smiled. 'Because I'm grateful to you. You showed me where the ocean is.'

CHAPTER 8

I lived in the reality of my own creation. I had put on my memory cap, however, and didn't know that I was both my own God and devil. I was Shari Cooper and I was alive on planet Earth and back in high school. It was my sophomore year and at the moment nothing was more important than Peter Nichols asking me to the prom. I could see him approaching in the crowded hallway. My heart pounded like a piston in my chest when he smiled at me.

'Shari,' he said. 'How are you doing?'

My hands were filled with school books and I worried they would be ruined with the sweat pouring off my palms. Peter looked so good then, his curly blond hair hanging in his blue eyes. Standing so cool in the hustle and bustle of the break between first and second period. Like he had just pitched nine innings of no-hit ball in the

453

World Series and was about to be handed the MVP award.

'Great,' I said. 'How are you?'

'Cool. Going to the prom tomorrow night?'

'Maybe.'

'Why maybe?'

I shrugged like it was no big deal. 'Haven't got a date yet.'

'Do you want to go with me?' he asked.

I managed to hold on to my books. 'Sure.'

'What time should I pick you up?'

'How about six?'

'Six is good.' He patted me on the back and stepped past me. 'See you then.'

Wow, I thought. Peter Jacobs. What a guy. Shari and Peter. What a couple.

Then it was Friday night, just like that, and I was upstairs finishing my hair and the doorbell rang. The noise startled me; my brush handle broke off in my hand, the bristles in my hair. But I just laughed; I was high as a kite. I ran down the stairs to find my mother and father opening the door for Peter. My father pumped his hand and my mother gave him a quick hug. They liked Peter, of course. He was a winner. He was my fastball. I was hoping for some fast times tonight as I hurried toward him. His tux was the colour of sand on an ocean floor. He smiled at me and handed me a corsage as large and as white as the moon.

'You look great, Shari,' he said.

'Thank you.' I accepted the corsage. 'You don't look so bad yourself.'

My parents stood nearby and beamed happily.

We drove to the prom in a silver limo that Peter had rented. The dinner and dance were in the same expensive hotel. There was steak and lobster, music and candles. We danced long and slow and Peter put his arms around me and told me how much he cared for me. I whispered the same. A vote was taken on fancy folded cards and not long after Peter and I were crowned 'Coolest Couple'. The band played us a special song – 'Stairway to Heaven'. I felt as if I had died and gone to heaven. And the night was still young. Peter kissed my ear and told me he had rented a room upstairs. Did I want to see it? Sure, I said. If that's what he wanted. He nodded and took my hand and we strode toward the elevator, while all my girlfriends watched in envy.

The suite was plush. There were flowers, a bottle of champagne on ice, soft music on the stereo. We drank a toast to ourselves. Then Peter kissed me and led me into the bedroom. The light was down low. He began to undress me.

'Do you want to make love?' he asked softly.

'Yes. Yes. Do you?'

'Yes,' he said. 'Help me get out of these clothes.'

'I love you, Peter,' I said as I unbuttoned his shirt.

'I love you, Shari.'

I opened his shirt and rubbed my palm over his hard muscles.

A metallic-coloured monster burst out of the centre of his chest.

'Eehhh!' I screamed and leaped back. In horror, I watched as Peter toppled to the floor, his blood and guts splattering the carpet. The monster climbed out of his ruined cavity and stood upright. Its head was enormous. As it peered at me, its mouth opened and a band of razor-sharp teeth protruded and snapped at the air. In the space of seconds it grew to eight feet tall. Too numb to shout for help, I backed into the corner and tried to be invisible. But the monster was hungry and wanted prime California girl flesh. Slowly it moved toward me, acid slime dripping from its mouth and burning the carpet. It would use the acid to digest me, I knew. I had maybe three seconds left alive. At last I found my throat and let out a bloodcurdling scream.

The monster stopped and peered at me curiously. It spoke in Peter's voice.

'Did I scare you?' he asked.

I was about to faint. 'What?' I gasped.

'It's me, Peter,' the alien said.

I frowned. 'Is that a costume?' I pointed to his dead body. 'What the hell is going on here?'

'We're at the prom,' he said. 'This is supposed to be the night of our lives.'

I was having trouble taking it all in. 'But are you inside that monster, Peter? It looks so real.'

'Oh, it's real enough.' It turned its huge head back towards Peter's body. 'You want to see it eat what's left of me?'

'No!' I cried. 'Get out of that suit now. You're making me sick to my stomach.' I was suddenly angry. 'I didn't like being scared like that. You almost gave me a heart attack.'

'I couldn't have done that to you.'

'No, I'm serious. I almost had a heart attack.'

The monster sat down on the floor. 'You can't have a heart attack, Shari. Don't you remember? You're dead.'

It all came back to me in an instant. Then I was really pissed. I strode over and whacked the monster on the head. 'We both agreed to block our memories. We were supposed to go to the prom like it was real. Since when have you known this was all make-believe?'

'Since it started.'

'That's not fair! Here I'm swooning under your attention and you're sitting in your fat head and chuckling at me. That's it, that's the last romantic fantasy I'm acting out with you. I'm going to find some other ghost. Maybe an Englishman from the last century. Those guys were supposed to have manners. I'm really angry at you, Peter.'

The alien shrugged. 'Sorry. I didn't mean to hold on to my memory. It just happened. Then as the night dragged on I started to get bored. I just wanted to liven things up.'

'Oh, thank you! I feel much better now! You get to go to the prom with me and screw me afterwards and you're bored. Thanks a lot, Mr MVP.'

'We didn't exactly screw afterwards.'

'We were about to. Why did you choose that moment to have an alien burst out of your chest? Do you know what that does for my self-esteem?'

'You're not supposed to have self-esteem problems.'

'Why not?'

'You don't have a body for one thing.'

'So? I'm still a person. I'm still walking around in the image of the body I had on Earth.'

'Why?'

I stopped. 'Why what?'

'Why don't you switch to another body?'

'What's wrong with this one? Is that why you got bored tonight? I wasn't cute enough for you? God, I'm happy I didn't date you when I was alive. I would have ended up killing myself. And would you get out of that stupid alien form? You really are making me sick. Not that the sight of your old self probably won't do the same thing.'

The monster vanished, as did Peter's dead body. He stood before me as I had met him at my funeral, wearing blue jeans and a baseball cap. 'I just wanted to experiment is all,' he said. 'You don't have to get all bent out of shape.'

I sighed. 'I suppose not. It's just that I never got to go to the prom with you. I dreamed about it so much and this seemed like a good chance to have a dream come true. You can understand that, can't you?'

Peter put an arm around me, and in that moment it felt pretty real to me, and wonderful, his touch, like the touch of my oldest and best friend. I was still having trouble with all this consciousness business but I supposed the Rishi would explain it to me more if I asked. Once again I was glad he had promised not to observe my fantasy life. He was so wise – I didn't want to act the fool in front of him.

'We can do it again, Shari,' Peter said. 'We can start

from when I asked you out. This time, I promise, I'll have my memory blocked. We can even have sex if you want.'

I looked at him. 'If *I* want? Don't you want?'

He shrugged. 'Sure.'

'What does that mean? Has being dead affected you more than you've let on?'

He took a step back. 'Are you asking me if I'm impotent?'

'It's nothing to be ashamed of if you are. We can talk about it.'

Peter was bored. 'Shari, think for a second. How can I be impotent when I can sprout a dozen tentacles and talons in two seconds and eat you alive if I want to?'

I paused. 'I see your point. Never mind.'

'Do you want to start the date over?'

I paced the hotel room. 'No. I want to do something more meaningful. Let's go exploring. The Rishi said we could go anywhere we wanted in the universe just by wishing it. I've always wanted to see the solar system. Interested?'

Peter smiled. Such a lovely boy and smile. 'Always,' he said.

We hung suspended above planet Earth, seeing it as astronauts, and more. For our eyes were sensitive to colours and feelings ordinary humans failed to perceive. I saw that the Earth had both a physical and spiritual dimension. Much of the Middle East, for example, was clean desert covered with dark astral clouds. Intuitively I understood the darkness was from the constant strife there, and that the area could not go on the way it had been and survive. While other parts of the Earth shone with soft white radiance. The Himalayas in India, in particular, were beautiful to behold, and the West Coast of America also had some points of brilliance, as did a few other spots on the globe. But it saddened me to see that the lights were few compared to the darkness.

'Too bad *Time* magazine never had a picture of the Earth like this on their front cover,' I said to Peter, who floated beside me.

'It is strange to see that hate is something you *can* see,' he agreed. He pointed to the Middle East. 'I do hope they get their act together there. It looks ready to explode.'

'I feel that way, too. It's almost as if it would take an explosion to break the tension there.'

'Or a huge wave of light,' Peter said.

I nodded thoughtfully. 'That would be preferable.'

'Well, there's nothing we can do about it right now. Where would you like to go next?'

I turned around, seeing an old friend behind me. 'Let's go to the Moon!'

There was no obvious sensation of speed as we soared towards Earth's natural satellite: no wind in our hair, no roar of a rocket engine. Yet the flight was exhilarating. Having the Moon rush steadily toward me, I never felt so free, so possessed by the certainty that all this was indeed my creation, as much as everybody else's, a playground made for all of us by God to learn in and enjoy. With a simple thought, I slowed as we neared the silver globe. But Peter was having too much fun and rammed headfirst into the Moon. We danced about on a crater-marked field, and then were off again, heading for the fourth planet from the sun, the red planet. Mysterious Mars.

Here I discovered both wonder and fear. On a purely physical level Mars appeared uninhabited, but studying it with the spiritual eye I was learning to use, I was treated to two interlocking visions. On what I can only describe as a low vibration, I saw a race of demonic reptilian beings. A cruel civilisation that fought and warred with itself and every other living being in its dimension. Here there was no light, no love, and as a result, only pain. I could only tune into it for a few seconds before being forced to shut it out.

'Do you see it?' I asked Peter.

He nodded gravely. 'It's like hell. Yet it's there with the other as well. How can that be? Two races on one world and our scientists on Earth can see neither.'

'I think there's a lot that science has yet to learn.' I focused on the other race. I say focused only in a manner of speaking. Actually, I found I could perceive more by 'letting go' inside. Several octaves above the reptilians were enchanted cities of beings who looked similar to people on Earth. Immediately I was reminded of the haunting civilisation the author Ray Bradbury had described in his book *The Martian Chronicles*. For these were a beautiful people with long shiny gowns, wine-coloured faces, and sleek bodies. Canals filled with luminous dark liquids crisscrossed their globe and they floated from town to town along these watery highways on delicate boats that could have been made of glass. Music filled their towns, sad and serious, yet uplifting and beautiful as well, echoing softly over the stark red deserts as well as into deep space. If these people – I preferred to think of them as the real Martians – were aware of the hellish dimension around them, they gave no sign of it. Peter seemed to read my mind.

'I wonder if writers on Earth somehow tuned into these two races and wrote about them,' he said. 'Mars is often described in literature as both evil and magical.'

'It's possible,' I replied, thinking that when I returned to Earth as a Wanderer I wanted to write about Mars, preferably about the beautiful race.

We took off for Venus next, and even approaching the second planet from the Sun, we were thrilled by the light and joy that emanated from that white globe. We had to stop far off in space to observe it; the vibrations were so high our ghost bodies couldn't stand it. Through the radiance I glimpsed – and it was only a glimpse – a race of beings much farther along the path of evolution than either humanity or the lovely Martians. It was as if Venus were inhabited by angels, and I understood why on Earth it was usually referred to as the planet of love.

'I don't think we can get any closer,' I said.

'We're probably too gross for them,' Peter agreed. 'I wonder why they are so much ahead of us?'

'I don't know if it's so much a thing of being ahead or behind,' I said, once more feeling for the truth inside, something I had begun to do out of habit since talking to the Rishi. I wondered if he had rekindled the ability in me, and if it would follow me back to Earth as a Wanderer. 'I think they started before us. They are as we will be in the future.'

Peter laughed. 'In ten millions years?'

'Maybe it won't take so long,' I said, once more feeling I had spoken the truth. The Rishi mentioned a transitional time on Earth, in the next few decades. I wondered if we might not join our cousins on Venus sooner, ghosts included.

Without consciously deciding on our next destination, we began to drift away from Venus and the Sun. Soon we were out among the globular clusters and nebula. Never in my wildest imagination as a mortal had I imagined such colours, such beauty and vastness of scale. It was as if all my life I had lived in a great palace, but kept my head in the closet. On Earth all I had cared about was who was looking at me and talking about me, while I lived in a universe of mystery and adventure. I made another vow to myself, to study astronomy when I returned as a Wanderer. I did not merely float through the star fields, I merged with them.

'We're all stars,' I told Peter.

'Yes. I was thinking how when my father died when I was ten years old I used to search for him in the sky.'

A wave of sorrow swept over me, but it was sweet as well, bittersweet like sour candy. 'When you died I looked for you in the sky.' I reached out, across the light-years, and took his hand. My love for him then was like the light of the stars that shone all around us, and I knew it would burn for ages. 'And now I have found you.'

He squeezed my hand. He didn't have to say anything.

We floated for ages, seeing more wonders than any

starship log could ever record. Eventually we found ourselves at the centre of the galaxy. Here the stars were older, as were the myriad races, and the peace and bliss they radiated were like that from a million Venuses combined. Inside, I understood that these people had learned all that this universe had to offer, and that they were merely waiting for the 'rest of us' to catch up so that they could go on, where, I didn't know, another dimension perhaps, another creation surely, where God was as real as the sky, and as easy to touch as water in the sea. In the centre of this floated what I believe our astronomers would call a galactic black hole. The light that streamed from both the stars and the worlds swirled around the object in a cosmic whirlpool, disappearing down a shaft that seemed to have no bottom. Fascinated, I moved towards it but Peter stopped me.

'We don't know where it goes,' he said, and for the first time since he had told me about the Shadow in the days after my death, there was fear in his voice.

'Nothing can harm us,' I said. 'I want to go inside.'

'If you go inside, you might not get out.'

I studied him. Throughout our starry journey he had been as enthralled as I was. But now I sensed not only his fear but the reason for it, something had happened to him while we were still on Earth. Yet I couldn't pinpoint the cause, and what it had to do with the portal to infinity that yawned before us. The black hole drew me like a magnet, and I realised we had not stumbled upon it by chance. I had to go in it before I could return to Earth and accomplish my mission.

'I am going,' I said. 'You can follow me if you wish.'

He hesitated. 'I'll wait for you, Shari. Take care.'

'I am taken care of,' I said.

I moved towards the portal.

As stars vanished behind me, so did the *I* that was Shari Cooper.

Words fail me here. How to describe the knowledge of anything without the presence of a knower? In the interior of the black hole the knowledge and the knower were one. I ceased to be aware of things. I was awareness itself.

Still, here, outside of all places, I sensed my true place and finally understood the Rishi's words.

'Our relationship is a beautiful thing. We are, ultimately, the same person, the same being. But if that is too abstract a concept for you, then think of a huge oversoul made up of many souls. Throughout many lives on many worlds, these different souls learn and grow . . .'

I was not singular. Many people were I, and yet we were one as well. All that they had experienced, I had experienced. The different lives the Rishi had spoken of, I had lived them all. I was the Master in Egypt instructing the young student outside in the pyramid. The student was also me. I was enlightened and ignorant at the same time, and I saw it was not possible to have one without the other. No light without darkness. No day without night. No compassion without suffering. No good without evil. Everything worked together, ultimately – a weave of different-coloured threads forming an unfathomably rich tapestry. How foolish we were to try to explain the mystery of life, I thought. The mystery could be lived but never explained. Any more than the mind of God could be explained. I felt so close to God right then I imagined myself a perfect fool. And I was happy.

I sensed something else as well. Peter was part of me, as much as the Rishi. It was right that he should be with me enjoying this glimpse of our higher selves. But he was not with me because he was still supposed to be on Earth. He had committed suicide, I remembered that now, and I could see the effect that act had set in motion throughout our oversoul, like a ripple set out across a mountain lake that was finally settling down to freeze for the winter. He had feared to follow me because his fear still followed him. Even this far into eternity. It was this realisation that jerked me back into normal space time. Normal as far as ghosts were concerned. I materialised outside the black hole beside Peter.

'What happened?' he asked.

'How long have I been gone?'

'Just an instant.'

'It felt like ages.' Looking at him I remembered his comment about how the situation on Earth was no longer our concern. I had not discussed what the Rishi told me about my going back as a Wanderer. Now I realised it was because his destiny was separate from mine. I could have fun with him for now, but the fun would have to end.

'What's the matter?' he asked.

'Nothing.'

'What happened to you in there?' There was an edge to his voice.

'It's difficult to explain.' I reached over and took his hand again. 'We have to go back. I have to speak to the Rishi.'

'Why?'

Would I miss him on Earth? I asked myself. I missed him now and I hadn't even left him. And he was a part of me. It was such a paradox. How could I succeed as a Wanderer without the love of Peter beside me?

'Because I need his help,' I said.

TO BE CONTINUED . . .

DYING TO KNOW WHAT HAPPENS NEXT?

GET HOLD OF THE NEXT FANTASTIC VOLUME ...

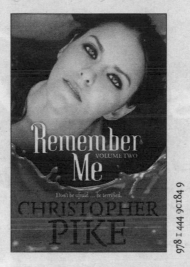

978 1 444 90184 9

Shari is alive once more,

but things on earth have changed. She will come to realise that she is no longer welcome ...

Shari is given a rare offer – to return to Earth in someone else's body. It is an offer she gladly accepts. But this new body isn't her own and she does not remember being Shari Cooper either. Initially she recalls nothing of the afterlife. Perhaps it is just as well. Not everybody on Earth welcomes those who return. Of the few who know of their existence, some want them dead. And others, the truly evil ones, wish them much worse than that ...

Sisters Red

'The wolf opened its long jaws, rows of teeth stretching for her. A thought locked itself in Scarlett's mind: I am the only one left to fight, so now, I must kill you …'

An action-packed, paranormal thriller in a gritty urban setting, with a charming love story and unexpected twist that leaves you wanting more!

THE DEAD.

Lazarus Stone is about to turn sixteen when, one night, his normal life is ripped to shreds by a skinless figure drenched in blood. He has a message:

THE DEAD ARE COMING.

Now Lazarus is all that stands in their way. To fulfil his destiny, he must confront not only the dark past of his family, but horrors more gruesome than even Hell could invent. And it all begins with the reek of rotting flesh ...

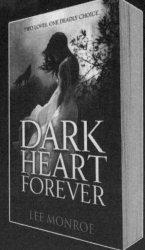

THE SECRET CIRCLE

THE INITIATION AND THE CAPTIVE PART I

Cassie is not happy about moving from sunny California to gloomy New England. She longs for her old life, her old friends … But when she starts to form a bond with a clique of terrifying but seductive teenagers at her new school, she thinks maybe she could fit in after all …

Initiated into the Secret Circle, she is pulled along by the deadly and intoxicating thrill of this powerful and gifted coven. But then she falls in love, and has a daunting choice to make. She must resist temptation or risk dark forces to get what she wants.

THE SECRET CIRCLE

THE CAPTIVE PART II AND THE POWER

Now that Cassie is part of the most alluring and deadly clique imaginable, she is starting to realise that power comes with a price – more dangerous than she knows. Torn between the opposing desires of the two leaders of the Secret Circle, Cassie is struggling again. Does she use her considerable supernatural power to save lives, or does she put all her energy into keeping Adam, the boy she loves.

Cassie's relationship with Adam is threatening to tear the circle apart, so where does Cassie's loyalty and strength, truly lie?

BEAUTIFUL DEAD

Not alive. Not dead. Somewhere in between
lie the Beautiful Dead.

A stunning series that will leave you restless.

Books 1-4
OUT NOW

NIGHT WORLD

Volume 2
Books 4-6
OUT NOW

Dark Angel

Angel saves Gillian from death in the icy wilderness and then offers to make her the most popular girl in school. But what does he want in return?

The Chosen

Vampire killer Rashel is torn between her feelings for her soulmate, Quinn, and her loathing for his thirst for human blood. She loves him, but is that enough?

Soulmate

Hannah's true love – Lord of the Night World, has come back into her life and reignited her passion. But her joy is threatened by the return of an ancient enemy ...

NIGHT WORLD

Volume 3
Books 7-9
OUT NOW

Huntress

In *Huntress,* Jez Redfern is leader of the Night World vampires, yet she has an instinct to protect innocent mortals from her former friends … But can she resist her own desire for blood?

Black Dawn

In *Black Dawn*, Maggie's brother, Miles, goes missing. Her search for him leads Maggie to the vampire, Delos. Whilst strangely attracted to him she knows it's him or her brother.

Witchlight

In *Witchlight*, Keller is a shapeshifter. She is seaching for a new Wild Power and battling her attraction to the dashing Galen. But it seems he can never be her soulmate…

www.bookswithbite.co.uk

Sign up to the mailing list to find out about the latest releases from L.J. Smith

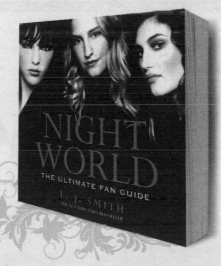

From the best-selling author of the Electra Brown series

RUNNING IN HEELS

FEB 2011

From riches ... to bitches.

Daisy Davenport has it all — stunning looks, a spectacular house, a seriously gorgeous boyfriend.

But when her father is sent to jail for corruption, Daisy's life is shattered. Forced to move into rooms above a kebab shop, she and her family have to readjust — fast.

And if life isn't hard enough already, Daisy's new school is a world away from her old one. And the school bully is going to make sure she remembers it ...

As hilarious as ever!

RUNNING IN HEELS

Helen Bailey

www.helenbaileybooks.com
www.hodderchildrens.co.uk

the Vampire Diaries

The Return – Shadow Souls

Forced to travel to the Dark Dimension with Damon, Elena is secretly terrified of letting her long-disguised feelings for Damon run wild. For, if Damon does lure her into becoming his dark princess, her new powers might not be used for good …

itv 2 Now a major itv2 series